Praise for Patricia Sprinkle's
Death of a Dunwoody Matron

"Sparkles with verve, charm, wit, and insight. I loved it."
—Carolyn G. Hart, award-winning author of
Scandal in Fairhaven

"Engaging . . . compelling . . . A delightful thriller."
—*Peachtree* magazine

"The sort of light entertainment we could use more of in
the hot summer days to come."
—*The Denver Post*

"Sparkling . . . witty . . . a real treat and as refreshing
as a mint julep,
a true Southern pleasure."
—*Romantic Times*

Also by Patricia Sprinkle

DEATH OF A DUNWOODY MATRON

A MYSTERY BRED IN BUCKHEAD

Patricia Sprinkle

BANTAM BOOKS
NEW YORK · TORONTO · LONDON · SYDNEY · AUCKLAND

A MYSTERY BRED IN BUCKHEAD
A Bantam Crime Line Book / November 1994

James Dickey, 11 word quote from the poem "Looking for the Buckhead Boys" from *The Whole Motion,* copyright 1992 by James Dickey, Wesleyan University Press by permission of the University Press of New England.

ISBN 0-553-56897-3

Published simultaneously in the United States and Canada

Bantam Books are published by Bantam Books, a division of Bantam Doubleday Dell Publishing Group, Inc. Its trademark, consisting of the words "Bantam Books" and the portrayal of a rooster, is Registered in U.S. Patent and Trademark Office and in other countries. Marca Registrada. Bantam Books, 1540 Broadway, New York, New York 10036.

PRINTED IN THE UNITED STATES OF AMERICA

RAD   0 9 8 7 6 5 4 3 2 1

WITH THANKS . . .

A book like this requires extensive research into both history and social ambiance. While I take credit for any errors, several people made the book richer and more accurate by sharing private insights into Atlanta's history and the book's locale: Franklin Garrett, official historian of the Atlanta Historical Society; Sol and Irene Kent; Jan Meija; Becky Baumhauer; Mr. Garrett's assistant, Lib Salter. Thanks to all of you!

Thanks, also, to the Historical Society Library's fine staff for steering me toward the right materials; to Cary Golden and Kitty Farnham for steering me toward the right people; to Shigenobu and Miriam Machida for help with Japanese and gracious hospitality; to Paula Rhea for insightful, sharp-eyed proofing; and to my children, for helping me get our house ready to sell and the family packed to move while I finished the manuscript. Finally, special thanks to my editor, Kate Miciak, who brings out the best in me.

"In 1838 Henry Irby of South Carolina erected a tavern-grocery store at the intersection of Peachtree, Roswell, and Paces Ferry roads which became . . . the center of the present Buckhead community, the most well-to-do and elegant residential area within Atlanta."[1]

A
MYSTERY
BRED
IN
BUCKHEAD

Part One

The Forties

Come as a cook,
Or butler, or maid.
The madame ain't home,
So don't be afraid.

      Buckhead party invitation, 1940[2]

Private Joe Brady was drunk. Gloriously, arrogantly, profanely drunk. A stream of curses flowed from his mouth into the Atlanta evening as freely as if he were drinking beer down at Fort MacPherson with the boys instead of swilling champagne on this god-awful snooty Buckhead terrace. Joe Brady had forgotten his chagrin at being in such exalted company. He had forgotten he was leaving next week to join General Patton's Third Army. He had almost forgotten the whole damned war.

When someone proposed a toast to the newly engaged couple, Joe raised his glass and blew them a raspberry. When he saw a sassy southern matron arch an eyebrow at his date, he bowed with alcoholic dignity. "Don't look down your nose at me, bitch. You fools lost the Civil War." She glided icily back inside.

He felt a shudder pass through the girl at his shoulder. Melody? Marianne? Joe had forgotten her name, and she had a face like a horse, but she had an accent like Scarlett O'Hara and he liked her shape. Especially in that strapless white evening dress. He eyed it speculatively.

She'd been pouring coffee last Tuesday at the USO. Obviously a pink, one of those high-class Atlanta teenage girls who spent most of their time with boys they called jellies. Jellies indeed. Joe was no jelly—he'd show her that before the night was through! When they'd met, she'd liked the way he looked. He knew the signs. So when she complained she was out of gas coupons and needed to get to an engagement party tonight, he'd offered to bring her. Now he was waiting for a little something in exchange.

He'd been dismayed, however, to discover just how much class her friends had. He had not expected an estate with high brick walls and an iron gate. He had not expected a nigger butler. He had not expected a house as big as City Hall back home, with a marble foyer, a live band, furniture that looked like it belonged in a museum, and a receiving line straight out of the society pages of the daily Constitution— Dorothy Connally and her fiancé Charles Davidson, Rippen Delacourt and his fish-faced wife Georgia, and Mr. and Mrs. Delaney Winwood, Georgia's parents, who were throwing this shindig in honor of Miss Connally's engagement.

Waiting in line to be greeted, Brady had growled, "I feel like a turnip on a rosebush."

"Shhh!" his date had cautioned. "The Winwoods'll hear you."

The buffet made up for the receiving line, but the bar had been risky. He'd run smack into Lieutenants Norton, Whitehead, and Maxwell, who he saw more than enough of at Fort Mac. They were bulling about the likelihood of Nazi spies down at the base, and they'd looked as startled to see Joe as he was to be there. When Dr. Maxwell, who'd just finished treating Joe for something he would rather forget, looked sideways at Joe's date, Joe had decided it was time to head for the terrace. He'd kept a lookout for the doc ever since.

Now, more than an hour and several drinks later, Joe raised his glass in a blasphemous salute to all officers who treated enlisted men as dirt. A short middle-aged redhead standing nearby cocked her head in obvious admiration. Encouraged, Joe embellished his lurid description. She gave him a smile as she went inside.

Mildred? Mollie? laid one hand on his arm and repeated her same old complaint. "Shhh! Somebody'll hear you!"

Joe didn't give a damn. He felt better than fine. A wisp of moon sailed overhead, and in this dim light, the girl beside him was almost beautiful. He cocked his head toward muted strains of "Stardust" floating out the open windows. "Let's dance, baby!" He pulled her toward him.

She squirmed away. "I need to speak to somebody first." She beckoned to another pink coming out onto the terrace, one with wide gray eyes and hair like honey—or was that her name? Joe was a bit fuddled on that point. In her red-and-white dress this girl looked as pretty as strawberries and whipped cream. Joe would trade his date for this doll any day.

"We'll have us a dance in a few minutes," he promised, giving her hand a damp squeeze. She smiled and went to join some other friends, but Joe knew he'd made an impression on her. He could read the signs.

Swaggering to take a drink from a passing tray, he didn't worry this time whether the butler noticed the black moons of grease beneath his nails. His date noticed, though. She laid her own hand on one of the stone pineapples that decorated the parapet of the terrace. Her nails were clean ovals, painted a delicate pink.

"It's honest dirt," he told her thickly, waving his grubby hand before her long pale face. "Mechanic's grease. I been getting Uncle Sam's troops ready to roll."

She shuddered and moved farther down the parapet without a word. Annoyed, Joe lurched after her.

The butler, bending to gather a couple of used glasses, stood and cocked one eyebrow. "Will there be anything else, miss?"

"N-n-no." The girl looked anxiously toward the glass doors leading to the dining room. "But if my brother—"

"I'll see can I find him." With portly tread, he returned to the party inside.

The few people at the far end of the terrace drifted inside, too. At last Joe and his date were alone. He flexed his large shoulders inside his uniform, leaned against the parapet, shakily lit a Camel, and blew three lopsided smoke rings into the dusk. She looked at him and her shoulders shook slightly.

He tossed the cigarette into a hedge of boxwoods just below. "Cold, sweetheart? It's that thin southern blood. How about you and me take a stroll through those bushes—" he jerked his head toward a bank of azaleas down the lawn "—and make a little fun to remember while I'm slogging through the muddy fields of France."

The way his tongue rolled around those words pleased Joe. Sounded poetical, it did. Showed he had as much class as the folks who owned this joint.

But his date—Melanie? Melissa?—darted a quick, anxious look at the French doors.

He laughed, a high bray that sounded even to his own ears as out of place on this elegant terrace as a horse's whinny. "Looking for somebody to rescue you from the Yankee soldier, honey?"

"There *are* Yankees with manners," she said, flaring her nostrils and starting to move away again. " 'Scuse me, I see my brother inside. I need to speak to him a minute—"

Joe grabbed her bare shoulder and squeezed. "Not so fast, babe." As she tried to get away, her skin slid beneath his fingers as powdery and soft as the inside of a balloon. It made him eager to get to the bushes. He gripped her with two fingers and let his pinky slowly creep toward her strapless bodice. With a cry, she jerked away. He laughed and pulled her back. "Come on, sweetheart, you want it as bad as I do."

"Take your hands off her, Private!"

The voice was low, but accustomed to being obeyed. Startled, Joe looked around. He saw a man silhouetted in the glass door against the brightness. With another small cry, the girl jerked free.

Joe grabbed her arm again. "Bug off—*sir*. You ain't wanted here. This is my date!"

"I said take your hands off her!" In two strides the man crossed the terrace and clutched Joe's uniform shirt. His fingers were unexpectedly strong.

Joe's vision was blurred. He couldn't see his opponent clearly. But he'd always enjoyed a good scrap as much as a roll in the hay. Tonight it looked like he'd get both. With a blunt and pungent reply, which included a pedigree of both his date and her protector, he shook off the lady and sailed into battle.

"Go inside, Sissy. Now!" the stranger commanded.

Joe scarcely heard high heels clatter across the rough granite or the door slam behind her. His juices were flowing. Joe had no doubts who would win. His only question was, how soon?

The drinks, however, had left him woozy and unbalanced. Twice he jabbed at the other man and flailed air instead. Then he was held by the shoulders and shaken in an iron grip of fury.

"Son of a bitch, you're really mad!" Joe marveled thickly. He balled his fist and struck the air again. "She ain't worth it, you know." He threw back his head and laughed.

The other jerked him forward and slammed him against the stone pineapple. "Hey!" Joe exclaimed. His head struck the pineapple a second time, and a third. Then it lolled to his shoulder.

That is how Private Joe Brady died in Buckhead.

Meanwhile, in a large upstairs linen closet, two people argued in hushed voices. "You needn't get out of the car, honey," the man wheedled, "and it's only once more, I swear. Double pay?" His voice was scarcely audible above "Stardust" floating up the stairwell.

In the darkness, the woman reached out for his arm. He

moved closer, knowing she needed something to hold on to while she debated with her conscience. He also knew why she dropped his arm as soon as she felt the long sinews beneath her fingers. She had recalled where they were—and the impropriety of being there. Resolutely she pressed her back and palms against the door. "What if we get caught?" she breathed.

"Did we ever get caught before?"

"No, but this time there's more at stake."

"We *won't* get caught. I promise. You know I wouldn't ask if I didn't need you." He fumbled for her hand and carried it to his lips.

She trembled, jerked it away. "Can't you get somebody else?"

Still holding her hand, he traced her cheek with his other forefinger. "Nobody good as you, sweetheart. Timin' is everything. You know that—and you're the *best*!"

"*You're* going to get caught someday," she said with conviction. "Even if I don't."

"Never! Nobody but you and Demolinius knows a thing. Whole world thinks I'm as pure as the driven snow."

"Georgia snow," she said wryly. They laughed together in the warm dark, then—again remembering where they were and that she really must go—she asked, "Can we trust Demolinius? If we did get caught, I could never explain—"

"You won't have to explain anything—ever! Just one more time, then if you want out, you're out." He paused. "I'll make it worth your while."

"Well—"

When she sighed, he knew she would do it. For him. He wondered how much more she might do, if asked—then shook himself like a dog coming out of water. He did not need complications at this point.

"Okay. Let me know where to meet you, and when. But it's got to be the last time. It just has to! If Mama found out, or—"

"Shhh. Nobody's going to find out." He reached behind her for the doorknob. His hand tangled for a moment in the waist of her soft blue evening dress and he tickled her gently.

She giggled and kissed him lightly on the cheek before slipping out the door.

As he had promised—for he was an honorable man, in some ways—he counted to three hundred before following. Stepping from the closet, he met the curious gaze of a petite woman with auburn hair, coming down the hall.

"Evenin', Peggy!" He offered her an elbow and a rueful grin. "Seem to have lost my way. May I escort you back to the party?"

"Actually, I was goin' outside for a breath of air. You may escort me to the back door."

On the Winwoods' back lawn, shaded by a dowager magnolia, two faces were splotches of white and gray. Their voices were desperate, but so muted that even someone standing just beyond the tree might not have heard.

"You cain't go! I cain't bear it!" His voice choked with tears.

The other voice was deeper, a rich baritone. "I have to. I have my transfer. Besides, being near you is torture, and it's getting risky to be seen so often together."

"I know but what will I do? I love you!" As the moon sailed from behind a cloud, his tears glistened for an instant in the silvery light.

His companion drew him deeper into the shadows and said roughly, "I love you, too, but I'm going. Tomorrow, at dawn. Now get back inside, and don't speak to me again tonight. That's an order!"

The first man stepped into full moonlight, was silvered from head to toe. "I'll follow, you know. *Wherever* you go! You just wait and see!" He turned and plunged toward the house, nearly colliding with a small auburn-haired woman standing on the kitchen steps.

"Sorry." He ducked his head away from the moon, hoping she could not see his damp cheeks. "I came out to cool off."

"That's what I came out for, too." She fanned the air with one hand. "It's hotter inside than—"

"Peggy?" a voice called through the open screen door.

She spoke over her shoulder. "Yes, John. I'm out here getting some fresh air. Just coming." She tucked her hand through the man's willing arm and together they went in.

In the enormous living room, Persian rugs had been lifted, furniture pushed to the walls, and one corner filled with a small live band. In spite of the humid heat most couples were dancing, taking what pleasure they could before facing a most uncertain future.

Rippen Delacourt stood in the doorway smoothing back his thick auburn hair. As the band struck up the first lilting notes of "Josephine," he searched for his wife. Failing to find her, he scanned the chairs lining the walls. Rip was, at bottom, a very kind young man.

Across the room, he saw a pair of eyes watching him anxiously. When their gazes met, she gave him a quick "I'm having a good time and I dare you to feel sorry for me" smile, but he could read that look. It was an act. Threading his way between dancing couples, he bowed. "May I have this dance?"

It was a mere act of courtesy. Rippen never expected such a transformation. But after one uncertain pause to see if he really meant it, her pale cheeks turned a happy pink and her eyes sparkled. "Why, yes!" She rose quickly.

After her first eagerness, however, she was strangely stiff in his arms. He began singing softly, adapting her name to fit the song, until she chuckled and he felt her begin to relax.

Her hair shone in the light of the big crystal chandelier and the scent of her perfume was delicate and sweet. He pulled her closer. "Don't stick yourself on my corsage pin," she warned practically. "It's awf'ly sharp."

He grinned down at her. "Maybe I better throw you away!" He gave her a twirl.

She followed his lead with surprising ease, then improvised a step of her own. Rip, who loved music, was enchanted. "You're a great dancer!" He executed a fancy step, almost as a challenge.

She took the challenge and bettered it. "So are you." She spoke over her shoulder with a flash in her eyes. Dancing had made her breathless and brought even more color to her cheeks.

"Here we go, Ginger Rogers!" Again he drew her close to his chest. As the music swelled around and within them, Rip danced as he had not danced in years—as he had only danced in his dreams. Their steps matched perfectly, and such magic flowed from them that other couples stopped to watch. After their final twirl when the music ended, the room filled with a patter of applause.

Flushed and perspiring, he bowed and his partner bobbed a mock curtsey. Then she turned and started for her chair. He drew her back, tucked her hand firmly into his arm. "That calls for champagne!"

She nodded without a word, but her eyes spoke her pleasure. He escorted her to the bar.

"Great dancing!" "Hollywood, watch out!" friends teased them.

Rip jostled them to a place at the bar and ordered champagne for two. "To you, partner." He raised his goblet and grinned down at her.

"To you!" she replied pertly, smiling at him over the rim of her glass.

Rip felt a surge of mingled elation and dismay. It was not the first time in his brief marriage that he had wondered what it would be like to love another woman, but the sheer impossibility of this one made it hard for him to breathe—or let her go. With banter and jokes, therefore, he kept her by his side until the others excused themselves and drifted away.

The band began the soft, seductive strains of "Marie." He held out his arms. "Shall we?" This one night, before it was too late, he would forget war, family, and respectability.

She came into his arms as if she had always belonged there.

As they twirled, however, Rip saw Delaney Winwood standing in the doorway beside Peggy and John Marsh. With a small bow, the older man left his guests, walked swiftly onto the dance floor, and tapped his son-in-law on the shoulder.

"May I cut in?" Delaney Winwood demanded softly.

"What on earth are you doin' out here? Don't you know everybody's been lookin' for you?"

The man by the parapet tossed his cigarette onto the lawn in a bright red arc, then turned, his face icy white in the moonlight. He didn't say a word.

"You look like you've seen a ghost! What on earth is the matter?"

They knew each other too well for him to lie. "I killed a man half an hour ago." He said it flatly, without emotion. Indeed, as of yet, he felt none. "It was an accident," he added.

His companion critically considered his pallor and trembling hands, then asked practically, "Where's the body?"

Grateful to be believed without fuss, he gestured with a quick movement of his head. "Lyin' under the boxwoods." He started for the French doors. "I guess I ought to call the police. No sense in stallin' any longer."

"Wait!" The newcomer caught his arm. "First, tell me what happened."

When the short sordid tale was finished, the two stood in silence, one too drained to move, the other thinking furiously. Then the latter asked, "You don't know who he was?"

"No. Some soldier. He was pawin' her. I just saw red."

"Is he from 'round here?"

"Yankee, I think. Probably stationed at Fort Mac. Where're you goin'?"

The other was halfway across the terrace. "To fetch your car. I'll bring it right up beside these steps."

"I'll never get away!" he protested.

"You aren't goin' to try to get away. You swear to me this was an accident?"

He nodded numbly.

"Then what difference does it make where he had the accident? I'll get the car, and we'll put the body in the trunk.

After the party, take him out to the Chattahoochee and dump him. With any luck, by the time he's found downstream, nobody will know who he is. The authorities will think he fell in and hit his head on a rock."

"I can't do that! I—" He stopped, changed arguments in midsentence. "Besides, *somebody* needs to know he's dead!"

"Okay." A grudging concession. "We'll leave him his dogtags."

"We have to call the police!" Blue eyes clashed with brown.

His companion clutched his arm. "Get sense in your head! Think who-all else would be drawn into this mess. You don't want that. Dump the body!"

He shook his head. "I can't do it! I can't!"

A sigh of exasperation as wispy as wind fluttered over the terrace. "I'll help. Now wait here. I'll be right back."

The man did not have the strength to protest further.

When he woke the next morning it would all seem like a dream. Bundling the heavy inert form into the empty trunk. Returning to the party to laugh too heartily and pretend to drink too much—while actually curbing his thirst for fear he'd say something he would later regret. Driving through the dark, finding just the right place on the riverbank, maneuvering the stiffening form out of the trunk, trying to carry the larger share of the load as was only proper. Awkwardly lugging it between them to the banks of the Chattahoochee and lofting it into the current. And then retching until he thought he'd bring up his very intestines.

Next week he would watch the paper daily until a paragraph appeared. Tonight, however, with the body safely locked away in his trunk, he went to the Winwoods' powder room under the foyer stairs and washed his hands with the intensity of Lady MacBeth. Then he returned to the party.

Near the buffet table he ran into a petite redhead whom he usually enjoyed very much. "Evenin', Peggy. How're you doin'?"

"Tolerable." She gave him an appraising look. "You had too much celebratin'? You look as pale as Banquo's ghost—and about as cheerful."

He laughed. "It's been a long night. Let me get you somethin' to drink."

A few minutes later, holding a martini as he mingled with the crowd, he just wished the small olive in his glass didn't look like that dead soldier's eye.

"Most of the conversation you overhear, among women, is concerned with the servant problem."[3]

On that sweltering day, Elouisa Whetlock should never have balanced a clean saucepan on the mountain of dishes draining by the sink.

The crash of the fallen pan reverberated across Atlanta. As Elouisa bent her long frame to retrieve it from the green linoleum floor, she heard the typewriter stop clattering in a room up the hall. "Here come dat sigh again," she muttered.

Sure enough, she heard a deep sigh followed by a weary question, "Elouisa, what on earth are you doing now?"

"Dishes, Miz Marsh." With a toss of her head, Elouisa reached for a plate smeared with buttery grits. She had been told often enough in her forty years to wash all the plates before she started in on pots and pans, but to Elouisa's way of thinking, it made no mind which you washed first. They all had to be done in the end, didn't they?

Miz Marsh was the one muttering now—probably wondering when her precious Bessie would be well enough to come back to work. If it hadn't been for the money, Elouisa would have been looking forward to Bessie's recovery, too. Miz Marsh was a hard woman to work for—home all the time, ranting about editors, publishers, and lawsuits, tending her worn-out husband, and wanting a maid to tiptoe around like some ghost. Elouisa was too solid to be a ghost, and she'd be damned if she'd walk soft or work quiet just to please some white woman, even Her Highness Peggy Marsh.

A bird darting past the kitchen window in a streak of scarlet and black caught Elouisa's eye. "Lordy!" she exclaimed, craning over the dishpan. "What a dress dem colors would make!" She reached absentmindedly for another plate, stiffened as it slipped through her fingers and crashed into the white porcelain sink.

A chair scraped in the front room. A light voice grew louder as it approached down the long hall. "You clumsy woman! What have you broken now?" A tiny woman with auburn hair raged into the kitchen. She stared in dismay at the china shards.

"Just a plate, Miz Marsh," Elouisa said sullenly, swiping her large hands down the front of her pink apron.

"I declare, you are the clumsiest creature! I wish to goodness Bessie would get back on her feet!" They glared at one another, the tall woman with ebony skin and smouldering eyes and the wan petite woman whose eyes were surrounded with lines of worry, whose once-pretty face had sharpened into something less appealing. Mrs. Marsh waved both small hands. "Just clean up that mess and go home. Go home, do you hear me? I can't work with you banging around, and you'll wake Mr. John. He needs his rest."

A sudden fit of coughing bent her almost double. One hand slapped her chest, the other clutched her spine. "Lord, my back feels like a streetcar ran over it!" Still coughing, she went to fetch her purse, counted out half a day's wages. "Go on home. I'll pick up the plate."

"I ain't started lunch." Elouisa stood sullenly. She wanted a full day's wages, to pay some of what she owed and put something down on a new dress.

Her employer flicked one hand impatiently and turned away with a swish of her green cotton skirt. "Don't worry about lunch. We'll walk across the street to the Piedmont Driving Club." She cocked her head, listening. "There! What did I tell you? You've wakened Mr. John. Take the money and go—and don't come back!" With another enormous sigh, she turned and hurried toward her husband's room, her heels clattering on the wooden floors.

Rage boiled inside Elouisa. Resolved, she tiptoed down the hall while Mrs. Marsh was busy with her ailing husband. If she couldn't have a full day's wages, she'd take a couple of Miz Marsh's movie star pictures. Some folks'd pay plenty for them.

In the front room entrance she paused, surveying towers of paper covering every surface and spilling untidily onto the floor. Her eyes fixed on large manila envelopes scattered here and there. One served as a back support for the typing chair. Another lay beside the desk. Others were piled in the bookshelf. Elouisa knew, however, that in spite of the careless way she treated them, Miz Marsh valued the envelopes higher than her movie stars. Elouisa had been told more than once not to move them, even to dust.

She licked her lips. Revenge tasted sweeter than greed. Furrowing her brow with purpose, she moved stealthily—more silently than she had ever worked—about the room, taking one envelope here, one there, until five rested beneath her damp apron.

Before Miz Marsh could finish helping her husband in the bathroom, Elouisa lumbered back to the kitchen, snatched up the paper sack that held her navy blue hat and street dress, and clumped down the apartment building's steep back steps. In the downstairs hall she slapped the hat every whichaway on her head, yanked off her pink apron, wrapped it around the bulky envelopes, crammed the bundle into her sack, and arranged her street dress on top.

Outside the back screen door she hawked loudly and spat against the granite foundation. The glutinous glob clung satisfactorily, shimmering in the sun. Lips exhaling small puffs of irritation, Elouisa descended the many steps to the sidewalk and trudged toward the streetcar stop. Before she reached the corner she was already regretting she hadn't taken time to change. What would people think of her, riding 'cross town in the middle of the day in her old gray work dress? One more grudge against Miz Marsh.

The bag was heavy. As she waited for the streetcar, Elouisa considered what she'd do with the envelopes. *Burn them!* Miz Marsh set such a store by them, it would be pure pleasure to watch them go up in smoke. But then her eyes narrowed. Could be they was worth something. Maybe she could send Lightfoot around to hint they could be had back, for a price.

When Elouisa climbed heavily onto the streetcar, she was already picturing her new red-and-black dress.

"They have acted like a hit-and-run driver that had damaged an innocent pedestrian. . . ."

> Margaret Mitchell, on copyright infringe-
> ment[4]

In spite of the heat, Elouisa stood on the sidewalk and watched the long funeral procession until it was out of sight. "Life sure is funny, Lightfoot," she said to the dusky man standing beside her. "Who'da thought Miz Marsh'd git run over by some fool taxicab? The way she carried on about suin' people, I'da thought one of dem would'a shot her."

"Just goes to show," Lightfoot said enigmatically, toss-ing aside the toothpick he'd chewed to a nub and bending to wipe dust off his new yellow shoes. Then he straightened and tugged at her elbow. "Come on, Weesa, I need a cold beer. She warn't nuthin' to you. You don't have to watch her all the way to Oakland Cemetery."

Elouisa gnawed the inside of her cheek. Little he knew! For two years she'd put off sending him 'round to the Marshes with them envelopes. Might as well burn 'em now. But she'd wait for a chilly day. That stack made a nice shelf in the back of her closet to keep her best shoes off the floor.

Part Two

The Nineties

"The Buckhead boys. If I find them, even one, I'm home."

> James Dickey, "Looking for the
> Buckhead Boys"[5]

Honey Norton was dreaming that she still lived in Buckhead.

It was her birthday. She was seventeen, waking in her dainty pink-and-white room in one upstairs corner of the enormous stone house. A soft breeze stirred her organdy curtains and the eyelet skirt on her dressing table. It carried up the scent of a gardenia blossoming just beneath her open window. She could hear Rollo, the yardman, mowing outside, and in a few minutes she would get up and tiptoe downstairs to make coffee. Before her father left for his insurance office, they would eat Wheaties together in the big sunny breakfast room. Saturday mornings, when he went in late, were always special for them both—an hour of private conversation and shared silences. Her mother, of course, wouldn't get up until Hattie, the maid, arrived, but Honey would carry up cups of coffee and sit on her bed to discuss plans. She and her mama shared a birthday.

Honey sighed and drew the covers to her chin, utterly happy.

Gradually, however, the summer breeze became a wisp of chill from an ill-fitting window. Rollo's mower dissolved into the drum of pouring rain. It lapped the edges of her consciousness until she remembered she was not seventeen, but nearly sixty-eight. Her parents were dead. And she no longer lived in Buckhead.

Hot, fat tears squeezed between her lashes to soak the pillow beneath Honey's cheek.

She turned over, consoling herself with the sleep-blurred knowledge that it was still Saturday. She would not have to go to the office in all that rain. Perhaps this afternoon she'd ask Jane Waterbury, across the hall, to come over for tea. She had enough flour to make cookies, and they could talk about art.

That was when, like a cruel brother yanking off her covers, full consciousness jerked away all consolation. This was not just any winter Saturday, when she would read in bed until lunchtime, do a bit of cleaning, and ask a neighbor in. This was The Day. At seven tonight Mary Beaufort's driver would arrive in a silver Cadillac and whisk Honey up Peachtree Street, back to Buckhead. Tonight was Rippen Delacourt's Christmas party.

"Ohhh." Honey groaned into her shabby green comforter. "Why on earth did I say I would go?"

She dragged herself out of bed and padded barefoot across the worn Oriental to her mirror, shivering with cold in her old pink flannel nightgown. Forgetting again for a moment who and where she was, she almost went to turn up the thermostat. Then she remembered. If she went back to bed with a cup of tea and read, lying first on one cold hand and then the other, she would not have to turn up the heat until almost noon. Half a day of heat on weekends was all her slender budget permitted.

Still shivering, she peered at the wan face in the mirror.

The harsh rain-dreary light showed a very beautiful woman, early prettiness stripped by years of want to the bare, exquisite bone. All Honey saw, however, were remnants of a lovely, luxurious youth. With one forefinger she stroked the wrinkles radiating from her fine gray eyes, then pulled a thick strand of still-tawny hair close to her cheek. "Perhaps you should wear it down tonight, like the debutante you will never be again," she told her reflection cynically. "Put a bow in it and see if anybody remembers."

By anybody she meant one somebody—and he would not remember. If he had not remembered for nearly fifty years, he certainly would not remember now.

Teeth chattering, she tugged the comforter off her bed and wrapped herself in it, fumbled with bare feet for pink slippers that had once been soft and fuzzy. They were hard now, but warmer than the icy floor. Padding across the small room to her closet—a mere wisp of a space, just enough for what remained of her once-lavish wardrobe—she considered and discarded everything there. Finally she sighed. "It will have to be the black. It's shabby, but at least it's a Chanel."

As she said it, she envisioned others who would fill Rip's spacious rooms tonight. Men who could buy this entire apartment building with next week's earnings. Their wives, whose greatest worry this morning was whether they had gained weight since ordering sleek new gowns from Neiman-Marcus.

Again she lifted the skirt of her black dress, saw how thin the silk had worn near the waist. Dropping it, she hurried to the phone, already composing sentences in her mind. "A touch of the stomach flu. So sorry. Please give Rip my warmest wishes."

Mary Beaufort, however, was at the hairdressers, having a final rinse put on her silver curls, then she and Sheila Travis, her niece, were meeting for lunch. Mary's housekeeper Mildred greeted Honey warmly, promised she would ask Miss Mary to call her back, then added, "Poor Mr. Rip is certainly looking forward to having everybody there tonight, Mrs. Norton."

Honey pressed three fingers to her mouth, so tightly she was in danger of cutting her upper lip, to keep from crying

aloud, "Have we come to that—poor Mr. Rip, poor
Honey?" Around her in the cold bare room swirled visions
of warm elegant rooms filled with music, cosmopolitan conversation, tables laden with more food than she ate in a year,
and eyes that said eloquently what words never would. Rip.
Dorothy and Charles Davidson. Winona and Philip Maxwell.
Mary Beaufort. Maybe even Lamar Whitehead. Could she
face them all, go back to Buckhead, just to please Rip? "Poor
Rip"?

"A lady never shirks her duty, nor fails to do a kindness." Honey could hear her mother as clearly as if that stern
pretty woman stood at her shoulder.

Honey squared those shoulders and took a deep breath.
"Mary doesn't need to call me back, Mildred," she told the
maid. "I just wanted to tell her I will be downstairs by seven.
Jason needn't get out of the car in all this rain."

As Honey was padding across her chilly bedroom on that
wet Saturday morning, Philip Maxwell was up in Buckhead
settling into his favorite chair—a navy leather designed and
crafted in Sweden to fit the contours of the human body. He
checked to be sure the morning *Constitution* waited on the
thick taupe carpet to his left before reaching for a steaming
mug of coffee on the small glass-and-rosewood table to his
right.

Sipping the coffee, letting it roll around his tongue,
Philip gave a satisfied nod. Delta, the new maid, had finally
learned to grind Colombian beans and brew them properly.
Unusually content, he put on silver-rimmed reading glasses
and unfolded his paper.

Through an enormous living room window, rain-laden
light gave a sheen to his silver hair and beard and reflected
off the exquisite streamlined graphic of a Sol Kent needle-
point in taupe, cream, and a touch of cobalt. Raindrops ran
down the window in dancing rivulets. If he craned his neck,
Philip could watch them dive toward pre-Christmas traffic
crawling along Peachtree Street eight floors below, but he
did not bother. Five years ago, he and Winona had moved to

this condominium from the large house he'd grown up in *precisely* so he could get above the snarl of traffic and shops the city fathers had permitted to clog upper Peachtree. Philip much preferred this ever-changing view of clouds and sky.

It had never occurred to him to leave Buckhead. It was still convenient for shopping in spite of the traffic, and only a short drive up Peachtree from the offices next to Piedmont Hospital where he still saw patients daily. His friends—the ones who were still alive and more or less kicking—lived nearby. And while he often deplored the fact that Atlanta seemed bent on turning what had once been a pleasant family-centered community into one long traffic jam, Philip deplored many things these days. In spite of his preference for modern surroundings, some people considered Dr. Philip Maxwell a testy old-fashioned man. He himself would have said that, like Queen Victoria, he did not suffer fools gladly, and as he aged, there seemed to be more and more fools around.

This morning, comfortably dressed in an ancient gray sweater, baggy plaid pants, and slippers he'd had long enough to shape them to his feet, he anticipated several hours of total solitude while Winona prepared for Rip Delacourt's party tonight. With any luck and this rain, her hairdresser's appointment and Christmas-related errands should keep her away from home most of the day.

With his usual forethought, Philip had instructed Winona last week to make certain that his tuxedo was clean and that Delta used enough starch when she pressed his shirt. He'd asked her to fetch his diamond cuff links and studs from the safe, and checked this morning to be sure she had put them in his jewelry box. Philip needn't think about the party again until seven.

Lazily he stretched, extended his short legs fully on the chair's matching ottoman, and let his slippers fall to the carpet. Wiggling bare toes and sipping excellent coffee, he adjusted his glasses and turned sharp brown eyes to a leisurely perusal of the morning headlines.

The news, while dreadful, was not unusual: continued famine in Africa, a retired admiral with AIDS, a plane crash in Europe, an unsolved Atlanta murder case reopened, an earthquake tremor in California, unrest in the Balkans, economic uncertainty in the Common Market, another tell-all book on World War II.

What was there in the paper to make Dr. Philip Maxwell freeze, touch his finger to one particular story, and groan?

While Philip was reading his paper, Dorothy Davidson was studying her reflection in a full-length mirror less than a mile away. The Davidsons lived on Cherokee Road, one of Buckhead's loveliest and most exclusive streets, and Dorothy's bedroom was a study in blue and lavender chosen especially to complement her delicate skin and startling eyes. Her stockinged feet sank nearly to the ankles in powder blue carpet as, tall and slim, she stood in an ecru silk-and-lace slip and critically considered her reflection.

In a less charming woman, that nose would have been called prominent and the chin sharp. Society writers usually referred to Dorothy as "distinguished," and preferred to dwell on her startling blue eyes. Her loveliness was not of feature, but of aura. Dorothy was a woman who tolerated only beauty around her—in her own body as in everything else. Even though she limped slightly from a recent hip replacement, a stranger would not guess (and friends never mention) that she was past seventy. A discreet plastic surgeon and a personal trainer who came in daily to help her work out kept her spare frame and long face almost as supple as they had been at fifty. But would her hair do for Rip's party tonight—or would she need to call Flossie to come comb it out again? She'd had it done yesterday for the Thompsons' reception, in a fluffy chic cap of silver-blue. Had it flattened too badly overnight? And was the color right?

Undecided, she padded into her well-filled closet and brought out a black crepe dress she had bought the last time she and Charles were in Paris. She hadn't worn it in Atlanta before. Holding it against her before the mirror, she was relieved. It would be fine for tonight, and her hair fine with it. No need for Flossie to come out in all this rain.

Still holding the dress against her, Dorothy moved slowly, languidly, to music only she could hear.

Charles Davidson came from the adjoining bedroom, lean and frosty in a navy pin-striped suit, crisp white shirt, and subdued red tie. His thinning white hair was combed carefully across his pink freckled scalp, and his face was ruddy from a recent shave. His pale eyes were softer than usual as he watched his wife, and his lips curved beneath his small white mustache. "Dancing already?"

Dorothy stopped dancing and flushed. "Daydreaming." She put the dress back into her closet, took out a soft blue wool, and stepped into it. "Zip me up?" She turned her back.

Charles did it efficiently—as Charles did everything—then turned her around and kissed her formally on the forehead. "I'll be home in time to dress for Rip's. We'll go late, I suppose, as usual?"

"If that's all right with you. But of course this year's party won't go as late as some. I told the Maxwells we'd try to get there about nine."

"Fine."

As he left, a small sigh escaped his wife. For one crazy moment she had thought Charles was going to sweep her into his arms and waltz around the bedroom—at nine o'clock on a rainy Saturday morning! The very notion made her smile. That was not the kind of man Charles Davidson was.

In the nearly fifty years they had been married, Dorothy had never known Charles to have one ungoverned passion, one uncontrolled thought. As her mother had said the first time Charles came courting, "He may not be much to look at, but he is one man you can depend on to do the proper thing."

Between them had hung the unspoken comparison: *unlike your father.* Dorothy's flamboyant father had died the previous winter—and left them barely enough to pay his car racing debts without selling the house. The shock of his improvidence had made Dorothy turn from the charming, volatile man she had begun to love to plain, dependable, honorable Charles.

"Fortunately," she whispered this morning in the still-ness of her bedroom. Over the years, more and more people had come to depend on Charles and his deep-down good-ness. By now he was one of Atlanta's leading financiers. And if sometimes he wasn't very exciting—

"You made your bed," Dorothy rebuked her reflection in the mirror. "By now you ought to have learned to lie in it."

But before she went downstairs, she waltzed, humming, slowly around her room, while rain spattered on the wide leaves of a magnolia just outside her window.

Up Peachtree Street near Lenox Square, Winona Maxwell clumped out of the dressing room of her favorite salon, gath-ered a teal kimono around her bulky body, and eased herself into Monsieur Paul's salmon vinyl chair. As always, it was a tight fit. While Monsieur Paul mixed her favorite shade— what Winona thought of as a vibrant, natural red—she peered at the profile topped with a white towel in the next chair. "Faith? Faith Andrews?"

The face that turned in her direction was wide, with a strong jaw and a heavy dusting of freckles. It was also a good twenty-five years younger than Winona's, so although Faith Andrews had been born in the middle of the Second World War and could now match Winona's five-eight in her stock-ing feet, Winona—who had met her as a tot of three—still thought of her as "the little Andrews girl."

"Getting ready for Rip Delacourt's party tonight." Winona meant it as a statement, not a question, but Faith nodded.

"Yes. Saturday's the only day I have to get beautiful."

Winona turned her head to hide a smile. Nobody in their right mind would call Faith beautiful. Her large bones were loosely knit, almost ungainly, until she seated herself at a piano. Then, when her strong hands touched the keys, Faith glowed with—what? Joy? Satisfaction? Winona didn't know what to call it, but it lit up Faith's plainness. She also had, Winona noted wistfully as Babette removed Faith's towel, a lovely head of naturally red hair.

While Faith sat beneath her stylist's busy hands, Winona probed her social life. "You're going to Rip's, too?" She couldn't remember seeing Faith at any of Rip's previous parties.

Faith flexed her long fingers. "I'm playing. Miss Mary Beaufort asked me to get up an ensemble of my students, but the pianist got flu yesterday, so I decided to fill in myself."

Remembering a juicy tidbit of gossip, Winona couldn't resist passing it on. "Do you suppose Lamar Whitehead will be there?" She leaned her lofty torso over the arm of the chair and whispered, totally ignoring the stylist (whom Winona tended to consider a mannequin, not quite human). "I heard yesterday he's been running all over town with a girl scarcely out of college! Can you imagine?"

"I can imagine almost anything where Lamar is concerned." Faith's voice was tight. Too late, Winona remembered that last year Lamar had dated Faith a few times, until Mrs. Andrews got so bad.

At that point Monsieur Paul arrived with his bottle of magic and Winona gratefully leaned her head back and closed her eyes. Hair coloring was the closest Winona got to sacrament, and she seldom spoke while it was being performed. While he combed and massaged, therefore, she relaxed under the gentle pressure of his fingers, half listened to taped Christmas carols, and meditated on the cloudy green crepe hanging in her closet. It had been subtly altered by Neiman-Marcus to fall without wrinkle over her ample form, and they were dying shoes to match. Which would look best with the dress's crystal beadwork, diamonds or emeralds? Both, she decided. Winona loved jewels with a child's passion for anything that sparkles.

"How's Doctor Max?" she heard Faith ask.

Forced to break her vow of silence, Winona replied shortly. "Couldn't be better. Still working," she boasted. Faith's cousin Prime, a radiologist, had recently retired at fifty-five.

"He's a marvel," Faith agreed. "I'll never be able to

thank him enough for all he did for Mother last fall before she died."

Monsieur Paul left Winona for her color to process. She wiggled to get more comfortable in her chair as she admonished Faith. "Don't you even try to thank him! He'd be offended. Philip sees disease as an enemy, and fighting disease as his personal war. The first time I ever laid eyes on him, he was patching up a sailor in the naval hospital in Honolulu. I was a nurse back then, you know. Philip was so engrossed in his sutures that I had to speak three times before he heard me."

Faith's face crinkled into delightful lines. "And you decided then and there to make him notice you? You certainly succeeded."

A sudden cloud passed over Winona's heavy face, darkening her bland eyes and turning her vivid mouth toward her treble chins. "No, that was later. Two years later." She forced a smile. "And just think—we've been married forty-seven years this month!"

"You're very fortunate," Faith murmured, then turned her attention to something her stylist was asking.

Winona felt a bit rebuffed, then smug. Faith must be jealous, she decided. What would it be like to be unmarried at fifty?

Faith, in the next chair, regarded Winona compassionately. It must be dreadful being married to an old fuddy-duddy like Philip Maxwell.

While everyone else was considering their appearance for Rip Delacourt's Christmas party, Miranda Wells—massive black arms akimbo—was considering Rip's dining room floor. Pleating the thick skin of her forehead like an accordion, she demanded, "Has you gone plumb crazy? Why you puttin' rat noses unnerneath that fine table?"

She had reason to be astonished. The room was thirty feet long and well proportioned, with heavy red brocade at the windows and elaborate hand-stenciled vines just beneath crown molding. Two enormous Persian rugs had been rolled and stored in the attic the day before, and Miranda had helped polish those heart pine floors until they glowed. Now, pine wreaths hung from the walls and scented the air. The buffet table running the entire length of the room was covered with soft white damask, and the huge sterling silver epergne rising from its center had been filled with red and silver poinsettias, bows, and greenery by the most distinguished florist in Atlanta. So why was Isaac Dokes carefully placing five long suede rats' snouts so they just peeped from beneath the tablecloth?

Isaac's bass chuckle filled the room. He twitched the last snout into place and rose, soft brown scalp shining under the crystal chandelier. "You ain't never been to one of Mr. Rip's parties, has you, Miranda? Peoples come to these parties to have *fun*. Mr. Rip gives the bes' parties of any *white* man I know!"

He picked up two holly wreaths, a sprig of mistletoe, and a large red bow. "Now le's decorate the Winwoods." Carrying a ladder to the Italian marble fireplace at the far end of the room, he climbed up and placed one wreath around the oil likeness of a man with thin lips, lank brown hair, and a disapproving stare. "Merry Christmas, Mr. Delaney," he said genially before climbing down.

Miranda grunted. "Doan' look too pleased to be decorated."

Isaac chuckled again as he moved the ladder to the other side of the fireplace. "Mr. Delaney Winwood never was one for levity, but Miss Fancy, now——" Almost reverently he climbed up to place his second wreath around the portrait of a woman with dimples in both cheeks and a twinkle in her green eyes. "Don't she look just like she's heard a secret and will share it if you come close enough?" Isaac beamed at the portrait. "Spittin' image, it is. And Miss Fancy—Mrs. Winwood, that was—loved a party as much as Mr. Rip. Gave a heap of 'em here in her time. So he allus fixes her up special for his." Isaac taped the mistletoe above her head and the crimson bow at a rakish angle just above her left ear. "Merry Christmas, Miss Fancy."

"Them ain't his parents?" Miranda demanded as he climbed carefully down the ladder and rejoined her.

"No, they was Mrs. Delacourt's parents, Mr. Rip's in-laws. His mama and daddy died when he was small an' his Aunt Carrie raised him, but after he married Miss Georgia, Miss Fancy took him in jus' like he was her own." He looked around to make sure they were still alone. "Some folks thought she cared more for Mr. Rip than for her own daughter. Co'se, Miss Georgia took after her daddy. They weren't much on parties."

"You knew all a' dem? You musta been here forever!" Miranda widened her eyes to feign astonished admiration. The longer Isaac talked, the longer before she'd have to get back to work.

Isaac puffed out his thin chest with pride. "Been here nearly thirty years, ever since the Winwoods moved down the road and give Mr. Rip and Miss Georgia this house. Gertie and I come then, an' we couldna found a better place. Most Buckhead folks doan' have live-in he'p anymore, but Miss Georgia was sick a long spell before she died, then afterwards, Mr. Rip was lonesome. Good thing he kep' us on, too. When he got sick, here we were. Now if you'll excuse me, I gotta put a few necessities in the powder room, then see to that awning."

He picked up a roll of toilet paper printed like five-hundred-dollar bills, and a large black mustache. "This here mustache goes over Mr. Rip's own picture, which he hung across from the toilet in the powder room soon after Miss Georgia died. Said he wouldn't have to look at it, and it might comfort his women guests to know their host was watchin' over them at all times."

Miranda shook her head in reluctant admiration. "Don't that beat all?" She moved ponderously toward the table and reached for a stack of sterling silver trays. "De son mus' favor his mama, den." She set one tray at a strategic place on the long table. "From what I seed of him, he's a regular prune-face."

Isaac drew himself up and spoke severely. "Mr. Walt had a great sorrow come to him last summer, woman. His wife was murdered, and he has not yet gotten over it.* Now

* *Death of a Dunwoody Matron.*

stop your gossipin' and get them trays ready." Chin rigid with dignity, he strode through the arch into the foyer and disappeared into the powder room.

Miranda moved along the table, grumbling to herself. "Murdered? Nobody said nothin' 'bout murder when they axed me to come in for dis party." She looked over her shoulder, suddenly aware how very huge the room was—and how empty. As quickly as a large woman can move, she scuttled toward the kitchen door.

SATURDAY, DECEMBER 11:
EVENING

"No one can deny that there's a need in Atlanta to build more affordable housing."[6]

The brick and granite Delacourt mansion and four-car garage stood on West Paces Ferry Road just down from the Georgia Governor's Mansion. A brick wall surrounded ten acres of landscaped lawn, and a sign on the iron gates reminded the uninvited that this winter wonderland, tonight atwinkle with fairy lights on every wintry dogwood and redbud, was a private residence, not a city park.

Drivers splashing through the chilling December downpour around the last curve noted gratefully that Rip had ordered an awning and a valet—who met them soaked to the knees. Some guests hurried up the wet granite steps. Others moved with the careful dignity of age. All exuded clouds of expensive perfume and whispers of fur, silk, satin, and velvet.

Inside, gleaming chandeliers and bright voices almost drowned out carols played by a small ensemble dwarfed by an enormous tree towering up the staircase curve. Women handed coats to a maid, lightly touched salon-perfect coiffures, and adjusted their jewels. Their menfolk shrugged off raincoats and tugged down tuxedo sleeves. Isaac's scalp glowed like milk chocolate and his soft gray fringe bobbed as he bowed in welcome. His honeyed voice provided a basso profundo to the music. "We're honored that you could come. Please wear this small Spirit of Christmas. Mr. Rip is there, in the center of the hall."

About nine an old racing green Jaguar pulled into the valet parking line. Its occupants—both tall, lean, and dark— were younger than most of Rip's guests, the man just past forty and the woman slightly younger. As they slowed to creep in sync with a gray Lincoln Town Car and silver Mercedes ahead of them, he objected, "You said we'd get here after everybody else."

Sheila Travis—who had been checking the mirror to see how badly her hair was frizzing—raised the visor and leaned forward to peer through the swishing wipers. "That's just Rip's cronies, Crispin. They come late and stay to close things down. Aunt Mary usually comes with them, but tonight she came early to serve as Rip's hostess." Her long fingers restlessly stroked her black velvet skirt. He reached out and covered them with his own, but said nothing to reassure her.

As a short man helped a woman of statuesque proportions from the Town Car and steered her resolutely up the steps, Sheila murmured, "The Maxwells. He's a crusty old sweetie and she's a dragon."

"Crusty and Dragon Maxwell." Crispin inched the Jaguar up as the Town Car was driven away and the Mercedes took its place beneath the awning. "I think I can remember that."

She felt a sudden surge of panic. "Be good tonight, Crispin! Please? Some of these folks helped raise me, you know."

He eased his well-built shoulders in his tux. "I feel like I'm being brought home to be vetted."

"Nonsense. You've met most of them before." But she

spoke crossly, because it was truer than she liked to admit. When they occasionally ran into Aunt Mary's friends at her aunt's penthouse, Crispin was merely a date. Once she had taken this tall, dark, and almost-handsome man through Rip's door, everyone who knew her inside would regard him as "Sheila Travis's new beau."

He must be having similar thoughts, for his voice had an edge as he inquired, "So what *do* I call these *in loco parens?*"

"Winona and Philip—or Dr. Maxwell. She was honorary chair of the Piedmont Ball a few years back, and will want to tell you all about that. And she's currently working on the hospital's latest fund drive, so unless you're prepared to write a fat check, don't let her get you into a corner alone. Oh, stop sighing, Crispin! We don't have to stay long."

"Will they all know I'm the half brother of Walter Delacourt's infamous murdered wife?"

"Only Aunt Mary and Walt, but she isn't speaking to you and he'll be busy helping his dad host. Oh, and Charles Davidson—" Sheila gestured through the rain toward the distinguished man now bent over the Mercedes door, helping out an equally distinguished woman swathed in mink "—but he's far too discreet to mention it." The man handed his wife a cane and escorted her up the marble steps with stiff dignity. "You remember him—Aunt Mary's financial advisor."

"Dear Charlie?" A chuckle rippled beneath Crispin's tone.

"Don't you dare call him that to his face! I don't know how Aunt Mary gets away with it. Even Dorothy calls him Charles, and she's not the least bit starchy—even if she is the last of a veddy, veddy old family. She's theatrical. Sits on the Alliance Theatre Board, loves to dance—"

"Sheila, why are you babbling?" Crispin pulled the Jaguar under the awning as the valet drove the Mercedes away. "I promise not to eat with my fingers or pick my nose."

She stole a quick look at him. He was a more than presentable date. So why was her stomach churning? Because she didn't want these people to simply accept Crispin. She wanted them to *like* him, and of that there could be no guarantee—especially with Aunt Mary so angry.

With a deep breath, she unfastened her seatbelt. "Ready?"

He shook his head. "I'm not letting a man with wet pants sit on *my* seat covers. Go on in. I'll join you in a minute."

"Don't chicken out, now," she warned him.

Inside, Dorothy was sweeping toward their host's wheelchair in a swirl of black crepe, her silver-topped cane making a musical shuffle-hop on the marble floor and her silver-blue hair gleaming above diamonds and sapphires. "Why, Rip, honey!" Her drawl was loud, rich, and very southern. "You're looking *mahvelous*!" Bending gracefully, she planted a scarlet lipstick flower on his forehead. People who made jokes about blue-haired old ladies, Sheila thought fondly, hadn't seen the elegant Dorothy Davidson!

Charles, meanwhile, was staring distastefully at something Isaac had just handed him. "Doan' look like that," Isaac told him. "It ain't spinach. Good evening, Sheila! Here's a little Spirit of Christmas for you, too!" He handed her a tiny white ghost stuck on the end of a pin.

"Must we?" Charles asked, stroking his wisp of white mustache.

"Pin it on, Charles," Rip called from the center of the foyer, flapping one hand for emphasis. "Later there's gonna be a prize!"

"God save me from any more of your prizes," replied his old friend fervently. In an undertone he added to Sheila, "One Fourth of July I won a live pig." He jabbed at his satin lapel with the pin.

"Maybe tonight you'll win an evening with Marley's ghost," Sheila told him cheerfully. "Here! Let me. You're going to ruin your tux. I love your cummerbund."

Charles gloomily peered down at the conservative burgandy, black, and silver leaves circling his waist. "Max has on turquoise and purple paisley. Dreadful! But you know Rip. 'Color required' on the invitations. Someday he'll make us all come in gorilla suits."

Attaching her pin, Sheila asked Isaac, "Where on earth did Rip get ghosts at Christmas?"

Isaac whispered, "Didn't. Bought them for a Halloween party, then didn't feel up to havin' it. Couldn't let all them good ghosts go to waste." Aloud, he added, "Take this one to Miss Dorothy, Mr. Charles. She went by me so fast I missed her."

"Next time," Charles assured him with dignity, "I shall pass you in a flash. Coming, Sheila?"

"You go on. I'm waiting for someone."

As Charles strode across the marble floor, Rip's right hand—his good one—awkwardly patted Dorothy's arm. "There's life in these old crocks yet, Dotty." His words slurred, and he slumped to the left in his wheelchair, but his mahogany brown eyes twinkled above a bright red cummerbund and emerald studs. "Next year, we'll rhumba. Shock the socks off old Charles!"

Charles thawed enough to bend and lightly clasp Rip's shoulder. "That's a shock I wouldn't mind getting, fella."

As tears stung her eyes, Sheila saw Isaac's were moist, too.

For most of his seventy-five years, Rip Delacourt had been a massive powerful man with a shock of mahogany hair and a laugh that filled any room. He'd made a fortune in what he called "the meat packing business," expanding his father-in-law's small women's foundation factory into the Winsome Company, internationally known for exquisite women's lingerie. Rip's love of good-natured pranks and lavish table ensured that any party he threw was worth attending. Tonight, if his guests were a bit restrained, it was because most of them remembered two years earlier, when a stroke had abruptly canceled Rip's annual Christmas party.

"Where's Walt?" Dorothy asked, looking about the foyer.

Rip flapped his right hand over his left shoulder and said thickly, " 'Round here somewhere. Can't keep track of kids these days."

"Even kids who are forty," Sheila murmured to Isaac.

His bass chuckle rumbled. "None of us think of you all that way, Sheila. We sure don't. Seems like you were both in high school just last week. But we all appreciate your clever detecting last summer that kept Walt out of jail. That was fine. Now, Miss Mary's in the conservatory, if you want her."

Crispin entered, brushing raindrops from his shoulders. Sheila linked her arm through his. "No, thanks, Isaac. This nice man is Crispin Montgomery, and right now Aunt Mary wants to kill him. If she asks, pretend you never saw us. Crispin, let's greet our host."

After he had welcomed the late arrivals, Rippen Delacourt's spirits plummeted. "Instant depression," he called the familiar phenomenon when he was well enough to joke about it. Just now he felt close to tears. Maybe he'd been wrong to have a party this year. He hadn't realized how much he'd miss mingling with his guests, fetching somebody a drink, dropping to the piano bench to thump out a tune instead of being marooned in the foyer, moored to this blasted chair. His old friend Mary Beaufort was drifting here and there, all gray satin and silver curls, making folks feel at home—but it wasn't the same as doing it himself.

A tear slid down the side of his nose. With a quick look to make sure nobody had seen it, he wiped it away. If only he could join the musicians and pep up their rendition of "Frosty the Snowman"! Sadly, his right hand lifted two useless fingers of the left one, then let them drop. Rip had thought he'd come to terms with what he could and could not do. Tonight, he knew he had not.

And there was more. Deep within he felt a throbbing loneliness as acute as a toothache. "Georgia," he whispered to his long-dead wife, "in spite of all our differences, I wish you were here."

Several miles and a cultural universe south of Buckhead, two women faced each other across a dim room.

"Doan' fuss, Mildred," the older one begged. "Jes' because I borried some embelopes—"

"You *stole* those envelopes, Ahnt Elouisa!" the younger one stormed. "Don't give me that 'borrow' business. You stole them!"

The room was small, stifling hot. The women's words had to compete for air space with thick odors of age, urine, baby powder, and fumes from a gas heater turned up high. Outside, the freezing December rain might be drenching Atlanta, but this room's windows were sealed with plastic. Not a breath of fresh air crept in.

The only light came from a double row of jets in the belly of the heater and the rainbow flicker of a color television in one corner—a television too big, too opulent for these surroundings.

The television was on, but nobody was watching. Elouisa Whetlock, ancient and shrunken in a huge recliner, nervously plucked at a colorful crocheted afghan across her lap while her head, covered with a myriad of tiny braids, bobbed with palsy and made dancing shadows on the wall.

Nearby, on a gray love seat, Mildred Anderson sat tense, hands clenched in her lap. In profile, Mildred's shoulder-length hair, smooth and curled under, gave her the silhouette of a medieval page, but she was no longer young. Her neat gray suit, white blouse, and black pumps contrasted sharply with the old woman's pink-and-blue cotton dress, bright green sweater, and fuzzy red slippers. Both women were dark, so dark that in the flickering light they seemed more shadow than alive. The mood between them was darker still.

The jingle of a commercial burst the silence. The younger woman raised her head and fixed the old one with a stern stare. "You stole 'em," she repeated, sick fear and fury catapulting her into the slurred syllables and rich idioms of her childhood. "Flat-out stole 'em."

"I'd of took 'em back." The old woman's protest was a high-pitched quaver. Fuzzy braids quivered with indignation. "I'd of took dem embelopes back, Mildred, if Miz Marsh'd of let me *come* back. But she got so high-'n-mighty I shook her dust off my feet. 'Twarn't my fault her plate got broke."

"It's your fault you stole 'em," her niece retorted, "and never said nothin' for almos' fifty years. Fifty *years*! Now you 'spect Miss Mary and Sheila to put it right? Cain' *nobody* put right what you did fifty years ago!"

"They can if anybody can," the old woman said doggedly, thrusting out her lower lip. "That Sheila is one clever chile."

"She's no child any more," Mildred pointed out. "She's fixin' to make forty, and she's honest, too. How're you gonna tell her you came by those envelopes?"

Arthritis had long ago frozen Elouisa's fingers into a permanent grasp. Now she plucked the afghan as if she could pick the right answer by choosing the right square. "Think of sumpin' to tell her, Mildred. I gotta tie up things, get ready to die."

"Die and go to hell," Mildred said bluntly. Her lips tightened. "You're one bad woman, Ahnt Elouisa."

It was the literal truth. At ninety-two, Elouisa was wizened and frail, but she had racked up a history of thieving, knifing, lying, and brawling that had kept her otherwise respectable family hopping to stay one jump ahead of whoever happened to be after her at the time—police, former employers, lovers, even other kinfolk. But while Elouisa had often been wild, nothing she had ever done had shamed or terrified Mildred like this.

"You gonna get yo' legacy," the old woman coaxed, almost whined.

Mildred sighed, a deep quivering that shuddered all through her. Seemed like Elouisa would leave a legacy behind her, all right. Theirs would go down in history as the family that—

It didn't bear thinking about. Shaking her head to clear it, she stood. "I'll tell Miss Mary tomorrow. See what she says. But don't go gettin' your hopes up. Ain't nothin' you ever did as bad as this. I wouldn't be surprised if you ended your life in jail. Ought to," she added, picking up her new blue raincoat.

"You cain' go 'til Junior gets home," Elouisa whined. "You promised you'd wait 'til he got back."

Mildred sighed, then sat back down. So she had. She glanced at the gold watch on her wrist. Only nine-fifteen? Junior might not get home until nearly eleven. He was park-

ing cars for Mr. Delacourt's party, and even as sick as Mr. D—
was, his best friends would stay past ten.

"I gotta stay," Mildred conceded, pulling one stockinged foot up under her and making herself comfortable,
"but I don't have to talk. Not one more word, Ahnt Elouisa,
until Junior gets here."

"Get me a Shasta grape, Mildred, and I'll be good as
gold."

Dorothy and Charles circulated only briefly before approaching Rip's festive buffet table. Conscious of Rip's
health, many guests had already gone. The rest were scattered through the spacious living room, conservatory, foyer,
and library. The dining room was practically deserted except
for Philip and Winona.

Emeralds sparkled on Winona's fat white fingers as they
hovered over a platter of new potatoes filled with red caviar.
Her dress might have enough material for a small tent, but
Dorothy noted that it hung smoothly. The low-heeled suede
shoes beneath it were precisely the same cloudy green.

"You know, my dear," Charles said softly at the door,
"Winona is not magnificent in spite of her size, but because
of it."

"Absolutely," Dorothy agreed, "but her hairdresser
really should tone down that red!"

She turned and caught Philip's sardonic gaze. Had he
heard? Her cheeks flamed, and she drew Charles to the buffet to hide them. At the meats, Charles reached first for the
ham, and then—seeing Maury Goldstein approaching the table—switched to smoked salmon instead. It was that kind of
thoughtfulness, Dorothy thought fondly, that made her quiet
husband popular with clients and friends, but *she* wouldn't
pass up Smithfield ham for anybody!

As her hand approached a pot of hot mustard, Philip
said in her ear, "Don't do it, Dotty. It'll bite you back all
night."

She turned with a smile. "Don't you hate getting old,
Max? Sometimes I wonder what we used to talk about in-

stead of joints, diet, and digestion, but we always had such good times here!"

Philip's face clouded for such a brief instant that she thought she'd imagined it, until he murmured, "Some of them, anyway." Before she could ask what he meant, he'd raised his wineglass toward the oil portraits over the mantelpiece. "I see that Rip's paid his usual tribute to Delaney and Fancy." He drained the glass. "May I get you something to drink?"

Dorothy browsed the vegetable trays while he went to fetch her a Perrier and himself another glass of wine. When he returned, they carried on a light conversation, but she scarcely knew what they discussed. She was wondering when Philip had developed that tremor in his hand. And was it her imagination, or was he unusually pale?

Winona, looming up with a well-filled plate, gave her husband an anxious, possessive look as she edged between him and Dorothy. "Rip looks a bit peaky tonight. Think he's still bothered by all that nonsense about Walter's wife?"

The sheer understatement of "all that nonsense" referring to a case of multiple murders left Dorothy speechless. "I . . . I really can't say, Winona." With relief, she noticed a pear-shaped man in a red-and-green plaid tie and cummerbund hovering diffidently nearby. "Lamar Whitehead! I haven't seen you in a hundred years!"

Lamar's age-mottled face grew ruddier, the dimple in his chin deepened. Beneath his white crew-cut, his light blue eyes beamed behind rimless glasses. He moved into their circle accompanied by a petite young woman whose radiance was more than youth.

Dorothy gave the young woman an appraising glance while Winona frankly stared. Framed by pale yellow hair, her face was wide at the cheekbones with a dimple in each cheek and slanting green eyes. She wore a bright red dress whose skirt did little to hide her spectacular legs, and she clung to the old man's arm.

Why, Dorothy wondered, would this girl go out with a man three times her age—especially Lamar Whitehead? Of course, Lamar *was* one of the major powers behind Georgia politics, but he stayed firmly out of the limelight and was always sure people wouldn't remember him. He often greeted a hostess by sticking out his liver-spotted hand and saying, "Lamar Whitehead, ma'am." Rumor even was that when he came back after two years' study abroad, he'd jumped off the train shouting, "Mama! It's me, Lamar!"

He was, Dorothy admitted, easy to forget. The kind of man about whom you said, after you'd made up your party list, "—Oh, yes, and Lamar." Perhaps that was why Philip said with gruff heartiness now, "Good to see you, Lamar! How've you been keeping yourself?"

Lamar puffed out his chest. "Not bad for a man of seventy."

Philip laughed. "Again? How many times does that make?"

Winona caught her husband's elbow in rebuke, but Lamar's beam didn't lose a watt. "More than I like to count. Isn't this rain awful? Reminds me of a party the Winwoods had back in '43, raising money for the second *Atlanta*. Do you remember?"

Philip laughed sourly. "How could I forget? I'd just enlisted. Last stop before hell." Again he downed half his wine in one swallow. Dorothy was perturbed. Philip seldom drank more than one glass in an evening. Why was he guzzling it like water?

Lamar chuckled. "That was a hell of a night, too. Rained cats and salamanders, and I ran out of gas taking my date home. Had the dickens of a time finding anybody to come get us. Nobody had gas."

"Speaking of dates . . ." Winona looked pointedly at Lamar's.

He seemed to remember for the first time that someone was attached to his arm. "This is no date." He fondly patted the hand tucked through his arm. "This is my granddaughter Clara, out from California to spend Christmas with her old granddaddy and look over Emory's graduate school. Get yourself something to eat, honey, then if you want to, run along and find some younger people."

The girl ducked in what would have been a curtsy if she hadn't had such an impish sparkle in her emerald-green eyes. "See you later, Pops."

She had scarcely gone when Winona said archly, "I'm going to call you next week, Lamar, about the new wing at the hospital. You, too, Charles," she added as he strolled back to them. "We're looking for ten million dollars."

"Don't look at me." Lamar speared a barbequed meatball with a red toothpick, popped it into his mouth, and spoke around it. "I'm practically in hock paying alimony."

"You should have married one wife instead of three," Charles chided him mildly.

"Would have saved me a heap of trouble," Lamar agreed.

In an upstairs bedroom, a lanky man with nut brown hair punched a control to raise the television volume, hoping to shut out the party below. He'd done his dutiful son bit—climbed into a tux, mingled with the guests, accepted condolences from people who didn't really give a damn that his wife had been brutally murdered six months ago—all they hoped to find out was whether the sordid stories in the newspapers were true. He'd had enough. If his dad thought Walter Winwood Delacourt was wading back into that zoo before closing time, he could think again.

Walt rearranged the pillows at his back, polished his glasses on his spread, and scowled at the screen. When he'd pulled it out, *Gone With the Wind* had seemed like a good choice. Tara in the sunshine to help him forget Buckhead in the rain, sparkling dialogue to replace the emptiness in his own head. He'd forgotten how much Melanie Wilkes looked like Yvonne. That saintly face, the gentle voice—*But Melanie didn't use people,* a thought niggled him, *or dispose of them when she was through.*

Abruptly he muted the sound and sat in stillness, holding his head in his hands. "How could I have been such a fool?" It was not a new question, nor merely his own. His father asked it with tedious regularity whenever another of Yvonne's creditors appeared.

Preparing to sink into a well of self-pity, he was irritated to hear someone knock lightly on his door. Which of the guests was unable to read? Grandmother Fancy's party sign rested halfway up the staircase: *No Snooping Beyond this Point. The Management.*

He padded in sock feet across the room, yanked open the door, and confronted a pair of laughing green eyes. "Hi! I'm Clara. Isaac said I'd find you up here, but he didn't say you'd be so tall." A young blond woman in a very short skirt looked up at him critically.

Walt held onto the side of his glasses and peered down at her. "I'm not tall, you're just short. And why should Isaac send you to find me? He knows I want to be alone." He'd meant to sound severe, but it came out—even to his own ears —petulant.

She laughed and reached for his hand. "He said you'd show me the house. Please? I just love old houses!"

Walt took a step back into his room. He was acutely conscious of his lack of shoes. "I'm sorry, but only the downstairs is open tonight. You can arrange with my father—"

"I already did. He sent me to Isaac, who sent me to find you. Look!" She held up one of the suede rat noses Rip had put under the dining table. "I swiped this to put on your father's pillow, where he'll find it when he's climbing in. But first I want to see the house. Come on!" This time she got his hand, and tugged. "Isaac says there's a real turret room, and a round bathroom, and a bed dating from before the Civil War, and—"

"It's not a museum," he pointed out stiffly. "We don't let people just poke around. The turret hasn't been used for years."

"I won't notice the squalor, I promise. I just want to see the structure. Come on!"

"No. This is a private house. We do not have to show it to anybody who wanders in asking."

Her eyes blazed. "I *didn't* wander in! I'm a guest of your father's, and he said I could see the turret." She fluttered her eyelashes at him with an impish grin. "Please?"

These days, Walt was impervious to that kind of charm. He opened his mouth for another refusal, but it was too late. With almost indecent strength the young woman dragged him from his lair and, with unerring precision, toward the staircase to the turret room.

Downstairs, the group of old friends had been joined by a tiny woman with silver curls and long-lashed brown eyes. She arrived with cheeks flushed and eyes still sparkling from recent conversations, but as she neared her dearest friends she fanned her gray silk bosom with one manicured hand. "Surround me, my dears, while I rest my face. If I have to smile one more minute, my lower jaw is going to fall off!" She reached up and massaged her cheeks. "Charlie, would you fetch me somethin' to drink? Anything, so long as it's ice cold and bubbly."

Dorothy looked down at her, concerned. "You've been going nonstop all night, Mary. How are you holding up?"

"I'm plumb worn out, and I haven't been so parched since the last time I crossed the Sahara."

"You crossed the Sahara?" Lamar questioned, surprised. "On a camel?"

Philip snorted. "A camel named Pan Am—or was it TWA?"

Mary shrugged. "Whichever, they ran out of ice and we had to make do with tepid drinks. Oh, thank you, Charlie, darlin'. You may have saved my life!" Her brown eyes sparkled over the rim of her glass at each of them in turn. "It *has* been a fun party, though, hasn't it?" Her voice brimmed with satisfaction.

"Wonderful," Dorothy assured her, "largely due to you. When do you leave for St. Petersburg?"

Mary sighed. "Not until the nineteenth. Rip threw his shindig this weekend so I wouldn't be tuckered out for my trip." None of the others showed a speck of sympathy. Mary Beaufort might sound like she was resting up to single-handedly drive an ox team to the Yukon, but they all knew she'd ride in a Cadillac cosseted by her driver Jason and her housekeeper Mildred.

Smile lines deepened beside Dorothy's clear eyes and

she drawled in her best public confidential tone. "We saw Sheila arrive with that *gaw*-geous man."

Mary Beaufort drew herself up to her full five feet. "Don't mention That Man to me. I'm so mad at him I could spit!"

"So we heard," Philip said, helping himself to chicken wings.

Winona jostled closer. "What on earth has he done? Surely they are still—"

Mary pursed her lips into a network of wrinkles. "Oh, yes, they are still—whatever. But can you imagine? He wants to take Forbes on a six-week jaunt to South American jungles, looking for plants for his old nurseries. A four-year-old!"

"This particular four-year-old *is* his nephew and ward," Charles pointed out. "If he wants to take the child—"

"Balderdash!" Mary tilted her chin like a rapier. "He only wants Forbes because *I* want to take him to Florida."

"*And* spoil him rotten." Sheila and Crispin had approached so quietly that no one noticed them until she addressed her aunt.

Dorothy reached out an arm to draw Sheila in next to her. "Aren't you *mah*-velous! You ought to wear black velvet every day of your life!"

"At least every winter evening," Crispin agreed, stepping to Sheila's other side.

Winona edged closer to the new man. Mary Beaufort, glaring at a point beyond his shoulder, said icily, "I told you, Sheila, I do not want to be in the same room with This Person."

"It's a big room, Aunt Mary." Sheila might be taller and darker than her petite aunt, but Dorothy noticed with amusement that tonight she held her chin at precisely the same tilt and had the same flash in her eyes.

Inside, however, Sheila was quaking. After successfully avoiding Aunt Mary for half an hour, she had seen the circle in the dining room and steered Crispin in their direction, thinking they could chat briefly and leave. She had missed Aunt Mary's head, hidden by Charles's taller shoulder. She was grateful when Charles inclined his balding freckled head with his usual excellent, if frosty, manners. "Good to see you again, Crispin."

"You're taking good care of Sheila, aren't you?" Winona challenged him. "Since we and Rip had boys and Dotty and Charles never had children, she's always been the only girl in our little group. We all consider her ours to some extent."

"And forget she's no longer a girl," Philip added testily.

Rebuked, Winona looked about her for diversion. "Look! Isn't that Honey Norton—at the same party with Faith? Honey!" She bustled toward a woman helping herself to salmon mousse. "What a surprise! Won't you join us?"

Honey, Sheila guessed, was younger than the others by nearly ten years, but care had etched lines beside the fine gray eyes. Her simple black looked well worn and was adorned only by a strand of fine pearls. The hair that must have inspired her pet name had apparently not seen a good salon in years. Long, it was pulled simply to her nape with a velvet bow.

"Hello, everybody." She named the faces around the circle mechanically, as if calling roll. "Dorothy. Charles. Philip. Winona. Lamar. It's good to see you all again." She gave Sheila and Crispin a puzzled look.

Dorothy quickly introduced them. "—and you remember Mary."

"Honey came with me." Aunt Mary tossed her curls with pride. "I told her we simply must all be here tonight, for Rip."

Honey's smile was forced. "Yes."

As if aware of her discomfort, Lamar changed the subject. "We've certainly had some fine times in this old house, haven't we?" He gestured genially about the dining room with his wineglass.

Charles held up his own glass and regarded it with disfavor. "If anybody'd told me we'd sink to serving water at parties, I'd never have believed them."

"*Mineral* water, dahlin'," Winona pointed out. "It's good for you."

"Filthy stuff," Lamar said, sipping his wine. "We were just talking, Honey, about parties Fancy held here during the war. You were too little for most of them, probably, but weren't you here for Charles and Dorothy's engagement party, the summer of '44? Wasn't it a blowout? I always wondered where Fancy got all that beef, butter, and liquor."

To Sheila's utter surprise, everyone was suddenly preoccupied.

Charles, apparently smitten with a fast-acting allergy, whipped out a linen handkerchief and blew his nose. Dorothy, who could recite entire Shakespeare soliloquies on one breath, choked on her drink. Winona patted her back and gave medical advice. Honey spilled her own drink and hurried to the bar for a napkin. Philip attacked his chicken as if hoping to win a Most Wings in One Minute contest. Even Aunt Mary started pointing out Rip's hand-stenciled ivy to Crispin!

Sheila herself was casting about for something to say to the baffled Lamar when Honey returned. "Good to see you again, Honey," Philip said, wiping greasy fingers and extending his hand as if she had only just arrived. "How long do you reckon it's been?"

"A long time," she acknowledged in a wan voice. "I don't go anywhere much since I gave up my car—" She stopped. An uneasy silence blanketed the group.

Sheila steered Crispin toward the buffet. "We don't need to be in on this reunion," she said softly.

"What on earth has she done?"

"Nothing. It was her former husband Winston—also known as Stack. According to what I've picked up over the years, Stack was part of this gang when he was young, and betrayed them all." Sheila helped herself to crab and followed him down the table toward the meats. "He was a banker, and one of many Atlantans who died in Paris back in '62 when a plane crashed taking off from Orly field. Honey's dad was on the plane too, I believe. The passengers were all patrons of the arts, and it was a tragedy for the whole city, but worse for Honey, because auditors discovered that Stack's generous gifts to the symphony in recent years had been embezzled from depositors, including his best friends."

"Whew!" Crispin signaled to the carver that he'd like rare roast beef. "But considering recent savings and loans history, the poor guy was just thirty years ahead of his time."

"Maybe so." Sheila chose salmon mousse. "And reading between the lines, I think Aunt Mary's friends are edgy tonight not because Stack took their money—heaven knows they've all got enough to spare—but because Honey is now a dentist's receptionist and dirt-poor. They know they didn't do what their mothers would have called 'the right thing by her' after Stack died. It's her sister, by the way, who is playing the piano. They scarcely speak, I gather, but I don't know the story behind that."

Dorothy joined them in time to hear the last sentence. Picking up celery, she nibbled it and asked brightly, "Isn't Faith's music superb? Don't you just love her arrangement of Britten's *Ceremony of Carols*?" She called over one shoulder, "That little sister of yours has magic fingers, Honey!"

Honey's eyes flicked anxiously toward the door. She looked so uncertain, so miserable at being where she was, that Sheila was suddenly tired of Dorothy's sparkle, Winona's insatiable curiosity, Lamar's jocularity.

Aunt Mary seemed to feel the same. "An excellent ensemble. Why don't we all go into the living room and enjoy the music?"

Down at Elouisa Whetlock's, the nine-thirty program had barely begun when Mildred heard someone on the front porch. "The party must have broken up early." Relieved, she fumbled for her shoes, then stopped, startled, when she heard a knock instead of a key. "Who on earth can that be at this hour—and in this storm?"

She tiptoed to the door and switched on the porch light, opening the door slightly on its chain. A wiry man stood there, dark as the night behind him. Water streamed from his cheeks and beaded on his grizzled hair. "What you want?" she demanded.

"Elouisa Whetlock. She in?" He pushed his face toward the crack in the door.

"Who is it?" Elouisa called from her chair.

"Who are you?" Mildred demanded in turn.

"Demolinius Anderson, her nevvy. Let me in, woman!" The man made a rude gesture. "I'm froze!"

Mildred peered at him in disbelief. "Step under that bulb and let me get a good look at you." When he did, she gasped, shocked to her core. "Why, it is! Where on earth—?"

He shivered, and she noticed he wore only jeans, a T-shirt, a light windbreaker, and run-down shoes with no socks. His hands were shoved into his jacket pockets, one of which bulged ominously. "Open the door," he snarled again, "afore I die of cold!"

"If that's a gun," Mildred instructed, "leave it in the mailbox there on the porch. Then you may come in."

Reluctantly, he turned, and she heard metal against metal. Not until he was back with flat pockets did she undo the chain.

The front door opened directly into the living room. As she held it wide, a wave of cold damp air bulged against the heat for a moment, then shattered into tiny sparks of chill. Mildred felt one flick her calf and another stroke her neck. But her shiver was from more than cold as the man came in rubbing bare hands together and shaping his lips into an ingratiating smile. "Ahnt Elouisa?" He approached the recliner tentatively, one hand extended. "Ahnt Elouisa?" He stopped, shocked.

"She's aged some," Mildred acknowledged, "but then, we've all aged some. You don't know me, do you?"

He turned and gave her face a puzzled scrutiny. Slow recognition dawned in his eyes, widened his lips in a sort of smile. "Millie? Lawdy mercy, baby sister, you done growed up! How's old Gracie?"

"Fine. She's a widowed schoolteacher, stays on the West Side." Mildred regarded him through half-closed eyes, trying to envision her big brother as she had last seen him.

When Demolinius moved out at fifteen, he'd been the kind of boy who liked to pour kerosene on anthills and watch them burn. Mildred and her older sister Grace had figured it was only a matter of time before he poured kerosene on *them* and lit it, too, so they were relieved he was gone. He'd bummed around town, then disappeared in the early fifties. His sisters had supposed him dead. What had finally brought him home after forty years?

When she voiced the question, his voice was soft and coaxing. "A man likes to come home after he's been wandering, Millie. A man likes to come home."

"You in trouble." It was not a question.

"Is that really my precious Demolinius?" Elouisa's voice made them both jump. They had forgotten, for the moment, that the old woman was there. Mildred had also forgotten the devious bonds that linked these two. "Come closer, boy. Let me look at you."

He bent over the chair. "I've growed some, Ahnty Weesa. I got bigger and you got littler." He stroked her bony cheek.

Elouisa looked sadly at her wasted body. " 'Bout gone, Demolinius. You come home in time to watch me die."

"You ain't dyin', Weesa!" He knelt and clasped her chair. "I come home to take care of you. Kin I stay here awhile?"

"You in trouble," Mildred repeated. "That's why you come."

He shook his head. "No, I ain't. Just down on my luck, that's all. And I cain' take living rough like I used to. I won't stay long, Weesa, I promise. There's a man I usta know—usta work for some—he'll give me something. I know he will. Just a few days. That's all I need." His voice sank to a soft wheedle.

Elouisa's twisted hands stroked his face caressingly and she crooned a welcome. Shut out, Mildred went to the kitchen and stuck leftovers in the microwave Junior's mother had sent when he moved in last year. By the time she had poured a cup of coffee and carried the makeshift meal in, Demolinius was warming himself close to the gas heater and she had reached a decision.

"You can't stay here. They's somebody else stays nights with Ahnt Elouisa, and they's no more beds. But here, eat this while I call Cuddin' Anthony. He owns Sweet Auburn

Bar-be-que, and has some beds upstairs where he lets his help sleep. He might put you up for a couple of nights."

"He can stay right here," Elouisa insisted, "sleep on my couch."

Mildred eyed the love seat. "If he cuts off both legs or folds in two." She turned to her brother and shrugged. "It's your lookout, but you'd be more comfortable at Anthony's. Freer to come and go, too."

She held her breath, wondering whether he'd take that particular bait. Sure enough, Demolinius nodded. "Doan' wanna put you out, Ahnty Weesa. You call Anthony, Millie. See kin I come. But you'll have to give me cab fare. I'm a little short tonight."

"I'll take you on my way to Grace's. I'm staying the night with her."

On her way to the phone, though, Mildred changed her mind. There was something wild about Demolinius she did not like—a sudden way of lifting his head and seeming to listen when there was no sound, a darting of his shrewd eyes to one corner and then another, a manner of tapping one foot and whistling soundlessly between his teeth.

So when Anthony agreed to have him for a few nights, Mildred asked him to please come pick her brother up. "I don't like to drive far in this storm," she told him, unwilling to admit the truth—even to herself.

But when Anthony rumbled a comforting, "Sho' will, honey. You just hold on 'til I get there," Mildred knew what was ailing her, because Anthony knew, too. She was knee-knocking scared.

When Rip's grandfather clock boomed ten, Mary Beaufort beckoned Isaac into the privacy of a large palm. Her dark eyes were anxious and more wrinkles than usual surrounded her pursed lips. "We need to send these people home. Rip's tired."

Isaac nodded. In the past half hour he too had noticed a tremor in his boss's crippled hand, a certain weariness in his laugh.

"You tell Gertie to stop putting out food," Mary continued, "and tell whoever you've got on the bar to close up. I'll
tell Faith to send the musicians home after one more number."

She trotted to where the ensemble was finishing a med-
ley of carols and laid one hand on the pianist's shoulder.
"The music has been beautiful, Faith. Simply beautiful!"

Faith lifted her square face just long enough to acknowl-
edge Mary's greeting, then gave an inaudible signal that led
into a jazz rendition of "Winter Wonderland."

Mary raised one silver eyebrow. "I take it Rip's been
making requests again?"

Faith's competent hands moved lightly over the keys as
she gave a deep, throaty chuckle. "How'd you guess? He
sent word by Isaac a few minutes ago to liven it up a bit.
Think this is what he meant?"

"Lord knows, honey. It nearly kills him that he can't
play himself." She closed her eyes and her drawl was more
pronounced. "We used to have pahties in this house when
Rip would play all night. Back durin' the war, when some of
the fellows would come home on leave, the Winwoods would
let us have the run of the place. We used to have a ball! We
always said if you could keep Rip in Co'-Cola and bourbon,
he'd keep the rest of us in music." Mary sighed. "Now we're
drinkin' water and—" She tightened her lips before they
trembled, and recalled her errand. "It's time to wind down.
When you finish this, play 'We Wish You a Merry Christmas'
and send your people in to get something to eat."

Faith nodded. "Thanks for persuading Honey to come,
Miss Mary. I can't imagine how you did it. She never goes to
parties."

"I just told her the gospel truth, that Rip's done a lot for
us all over the years, and now he needs us. Why, you ought
to hear Rip tell how when he was twelve, his aunt used to
corral him to take little Honey Andrews riding on the streetcar so your mother and she could have luncheons. Honey
was about four, I think, and she must have kept him hopping!" Mary sighed. "I still miss your sweet mother, dear.
You took such good care of her in her last years." She patted
Faith's broad shoulders, scanned the three rooms she could

see from the foyer, then spoke with exasperation. "I declare, I haven't seen Sheila for thirty minutes. Probably off in a corner somewhere with That Man, just when I need her. Join us back in the library for coffee later, Faith—if I can get everybody else out!"

Faith bent her head to conceal a smile. Nobody could steer guests home as charmingly—and firmly—as tiny Mary Beaufort.

As predicted, Sheila and Crispin were settled on the big leather couch in Rip's empty, peaceful library at the far back of the house. She had her head on his shoulder, her long legs propped on the coffee table, and a glass of champagne in one hand. Logs burned cozily in the fireplace, drawing gleams from Rip's famed collection of Coca-Cola memorabilia and warming Sheila's outside to match what the champagne was doing to her insides.

"I might never move again!" she murmured lazily. "One of the nicest parts of being nearly forty is that when you find a quiet corner in the middle of a party, you can stay there—and not care about what anybody else, even Aunt Mary, will think."

Crispin chuckled, and rubbed one cheek on her hair. "Want another drink before we go?"

She considered. "How about coffee, and a piece of Gertie's chocolate pound cake?"

As he rose, a voice complained behind them, "Lord! That woman nearly wore me out!" Walter Delacourt loped around the end of the couch and flung himself into one of the twin leather wing chairs flanking the fireplace. He stretched his long legs across the hearth and let his head loll to one side.

Sheila, more irritated by this interruption than curious about which woman had done what, nudged one of his calves with her toe. "Don't hog the heat, Walt. Leave some for the rest of us. You remember Crispin, of course."

Walt held his glasses with one hand and peered at her date. "Sure," he said vaguely.

If he hadn't looked so bushed, Sheila could have shaken him. The two men might not have met until after Yvonne's murder, but Crispin was still Walter's only brother-in-law—and legal guardian of a child with whom Walt had lived for over a year. Sheila could understand why Walt had sold their Dunwoody home, moved in with his father, gone to work every day as if none of it had happened, but couldn't he occasionally inquire about the child? She wondered if he even remembered Forbes existed.

She was about to ask when he said, instead, "That sounds like sleet on the windows. Remember that ice storm in high school, Sheila? You came up here to work on our project on unsolved mysteries—" He jumped up and went to the shelves. "I saw it just the other day—here! It still makes good reading!" He waved an old green binder at her, then shoved it back, loped to his chair, and continued with a story Sheila would rather he didn't tell.

"*Everything* froze up." Walt flapped his arms expressively. "The drive, bushes, trees, even the steps. On her way out, old Sheila slipped, and hit every step with her tailbone—then slid halfway across the drive. She looked like a giraffe on ice!" He threw back his head and slapped his thigh in merriment.

Sheila regarded him sourly. "You laughed then, too, if I recall. Now go to bed. You're stinking drunk."

Walt slid low on his own tailbone and shook his head. "I'm not drunk, I'm whipped. Isaac and Dad sicced a girl on me who wanted to see every blasted closet in the house. The turret, too. Lord," he intoned piously, "deliver me from women with energy."

Crispin reached for Sheila's glass, touching her fingers with his own and doing funny things to her nervous system. "I was heading for coffee, Walt. Want me to bring you some?"

Walt shook his head, then stood in an abrupt change of mind. "I guess I ought to go see how things are going. Maybe," he added hopefully, "the *people* are going."

Walt and Crispin left the room shoulder to shoulder. Not best buddies, but at least it was a start.

Left alone, Sheila closed her eyes. Could any place on

earth be as delightful on a stormy night as this book-lined room with its bronze velvet drapes, walnut paneling, and sleet-slung windows? The only thing missing was the old green and bronze Oriental, which had been lifted to accommodate Rip's wheelchair.

Her mind drifted through a parade of holiday memories: Christmases as a missionary child in Japan, when she'd wistfully wondered what an American Christmas would be like. High school Christmas parties in this very house. Huge, unwieldy embassy parties which her husband Tyler had expected her to manage with grace and aplomb—and which left her too drained to enjoy the rest of the holidays. Christmas two years ago, just after Tyler's fatal climbing accident, when she sat numb in her parents' Alabama living room and tried not to panic at having to make a life for herself. Now, this year, she had Crispin. Sometimes that thought worried her like a cricket loose in a bedroom. Tonight, however, after champagne, it was lovely.

Demolinius was wiping bacon grease from his plate with white bread when Mildred heard Junior's key in the lock. Not until she exhaled did she realize she had been holding her breath.

For Junior, Mildred could smile. He looked just now like a child, tugging off his yellow slicker, with his pants soaked to the knees. It always astonished her that a reprobate like Elouisa could have such a great-grandson. Even more astonishing, Junior managed to put up with Elouisa. After he'd finished high school, the family had gotten together and pointed out to him that the old woman was too old to live by herself but obstinate about staying in her own home. They'd offered to pay for his Atlanta University degree if he'd move in with her. For two years now, Junior had faithfully checked on the old woman during the day and persuaded his many girl friends to come cook them both a good meal at least twice a week. Yes, Mildred could smile at Junior. She enjoyed looking at him, too.

At twenty, he was not particularly tall; but he was mus-

cular, and the color of fresh ground coffee. Mildred did not
share his admiration for the curves a barber carved in the
side of his hair, but she was willing to agree that his small
black mustache was worth the care he took with it.

He slammed the door behind him, shook the dripping
slicker, and exhaled a long breath. "Man, I am one wet human being! When Isaac said I could come on home, I didn't
ask him to repeat it. Whew!" He paused to flick their guest a
curious look.

"Junior, this is my brother, Demolinius. He's been gone
a long time, and just got back tonight." Mildred said it
evenly, her eyes willing Junior, *Let it go, don't ask questions
right now.*

He got the message. "Glad to meet you." He went to the
bathroom, came out toweling his head. "You and Mama
Weesa have fun tonight, Mildred?"

She made a wry face. "Not much. I've had about as
much of Ahnt Elouisa as I can stand for now."

He threw his great-grandmother a tolerant look. "She
ain't bad, Mildred, if you don't rile her."

"You tell her, Junior!" Elouisa quavered.

"Rile her nothin'," Mildred retorted. "She's been riling
me. I'll talk to Miss Mary tomorrow," she told Elouisa,
reaching for her coat and gray gloves, "and Anthony's on his
way for you, Linus. Says you can stay a week if you need to."

"I gotta change. I'm soaked." Junior went to his room.

"Call Miss Mary rat now, Mildred," Elouisa demanded,
plucking the air with one claw as if to draw Mildred into her
web. "Go in dat kitchen and call her rat now! I might die
'fore morning."

"You ain't dying, Weesa," Demolinius crooned softly.
"I'm here to take care of you now."

"Miss Mary won't be home yet, anyway," Mildred told
her.

"They're probably still at Mister Delacourt's," Junior
called. "Gertie was fixing decaf to take back to the library
when I left. Looked like some folks were going to be there a
little while yet."

"Well, I can't bother them there." Mildred picked up
her bag.

"I might *die!*" Elouisa insisted again, waving both hands in the air. They made huge shadows like deformed birds on the wall. "Might die tonight, wit' dis on my soul! Call and tell Miss Mary to come out here and let me tell 'er all about it. She gotta make it right. She just gotta!"

"What's troublin' you, Weesa?" Demolinius's eyes darted from one woman to the other.

"Some papers I borrowed from a lady I worked for. I want to get 'em back afore I die."

"Don't sound so goody-goody. You stole those papers," Mildred reminded her.

Demolinius wheeled back to the old woman. "Stole 'em, Weesa? Is they valuable papers?"

"Not anymore, Linus. Woman who'd pay for 'em is daid."

"Burn 'em, den."

Mildred swiftly intervened. "They aren't hers to burn. They need to be returned to the family."

Demolinius narrowed his eyes. Mildred remembered that look. Her brother was wondering what there might be in all this for Demolinius. "Want me to help you?" he crooned. "Tell me all about it, Weesa."

"It ain't much, precious, but I don't want to die with it on my soul."

In the process of shrugging on her coat, Mildred hesitated. She had no doubts about Elouisa's soul. It was so heavy with sin that this one theft wouldn't sink her deeper in hellfire. But if Elouisa did die tonight, Mildred would hate having it on her own conscience that she had failed to honor a dying woman's wish.

And if Demolinius got his hands on the papers before Mildred could hand them over to somebody responsible—

She wasn't due back at Miss Beaufort's until late tomorrow. Who knew what might happen by then?

"I'll call them at Mr. Rip's." Mildred dropped her things back onto the love seat and headed for the telephone. "But Miss Mary isn't going to like this. Not one bit."

∙ ∙ ∙

"Sheila?"

Sheila opened her eyes to find Rip's cook Gertie hovering near the end of the couch. "Mildred's calling Miss Beaufort. Will you talk?"

Sheila sat up, drowsy and concerned. "What's the matter—did she say?"

Gertie shook her head. "No, but she did say it's urgent. Walt's got the liberry phone up in his room right now. Come to the kitchen." She led the way.

Gertie's kitchen wore the rumpled tired look of a party just ending. Smeared silver trays dotted the green-tiled countertops, surrounded by wadded scraps of waxed paper and aluminum foil. The dishwasher chugged, and a large ebony woman hummed as she rinsed a crystal bowl and set it to drain, then reached for a stack of serving spoons and slid them into a pan of soapy water. Real Thing, Rip's red-and-white spaniel, snoozed uneasily in one corner. Two women conferred near the refrigerator over a plate of leftover mousse. Gertie waved toward the phone and hurried toward them. "I *tole* you, put leftovers in the icebox! I'll sort 'em tomorrer."

The receiver was perched on top of a box of water crackers.

Sheila could hardly hear the voice on the phone over the kitchen noises. "Say it again, Mildred, louder."

"I said, I hate to bother you and Miss Mary, but I got a bit of trouble down here at my Ahnt Elouisa's." Mildred launched into a long rambling story. By the time she reached ". . . so Ahnty Weesa got mad and stole some manila envelopes from Mrs. Marsh, which need to be taken back—except we don't rightly know how to go about it," Sheila felt like she'd stepped onto a pile of marbles and was heading off in four directions. Why would Mildred consider this urgent enough to call Aunt Mary at a party?

"Taken back to Mrs. Marsh?" she ventured, hoping for at least a glimmer of clarity. Instead, things got worse.

"Of course not, honey! *She*'s been dead nigh on fifty years."

"Mildred," Sheila asked gently, "have you been drinking?"

"Sheila!" Mildred was getting huffy. "Look, *you* may not realize what-all this means, but Miss Mary will. Tell Miss Mary what I told you. Then, on your way home, Ahnt Elouisa wants you to run by and pick up the envelopes. They're full of papers, and she doesn't want to die with this on her conscience."

"Call her preacher," Sheila longed to say. Instead, she ripped off a scrap from a paper sack and wrote down Mildred's directions. You don't refuse favors for someone who stayed up all night rubbing you with calamine lotion when you had chicken pox in tenth grade.

The thought of how long ago that had been, however—and that she was, after all, now a grown woman able to make competent decisions—made her suggest, "How about if I get them in the morning? It's pretty nasty out just now. Or why don't you bring the envelopes when you come home tomorrow night? You and Aunt Mary can spend a cozy evening discussing this beside the fire."

Mildred sighed. "Ahnt Elouisa is real set on getting rid of them tonight, Sheila. It shouldn't take you long, and it would surely make an old woman feel better. Me, too, to tell the truth."

The first commandment for any girl raised by a southern mother—even in Japan—is "Be sweet, now." Sheila didn't feel up to bucking her entire heritage so close to Christmas. "It'll take me at least an hour." First she'd go back to the haven of the library to drink her coffee and eat her cake.

As she hung up, Gertie muttered wryly, "You got on your persimmon face. Why can't you be like Miz Norton, now? That woman's been a honey all her life. She come all the way in here a while back, just to thank me for the nice party."

Sheila eyed her sourly. "If you want me to be sweet, next time give Aunt Mary her own telephone call."

Gertie's eyes rounded with indignation. "I tried, but she wouldn't take it. Said it couldn't be a real emergency—Mr. Davidson was *here*. Now tell me what *that* means!"

Sheila snorted. "Aunt Mary handles only financial emergencies, Gertie. The minor ones she leaves to us lesser mortals."

Gertie flapped her hands toward the door. "Get out of my kitchen with your big words, and lemme get back to my business."

Sheila started for the door, then turned. "Thank you for the nice party, Gertie," she said sweetly.

The library was no longer a haven. The fire still burned low, reflecting off the book-lined shelves. The casement windows still shut out the sleet that drove relentlessly against them. But now Rip's wheelchair sat near the desk. Aunt Mary perched on a chair beside him. Philip sat drumming his fingers on one fat arm of the couch. Winona sat bulkily between him and Lamar at the other end. Charles stretched his legs on one side of the fire and Dorothy sat regally on the other. Honey browsed the bookshelves while Isaac poured coffee at the desk. Walt was draped over the globe in a distant corner, warily eyeing a young blond woman in a short red dress who stood with Faith by the window, surveying the weather.

As Sheila entered, the unknown young woman hugged her bare arms and laughed toward Walt. Sheila wondered where she'd gotten that natural tan at this time of year.

Crispin was propped against the bookshelf flipping through the pages of a *National Geographic*. He pointed mutely to a steaming cup of coffee and generous slice of cake on a piecrust table. Sheila edged over to them and began to eat greedily as Dorothy relentlessly continued a previous conversation.

"Thanksgiving of '44 wasn't any picnic, either. Remember? Rip and Charles home before shipping out to Europe, Georgia in bed with the flu, us deciding to get married before Charles left—which sent poor Mama into a perfect tizzy wondering what food and flowers she could afford, if she could find any to buy. We couldn't afford servants if there had been any to hire, so we had to do everything ourselves. And the weather was dreadful! We lived like pioneers!" Dorothy shuddered. She held her hands out to the fire, sapphires glittering on her fingers. "When you got married two years later, Honey, I was downright jealous. Orange blossoms, champagne—we didn't have any of those things at our wedding."

"Philip and I were married in a naval hospital chapel, and didn't even get leave," Winona barked, not to be outdone in suffering for her country.

"How romantic!" exclaimed the young woman in red.

Philip peered up at her with the look of suffering tolerance he reserved these days for the young. "Must sound better now than it was then. Nothing romantic about naval hospitals that I remember."

"Full of queers today," Lamar grunted sourly. "In our day, we wouldn't have tolerated it. But nowadays—"

"Don't you start on that," Aunt Mary said firmly.

"When did you get married, Pops?" the girl asked, quick to Lamar's rescue and answering Sheila's question about who she was.

"I was smart enough not to get married until after the war," Lamar rumbled genially.

"Not smart enough to stay married," Charles pointed out.

His wife blew him a kiss across the hearth. "Darling Charles, would you do it all again?"

Charles reddened and made a harrumphing noise. Rip guffawed. "Not France. Without me, he'd have starved. I did the parley-voo-fransaying and he slogged through the mud for daily mail call."

"I'm surprised you didn't both starve," Mary told him dryly.

"Speaking of starving," Charles said over their laughter, "where did Sheila get that chocolate cake she's devouring?"

Everyone finally noticed she had joined them.

Rip looked up inquiringly. "More, Isaac?"

"Yessir, we surely do."

Walter turned. "I'll bring it in."

"I'll go with you." The girl in the red dress hurried over to take his hand and lead him from the room.

"Remind you of anybody?" Dorothy asked with a ripple of amusement, watching them go.

Charles nodded. "Fancy to the life! Don't know how you did it, Lamar."

"Fancy and Daddy were first cousins, you know." Lamar rubbed his hands and leaned toward the fire. "Must be in the genes."

Meanwhile, Aunt Mary had risen and trotted to Sheila, giving Crispin a cold shoulder. "What did Mildred want, dear?" She had spoken softly, but at least one outsider had heard.

"I thought Mildred was keeping the child." Winona made a question out of a statement.

"He's with his grandmother, down on Juniper Street," Aunt Mary told her shortly, "and her wonderful companion Lucky. What did Mildred want, dear?" she repeated, lowering her voice to remind the others—including Crispin, whom she ignored—that this was a private conversation. To Sheila's delight, Crispin casually shifted so they stood shoulder to shoulder against the diminutive enemy.

Sheila sipped her coffee before replying softly, "Why, nothing important, Aunt Mary. After all, Charles Davidson is *here*."

Aunt Mary gave a small puff of exasperation. "I was busy sending people off. I didn't have time to talk on the phone."

Remembering how hard her usually indolent aunt had worked on Rip's party, Sheila relented. "It really wasn't urgent. From what I could gather, Mildred's aunt is all het up because fifty years ago she stole some envelopes belonging to a woman she worked for, a Mrs. Marsh. Now she wants to return them."

She still spoke softly, but a sudden silence had made her voice audible to the whole room. Conscious of curious eyes, she decided to tell everyone. This crowd always got a kick out of the bizarre.

She continued, "Mrs. Marsh apparently reprimanded Mildred's aunt for breaking a plate, and she took the envelopes for spite. Now—this very night—she is suddenly terrified she's going to die and wants *us* to take them back." She gave a short laugh and shrugged. "I told Mildred I'd pick them up on the way home. Sorry, Crispin, but Mildred insisted. I'll bring them to you tomorrow, Aunt Mary, and you can figure out how to find this Mrs. Marsh—if she's still alive —and return her precious envelopes."

She had expected roars of laughter. At least a few chuckles.

She was wholly unprepared for electric silence.

"Mrs. Marsh?" Dorothy finally asked, in an I-don't-really-believe-this-but-it's-worth-a-chance voice. "Not *Peggy* Marsh?"

Sheila shrugged again. "I don't know. Somebody Mildred's aunt worked for fifty years ago. Do you know any Marshes?"

Around the room, eye met eye and heads were shaken, but it was incredulity, not negation. For a long minute nobody spoke.

Finally Charles asked, in his noncommittal way, "What kind of envelopes are they, Sheila? Did Mildred say?"

Sheila shrugged. "She just said envelopes—full of papers."

The air grew even more electric. Winona's mouth was a perfect "O" and even Philip looked mildly excited.

"What do you all know that I don't?" Sheila asked, baffled.

Aunt Mary turned. "Please get Sheila's coat, Isaac. Crispin, the valet's gone, so you'll need to fetch your car. Even with the storm you should get there and back in an hour."

"Back?" Sheila protested. "We aren't *coming* back. You can look at those papers tomorrow. After all, how important can they be after fifty years?"

"They could be very important." Dorothy's charming voice wasn't quite steady. "You see, Sheila, Peggy Marsh was born Margaret Mitchell."

*Department store publicist, explaining why Margaret
Mitchell's first autograph party should be a small af-
fair: "I have known Peggy Mitchell always, and I
don't believe she could write anything earth-shatter-
ing."*[7]

Sheila looked around the room in amazement. "Margaret
Mitchell?" Her own voice wasn't terribly steady, either. "The
one who wrote *Gone With the Wind*?"

The only sounds in the room were sleet and fire.

Dorothy broke the silence. "Remember how Peggy kept
chapters in envelopes scattered all over the house? These
might be from an early draft!"

Philip formed the skeleton of a ball with his fingers and
nodded judiciously. "Or some she omitted in the final version."

"Maybe it's a sequel!" Winona clapped her fat hands

and drummed her stockinged feet against the couch. "A *real* one!"

"Surely she would have missed anything important," protested Mary. Rip flapped his good hand in agreement.

"Not necessarily." Lamar puffed himself into legal pomposity. "I knew Peggy well, you remember, and her last years were sheer torment. Her own bad health, John's, and a swarm of vultures out to get what they could from her book. She was so busy, she could have overlooked a few missing envelopes."

"But someone would have said so if she'd started a sequel," Honey said softly, leaving the window and hesitantly taking the desk chair near Rip. "Wouldn't they?"

Rip started to speak, but Lamar got ahead of him. "The Marshes were very private people. Seems to me I do seem to recall Peggy once saying something about another book."

"Pshaw!" Their enthusiasm had cooled Mary's. "These papers will probably turn out to be nothing more than tax receipts or unanswered letters."

Rip finally spoke, his speech slurred with weariness. "Couple time . . . Couple times John hinted . . . new book in works."

Sheila leaned toward Crispin and whispered, "Wouldn't that be marvelous?"

His eyes laughed down into hers and he asked softly, "I take it you've read her first one?"

They hadn't talked about everything in the six months since they'd met, but Sheila was surprised he didn't know how much *Gone With the Wind* had affected her life. "Three times. The first time, when I was thirteen, I cried so much my daddy suggested we plant rice. I spent most of high school trying to be more like Melanie Wilkes—"

"—until you found out you're more like Scarlett."

"Unflattering of you to notice, but true. I even came to Atlanta for high school hoping to find Tara."

"Did you?"

"Not yet, but I'm still looking. I'll gladly drive across Atlanta to have a look at those envelopes."

"Not in my car you won't. But you may ride in the passenger seat, if you promise not to babble."

"I'll try. But you've got to admit this is not your usual party ending." She started for the door. "We'll go get them, but we won't come back if the weather is too dreadful."

"You *must,* dahlin'!" Dorothy reproached her. "We'll none of us get a wink of sleep 'til we've seen those pages with our own eyes!"

As they left, Walt and Clara carried in a plate of cake. Real Thing padded after them and flopped down by Rip's chair.

"Here's what's left, folks." Walt set the plate on the desk. "I think I'll call it a night."

"You can't!" Winona's fluttering hands set her diamonds atwinkle. "The most incredible thing has happened!"

When he'd heard, Walt yawned. "I don't care enough to stay up all night. Let me know in the morning, Dad, if Sheila's discovered a masterpiece. Night, all."

"You're not going to bed, you're going up to finish watching *Gone With the Wind*!" Clara accused him. "You were watching it when I went up to your room earlier. Admit it—aren't you?"

Walt looked a bit embarrassed. "Well, maybe—"

The girl took his arm. "I'll go watch with you. You all call us the minute they get back!"

Isaac's eyes followed them to the door. "She's good for Walt, Mr. Lamar," he said, when the pair had gone. "I'm glad you brought her."

The group sat in the silence of old, old friends, until Dorothy rose and moved restlessly about the room, the silver head of her cane gleaming in the firelight. Finally she paused in front of the wheelchair. "Did John really hint at a new book, Rip? A sequel?"

"No sequel could be better than the first one," Winona declared, squirming to get her thick thighs more comfortable.

Charles had been lost in thought, forefingers resting across his mustache, eyes fixed on the fire. "It might not be a sequel," he said in his deliberate way. "Remember the big party Georgia's folks had right after the war?"

Lamar nodded. "Half of Atlanta was here."

"My first party in this house," Winona added, as if she and not victory had been the occasion for the celebration.

"I don't suppose you remember much about it, Faith." Philip buffed his nails against his thigh. "You came in diapers and crammed a whole piece of cake in your mouth. Perfectly disgusting!"

"I could do it again," Faith said with a grin. "I'm famished."

"—been working all night," Rip remembered. "Give— cake and coffee, Isaac!"

As Isaac served her a generous slab, Charles continued as if to himself. "Even though she was in considerable pain, Peggy came, out of love for Fancy. She spent most of her time sitting right in here—maybe that's why it's so vivid to me now. I asked her if she ever planned to write another book. Do you know what she said?"

Nobody did.

"She laughed in that marvelous way she had and said, 'If I do, I'll put you all in it.'"

No one spoke for a moment. Then Philip voiced the opinion of all: "Good Lord! *What if she did?*"

Driving was dreadful. The rain had indeed turned to sleet. Crispin negotiated Rip's winding drive and West Paces Ferry Road in silence, then looked her way to inquire, "Well, did I pass muster?" He swerved to avoid a sleety puddle.

She nodded. "You even got a few words out of Aunt Mary. I was impressed. But I don't think she's ready for a truce yet."

"And what are you ready for?"

His question hung between them in the dark. Sheila leaned her cheek against the car window to cool it, annoyed because she didn't have an answer for him. Her feelings baffled her. She seemed caught in a deep tide that nudged her ever closer to him, then sucked her back. When he was not there, she could equally convince herself that she wanted to spend her life with him, or that she could live happily without seeing him again. When he was near, she had no idea what she felt. To complicate matters, Crispin seemed caught in a similar tide—rushing closer, then backpaddling into banter.

Now, when she hadn't answered after several minutes, he laughed softly in the dark. "I shouldn't tell Aunt Martha to pick orange blossoms and thaw out the groom's cake she's got in the freezer?"

"Just tell her to send it up!" she suggested. "We could go ahead and eat it."

"You'd eat anything. But that cake gets eaten only if and when I marry. Aunt Martha has made that perfectly clear."

"She needs a magnet I saw the other day: 'Life is Uncertain. Eat Dessert First.' Think it would convince her?" Sheila was not actually convinced Crispin had an Aunt Martha. She came into the conversation only when he was trying to change a mood.

"Not a bit. Like the pilgrim in the hymn, nothing swerves Aunt Martha from her avowed intent. And speaking of swerving—" He spoke between clenched teeth. As they rounded a downhill curve, Sheila felt the car shimmy. "—this is neither the time nor place for this discussion. Are there no straight, flat roads in Atlanta?"

When they finally reached one, it was icy and its traffic lights were out. "I don't know, Sheila," Crispin said, steering down the center of the road. "This is getting worse block by—"

A glare of lights filled the windshield. He wrenched the wheel to the right, and the Jaguar went into a slow, dizzy spin.

This isn't really happening.

Sheila had time to think that clearly while she watched trees whirl past, then a building, a pole, the trees again. Finally, with a bone-thudding crash, the Jag stopped and she was dashed against the door.

She sat, stunned. Shaking her head to clear it, she asked

in a wobbly voice, "Crispin?" Her head throbbed and her right shoulder hurt terribly. "Crispin?"

He said nothing. In the dimness she saw him slumped over the wheel.

"Crispin!"

Her own scream shocked her into action. She reached out and touched him, but he neither moved nor groaned.

"Oh, God, no! Not again!" Icy memories doused her. A stranger on the phone, a clipped professional voice, "Mrs. Travis, your husband has been injured." Tyler in his coffin, cold and still. A silent house, creeping servants, herself shivering, frozen, burrowing into her husband's favorite big blue chair for warmth.

"No!" She grabbed Crispin's arm, fumbling under his cuff for his wrist. She was so relieved to feel a faint pulse that her stomach heaved. "An ambulance," she mumbled to herself incoherently. "Ambulance." She unfastened her seat belt, seized her door handle, and shoved, dizzy with pain. But the door did not budge. Craning her neck—an almost impossible proceeding—she saw why. Her side of the car was crumpled around a light pole. She would have to climb between the seats and get out the left back door.

"Hey, folks, you okay?" A shadowy face peered through Crispin's window.

"How could you do this to us?" she wanted to shriek. If she could have reached him just then, she would have flailed him with her fists. "We're trapped!" she cried.

He jerked open Crispin's door and Sheila felt a stab of sudden fear. She envisioned tomorrow's headline: *Couple Murdered and Robbed After West Side Accident*. Instead, enormous brown hands felt Crispin's neck, checked his pulse, gently moved his head. "Just knocked out," the man said gruffly. "Can you crawl over the seat?"

Relieved but still furious, Sheila bunched her coat and the slim skirt of her dress into her left hand. "Not modestly."

"Ma'am, this is no time for modesty. Give me your hand."

It was an agonizing process. When at last she stood beside him in the relentless sleet, he looked down at her evening sandals and clucked in dismay. "You'd better get back in that car, or your feet will freeze before help gets here."

After running them off the road, he was worried about her feet? Without replying, Sheila bent to make certain a pulse still flickered in Crispin's neck. As she stood, she caught sight of the bloody mess where his knee used to be. Retching, she backed away from the car and lost all Rip's lovely food in the slush.

"You gonna be all right?" the man demanded, standing near but not touching her.

"I don't know," she told him shortly, wiping her mouth on her sleeve. "We need an ambulance." She peered up and down the road. Where on earth would they find a telephone in this streaming bleakness? A sudden squall of sleet made her shiver.

"You get back in your car and wait. I gotta phone in my car. Just a minute." He sloshed down the street, hatless in the gale, to a green Toyota parked a short distance behind them and facing in the same direction. As she realized the implications of that, hot shame swept up Sheila's neck and face. This man had not come toward them in the storm. That driver had probably backed up and run. This stranger was that rarity of the road, a good Samaritan.

Almost weeping with gratitude and shock, Sheila slumped against the back seat, clutched her coat around her, and shivered.

The man returned in a minute talking on a cellular phone. When he hung up, he said with satisfaction, "My wife laughed at me for getting this thing, but she'll never laugh again." While he trudged back to his car to put it back, Sheila repented of half the nasty things she'd ever said about car telephones.

The next half hour was a blur of sirens, lights, and a breathless ride through the city to Piedmont Hospital. Not until she had seen Crispin rolled into an examining room did Sheila take time to call Rip's.

· · · ·

After she'd explained what had happened, she could hear Gertie going down the hall. "Miss Mary, oh, Miss Mary!" This was one urgent call Mary Beaufort did take.

The emergency room was full of storm casualties. When Aunt Mary swept into the hospital with Philip half an hour later, Sheila had heard nothing about Crispin and had not yet been seen by the doctors. Philip soon remedied both.

She was x-rayed and informed she had a badly bruised collarbone from her seatbelt, but no fractures. Given a shot, she floated in a world where pain no longer mattered. She scarcely noticed when Aunt Mary left her to call Rip's and send Jason for a robe and pajamas Sheila kept at the penthouse for emergencies.

Crispin, meanwhile, was sent upstairs to a private room. He had several broken ribs, a smashed kneecap, and a slight concussion.

"How long will he remain here?" Sheila drowsily asked Philip when he returned to the emergency room.

"Three days or so. We'll wait for the swelling to go down, sew up his knee, and make sure he's healing well without infection."

"Do," Aunt Mary told him crisply. "You may want to keep him a month."

Once Mary had called back with a report, Rip's party broke up with a definite sense of anticlimax. As Faith's red Plymouth made slippery progress down Peachtree Street toward midtown, Honey sighed. "I appreciate your going all this way, Faith, to take me home."

"Don't be silly," Faith protested with asperity, slowing to ease through a particularly slushy patch. "You're my sister." She strained to peer through a windshield blurred by sleet.

Honey clasped her purse tightly in her lap. "Your music was lovely," she said formally, with a trace of desperation. "Do you like teaching at Emory?"

"Yes, very much." Faith decided to get something off her chest. "I think you know I was pretty upset when I couldn't go to Juilliard after Daddy died." Honey said nothing. Faith ploughed on. The car and darkness outside provided both privacy and intimacy, and she saw Honey too seldom to let this chance pass.

"I thought *you* should move in with Mama, especially since Stack had just been killed, too. But if I'd gone to school up North, I might have stayed, not gotten a doctorate at Emory or been right here when a faculty position came open. I love our house, and I love Atlanta. So I am glad—do you hear me?" Giving her sister a quick glance, she saw that Honey was gazing out the far window. Maybe not even listening, but Faith persisted. "I'm *glad* I stayed here—and sorry Mama left me all the money."

Honey made a swift movement with one hand, but Faith ignored it. She'd been wanting to say this too long to stop now. "It seemed fair at first, since I'd cared for her all those years, but now I want you to have some of it—and come home. I spoke with Lamar Whitehead tonight, and he's going to draw up some papers. It's silly for you to live in a pokey apartment while—"

Faith had anticipated a gentle protest. Honey's fury took her by surprise. "No!" It was a harsh, raging cry. "I won't take a penny of Mama's money, do you hear me? Not a penny!"

The car skidded wildly over the road. Faith had to battle for several seconds to bring it under control. "Thank God nobody was coming!" she gasped, trembling.

She could feel Honey trembling beside her, too, and sensed more than saw Honey's fingers pressed against her lips.

Baffled but determined, Faith said with a breathless laugh, "Life's too short for us to fight, Honey. At least think about what I said. After all, we're all the family we have. Don't shut me out of your life any longer."

"You've never been *in* my life!" Honey's voice was raw, ragged. "I got married when you were two, remember. I hardly know you. That may be my fault. I admit it. But *you* took care of Mama. You earned the money, and the house. And—" she paused, then finished lamely, "—we have nothing in common."

Before Faith could reply she added, in an abrupt mood swing. "But I have an idea—let's drive over to Elouisa's and get those envelopes now! She's probably still up waiting for Sheila, and it won't take me but a minute to run in and pick them up. Please," she added coaxingly.

Faith had no intention of driving to the west side on this dreadful night. To plead her case, she permitted the yawn she'd been swallowing for the past hour to engulf her. "I'm nearly dead. I've been playing all evening, remember." She flexed her fingers against the steering wheel to relax them. "And we could never find the place."

"I know where it is!" Honey crowed triumphantly. *Like Mama used to,* Faith thought, *when she figured she'd convinced you to do something you didn't want to do.* "Elouisa worked for me once or twice when I couldn't get anybody else. It won't take me but but a minute to run in and get the envelopes," she repeated, as if it were that, and not the hour's trip, that held her sister back.

"Not tonight, Honey. I'm exhausted, and these roads are wretched. Look what happened to Sheila. But if it clears up, I'll take you tomorrow afternoon after church."

It was a generous offer. Faith's Sunday afternoons were cherished for puttering and rest. But Honey shook her head. "Never mind."

When they reached her apartment, she did not invite Faith in. Faith would not have gone, of course, but she did expect to be asked. Instead, Honey opened the car door almost before the car stopped, made only the sketchiest of good-byes, and carefully maneuvered steep steps leading to the front door, head bent against the sleet. She remembered her manners only long enough to sketch a wave before she went inside.

Faith sat a moment longer at the curb, shoulders bowed with defeat. She hadn't realized how much she had counted on that conversation. Now she knew she'd been rehearsing it in her mind ever since she'd heard Honey would be at Rip's party. She had played Honey's part many ways—injured, tentative, even grateful—but she'd always envisioned one happy ending: two sisters sharing the family home.

"You didn't have to be rude," she muttered to her absent sister as she backed down the drive. "Mama never raised us to be rude." Then her wide mouth curved in her usual smile of good humor. "I guess Mama practiced on you and got it right with me."

As she climbed into bed later, however, Faith brushed away tears. "You should have gone for the stupid papers," she chided herself. "So what if it took an hour of your life? The only time your big sister ever asks you a favor, and you turn her down."

When Jason glumly pulled Aunt Mary's silver Cadillac to the emergency room door, Sheila was stricken with guilt. "The Jaguar! I completely forgot about it! It will be stripped by morning!"

"Lamar tended to that," Aunt Mary replied. "While you were in X-ray, he came by for Crispin's keys and car insurance card. He'll have the car towed tomorrow to a body shop —but don't get maudlin with gratitude. Lamar never does a favor without remembering you owe him one."

She settled her tiny body into the Cadillac's plush back seat and arranged her furs on her shoulder. "Home, Jason, please. Philip and I agreed you should stay with me tonight, Sheila. You can go to your place tomorrow when you feel like it. Don't mention your dog, either. I've already taken care of it."

She might sound like she had personally fed, watered, and walked Lady through Hurricane Andrew, but Sheila now understood why Jason looked glum. In his years with Mary Beaufort, her driver had embarked on a course of self-improvement that had built his body, his vocabulary, and his self-esteem. His employer encouraged him, flattered him, and deployed him on a number of assignments connected with the running of her modest empire. None of them, Sheila suspected, had seared his soul like being sent to walk a sheltie in the sleet.

"Thanks," she murmured gratefully, summoning a smile and willing Jason to look in the rearview mirror. When he did, he did not smile, but his shoulders relaxed. At least one person understood his outrage.

No one spoke again until they pulled into the parking garage of Aunt Mary's apartment building. As she climbed from the car and headed for the elevator, however, Mary Beaufort exuded satisfaction. "I knew the good Lord wouldn't let That Man take Forbes to South America."

"The last chapter of the book was written first and
from then on Miss Mitchell wrote any chapter that
happened to be uppermost in her mind. . . ."[8]

Honey knocked again, peering anxiously over her shoulder
toward the cab at the rain-pelted curb. If that driver left her
here, she didn't know what she'd do! This little brick house
looked respectable, if tacky, with sheets of plastic nailed
around each window, but she could never seek assistance
from its neighbors. Honey's imagination conjured menace
behind every curtain.

"Come on, Elouisa," she pleaded under her breath,
scrunching her neck lower in the collar of her shabby London Fog and shivering. A sheet of wind-driven rain flapped
across the small porch, rustling the red bow of a plastic holly
wreath and soaking her ankles.

She checked her watch. Only nine-thirty. Surely Elouisa wouldn't have gone out early on a day like this!

When the door finally swung open, a muscular young man regarded her curiously. "May I help you?"

"I . . . I'm Honey Norton. I've come to see Elouisa Whetlock."

Honey hated herself for stammering, wished Elouisa had opened the door herself. This young man in ironed jeans and a white Atlanta University sweatshirt disconcerted her. Barefoot and smelling like he'd just stepped from a shower, he looked too clean, too intelligent to live on this shabby street.

"She's inside. Come on in." He stepped back and motioned her inside. With one last anxious look toward her cab, she entered.

The room was hot, its air thick and fuggy. She nearly went back to the damp cold outside, until she saw, on the coffee table, a stack of ancient manila envelopes.

A quavering voice called from a recliner in the corner. "Izzat Miss Honey? What brings you out dis way? Sorry I cain' get up, but I'm poorly today. This here's my great-grandson, Junior."

The change in Elouisa since she'd seen her last shocked Honey. Was this the way she herself would be in twenty-five years—a prattling skeleton with precious little camouflage? At least, she consoled herself, she wouldn't keep a spitting can by her chair.

Forcing her lips into a smile of greeting, she crossed the room and bent to grasp one gnarled old hand between both of hers—for Junior's sake. But when she touched the deformed dry claw and felt it warm in her hand, she held it a moment longer out of compassion. If Elouisa had been difficult in her youth, she was being amply chastened by old age.

"Call me if you need me." Junior left, and Honey heard him speak to someone in the kitchen.

She perched on a gray love seat, set her purse beside her, and reconsidered the speech she had prepared. She would have come straight to the point with the Elouisa she'd expected to see. But this old woman, still babbling a steady stream of welcome from her chair, required a warmer, more circuitous approach. She spent several minutes, therefore, in recollecting people they had both known and memories they shared. Only then did she ask casually, "I guess you knew about Mr. Delacourt's party last night?"

Elouisa nodded and smiled to show toothless gums. "Mildred was over here all eeb'nin', and Junior—" she jabbed one hand toward the back of the house "—he parked cars for the party."

"I thought I'd seen him before." Honey finally stopped worrying about her cab. If he left, she could ask that nice young man, known to both Rip and Mildred, to drive her home.

She had already rehearsed her next sentence on the long dreary ride across town. "Did you hear about Sheila's accident on her way to your house?"

Elouisa's head bobbed in distress. "Accident?" She waved her clubby hands. "Nobody called 'bout no accident! She was s'posed to git some stuff from me. I wondered why she never showed—"

"She had a wreck, not too far from here. The streets were treacherous. We were all still at Mr. Delacourt's when she called from the hospital."

"She didn't die, den."

Honey couldn't tell whether Elouisa was glad or disappointed. "No, but she's badly bruised, so I came for the envelopes."

It came off as well as she'd rehearsed it. Even so, she felt her conscience clutch within her. Honey was not accustomed to grasping opportunities for herself. She could hear her mother's frequent admonition, "Don't be selfish, now!" If she were not desperate, Honey would not be here.

Last night at Rip's, she had been only mildly interested in the conversation. Her own finances were too precarious for her to care about a manuscript to which she had no claim. But as Faith drove her down Peachtree, Honey suddenly realized with dizzying clarity that in this case, possession might truly be nine-tenths of the law. She also realized that she, Honey Andrews Norton, possessed an advantage which Mary Beaufort, for all her money, did not: She'd known Peggy Mitchell's heirs all her life. If Honey returned the papers instead of Mary, she believed Peggy's nephews would be both grateful and generous.

Most nights Honey lay awake tortured by one unanswerable question: *How can I ever afford to retire?* Her training and skills had not prepared her to earn a living, and the work she had found provided no pension. Last night after Faith left, she had paced the apartment all night, wondering if this, finally, could be the miracle for which she had prayed. By dawn she had convinced herself by a simple formula: She needed money and Mary Beaufort did not. She *must* seize her chance to return Peggy's papers to the Mitchells and reap the reward!

She had dressed, eaten Mini-Wheats, and called the cab in a euphoria that saw no obstacles in her path. Only on the chilly windswept porch had she felt her first wispy doubts.

Now, as Elouisa silently peered across the room with hooded, filmy eyes, Honey had an awful thought: What if Mary had already called this morning to say *she* was coming, or was sending Jason? Why hadn't she called Mary before she left? She couldn't have asked straight out, of course, but she might have gotten a feel for Mary's plans.

To convince herself, as well as Elouisa, of the validity of her claim, she lifted the five envelopes onto her lap.

Struggling with her palsy, Elouisa shook her head. "Sorry, Miss Honey, but I ain' lettin' nobody take dem embelopes out of here butten Miss Mary or Sheila."

"But since I'm already here," Honey willed her voice to sound reasonable, not desperate, "I can save them the trouble. Sheila is in no condition to drive. And these papers belong to Mrs. Marsh's family. They should be returned as quickly as possible."

Elouisa wasn't too old to be shrewd. " 'Pears to me somebody might be willin' to hand me sumpin' to get 'em back."

"Nonsense! They don't belong to you!"

"Don't belong to you, neither, lady."

She whirled. Another man lounged in the kitchen doorway. A lean man with a scarred black face, grizzled hair, and the meanest eyes she had ever seen. He, too, looked vaguely familiar, but Honey was too mesmerized by the butcher knife in his hand to wonder why. He dug the point into one of his fingers, pulled out a splinter, wiped the knife on the seat of his pants, and balanced it on one palm. In short red T-shirt sleeves, his biceps looked like iron oranges and his muscles like wisteria vines implanted under his dusky skin.

She blinked. Her lungs felt paralyzed, and motherly cautions flooded her brain: *Don't ever go into colored houses alone. Always take a man with you, and stay near the door.* In years of picking up maids and taking them home, Honey had considered the admonitions foolish folklore. Now, darting a look at Elouisa and finding the old woman watching the stranger with hooded approval, she felt utterly alien and alone.

Instinctively Honey fell back on generations of privilege. Standing—she felt less vulnerable meeting him eye to eye—she said firmly, "I'm going to return them to the people they do belong to." Resisting an impulse to clutch the envelopes to her chest, she moved casually toward the door.

"Belong to Weesa rat now." The man's low voice was both pleasant and menacing. "Set 'em on the sofa and git along home."

Junior called from the back. "You all got a problem out there?"

The older man turned his head. "Nothin' I cain' handle, Junior."

In that instant, Honey fled.

Dashing desperately for the door, she jerked it open and pelted onto the porch. Elouisa screeched. The man shouted. Honey heard him pounding across the living room.

She reached the steps before he grabbed her arm. Wrenching away, she reeled down the steps and fell to her knees in red mud. All the envelopes but one shot out of her arms.

"Hey!" the cab driver called through his open window.

Heedless of muddy knees and torn stockings, Honey abandoned the scattered envelopes. Without waiting to see whether the man was picking them up or coming after her, she covered the space between the house and the taxi faster than she ever knew she could run. The driver, bless his heart, flung open the cab's back door. Honey, clutching one precious envelope, fell inside. Tires squealed. They roared off into the rain.

An hour later, she stared in dismay at the typewritten pages spread across her mahogany coffee table.

"How did she know?" she whispered, hugging herself tightly with both arms and rocking forward on the gold brocade sofa to read the pertinent parts again. "How could she possibly have known?"

Her knees were bare and skinned beneath the old plaid flannel robe she had put on when she peeled off her soaked clothing. Her thick hair was still damp, heavy against her neck. Her hands had not stopped trembling. She had been to hell and back for these papers, and she had no idea what to do with them.

How she missed Stack! Worldly-wise irresponsible Stack. *He'd* have an idea. Only two alternatives presented themselves to Honey's own, more orthodox brain: *Sell them* or *Burn them.* Which could she bear to do?

The papers before her were, apparently, the final chapter of a novel. Honey believed Margaret Mitchell had written it. Her swift, lively style filled every line. Honey could not bear to think of destroying what could be precious history. And while this one chapter might not bring a fortune on the open market, she suspected it might bring enough to let her leave this worn-out apartment in a seedy part of town and buy a small Buckhead condominium. Above all things but two, Honey yearned to live in Buckhead.

But how could she let others read these pages?

"Who told?" she wailed to the empty room. "Who told Peggy?" Enraged, disappointed, flayed with betrayal, she grasped at a fleeting thought. Could one stipulate that something not be published for forty years?

She didn't know, but she knew who might. Still trembling, she reached for the telephone book.

•   •   •

Mary Beaufort dropped her telephone onto the rose sofa cushion beside her. "Where can Honey have gone in all this?"

"All this" was the new downpour that had been falling since dawn, warmer and heavy, to melt all traces of ice. Now, at noon, Atlanta wore its most common winter face—sodden and gray.

Aunt Mary's living room, however, was a cozy haven, if you didn't mind so much rose and white. Even the Christmas tree by one window was white with rose balls, and Alfred, Aunt Mary's Persian, was a snowy mass on an azalea pink cushion by the other window. Sheila, who knew this room so well she no longer noticed the preponderance of pink, more lay than sat in her favorite ivory overstuffed chair with her legs stretched out on its enormous matching ottoman. Wrapped in the same large white terry cloth robe Jason had fetched the previous night, she was so engrossed in the Sunday comics that she scarcely heard Aunt Mary's question. Beside her chair was *Gone With the Wind,* which she had found on the guest bedroom bookshelf and begun while Aunt Mary was at church. She'd temporarily abandoned Scarlett and Rhett when Jason brought up the thick Sunday paper, but she planned to read all afternoon while the dull patter of rain on a window ledge outside reminded her just how warm, cozy, and downright blessed she was.

She'd wakened stiff and sore, but smelled maple pecan muffins and thanked God that Aunt Mary had brought her here instead of taking her home to a lively sheltie. After a shower, she'd made a couple of phone calls. A neighbor agreed to feed and walk Lady this morning, and Crispin said —grumpily and drowsily—that he didn't want to see anybody until later in the day. Now, freed of responsibilities, she wallowed in comfort; Handel's *Messiah* on the stereo, paper on her lap, and steaming coffee at her side.

It took her a while to realize Aunt Mary expected a reply.

"Maybe out to lunch?" She was more interested in figuring out how to open and hold the paper with her good arm. That achieved, she reached for her coffee, emitting an involuntary "Ouch!"

"Does it really hurt that much, dear?"

"Yes, it really hurts that much—which is why I'm not terribly worried about Honey Norton right now." She didn't mean to speak so sharply, nor to wobble on the end of the sentence.

Aunt Mary reached into a drawer beside the sofa and handed her a lacy handkerchief. "Then a small measure of self-pity is appropriate. Get it over with while I try Honey again." She reached for the telephone beside her.

Sheila laughed midsniff. "I can't get used to you and that portable phone! After years of insisting you'd never have a telephone in *your* living or dining room—"

"I still won't have an infernal instrument at my elbow ready to bother me at any time," Aunt Mary replied, unperturbed, "but I can turn this off and stick it under a cushion when I want to."

Sheila returned to the paper. She looked up a few minutes later to see Aunt Mary still holding the telephone with an expression of utmost concern. "Honey's probably lunching with friends after church," Sheila assured her. "You'd be starting your peach cobbler at Morrison's about now if you hadn't come home to feed me soup."

If she'd expected a sentimental reply about families sticking together in times of trouble, she should have saved her breath. "I hoped you'd have found that scrap of paper with Elouisa's address. You're quite sure you've lost it?"

"I've lost it," Sheila said for the fifth time. "It must have fallen out of my purse in the emergency room, when I was rummaging around for my insurance card."

"If you would straighten that purse occasionally, Sheila—"

"I keep meaning to, Aunt Mary, but it never rises to the top of my to-do list. You don't have Mildred's sister's number?"

"Yes, but they were leaving early for a family reunion down near Jackson. Not Elouisa's side of the family, the other one." Aunt Mary sighed. "I cannot understand why Mildred wanted to go."

"Admit it," Sheila told her. "You're just put out because you'll have to wait until she gets home tonight to find out where her 'Ahnt Elouisa' lives—and satisfy your friends before they burn up the telephone system with their curiosity."

While Aunt Mary was at church, Sheila had taken calls from everyone who'd been in Rip's study last night except Honey—which, she admitted, was mildly strange. "Call Faith," she suggested now.

Deep in Hagar and Beatle Bailey, she only vaguely heard Aunt Mary asking ". . . Church in all this rain? Yes, that's what I thought, too. Especially without a car. But maybe we're wrong. Where else could she have gone?"

Whatever Faith replied took her a long time, and set Aunt Mary to tapping her left cheek with one rose-tipped forefinger. "Oh, my!" she exclaimed. "Do you think she might have gone alone, dear?" She sounded so worried that Sheila looked up, surprised. A deep crease separated Aunt Mary's delicate brows as she listened. ". . . But if she doesn't have a car . . . well, yes, I suppose a cab . . ." (in the dubious tone of one who had forgotten such things as taxicabs shared the planet).

When she hung up, she tapped her cheek again, lost in thought. "If only I hadn't given Jason the afternoon off—" She picked up the phone and dialed again. "Hello, Rip, is Walter there? Would he like to drive Sheila on an errand for me?"

Exasperated though she was, Sheila retained enough sense of humor to recognize that bright tone of voice. It harkened back to days when Sheila and Walt had brand-new driver's licenses and were delighted to run errands for their elders.

"No, nothing you need to worry about, Rip, dear, just something I need her to do for me. She's not able to drive. Her shoulder's a little stiff."

"My shoulder is very sore, Rip!" Sheila called across the room.

Aunt Mary waved her to silence, listened, replied, and finally hung up. "Walt's on his way." She slid off the couch and stood, full of purpose. "You'll need to dress, dear."

Sheila played her trump. "I have nothing to put on. The hospital sliced up my dress. They also," she added grumpily, "sliced up my best underwear. And Mother used to tell me to wear good underwear in case I have a wreck. Ha!" She slid lower in her chair and turned back to her paper, then added as if suddenly inspired, "*You* go with Walt, instead."

"Pshaw," Aunt Mary said bluntly. "I can't go out in all this rain. And you must not have looked in your closet, dear. Come see what I have for you." Before Sheila could reply, she had headed down the hall.

When Sheila reached her room, Aunt Mary was perched on the fat turquoise comforter, short legs dangling down the side of the high mahogany four-poster. "Look in the closet and the top dresser drawer, dear."

Even knowing it was a bribe, Sheila looked.

Last night she'd been too groggy to do more than drop her coat in a heap on the floor. This morning she opened the closet with a small tingle of anticipation. Aunt Mary's surprises were often wonderful.

This one certainly was. Inside the closet she found a Neiman-Marcus garment bag containing a sweater and skirt in soft taupe wool flecked with forest green, teal, and rose. In the drawer was a Victoria's Secret box. It contained a complete set of exquisite rose lingerie.

"How lovely!" Sheila exclaimed involuntarily—then remembered the use to which it was being put. "But not lovely enough to make me limp through a downpour looking for a woman who'd rather be left alone." She gave her aunt a severe look. "Were you out buying this when you said you were in church?"

Aunt Mary's eyes widened. "Of course not, dear! I got it weeks ago, for your Christmas present. But you need it worse today. Here, let me help you with the sleeves. And when you get to Honey's, don't just knock and come home. Be sure you look inside to be sure she hasn't fallen. A neighbor must have a key."

•   •   •

Sheila lowered herself into Walt's car feeling ninety instead of merely wounded. "This is the king of wild-goose chases," she informed him, wincing as she tried to find a comfortable position in his passenger seat. "Honey Norton is at a friend's house drinking tea."

He slid into the driver's seat and started the engine. "So why are we going? And why are you so dressed up?"

Walt himself was comfortable in a brown sweater, tan corduroy slacks, and loafers. He'd come out, as usual, without a coat.

Sheila's own raincoat was draped around her shoulders in deference to pain. She brushed her new sweater lovingly. "Isn't this gorgeous? I'm wearing it because I had nothing else at Aunt Mary's except a bathrobe. And we're going because Aunt Mary has a vivid imagination and nothing better to do on this rainy day than exercise it. Faith says that on their way home last night, Honey wanted to go pick up those envelopes. Since Honey hasn't called this morning to find out if we've gotten them yet—and, not incidentally, knows where Elouisa lives—Aunt Mary wants to track Honey down. Her excuse is that maybe Honey's in some kind of trouble. Barring that, she suggested we ask Honey for the address—which I managed to lose at the hospital—and fetch the envelopes. Aunt Mary likes a little excitement in her life and it's been a long time since her last mystery." She could have kicked herself. The last mystery had been Walt's.

"I certainly gave her my share," he said bitterly, nosing the Buick onto Peachtree Street and heading south. To her relief, however, he added, "What kind of trouble could Honey be in?"

"Oh, you know Aunt Mary! She's imagined everything from gang rape to white slavers." As always, Walt's driving made her too nervous to give more than half a mind to their conversation.

With great forethought, he slowed as they approached a light a full block down the street that *might* turn red half a minute after he'd passed under it. When it stayed green, he resumed his usual twenty-nine miles an hour. "Well, if Honey did go out this morning to get the purported Mitchell manuscript—"

Sheila laughed. "The purported manuscript—I like that! Sounds like you're swearing when you aren't. But I know what you're going to say. What if Honey did go get it? We can't wrest it from her grasp and bring it back to Aunt Mary like a bone. And if she doesn't come to the door, how will we know whether she's not at home or merely not answering her door and phone? I don't want to barge in on a very private person."

"You're the sleuth, Sheila. Think of something. I was just glad to get out of the house. There's nothing on television." He slowed again. He'd need to turn in a couple of blocks.

A car whizzed by in the next lane, spraying water onto the windshield. Sheila clutched Walt's arm. "Watch out!" she cried. Then she cringed with embarrassment.

"I saw him, Sheila." Walt was mild, but cross. "You're going to make me have a wreck! What's the matter with you?"

"I was remembering our accident," she admitted.

"Those roads were icy," he pointed out, shoving his glasses up his nose. "These are merely wet. And *I'm* a very careful driver."

She wasn't certain whether he was implying that Crispin wasn't, or reminding her that it was she, not Walt, who'd had several minor fender benders in their early days of driving. Instead of pursuing that (and to distract herself from the road), she asked, "How's it going, living with your dad?"

Walt shrugged. "Not bad, not good. We don't see each other much except at dinner three or four times a week, and on weekends if I don't go to the office. Mostly we rattle around like dried beans."

Sheila couldn't speak. Her eyes were fixed on her outside mirror. Walt was about to turn, and a black car was hurtling toward their rear at a devilish speed!

Walt made the turn with time to spare. "You can breathe now," he said mildly.

She glowered at him. "Wait 'til you've had a wreck."

"I don't have wrecks. Except my personal life," he added gloomily. "You understand, don't you, Sheila? You lost Tyler. But there's one thing that's different about me. I can't trust myself to love again. I was so stupid! What if I'm that stupid again?"

"You weren't stupid, Walt," she assured him, "you were flat out deceived. That's not your fault."

As she said the words, they sank into her own soul with a silent "Aha!" She was still getting acquainted with their truth when Walt pulled up to the curb. "Well, here we are."

"Here" was a two-story brick building perched high on a hill. Modest single-family houses crowded it on either side. Walt's black umbrella kept them only moderately dry as they negotiated a stream slithering down the steep driveway and climbed fourteen slick granite steps to the front door. "Miss Mary would have gotten soaked," he panted.

Sheila was too out of breath to make the obvious retort. She was also looking at a security lock hanging on the front door.

"What do we do now?" Walt peered upward, angling the umbrella so that icy drips scuttled down Sheila's neck.

"Go home." She turned on the steps.

"Don't quit yet!" He pounded loudly on the door.

Eventually a voice called from inside, "What do you want?"

"Honey Norton," Walt called back. "We're friends of hers."

Friends, Sheila amended silently, who hadn't laid eyes on her until the night before and were now bent on disturbing her Sunday rest.

The door was shoved open. As they entered, they caught a glimpse of a skinny woman scuttling back through a nearby door.

"Not a bad place when it was built," Walt commented, closing his umbrella and letting it drip on the brown tweed carpet of the long yellow hall. "Neighborhood was better then, of course."

Sheila nodded. Originally, four apartments with high

ceilings and six enormous rooms would have stretched the length of the building, two up and two down, separated by wide halls. Every one would have sported both a back and a front screened porch. Today, if the number of mailboxes lining one wall was correct, the building held eight smaller units. Not as bad as some buildings, subdivided into twelve tiny efficiencies. The neighborhood was a haven for singles, the elderly, drug-pushers, prostitutes, and the flotsam and jetsam that large cities use as a buffer between affluent citizens and the poor. Sheila doubted that women or elderly residents left home unaccompanied after dark.

Walt browsed the mailboxes. "Upstairs, right front."

They each knocked on the door, without result. "What now?" he asked, willing to abdicate leadership now that they were inside.

As Sheila waited for inspiration, a dog began to bark across the hall. It sounded mean and enormous. Again Sheila turned to go, but Walt crossed the hall and knocked on a door decorated by a small but pretty wreath of pine and real holly. "Who is it?" a quavering voice called over the din.

"Friends of Mrs. Norton," he replied. "Have you seen her today?"

The door opened a crack. A bird's nest of uncombed gray hair and one gray eye bobbed just above a low security chain. The eye was faded with age, but it conveyed intelligence. It also conveyed a good deal of suspicion.

Sheila joined Walt, although it made them look like a team of Jehovah's Witnesses seeking converts in the damp, unheated hall.

Walt bowed slightly and addressed the suspicious eye. "Good afternoon, ma'am. Have you seen Honey Norton this afternoon?"

The old woman put her wrinkled mouth to the crack and spoke loudly above her dog's clamor. "I think she's home. She went out earlier—called a cab and went out in all this rain!—but she was home by eleven." Her voice was rich and musical, younger than her face. She started to step back inside, then added, "She had a visitor later, I think—while I was heating some soup. At least, I *thought* I heard somebody knock at her door. Perhaps it was another one down the hall."

Walter nodded and turned to leave. "Thank you."

"Don't quit yet," Sheila muttered. She stepped forward. "You don't know who keeps her spare key, do you? My aunt is concerned, because she's been trying to reach Honey all day."

Walt stiffened. Sheila knew what he was thinking. This old woman wouldn't just hand over Honey's key to two strangers. How could she know they weren't thieves, waiting to hit her over the head and steal Honey's treasures?

Sheila could see the same question reflected in the shrewd gray eye. "You say you are old friends of Mrs. Norton's?" She fumbled for spectacles hanging on her sagging bosom, donned them, and considered the two of them dubiously through the crack in the door.

Sheila bent closer, to make herself heard above the dog. "My aunt, Mary Beaufort, has known Honey for years. If you would like to call her to verify that she sent me—" A pity that Mildred wouldn't be there to answer, with reassuring formality, "Miz Beaufort's res-i-*dence*."

Walt pulled a card from his case and stuck it through the crack. "I am Walter Winwood Delacourt—"

The response was unexpected. The old woman stepped back, peered up at him across the narrow length of chain barring the door, then broke into a smile that showed full white dentures. "Delacourt? Why, you must be Rip's son!"

Before he could do more than nod, she had slid the chain and opened the door wide. Now they could see how thin she was, and how stooped. They could also hear the dog's snarls even clearer.

"Rip and I went to school together a hundred years ago!" She beamed up at Walt. "Does he still run his meat-packing business?"

Walt flushed, but manfully pumped the small proffered hand. "I'm running the business these days, ma'am."

"Pardon the way I look," the old woman apologized, rubbing her nappy gray sweater with one hand and futilely trying to order her hair with the other. "I didn't expect to see anybody today."

Sheila hung back, wondering where the barker was—and how securely penned. Then a flutter of color near the ceiling caught her eye. "Origami!" Impulsively, she took a step forward.

The old woman half turned, nodding with pride at a multitude of brilliant birds, fish, and small paper animals floating in midair. "You like origami, dear?" She reached up and touched a golden fish, setting it and its companions bobbing.

"I love it!" Sheila started to step past her, then caught herself just at the threshold. "Is your dog safe?" It was a dumb question. Any fool could tell that that animal was a killer.

The old woman twinkled as if Sheila had made a joke. "Oh, he's quite harmless, dear." She hobbled arthritically back into the room and pushed a tape recorder switch. The din ceased.

"There! That's better, isn't it?" She chortled, obviously enjoying her guests' astonishment. "Fido's lots cheaper to keep than the real McCoy, and he doesn't require exercising. Now come on in and see my pretties." She moved heavily toward the fireplace at the rear of the room, where a few Christmas cards decorated the mantel.

Sheila followed, enchanted. She scarcely noticed the furniture, except that the dining table was littered with colored paper. She was too entranced by what must be a hundred origami mobiles hanging from wires strung several feet below the ten-foot ceiling.

"They are exquisite." She reached up and lightly set pastel cranes flying, moved on to a swirl of red, blue, and gold fish, then to a herd of small brown antelopes. She picked her way slowly, admiring the craftsmanship. "Where did you get them all?"

"I made them." The old woman glowed with a creator's pride. "My husband was stationed in Japan during the Korean War, and I could only see him on weekends. To fill up my time, I started doing . . . this." Her small bony hands rose in praise of her art.

Sheila fingered the pastel cranes again. They would be

lovely in her living room. "Do you ever sell any?" she asked hesitantly, not wanting to offend.

A throaty laugh filled the room. "Of course I do! Whenever I can. I'm getting too old to sit at craft fairs much anymore, but my daughter goes for me. I'd made all these for Christmas fairs, but this rain—" Her hands fluttered like one of her mobiles.

Sheila rummaged in her purse to hide her flush. She'd gotten so used to Aunt Mary and her well-heeled friends, she'd forgotten how many elderly women supplement fragile incomes with cottage industries.

"If you like these cranes," the old woman hobbled to fetch a long forked stick and neatly hooked them as they moved lazily through the warm air, "I can let you have them for fifteen dollars. They'd go for twenty at a fair."

They would go for far more than that at a gallery or boutique. Sheila had finally found her checkbook, but Walter, bless him, was whipping out his wallet. "A fifty's all I have, ma'am. I'll take the antelopes, and you just pretend we got them at a fair."

The old woman did not protest. The fifty disappeared into her pocket.

Walt cleared his throat. "Um, Sheila, perhaps we ought to call the building supervisor for a key, if Mrs. er—"

"Waterbury, Jane Waterbury."

Sheila knew they'd get the key. Their southern bona fides had been established: They were Rip Delacourt's son, and paying customers.

Sure enough, Jane Waterbury shuffled to the corner, rustled around in an overflowing drawer of a small cherry desk, and found a brass key. "Honey left this with me in case of emergencies. Since she's not answering the door, if it will reassure your aunt—" She hobbled across the hall and fumbled to get the key in the lock.

As the door swung open, Sheila saw at once that Aunt Mary would not be reassured.

Honey Norton sprawled on her living room floor, pale and still.

• • •

Sheila and Walter made a good team. He hurried to the telephone while she knelt and found, to her great relief, a pulse.

Jane Waterbury collapsed into a brocade wing chair. She was breathing heavily and clasping her thin chest. When Sheila brought her a glass of water, she accepted it gratefully.

While they waited for the paramedics, Walter prowled around the room. "Might as well look for clues," he said to Sheila, giving Honey a quick, uneasy glance. Sheila couldn't imagine what clues he expected to find. They'd already tramped all over the carpet and left their fingerprints on her door. Besides, from the way she was lying, Honey could possibly have tripped and hit her head on the corner of the fireplace. When Sheila checked for a pulse, she'd also checked for wounds. Except for a bump on the head, she'd found nothing.

"Look at this!" Walt peered at a small oil painting over a small walnut secretary. "It looks like a genuine Manet!"

"Oh, it is," Mrs. Waterbury assured him. "Honey still has a few very fine things from her married days."

Sheila's eye was drawn to discolored squares on the green walls. Other paintings had once hung there. "Maybe I should pack a few things for the hospital. Would you help me, Mrs. Waterbury?"

"I don't think I trust myself to stand yet, dear." She struggled to breathe normally. "This has been such a shock! But you go on, dear. I'll be all right in a minute."

Sheila headed to the bedroom. When Walt followed, she said softly, "Don't disturb anything, but let's have a look for those envelopes."

They did not find them. They did find, however, more than Honey would have wanted her Buckhead friends to see: a cheap worn comforter on the antebellum mahogany four-poster, a very few (carefully preserved) good dresses, a thin and ragged towel over the tub, careful darns in the brocade covering the fine old sofa and chairs. There was Limoges china in the kitchen cabinets, but— "She must eat out a lot," Walt said, peering into the almost empty pantry.

Sheila, swallowing a lump in her throat, was glad to hear emergency vehicle sirens arriving outside.

While the paramedics worked with Honey and carried her out, two police officers interviewed Sheila, Walt, and Jane Waterbury. After Sheila gave an edited version of why they were there, the officers were inclined toward a household accident or an intruder bent on robbery for drugs. "We get a lot of that in this neighborhood," one explained to Sheila. With no evidence to the contrary, she saw no reason to protest. She and Walter left the officers and Mrs. Waterbury summoning the apartment manager from across town.

As he slid into the driver's seat, Walt handed Sheila a small ghost on a pin.

"Why on earth did you bring that?" she demanded.

"I found it on the living room rug, and didn't want the police tracking it back to Dad."

She held the pin by its point and twirled it rapidly, but not as rapidly as she was thinking. Honey's pin was in a small Limoges egg on her dresser. Sheila had seen it not half an hour before. Her own had been in her ruined velvet dress, and Walt wouldn't be caught dead wearing one.

Who else from Rip's party had been in Honey's apartment since last night—and why?

"I want to know where everyone was this morning," she told Aunt Mary softly but firmly. For the second time in twenty-four hours, they stood in a hospital corridor.

Aunt Mary drew her black raincoat closer around her and took an indignant step backwards. Dorothy, who had overheard, spoke first. "Surely you don't think any of us had anything to do with this!"

They were all assembled at Piedmont Hospital outside Honey's room: Charles, Dorothy, Rip, Lamar, Aunt Mary, Walt, and Sheila. Sheila supposed Aunt Mary had summoned the others. Since they hadn't seen Honey for years before last night, why should they have come otherwise?

They'd waited half an hour for Faith and Philip to come out with a report. Sheila, who knew most of them so well, also knew something had them all strung taut. But was it Honey's accident, or their own embarrassment that it had taken this to bring them to her aid? Was one of them even more anxious, waiting for Honey to point an accusing finger and say, "You struck me down!"?

Whatever the reasons, they now exchanged uneasy looks and shuffled their feet. Rip held up a hand as if requesting permission to speak. "Walt said . . . probably an accident."

The others nodded, but looked to Sheila as if seeking reassurance, not giving affirmation.

They continued to wait. Charles and Lamar carried on a halfhearted conversation about the upcoming Olympics, casting what Sheila in her present mood considered furtive looks at Honey's door. Walt held up the wall. Rip played a tattoo on the arm of his chair while Dorothy—charming in a rustling silver raincoat and a blue scarf that exactly matched her eyes—exclaimed over and over how awful it all was— breaking off midsentence to look fearfully at the closed door.

Sheila found it hard to believe that any of these people had anything to do with Honey's being here. But where did that little ghost come from if not from one of them? She tried again.

"I still think we ought to remember now where we spent the morning, in case we're asked later."

She had carefully avoided Aunt Mary's eye. Nevertheless, it was Aunt Mary who replied. "In church, of course! Where else would any of us be on a Sunday morning!"

Lamar took off his glasses and polished them. "Well, now, Mary, I didn't make it to church this morning. I was busy seeing about Crispin's car." He fished in his jacket pocket and pulled out a business card. "Here's the place to call tomorrow, Sheila. I drove it over, and spoke with the owner at home. Friend of mine. Says he'll get right on it. It won't take too long."

How could she suspect someone who'd spent so much time on her own problems? "Thanks, Lamar." She shoved the card into her purse, then, catching Aunt Mary's eye, retrieved it and put it carefully into her wallet.

"What about you, Rip?" Lamar asked genially. "Got an alibi?"

Rip grunted. "Missed church, too, Mary. Tired after last night. Ask Isaac—"

A smile twitched Charles's lips. "Everybody knows Isaac would lie himself blind for you, Rip. You're just lucky Honey's apartment has stairs." He turned and said formally, "Dorothy and I made up for everyone else's shortcomings, Sheila. We were at the cathedral for early services *and* Sunday school, and I stayed afterwards for a brief meeting while Dorothy rode home with the Maxwells. Could they testify, dear, that you remained there instead of going over to Honey's?"

He had spoken without a trace of humor, but Dorothy laughed. "Don't tease me, Charles Davidson! You know Meredith and Gaines were coming for lunch." She turned to Sheila. "His brother-in-law is Gaines Wiggins, the golfer. And don't try to pin this on Charles, either. He couldn't hit someone—they might bleed, and he can't even eat rare meat without getting queasy."

He looked a bit queasy this afternoon, actually. He kept looking at Aunt Mary and stroking his mustache as if trying to decide whether to speak or not.

"Speaking of pinning—" Sheila pulled her ghost from her purse and stuck it on the front of her sweater.

If she'd hoped for a guilty gasp, she was doomed for disappointment. She got only two responses. Aunt Mary turned away, and Dorothy exclaimed, "Who won the prize? And what was it?"

"Two tickets to *A Christmas Carol* for Friday night," Walt replied glumly. "Clara won them."

Lamar nodded. "She was tickled pink, and has already roped Walt into going with her."

Walt tugged on his collar. "I don't know yet if I'm free—"

"Of course you're free," his father growled. "Never do a thing on Friday nights except sit around moping."

Faith's voice could be dimly heard through the closed door. Dorothy leaned on her cane and spoke so softly that only Sheila, Aunt Mary, and Rip could hear. "The only silver lining in this dreadful cloud is that maybe now Faith will make things right."

"Make what right?" Rip rumbled with obvious curiosity. Aunt Mary shot Dorothy a warning look.

Dorothy cocked her silver head and said defiantly, "He ought to know, Mary. After all, Maud Andrews was his Aunt Carrie's best friend." She bent nearer Rip and confided, "When Maud died last fall, Rip, she left everything to Faith. *Everything.*"

He knitted his bushy brows and didn't bother to lower his own voice. "Why'd Maud do a damn-fool thing like that? Adored Honey."

Dorothy shook her head. "You men never notice anything! Maud and Honey quarreled right after Honey's wedding, and barely spoke for years. They made that up a bit, and Honey often lunched with her dad at the Driving Club, but she seldom went home. Then, after Stack and Henry both died, Honey and Maud had a royal set-to."

Rip shook his head, obviously deeply troubled. "Not like Honey. Sweet kid."

Dorothy chuckled. "You're remembering her at four, Rip, riding the streetcar."

Lamar, who had silently joined them, guffawed. "I remember you at eighteen, driving one!" He winked at Sheila. "She looks harmless, but Dotty's a madcap. Used to drive through town like it was the Monte Carlo, and one night, on a dare, she got somebody to lure away the streetcar driver and—"

"Hush!" Dorothy stopped him with a teasing smack on the shoulder. "Don't tell my past sins! We all grow up different than we started. Look at Honey. A sweet little girl, but she turned out as stubborn as her father. My Bertha's mother Hattie worked for Maud for years, and—"

"Dorothy!" Mary Beaufort reproved her. "Surely you aren't going to repeat servants' gossip!"

Sheila shared her distaste, but wanted to hear the story. Faith, after all, was the person most likely to have been in Honey's apartment after Rip's party. She had taken Honey home.

"It's not gossip, Mary," Dorothy protested. "Hattie was there! And Bertha didn't breathe a word to me until I said one day how strange it was that Maud left everything to Faith. Then Bertha flew to Faith's defense. Hattie practically raised Faith, remember. Maud was forty when she was born.

And Bertha and Hattie think people *ought* to know what happened, so they won't blame Faith for getting all the money."

She bent back to Rip. "Bertha said that after Stack and Henry died, Maud invited Honey to move in with her. But there was something Honey wanted Maud to give her first. Maud got huffy—you remember how self-righteous she could be—and refused, but Honey said she'd never move back unless she got it. Bertha said they went round and round one whole afternoon, until finally Honey had a fit!" Dorothy added for the women's benefit, "Hattie wondered if she was wanting that set of china that's been in the Andrews family since before the Revolution. Honey might have thought she should have it once her daddy was gone. Anyway," she turned back to Rip, "whatever it was, Maud said Honey was being selfish, and Honey said she wasn't selfish, she didn't want one red cent of her mother's money, but just that one thing. Maud said no again, and Honey stormed out. She never went back, not these past thirty years! That's why Maud left everything to Faith. But now," she stood erect with a bright, hopeful smile, "who knows? Maybe—"

She stopped. Philip stepped out of the room. Six pairs of questioning eyes met his. "She's unconscious. Faith will stay a while, but I've ordered round-the-clock nurses. Won't come cheap. I hope she has good insurance."

Mary arched silver brows. "And if she doesn't, Max?"

He peered at her over his half-glasses. "I suppose you'll insist that we all make up the difference, Mary."

Soberly, they all agreed.

Before Philip could return to the room, however, Lamar held him back. "Wait, Max. Sheila here wants to know where each of us was this morning. She thinks maybe one of us clobbered poor Honey and snatched that manuscript."

Philip's face darkened above his short beard. "This is no joking matter! Why should any of us be responsible for this dreadful thing?"

Dorothy linked her arm through her husband's and spoke quickly. "Let's all go out for a bite to eat! I, for one, am stahvin', and Charles is gettin' moody. Time to feed him. Who's coming?"

But Philip shook his head. "Winona's in bed with a migraine. I'd better go on home when I've seen a couple of other patients."

Rip raised a tremorous hand. "Better get back, too. Isaac's downstairs." Slumped in the wheelchair, he looked drained and weary.

Walt seized the handles of the chair. "I'll take you down, Dad, and follow you home. Not much I can do here."

"Get me a Coke before we go," Rip commanded. "Saw a machine."

Dorothy leaned very near Sheila's ear and murmured, "Rip would notice a Coke machine on the way to a cannibal's cooking pot."

Sheila's eyes twinkled. "And would probably ask for one." She saw Walt reaching for his wallet. "Oh! I owe you!" She fumbled for her own.

"Don't worry about it." He riffled through several bills.

"A magic wallet?" she teased softly. "Only one fifty at Mrs. Waterbury's, and now—voilà!"

He looked embarrassed. "Yeah, well, what can I say?"

"How about, 'I'm a nice guy, Sheila'?"

He shook his head and replaced his wallet. "How about 'Buy Dad a Coke, Sheila'? I don't have a single."

She handed him a dollar. "Don't forget the cranes are mine," she reminded him as he reached for Rip's chair. "Don't let anybody sit on them!"

"Cranes?" Again Aunt Mary arched her brows. Sheila explained, adding, ". . . and if anyone's looking for a good investment, you might form a partnership with Mrs. Waterbury. Her mobiles are exquisite."

Aunt Mary pursed her lips and said frigidly, "I didn't send you shopping, Sheila. You could have found Honey sooner if—"

"I couldn't have found Honey at all without Mrs. Waterbury's key, Aunt Mary. Besides, she heard a visitor arrive. I may go back tomorrow and see if she saw anything, or could recognize the voice."

"Don't waste your time, dear." Aunt Mary spoke briskly, gathering her coat about her. "For once, the police are surely right. If Honey didn't fall on her own, she probably let in a stranger. In that neighborhood, anything is possible. Lamar," she put a black-gloved hand through his arm, "shall we go with Dorothy and Charles?" When he nodded, she turned back to Sheila. "I suppose you will want to look in on Crispin. Don't stay long, dear. He's so very ill."

A Brief and Private Interlude

*"Beware the straying wisp of hair, the too-tight curl,
the ungroomed eyebrow, the smudged lipline."*[9]

Even as Sheila hurried toward Crispin's room, she was knitting her brows in thought. Aunt Mary turning down a mystery? That was the greatest mystery of all!

Then she rounded a corner, saw Crispin's closed door, and forgot all about Honey Norton and Margaret Mitchell. She stopped to run a hand through her curls, wondering how badly they'd frizzed in the rain. Her stomach was fluttering like a paper crane, and she felt inexplicably shy. She paused, put on a touch of lipstick, caught a deep breath, and squared her shoulders before giving the door a gentle push. Was he dozing?

He most certainly was not. His right arm might be bound to his chest and his right leg, resting outside the sheet, might be bound and packed with ice, but his left fingers awkwardly held a hand of cards and he whistled through his teeth to aid serious thought.

Next to the bed, in the room's only extra chair, hunched a young man in a ratty maroon bathrobe, studying his own fan of cards. When he saw Sheila, a smile lit up his homely acne-pocked face. "Rescue! Distraction! Do come in, lovely lady, and tell this man to have mercy on me, a sinner!" His eyes, bulging slightly, were so pale they looked colorless beneath his uncombed mop of dark red hair, and gave him the look of an engaging gnome.

Sheila looked from one to the other and shook her head admonishingly. "Cards on Sunday, Crispin? Dangerous for a man already struck down once by divine wrath."

He grinned and indicated his knee. "I *am* suffering, Sheila. Do, at least, include that in your report to Saint Mary." To his baffled partner, he added, "Her aunt prays hourly for my downfall, because I have designs on my own nephew—and her niece."

"My kind of woman," the red-haired man murmured, searching for a discard. "Smite all mine enemies, O Lord—" he rolled his eyes heavenward "—and don't let him win any more of my money."

Crispin grunted. "Come keep an eye on this buzzard while we play out the hand, Sheila. He's likely to cheat."

"Unlikely to win otherwise," his partner grumbled, licking his lips as he again considered his hand. His mouth was too small to hold so many large white teeth.

Crispin held out his one good arm and sent her a look of clear invitation, but Sheila declined. It wasn't just that she disliked public affection. It was also that the mat of dark hair curling at his throat was doing funny things to her knees and breathing apparatus. She was grateful for the visitor. If Crispin had proposed at that moment, she might have foolishly accepted.

"Have my chair." The young man rose, standing several inches shorter than Sheila. "And since your friend Crispin is a social boor, let me introduce myself. I'm Sean Bagwell, gentleman, scholar, and pauper since Crispin won all my dimes. You can make it up to me by going to dinner with me tomorrow night. I'm busting out of here in the morning and have a paycheck due me."

Crispin waved him imperiously back to his seat. "Sheila,

this rogue is neither gentleman nor scholar, merely a poor poker player and a reporter for the *Atlanta Constitution*. Sean, this is Sheila Travis, who will be busy tomorrow night wiping my furrowed brow after surgery. Here, Sheila, come demonstrate your brow-wiping technique." He shifted on his pillow to give her room to sit.

She sat gingerly, trying to hurt neither him nor her own sore shoulder. It was good to see him so cheerful. It was good just to have him alive.

When they finished the hand, Sean stood and fished in the pocket of his robe. "Well, that's my last dime." He dropped it onto a small pile on the bedside table and jingled his pocket. "Time to go before you start on my quarters." He collected the cards, then left with a jaunty wave.

"Pleasant fellow, but I thought he'd never go. Come here!" Crispin awkwardly lifted his head.

Ignoring her own pain, she bent to meet him, as eager as he.

As their lips met, however, something inside her seemed to freeze. She lifted her head, biting her lip and fighting back stinging tears. What was the matter with her?

"Hey!" Crispin jerked her hand to make her look at him. His eyes were both puzzled and hurt.

She stood, and moved around the bed. "Give me a minute, Crispin. Tell me how you feel."

"Just fine, Mrs. Travis. And how are you—besides running hot and cold?" He snatched the pillow from underneath his head, punched it savagely, and tried to put it back. Unsuccessfully.

"Here." She reached for it.

He pulled her down to him, and kissed her thoroughly. "There."

Breathless, she sat in the chair. "Was that necessary?"

He gloated. "Very. Now, tell me what you've been up to this awful afternoon. You said you planned to rest and laze around all day, but when I called, Miss Mary said you'd gone out—in such a chilling tone, I didn't dare ask where."

She told him—and what she had found. He whistled. "Do you think Honey really did go after the manuscript, and someone slugged her to get it?"

Sheila shrugged. "We won't know, I suppose, until she comes to—if she does. Philip wasn't real convincing on that point."

Crispin shook his head and looked at her admiringly. "You have a knack for getting messed up with the wrong people, don't you?"

"You are referring to people I've known all my life," she reminded him with dignity, "except for Honey. And she could have tripped and fallen, or let the wrong person in."

"The wrong person wearing a Christmas ghost," he retorted.

Before she could reply, his supper arrived.

When she had finished helping him ("I meant help feed me, not help eat it," he protested halfway through), he lay back on his pillows. "Now. Sit over there where I can't touch you, and tell me about your husband."

She regarded him in bewilderment. "Tyler?"

"That's him." Crispin, hunching his shoulders to get more comfortable, winced with pain. "I've been thinking about you and old Tyler a lot today—and don't look at me like that. I'm not afraid of ghosts. Until I know something about him, I won't really know about you."

Wary, she gained time by rearranging the toiletries on his bedside table. "What do you want to know?"

"Well, let's see. Your Aunt Mary has already told me he was very important in international circles, so you can skip that. And I know he was killed climbing a mountain, so you can skip that. Why don't you just tell me what he did to make you flinch every time his name is mentioned?"

"I do not!"

"You most certainly do."

She could feel her face setting into what her mother called her balky look. "Don't all widows flinch a bit for a year or two?"

"No, divorced women flinch. Widows burst into tears, or go around looking like they are being eaten alive from within, or maybe even go about their business looking relieved. You do none of the above. And most widows like to insert the old man's name into conversation." His voice rose to a falsetto. " 'Dear Jack used to just love this place.' "

"Or 'Jack, the cheapskate, never brought me here,' " she said sourly.

"Sure. But at least old Jack gets a word here and there. You never mention Tyler unless someone else brings him up. Then, if they criticize him you defend him. If they praise him, you agree with them. But first, *always,* you flinch. Why?"

She shrugged and managed a tiny smile. "Different people grieve in different ways, I guess. Do we have to talk about this?"

"Yes, we do." He reached for her, then drew back his hand. "No, I said I wouldn't touch you, and I won't, until I understand all this. I don't want to hurt you like he did. There—see? You did it again! You flinched!"

"I did not," she said, but even she knew it lacked conviction.

"Okay, you didn't. But tell me a bit about him. Where did you two meet?"

"At a women's college dance in Virginia, my junior year. Tyler was six years older, so he'd already finished graduate school and was working in Washington. A girl I knew was engaged to a friend of his, so they introduced us." She stopped.

"And then?" he prodded.

Her lips curved in a smile. "We danced all evening, and I fell head over heels in love. He was everything a girl dreams of—tall, handsome, witty, charming, and above all, persistent." Her eyes got dreamy and she laughed deep in her throat. "He sent flowers, took me to wonderful places, and sometimes he'd even come take me to dinner on Wednesdays. At a girl's school, any man who'll take you to dinner on Wednesday is irresistible."

Crispin reached toward his bedside table. "Let me make a note of that."

She laughed scornfully. "See? I knew you didn't really want to hear about Tyler."

He shook his head. "I'm not hearing about Tyler, yet. So far this sounds like an interview for a women's magazine. If I looked up old magazines, Mrs. Travis, would I find that very same script? With pictures showing that same practiced sparkle in your eyes?" His voice was grim. "This is the first time since I met you, Sheila, that you've gone false on me. I much prefer you climbing trees and felling gunmen with a single blow."

"Then let's climb trees and fell gunmen, Crispin. Tyler seems very long ago and far away."

He shook his head and sighed. "As long as you are working, or poking around into mysteries, maybe. But whenever I try to get close to you, I feel you recoil. Now I'm not inordinately vain for a charming, handsome fellow, but I've never had a woman recoil before, so I'm putting my money on it's being Tyler's fault. Am I right? What did he do to you, damn it?"

She rose and went to the window. Across the treetops she could see maybe fifty lighted windows. She would gladly trade places with people behind any of them, sight unseen. The last time she'd felt this apprehensive was just before she'd had her appendix out. "Can't we just skip this?" she'd shouted to the nurses as they rolled her down the hall—or so they told her later. She wanted to shout the same thing at Crispin, too. But she could feel his will like a huge magnet pulling the words out of her.

She spoke without turning around. "Tyler sucked the life out of me, Crispin. I don't want it to happen again."

"Tell me," he commanded.

She stood silent until she could control her voice. "There's not much to tell. In Hawaii, on our honeymoon—" she turned, and the expression on his face made her stop. "You *don't* want to hear this."

"Yes, I do," he said in the tone of one commanding his own firing squad. "I suppose he abused you."

She laughed, and this time it was genuine. "Heavens, no! Or at least not physically." She propped herself against the window, arms hugging her chest. "He was gentle, courteous, and kind, and I really was the happiest girl in the world. When other women looked at us, I knew they were wishing they could trade places with me. For two days I lived on a cloud of pink fluff."

She waited so long to continue that he prompted her. "But?"

"I just said I was a girl. It was true. I wore ruffled dresses, styled my hair like I had in high school. Aunt Mary had suggested a more sophisticated style, she'd even bought me a few mature dresses, but I was sure Tyler loved me for my girlish simplicity." This time her laugh was blunt and humorless. "Until . . ." She took a deep breath to get control of her voice. "Two days after we were married, he said he had another wedding present for me. He'd made dinner reservations at a marvelous restaurant, but first he was treating me to a salon make-over. He went with me, and he and the hairdresser discussed a new haircut and shades of eyeshadow."

"You were furious." Crispin nodded confidently.

"Oh, no! I was grateful! I thought it was wonderful that my husband cared that much. He chose a good hair style, too." She looked quickly toward his mirror and back. "Not very different from what I wear now, in fact. I suddenly looked adult, and very chic. Afterwards, he took me shopping for sophisticated clothes—a whole new wardrobe."

Crispin wiggled a bit on the bed and groaned. "Dang shoulder. So he bought you clothes. Why don't you sound thrilled?"

She took another breath, then blinked her eyes to clear them. Why should it hurt so much now, twenty years later?

"Because when—when we got back to the hotel, I found out why we'd bought the clothes." She had to go slowly now, set each word down and make sure it didn't wobble before she chose the next one. "While I was getting my hair cut, he'd gone back upstairs and given every stitch I owned to the hotel maid. Even my favorites, and things I'd bought for my trousseau." She turned and stared out the window, her eyes burning from eighteen years of unshed tears.

Crispin spoke to her back. "Did you cry?"

She shook her head and swallowed. "He was so pleased that I didn't want to hurt his feelings. I loved him very much, you see."

"Come here." She turned, and he reached out a hand. She took the chair beside him and he gently stroked her hair. "It was a beastly thing to do."

His compassion undid years of self-control. She laid her

forehead on the sheet near his waist and wept until the sheet beneath her face was soaked. She was amazed at how good it felt to let that old poison out of her system. At last he gave her a shake. "Hey, are you in league with my surgeon? Did you promise to drown me so he can play golf tomorrow?"

She sniffed and sat up, giving him a watery smile. "I really ought to go so you can rest up."

"I'm resting. You're doing all the work." He stretched and wiggled his toes. "So that's how your marriage started— Tyler telling you how to dress and cut your hair."

She mopped her eyes with his sheet. "And that's how it went. He told me how to sit, stand, speak, entertain, even enjoy myself. At first he was diplomatic. Eventually he didn't bother." She paused, added automatically. "He worked so hard being tactful everywhere else, he needed to feel he could relax, even be nasty, at home."

"Don't defend him, Sheila!"

She jerked upright. "I'll defend him if I damn well please!" Then she bit her lip and flushed, as astonished as he at the rage behind her words.

"You still love him." He said it flatly and turned his head away.

She reached out and turned him back. "No. That's not it. What made me mad just now was that all my married life, Tyler issued orders in just that tone of voice—and I obeyed. I will *never* let another man, you or anybody else, tell me what to do when I know what I am doing is right!"

He grinned. "I guess not! But I don't promise to stop using that tone of voice just because it makes you mad. Fair enough?" She nodded with a smile. He smiled back. "And what I meant to say was, I never met the guy and he's not running for reelection, so you don't have to talk nice about him just because he's gone."

She stood and began to pace the room. "But I truly am grateful for some of what he taught me. A lot of it, really." She sighed. "I just wish I hadn't given myself away in the process."

"Behold," he said sarcastically, "the grateful victim."

"I was not a victim!" she blazed. "I was a wimp! Tyler was a whole person. He knew what he wanted, and went for it. I wasn't even half a person. I let him make me over without a single protest. I accepted his criticism, catered to his whims, and never once did I say 'No' or 'Enough!' Tyler and our marriage would both have been better off if I had."

Crispin shoved his fingers through his hair, making it stand in sweaty little spikes. "*Do* you still love him?"

A certain wistfulness behind his words drew her to him. She returned to the chair and sat by the bed, aware of what a brave and hard thing he was doing for her. Taking his hand in hers, she stroked his fingers and said gently, "Crispin, I have never in my whole life been loved as fully as tonight. Nobody has ever cared enough to make me talk and really listen. So I'll tell you the whole sordid story—the part that hurt the worst, and still makes me scared to ever love anybody again. But if you ever breathe a word of this to my parents or Aunt Mary, I'll cut out your tongue."

He took back his hand and traced her jaw with one finger. "The only time you look like your aunt is when you get indignant. So," he stretched his good arm above his head, "tell me the whole sordid story."

"I've already said I loved Tyler. I went into our marriage loving him completely, the way a young girl loves for the very first time. And all those years that the great god Tyler was making me over in his own image, I was willing to be made over, because I believed that that was the way he showed his love. Even when he was rude to me, I comforted myself that after being diplomatic all day, he needed somebody to be rude around. But then—"

She stopped and got up again, went back to the window. "I can tell this better if I don't have to look at you, okay? Well, I said before that I met Tyler through the fiancé of a friend. They didn't get married, but Tyler stayed in touch with him." She laughed wryly. "Tyler stayed in touch with anybody who could conceivably be of any use to him. Well, four years ago—two years before Tyler died—Barry visited us in Japan. Tyler had to go out one evening, and after dinner, Barry got drunk. Very drunk. And he tried to get amorous. When I pushed him away, he said—" she took a deep breath and spoke quickly. "—he said, 'Come on, Sheila,

Tyler won't care. I always liked you better than he did, anyway.' " Unconsciously she mimicked his voice.

" 'But Tyler decided to *marry* me,' I pointed out.

"He made a rude sound and shook his head. 'Tyler decided to marry you before he ever laid eyes on you—unless you were as ugly as a junkyard dog. Those were his very words, Sheila. He came into my office waving a piece of paper and raving that he'd found his wife. A girl who grew up in Japan, spoke the language like a native, came from the South Carolina Beauforts—the *rich* ones—and the Alabama Daughterys. And tall. Old Tyler always liked 'em tall.' "

Sheila reached over, poured herself a glass of water, and sipped it. Crispin, she saw gratefully, had turned his face to the far wall. She forced herself to finish. "Barry proceeded to tell me how Tyler had arranged to meet me in the romantic setting of a dance, how he had continued to woo me with flowers and dinners, because—and I quote Barry quoting Tyler—'She's the partner I need to go where I plan to go, Barry, and I'll have her, unless she's ugly as a junkyard dog. I can fix anything else, but I can't fix ugly.' "

She laughed and tossed the opaque plastic cup into the wastebasket. "That's when I learned that my entire marriage was a sham, prearranged between Tyler Travis and his colossal ego."

She stopped. She had told Crispin enough. He did not need to hear the rest: Barry's affectionate pleading—"So if you sleep with Tyler who doesn't care diddly squat about you, Sheila, how about a tumble with a man who could?"—and the dreadful, shaming episode that followed.

"Did you ever think of leaving him?" Crispin sounded farther away than across the small room.

"Not seriously. I was raised to believe that for better or worse doesn't just mean for better. Besides, I couldn't bear for my parents or Aunt Mary to know how I'd been deceived. Most of all, I didn't know who I was except Tyler's wife. The most frightening part of Tyler's death wasn't losing Tyler, but the terror that I could never be anything or anybody apart from him—and that I'd never be able to know again if I was truly loved, or being fooled once more."

He didn't reply. As several minutes passed, she began to

wonder if he'd fallen asleep. Then she saw that his hand was clenched on top of the sheet.

"Crispin?" She neared the bed. His face was pale and drawn with pain. "I knew I shouldn't have told you!" she cried.

He shook his head and spoke between clenched teeth "Not you. Dratted knee. Spasm. Call a nurse!"

She arrived at the nursing station at a quick lope. Before she arrived, a nurse had picked up a waiting tray and started in the direction of his room. On their way back, Sheila asked angrily, "Why hasn't somebody come before with his medication? He's in agony!"

The nurse gave her an indignant look. "He told us not to come until he sent for us. Said you had serious matters to discuss. But he's an hour overdue. I don't know how he's stood it."

When he was a bit easier, Sheila bent awkwardly to give him a gentle kiss. "Don't ever be that brave again, do you hear me? Like Rip told Dorothy last night, we're a pair of crocks. Will you be all right?"

"Fine," he murmured drowsily. "How will you get home?"

"Take a cab to Aunt Mary's and ask Jason to take me home from there, if he will. Last night while you and I were getting patched up, Aunt Mary sent him over to walk Lady in all that icy rain. A lowering experience for the poor man."

"Marvelous woman, your aunt. Takes care of a dumb animal she doesn't like, but objects to a poor little guy going to South America with his loving uncle."

"His wicked uncle," Sheila amended, bending to kiss him again. "I'll see you first thing tomorrow, before your surgery."

"Don't. I'll be quaking in my bedpan. Don't want anybody around. Come after work. And find out who coshed Honey by then."

Black Atlantan recalling days of white-only police:
"One night somebody tried to get in one of the windows. . . . My father called the police. And after a while the police did come and asked my father didn't he have a gun. He told them 'Yes.' And they said, 'Well, why didn't you just shoot him? Why would you waste time calling us?' "[10]

One floor down, the elevator stopped for Faith Andrews. "Let me give you a lift to Miss Mary's," the musician insisted when she learned where Sheila was headed. "It won't be a block out of my way, and I'd like to thank you for finding Honey. If you hadn't—" She pulled her black trenchcoat around her and shuddered.

Sheila wanted to ask her some questions, but Faith was so tired the freckles stood out on her square face. In spite of her weariness, however, she was a pleasant companion. The two women made easy, casual conversation as they rode.

As they waited on the light where West Peachtree joins Peachtree, Faith asked curiously, "Are you from Atlanta? I don't remember you growing up, and you don't talk southern."

"I grew up in Japan. I only visited occasionally until high school. You're a native Atlantan, aren't you?"

Faith laughed. "I ought to be, but I've never known if I really count. The family's been here for four generations, but when Mama was pregnant with me in '44, Daddy was afraid somebody would try to bomb Fort Gillem or Fort MacPherson and hit Buckhead instead, so he sent Mama, Hattie, and Honey up to our house in Cashiers, North Carolina that June." (Faith pronounced it "Cashes," but Sheila knew what she was saying. Aunt Mary had a house in the same part of the Blue Ridge Mountains.) "I was born the end of August, and we all came home two months later. What does that make me?"

Sheila chuckled. "A southerner, at least. Since I was born and raised in Japan of American parents, I've never felt I really belonged either place. And you have a family home and a sister. I've always wanted both."

Faith shook her head. "These days I have a house, period. It used to be a family home, but I rattle around in it now. And Honey doesn't seem like a sister. We're too far apart in age. She got married before I was walking good, then she and Mama never got along, so she didn't come home much. We're virtual strangers. In high school, when I'd run into her up at Lenox Square with my friends, we were so formal my friends didn't believe Honey was really my sister. But," she added thoughtfully, "at least she never tried to run my life like some big sisters do."

After that, they rode in silence up an almost deserted Peachtree through the gloomy wet night. The rain had stopped, but the moonless sky was hung with thick gray clouds. Sidewalks gleamed murkily under streetlights.

Sheila didn't know where Faith's thoughts might be, but her own were back in Crispin's room. She wished she hadn't told him so much. She wondered how much he'd absorbed through his pain. She wondered what he would do with what he'd learned. She wished she hadn't told him so much— Ruefully, she realized she'd come full circle to where she'd started.

To keep from thinking, she mused aloud, "I wonder if Honey did go after those envelopes this morning, and if so, where they are now. Walt and I didn't see them at her apartment."

Faith sighed. "I hope we can ask her soon."

"Mildred will know—or could find out. She ought to be home by now. Want to run up and see?"

Faith pulled into the parking garage beneath Aunt Mary's condominium. "Frankly, Sheila, I don't care enough to make the effort—and I need to get back to the hospital. I'm just running home for a few things."

Watching her drive away, Sheila couldn't help wondering: Was Faith really that disinterested in whether Honey went for the papers? Or did she already know?

She walked slowly through the garage and jabbed the elevator button. She was exhausted, and her shoulder throbbed. *With any luck,* she told herself, *you can be in the tub in an hour.*

In the upstairs hall she found Mildred and a stocky young man. Mildred introduced him as "my cousin Junior," adding, "Miss Mary called Grace's and asked me to have Junior follow me home, for some reason. Do you know why?"

Before Sheila could answer, however, Aunt Mary trotted out of Forbes's room. "He's asleep," she whispered.

She looked at Junior, her head cocked to one side like a small bird's. "Mildred, is this the young cousin you've told me so much about? The one who lives with your Aunt Elouisa?"

"Sure is, Miss Mary. James Martin Turner. We call him Junior. Junior, just carry my bag to the first room beyond the kitchen."

When he'd disappeared through the swinging door,

Aunt Mary turned to Sheila. "I asked Junior to come so you and Jason can follow him back."

"Back where, Aunt Mary?"

"To Elouisa's, of course, to fetch those papers." Sheila opened her mouth to protest, but Aunt Mary continued, "You look surprised, Mildred. Didn't you know Sheila didn't get them last night?"

"No, ma'am. I went on to my sister's after I called."

"Well, they had a little accident on the way—"

"Not on purpose, no matter how she makes it sound," Sheila contributed.

"Were you hurt?" Mildred's eyes roved over her, concerned.

Sheila started to answer, but Aunt Mary gave her no time. "You and Jason can follow Junior now. Don't interrupt me again, Sheila! I want to ask Mildred something else. Mildred, did you and Elouisa tell anyone about the envelopes except us?"

"We sure didn't, Miss Mary. Telling you was bad enough. I am so ashamed of that old buzzard—"

"Never mind that now. But the sooner we get them, the sooner you can stop worrying. Call down to tell Jason that Sheila's ready."

"Honey—" Sheila began.

"Pshaw, Sheila! Honey didn't get those envelopes." Aunt Mary checked off her logical deductions on her slim fingertips. "You didn't find them. None of our friends has them—I'd have known if they were lying. And nobody else knows about them. So go fetch them now." She gave Sheila a gentle prod toward the elevator.

"I'm worn out!" Sheila objected.

Junior had been hovering in the background for a couple of minutes. Now he stepped forward and said, politely but firmly, "I'm sorry, ma'am, but you'll have to wait 'til morning. Mama Weesa is already asleep, and she needs her rest."

Aunt Mary's lips tightened in exasperation, but his gaze did not yield. To Sheila's amazement, her aunt finally gave a reluctant nod. "Very well. Since Sheila works," she made it sound like an eccentric aberration on her niece's part, "I'll go myself first thing in the morning."

Sheila sidled over nearer Mildred. "We'll have to keep him around. Anybody who can stare Aunt Mary down—"

"Hush!" Mildred told her, and turned to her employer. "You're getting your teeth cleaned at nine-thirty, remember."

"Oh, pshaw! I suppose I'd never get another appointment before I leave town. You can try first thing in the morning, though."

"Then we have Forbes's nursery school Christmas program. You can't miss that. He's gonna be a Wise Man," Mildred added to Sheila.

"Certainly can't miss that," Sheila agreed solemnly.

Aunt Mary pursed her lips in dismay. "You'll have to go after all, Sheila."

"I work, Aunt Mary, as you just said."

Aunt Mary fluttered her hands to dismiss that inconsequential complication. "If you must, go on your lunch hour. But bring them straight back here—and don't you dare read them first!"

Before Sheila could protest at this high-handed planning of her schedule, Mildred quickly said to Junior, "Sheila's the one I told you about who works for Hosokawa International."

The young man whirled, eyes wide. "No kidding? I'm planning to do a paper next term on U.S.-Japanese trade relations." His voice had a little gurgle behind it, like a stream of laughter. "You don't happen to know anybody who'd talk to me about difficulties in intercultural communication and bridging intercultural gaps, do you? It'd be great if I could get a head start on my research."

"You could talk to me. That's my job."

"No kidding?" He was so happy his little mustache quivered. "What do you do, exactly?"

She laughed. "I bridge international gaps—which is terribly hard to describe. Sometimes I sit in meetings between Japanese and American executives to help them say what they really want to say, rather than what dictionaries make them think is proper. Other times I help negotiate bi-lingual

contracts. Since I understand the customs and what consti-
tutes insult in each culture, I also have to review some ads, to
be sure they aren't offering unintentional offense. Sometimes
I prepare materials and conduct seminars to help corporate
families adapt to an overseas assignment in either country.
And since I have embassy training—" her thoughts flew to
the hospital room and tonight's conversation, but she
dragged them back, "—I sometimes represent our U.S.
CEO, Mr. Hashimoto, at business functions. I'll be glad to
talk to you further about it sometime."

Junior snapped his fingers. "How about if I bring those
envelopes to your office tomorrow, and you answer a few
questions while I'm there. Fair?"

"More than fair. As hard as it's going to be for me to
drive for a few days, it's downright kind."

"About ten?" When she nodded, he gave Mildred a
quick kiss on the cheek and left, calling, "See you tomorrow!"

"Don't you open those envelopes before you get here,"
Aunt Mary warned Sheila. "Now go home and get some rest.
You stayed far too long with That Man. You look half dead.
And I have some calls to make."

Probably alerting the gang, Sheila thought as she descended to Jason and the waiting car.

Her deduction must have been correct. By the time she'd
fetched Lady and given her kind neighbor a thumbnail
sketch of the accident, Dorothy called. "It's been so good to
get glimpses of you these past two days, Sheila! I'm realizing
how little I've seen of you since you moved back to town.
Why don't you come up to the Swan Coach House for lunch
tomorrow? And if you've gotten Peggy Marsh's papers by
then, I'd love to take a peek at them."

It took considerable diplomacy to decline gracefully.

Then Philip Maxwell called to say gruffly, without pre-
amble, "Thought you looked a bit peaky this afternoon,
Sheila. Why don't you come in on your lunch hour tomorrow and let me give you a once-over?"

Whatever his motive, his concern was genuine. Touched, she unconsciously reverted to her childhood name for him. "I'm fine, Uncle Max—really. I look peaky because of finding Honey, and the accident. A good night's sleep will help. And if you were also going to suggest I bring you Margaret Mitchell's envelopes, I'm taking them to Aunt Mary's right after work. She'll probably invite you all over to see them later."

Lamar, when he phoned, didn't beat around the bush. He also offered genuine good advice. "Mary says you are finally going to be getting Peggy Marsh's envelopes tomorrow, Sheila. You be sure to have a witness present when that young man hands them over, then you seal them in his presence and that of a witness, and have both the witness and the courier initial the seal. Don't you even *think* about opening them except in the presence of a lawyer! You don't want someone going to court at a later date claiming something's missing."

"Very wise, Uncle Lamar." She spoke before she thought, then wondered ruefully: *Will I ever really grow up?*

To assert her adulthood, she added, "I'll ask one of Hosokawa's lawyers to—"

She was amused when Lamar responded as she'd expected. "I'd rather keep it in the family, so to speak. Let me check my calendar—yes, I'm free for lunch. Know the Mitchell lawyers, too. Why don't I pick you up, and—"

It was a kind offer. Tempting, too. On the other hand, Aunt Mary would never forgive her if Lamar got to see those papers before she did. "How about if you come over to Aunt Mary's tomorrow evening, and we'll all open them together?"

"Good idea. Let me know what time, and I'll invite the Mitchell lawyers. Tell Mary *not* to serve mineral water."

Sheila hung up, chuckling, and went for Lady's leash. When she had walked the dog, fixed herself a Swiss-cheese-and-mushroom omelette, and managed an awkward bath, she climbed into bed with a grateful sigh. "Thank you, God, this day is over."

•   •   •   •

It wasn't, for everyone.

When he got home, Junior tiptoed to the table beside Mama Weesa's recliner. The stack of muddied manila envelopes was right where Mama Weesa made Demolinius put them after he'd picked them up out of the yard that morning. "I ketch you botherin' dem embelopes, I'll skin yo' hide," she had told both men.

To Junior's surprise, beyond darting curious looks that way from time to time, Demolinius had left the envelopes alone. When Uncle Anthony had come at three to take Demolinius back to where he was sleeping, he'd gone meek as a lamb.

That worried Junior. He was certain something was hatching behind those smouldering eyes. So after Demolinius had gone, Junior and Mama Weesa had a heart-to-heart talk.

When he went to bed, he took the envelopes with him. Propped comfortably on two pillows, he switched on his bed light, tipped the pages from one envelope, and started to read.

Junior had never cared much for historical fiction, and while this was well written, it was not a period of history in which Junior was interested. Also, no blacks appeared in important roles. Soon his eyelids began to droop.

He slid the pages back into the envelope, shoved the entire stack between his springs and mattress, and switched off his light.

About one o'clock he lifted his head off his pillow and listened intently. He heard again what had wakened him: a scraping at the back door!

He crept from bed, pulled on his pants, and reached into the corner for a steel bat. He'd rather have had a gun. Gently bred, Junior found this neighborhood rough, full of strange sounds and stranger people. But when he'd suggested to his parents that he'd sleep easier with a gun in his drawer, they'd had a fit.

"You'd be more likely to shoot yourself," his mother said.

"Or an intruder would shoot you with your own gun," his father added. "Guns do too much permanent damage to people, son." The next day, though, he'd brought Junior the steel bat.

Barefoot, on tiptoe, clutching the bat, Junior left his small back bedroom and eased across the darkened kitchen. Mama Weesa was snoring to beat the band at the front of the house, and he could still hear something scratching softly at the back door.

Straining to see through the plastic, he wished they could have persuaded Mama Weesa to let Dad put in storm windows this year. She wouldn't hear of it—"Don't want to attract no storms to my house," she'd declared, holding fast to her opinion that storm windows drew storms like lightning rods drew lightning. Now, though, Junior could discern only a dark shape huddled on the small back porch, fumbling at the lock. Thank goodness Dad had put up a solid door with a deadbolt! But had Mama Weesa remembered to lock it after she'd set out the garbage?

Crouched low, Junior crept to the door and slammed it with his left fist. "Hey!" he bellowed.

Trembling and covered with sweat, he pressed himself against the wall, expecting gunfire. Instead, he heard feet scrambling down the steps. As a crouched shape dashed past the window, Junior again let out a tremendous yell. Elouisa's snores continued unabated.

For five minutes afterward, James Martin Turner leaned against the doorframe trembling, praying he wouldn't wet his pants. He wasn't big enough for this sort of thing. Tomorrow, family or no family, he'd get him a gun.

"To my household, my children, and . . . the generations to come, I bequeath my good name as it has come to me from an honorable and honest ancestry. My chief aim in life has been to help and not hurt my fellow man. . . ."

Asa Candler, founder of Coca-Cola, in his will[11]

Monday, the winter sun finally returned. It was just brightening the horizon when Charles Davidson stood at his office window high above North Peachtree Street watching a rosy glow backlight office towers up near Lenox Square.

Normally, Charles would have been at his massive mahogany desk checking market reports. By dawn in Atlanta the financial day was finished in Tokyo, closing in Frankfurt, and bustling in London. Charles liked to know early what the market was doing.

This morning, however, he was having difficulty concentrating on the familiar columns of figures filling his terminal screen. He'd come to the window hoping to rid himself of a gut-strangling indecision that made him feel far younger than the age-gnarled forefinger lightly stroking his mustache. Standing there, tall and spare against the dark paisley drape, he looked much as usual: confident, competent to hold a financial empire in those large hands. Only a caring observer would have noticed a tremor in the finger that stroked his upper lip, and beads of sweat beneath the few strands of hair combed across his skull.

Finally he spoke aloud a decision it wrenched his soul to make: "I've got to do it—*whatever* the outcome!"

He jotted instructions for his staff, checked an address, and made one call. Then Charles Davidson put on his black overcoat and left the office on a most unpleasant errand.

In his home study several miles down Peachtree, Philip Maxwell had also welcomed the dawn, but Philip had sat up most of the night. Elbows on his rosewood desk, chin propped on interlaced fingers, the doctor stared at a clipping on his otherwise clear blotter. He needed to think. Why couldn't he think?

He read each word again, then buried his smooth silver head in his hands. "Oh, God," he groaned, "what should I do?" Tears dripped between his fingers. "What shall I do?" Unconsciously, he had changed tenses. He was already moving toward a decision.

At last he sniffed, took a tissue from his bottom drawer and blew his nose, then said to the empty room, "I'll do it. I must!"

"Do what?"

Winona stood in the doorway, looking larger and more shapeless than usual in her green robe. Her hair was awry; her face glowed with cream. A stranger seeing them thus—Winona lumpy and plain, Philip dapper even after a sleepless night—would have wondered as others often did why he had ever married her.

Philip had no such thoughts this morning. All his attention was focused on keeping his wife's attention off that clipping. Covering it with his palm, he held her gaze while he scrabbled his fingers to wad it. "Nothing that concerns you, Winona," he said testily. "Just a touch of indigestion. What are you doing up so early?"

"You didn't sleep all night," she accused.

"Old people often don't." He rose and slid the wadded clipping into the pocket of his robe. Heading for the bedroom, he said over one shoulder, "I'm going on down to the office to catch up on some paperwork. Go back to bed."

Hurt and angry, she returned to their room.

Not until he was riding the Sheffield Building elevator to his office, the clipping secure in the pocket of his black overcoat, did Philip identify something else he'd seen in his wife's eyes: fear.

If she knew what he was going to do in a few hours, he thought grimly, she'd be terrified.

Winona waited until eight o'clock. Then she could stand it no longer. Hurrying to her bedroom, she reached for her telephone.

"Dorothy," she said breathlessly as soon as her friend mumbled a sleepy greeting, "what on earth is going on? Philip came home last night saying Honey'd had an accident, but he wouldn't tell me what happened. Now he's been up all night. I found him early this morning sitting at his desk looking as worried as he did when our older son got meningitis. What's going on? Is Honey all right?" She paused at last for breath, giving Dorothy a chance to reply.

She could hear a rustling on the other end. Dorothy was probably sliding up in bed and propping herself on her lovely blue-and-lavender designer sheets, while Winona had been up and worrying for hours! When Dorothy got herself settled to her satisfaction, she would finally deign to reply— or that's how Winona saw it. In fifty years she'd never quite gotten over a feeling that native Atlantans, those not only born in the city but with Atlanta-born parents, considered themselves better than those who'd only spent their entire adult lives there.

Dorothy, meanwhile (wholly unconscious either of the accusation or of any intention of living up to it) had been trying merely to bridge the gap between an exceedingly pleasant morning snooze and Winona's sudden demand. She was also troubled by Philip's worry over Honey. "I thought she'd had a simple concussion, dear. But if Philip is worried—"

"He is." Winona's bluntness revealed instantly to Dorothy how worried *she* was. Normally she was as protective of Philip as a mother 'possum—and about as forthcoming.

Intrigued, Dorothy tucked the covers more comfortably about her spare chest and prepared for a long chat. "Well, apparently Honey either fell or was shoved in her apartment yesterday. Sheila and Walt found her—"

Winona was momentarily diverted. "Sheila and *Walt*? I thought Sheila was practically engaged to Crispin. Has she—?"

"I don't know about that," Dorothy said with a trace of waspishness. She hated being interrupted. "But Mary was worried sick. She'd been trying to reach Honey all yesterday morning, and couldn't get an answer, so she asked Walt to drive Sheila over to check on Honey—because Sheila's shoulder is so painful. Mary just *knew* something must be wrong. She was proven so dreadfully right!"

It must be remembered that Dorothy's passion was for drama.

Winona, without a dramatic streak in her ample body (except in the matter of clothing and decorating it), drummed bloodred nails on her bedside table. "What *happened* at Honey's?"

"There's no way of knowing until she wakes up. She's in a coma. But," Dorothy suddenly remembered, "it was the oddest thing. Do you know, Sheila actually asked us where we all were yesterday? As if we'd had something to do with it!"

She'd expected shared indignation, but Winona surprised her. After a brief pause, she asked, "Did she say why? And who?"

"Winona! You're as bad as Sheila! As if any of us would hurt Honey—or anybody else!"

"Well, if Sheila thinks so," Winona said, digging in her heels with a stubbornness committees had come to dread, "she must have a reason. I wonder what it is."

"Thank you," Dorothy murmured, then hastened to add, "I wasn't speaking to you, dear. Bertha just brought me some coffee." She paused to take a sip. "Ummm. Well, as I was saying, Sheila asked where we'd been all morning. We, of course, were in church. You all brought me home."

"Yes. Then we ate a bite of lunch and Philip went to the hospital. I lay down for a bit, and woke up with a dreadful migraine."

Dorothy's musical laughter tinkled through the phone. "I wasn't asking where *you* were, Winona. Sheila was asking *us*. We told her, of course, except Philip. He got furious—as we all should have done! I think she's gotten so used to stumbling over mysteries, she doesn't recognize an ordinary accident when it happens. That's what Mary thinks, too, by the way. At dinner last night she cautioned us several times not to encourage Sheila in this—that she has enough other problems at this time. Charles thought Mary was talking about Crispin, and told her that handsome man is the best thing that ever happened to the child. That's the first time I can ever remember Mary and Charles disagreeing, but—oh! There's a call on my other line. Please keep me posted if you hear anything about Honey, will you?"

They both knew she wouldn't. Philip would have a fit if he caught Winona discussing his patients. But her own worry had deepened considerably. As much as Winona hated going out early on a cold winter's day, this morning she knew she would have to.

Mary Beaufort hung up her phone and headed for the kitchen. "Mildred, can you drive your car and meet me at Forbes's school for the program?"

Mildred turned from the sink in surprise. "Instead of going with you and Jason and waiting while you're at the dentist's? I can if you need me to. Has something happened to your car?"

"No, but something has come up. I'll see you there, dear."

Mildred returned to scrubbing the frying pan with a question knitted between her delicate brows. Mary Beaufort hadn't mentioned the dentist in that conversation. Where else could she be going?

Mr. Rip was fidgeting again, driving Isaac nearly crazy. Wouldn't eat all his toast. Didn't drink his coffee until he'd let it get cold, then fussed that it *was* cold. Didn't want his blue suit, wanted his brown one, then didn't like the tie Isaac chose to go with it. Real Thing, catching his mood, was whining constantly.

"You only goin' to see Dr. Maxwell," Isaac finally pointed out. "You doan haf to doll yo'self up like you was lookin' for a job."

"Don't want to look sloppy." Hearing echoes of the Old Rip in that growl, Isaac turned to hide a smile of pure delight. This wasn't Mr. Rip's usual sickly fidgets. What was he up to?

Although often exasperated by his boss's eccentric whims, Isaac used to boast that working for Rip Delacourt was like working for a politician. "You never know what them rascals'll be up to next!" These past two years had nearly broken Isaac's big heart. He had watched his boss struggle to learn how to feed himself and comb his hair. He himself had struggled to maneuver the chair without hurting either the shrunken body or the fragile dignity. "I could just cry," he'd told Gertie many evenings in the kitchen, "or spit!"

"Doan' you spit in my kitchen," she would warn him. Then she'd give him a big, soft hug. "Seems like that stroke lef' us all jes' a little bit crippled."

Now, as Isaac reached for another tie in the closet, he beamed. Before he turned, however, he rearranged his features into an expression of dignified outrage. "Will this one do, then?"

Rip considered the tie and nodded. "Yeah. Now call Walt and tell him I want him to drop me off."

"Mr. Walt has to get to work. Can't be drivin' you all over town. I'll take you myself, soon as I get my own bit of breakfast."

"I don't want you." Rip poked out his lower lip. "I might be a while. I'll call you when I'm ready."

Now Isaac's outrage was genuine. Mr. Rip *was* up to something, for sure—and leaving old Isaac out!

"Be like that, then," he said huffily, "but doan' expect me to come runnin' to pull you out if you get in over your head."

"I can still swim in certain ponds," Rip replied blandly.

Elouisa Whetlock couldn't swim, and she might nigh couldn't see, but she could hobble after a fashion and there was nothin' wrong with her hearin' that a good strong hearin' aid couldn't fix. At nine o'clock in the morning, therefore, she turned the volume up high and pressed her forehead to the front window, straining to find out who Junior was talking to on the sidewalk.

She heard the voice say, "I can take them. It's no trouble at all," then Junior's light baritone insisting, "No, I'll take them myself. I promised Sheila." He sounded like he was getting riled.

For the first time all winter Elouisa regretted that she'd made Junior cover her windows. The plastic and Elouisa's own poor eyesight defeated her. All she could make out was somebody in a black coat, dark hat, and gloves. Couldn't even tell if it was a man or a woman. White, though. She was pretty sure of that.

Curiosity propelled her old knees toward the front door, but before her trembly twisted hands could get all the locks open, she heard Junior drive off. She'd strained to hear that Toyota so many evenings now, she'd know it anywhere. She got the door open just in time to see a big gray car head off after it. Looked like a Cadillac—but all big cars looked like Cadillacs to Elouisa.

Junior burst into song. The sun had come out, he had a date with his currently favorite woman this evening, and his upcoming interview with Sheila Travis would give him a leg up on next term's work that might boost his GPA to the top of his class.

"There's a bluebird on my shoulder," he caroled, then grinned. Mama would be tickled to hear him singing Uncle Remus songs, after all the grief he used to give her about going to kids' story afternoons over at Joel Chandler Harris's Wren's Nest!

He was going almost too fast for the turn into Magnolia Cemetery—a quick route if the police were busy elsewhere. Junior fervently hoped they were, because he was running late.

"Old fool," he muttered, grabbing to keep the mud-stained envelopes stacked beside him from sliding to the floor. Even Junior didn't know if he was referring to his recent encounter or to his great-grandmother, who had landed them in this mess.

The big gray car came up so quickly he didn't see it until it loomed in his rearview mirror.

Junior stepped on the gas.

As they started down a steep hill, it stayed on his tail.

Junior edged to the right of the narrow road. "You wanna pass, go right ahead. Better you get a ticket than me."

As he had expected, the car started to edge by on the left. When they were neck-and-neck, however, the driver tooted the horn. Junior turned his head and, startled, looked into an open window and the barrel of a gun.

The shot was accurate and deadly.

Junior's Toyota lurched out of control and made a haphazard path through the granite and marble tombstones.

The driver of the big gray car slowed, shoved the gun under the seat, and watched the Toyota roll. It should stop in a minute or two, and no one else was in sight. Getting the envelopes would only take a minute. If anyone came along, what could be simpler than to say you'd seen the accident and stopped to help? This had been easier than it could have been. Easier than it *should* have been. That young man should have had sense enough not to head through the cemetery when he was being followed.

The driver was not without remorse. The hand that had steadily pulled the trigger now shook uncontrollably, and a whisper wafted heavenward: "Why wouldn't he just *give* them to me?"

The whisper was followed by a grunt of surprise. The erratic Toyota had straddled a short, broken monument and ripped a hole in its gas tank. Seconds later, it exploded.

The driver of the big car sped away without looking back. No need to worry about those envelopes now. Just be gone before somebody called 911.

Across Atlanta, in Hosokawa's plum-and-gray boardroom, Sheila shifted in her large upholstered chair to ease her shoulder and sneak a look at her watch. Ten-thirty. Surely Junior would rescue her soon!

Knowing that in a short time she could be holding envelopes that might have once been held by the author of *Gone With The Wind* made it hard to concentrate on the lugubrious prose of Toshio Ohta, unexpectedly down from Chicago to discuss Hosokawa operations there. Ohta-san was a dark sallow man, with cheeks so plump they almost swallowed his small black eyes, and stiff hair that bristled above a wide forehead. He looked, Sheila had always thought, like a young pig. As he glanced up from the elaborate chart he'd spread on the black laquer table and caught her checking her watch, his eyes took on a most piggy gleam.

"Mani-ka aru no deshitara, mata, jikai ni," he said politely, making a motion to gather up his papers.

That, she noted, was a good illustration of how dictionary translations could mislead. Who would know, without assistance, to translate a mere "If you have something else to do, maybe next time" into the stinging rebuke he'd intended?

"Dozo, dozo." ("Please, please.") Sheila gave him a small bow and hoped he hadn't seen her flush. Ohta-san had strong opinions about women in executive positions. This morning she was doing little to counteract them. She bowed again. "I was expecting someone, but he has not yet arrived. Until he gets here, my time is yours."

Taking her at her word, Toshio Ohta also took her entire morning. Then he rolled up his charts and suggested lunch.

"I regret that I have other plans." She did. She hoped to talk with Junior. If he'd called to say he'd been detained, she planned to walk three times around Hosokawa's landscaped lake to ease the numbness of mind and body that always resulted from a morning in Ohta's earnest company. But he looked so crestfallen, she took pity on him. She knew how he felt—a short-term visitor at loose ends until his return flight. "Perhaps Masako Nanto—"

He brightened. Masako, Sheila's administrative assistant, was a petite young woman with skin the color of a ripening apricot and smooth dark hair cut to frame her gamin face. She was single, as was Toshio Ohta. And if Masako liked her men slender, golden, and young, Sheila knew she also liked to eat. Masako would not turn down a free lunch.

"A fine young woman." Ohta-san blinked his little eyes and almost licked his lips in eagerness. "She has not lost her Japanese heart."

Sheila bowed and went in search of Masako, reflecting that Toshio Ohta was like thousands of other Japanese in the United States: They might wear Western clothes, live in ranch-style houses, eat fried chicken and take-out pizza, learn idiomatic English, and more than master Western business practices, but deep in their hearts they worried about losing *yamato damashi,* the essence that made them Japanese.

Masako at the moment had lost all heart whatsoever. "I will *never* finish editing these reports," she wailed when she saw Sheila. "You never told me there were *thousands* of pages."

"It only seems like thousands," Sheila comforted her, "and if you'll do me a favor, you can forget them for the next two hours."

When she explained, Masako was delighted. "I can order anything I like? For that, I will gladly endure Ohta-san's heavy charms."

"Watch out for his heavy hands," Sheila warned, handing her a corporate credit card. "I'd sit across from him, not beside him."

Masako tossed her head. "I was not born yesterday."

Sheila chuckled as she scanned her desk. "Ah-so, oh ancient one, did anyone come by and leave a stack of envelopes for me?"

"No, but you had several calls." Masako handed her a sheaf of notes and went to fetch her coat. "See you later—much later!"

Sheila rifled through her phone messages. Most could be returned after lunch, especially the three from Aunt Mary. No doubt about what *she* wanted! But she was puzzled to find nothing at all from Junior.

He'd probably changed his mind about interviewing her for his paper, and decided the envelopes could wait. But she felt as disappointed as if she'd been stood up for a special date—and more surprised. Junior had looked like a man of his word.

Giving her phone a quick, hopeful look, she used Masako's line to check on Crispin. He was in the recovery room, and no one was willing to give her an over-the-phone report on his condition. She also tried Philip, without success, and left a message for him to call her. When her private line rang almost immediately, she pounced on the receiver.

"Are you sitting down, dear?"

"Yes, Aunt Mary." Sheila had been hoping it was Philip. Disappointment made her tart. "Is that what you called to ask, or are you wondering whether I've sneaked a peek at a certain manuscript?"

"There are more serious matters, Sheila, than the possible contents of those silly envelopes. Mildred's nephew Junior was killed this morning. On his way to your office, apparently."

Sheila felt like the bottom had dropped out of her elevator. She took a deep breath and closed her eyes, struggling to concentrate on what Aunt Mary was saying. "——out of control, ran over some tombstones and exploded."

Sheila caught her breath. Crispin's Jaguar spun, spun on an icy street, crashed. Dizzy, she propped her head on one hand and repeated a puzzling word. "Tombstones?"

"It happened in Magnolia Cemetery. Mildred's gone to his parents', and will call when she learns anything more. You might contact that police detective friend of yours and see what he knows."

Sheila forced herself to drag her mind back to Aunt Mary's practical level. "If you are referring to Lieutenant Green, Aunt Mary, he's not exactly a friend. When I saw him last, he was barely civil." Aunt Mary merely waited. "Okay, I'll call and see what I can find out. Tell Mildred to let me know if there's anything I can do."

It was such an inane thing to say. What could anyone do at a time like this?

"You can pray for his family," Aunt Mary reminded her. "Would you like to come over here for dinner?"

"No, I'm going to see Crispin." She yearned to go now, this moment, and let him hold her fast while this crazy world spun around them.

Aunt Mary, however, had other ideas. "We'll all go. Are you driving?"

"Not yet," Sheila admitted. "It's still a bit beyond me. I'll use a cab."

"Nonsense, dear. Jason will fetch you at five, and you can swing by here to pick us up. I'll pop in to see Honey while you take Forbes up with you. He's dying to visit a hospital."

"Crispin had surgery this morning, Aunt Mary. He's not likely to want to see a four-year-old tonight, even if the hospital would let him in—which I doubt."

"Pshaw! Philip can arrange a little visit, and Crispin's got to learn he can't just put up with the child when it's convenient and let others care for him the rest of the time. And you won't want to stay long. Too much company isn't good when someone is trying to recuperate."

"How sweet of you to care."

When they'd hung up, Sheila sat, chin on hand, staring out her office window where the weak sun could not overcome a general soppy bleakness: tan grass, empty ornamental lake, maples mere skeletons against a white, cold sky.

An ugly day, she thought. Nausea cramped her stomach. For Junior, this had been an especially ugly day.

Before she called Police Lieutenant Owen Green of Atlanta's Homicide Division, Sheila considered carefully what she would say. She decided to identify Junior as the young cousin of a close friend. "The great-grandson of my aunt's housekeeper's aunt" sounded much too remote for the rush of liking she'd felt when they'd met last night—and, she admitted with a rueful smile, would give away how truly remote their relationship was.

Green was cordial, but wary. Since their first meeting,* the police lieutenant had persisted in thinking she was more nuisance than help. "You aren't calling to suggest that this vehicular accident was murder, are you, Mrs. Travis?"

"Not at all," she assured him, but once he'd suggested it, the idea began to niggle. "It couldn't have been, could it?"

Green grunted. She pictured him at his desk, small and as brown as his suit, with a kinky gray fringe and eyes that had grown tragic from all they had seen of the world. Right now, his mobile lips would be working in and out as he considered what he would say next. "No reason to think so, no. Looks like he lost control of the car and went over the curb, striking a broken tombstone that pierced his fuel tank. At least, that's what we're surmising at this time. Forensics isn't finished, of course."

Sheila was both sorry and glad. Sorry because she had genuinely liked Junior. Glad because the young man's death had had nothing to do with Elouisa's stolen envelopes. "Did anyone see it happen?" she asked.

Green decided she was still being difficult. "No, but if

---

* *Murder on Peachtree Street.*

you'd care to take a look at the site for yourself, you can see how easily—"

"Oh, no! I just wondered who found him. He was a very special young man," she added.

As she had hoped, Green was mollified. "There are houses nearby. A resident saw smoke down in the cemetery and dialed 911. The car was burned and smouldering by the time fire engines arrived. A tragic accident," he concluded in the tone of one who considers the conversation over.

But she was not quite finished. "Junior was supposed to bring me some papers this morning."

"I shoulda known," Green muttered—probably not for her ears. The sigh that followed came from the toes of his soft brown Hush Puppies. "Before the young man agreed to make that delivery, did anyone tell him that people who make dates with you, live across the hall from you, or marry your high school buddies have had a high fatality rate lately?" His voice sounded as if he was about to drop the receiver into its cradle.

"Wait! Just tell me if you found a stack of envelopes—"

His laugh was short and brutal. "Mrs. Travis, anything that could burn did burn. Also some things you wouldn't *believe* could burn. We're still waiting for the car to cool down before we sift through the debris and remove the remains."

She hung up, feeling worse than when she'd called. She appreciated his distinction between a body and remains.

"The Ku Klux Klan, through its Buckhead robe factory and other enterprises, pumped millions of dollars into the city's economy . . . and gave to local charities."[12]

About her visit to Crispin that evening there is little to say, except that Philip had—with some prodding from Aunt Mary—arranged for Forbes to go along.

Crispin was groggy and in obvious pain, and Sheila was inhibited equally by a certain nervousness after Sunday's revelations, Forbes's lively chatter, and the likelihood that if they stayed too long Aunt Mary would come after them breathing fire. Therefore, while Forbes investigated the room and bathroom, she whispered that Mildred's cousin had been killed in a tragic car accident, then left nephew and uncle to manly conversation.

"—'n I carried frankamints, an' I didn't even drop it.

An' you know what? I got to keep my crown. You can wear it as soon as you get out of here. An' you know what else? We got to go to HotDonald's for lunch! Aunt Mary and Mildred ate Big Macs and I had a Happy Meal, an' . . ."

At that point Sheila stopped listening. She was trying to picture Aunt Mary and Mildred sliding into a fast-food booth and unwrapping their burgers.

However, when Forbes reached the stage of "How does the bed go up and down? Do you just push this button?" Sheila rose.

"I think it's time to go, now, Forbes. Aunt Mary will be finished downstairs."

Crispin reached out and ruffled Forbes's dark curls, so like his own. "Do me a favor, boy. Go to the hall and wait just outside the door for one whole minute while I tell Sheila something. Okay?"

Forbes's long-lashed gray eyes danced mischievously. "No! I want to watch you kiss her!"

"She'll get to watch me paddle you, instead," Crispin warned, raising himself with effort on one elbow.

Forbes scampered out.

Sheila bent for a quick farewell kiss, but he caught her face in his two hands and held her a few inches from him. "I haven't had time to process last night, Sheila. Can it wait until I feel better?"

"It can wait longer than that." She put a finger in the dimple in the cleft of his chin. "I've wished all day I'd stopped sooner, noticed sooner you were in pain."

He smiled. "Still am. Weren't you going to do something about that?"

She had the most enjoyable few minutes of her day.

Downstairs, outside Honey Norton's room, Sheila and Forbes found not only Aunt Mary, but Walt, Rip, Lamar, and Winona. Walter was still dressed for work, in a dark, three-piece pin-striped suit. Rip also had on a suit, but it was rumpled into comfortable folds. Lamar was freshly turned out in gray silk and a bright red tie. Even his glasses looked freshly polished. His pungent aftershave competed with Winona's perfume, but nothing could compete with Winona's dress. It draped her bulky figure in startling swaths of peacock blue, kelly green, and lavender. Beside her, Aunt Mary looked smaller than usual.

"—went up in flames," Aunt Mary was saying to Winona, "and I, for one, cannot say I am sorry. Don't look at me like that, Sheila! I was not referring to the young man, but to those papers. We were making a mountain out of a hump in the grass. Of *course* I am sorry Junior was killed. Just devastated!"

She looked it. Above her heather tweed suit and amethysts, her wrinkled face looked pinched, her eyes haggard. Sheila was mystified at the depth of her concern—and whatever had possessed her to speak of Junior's death before the child?

Forbes's ears were wide open. "Who was killed? My mama was killed," he informed Lamar and Winona, who might not know.

Sheila had been raised to believe children need to regard death as a part of life, but it pained her to see him accept it so matter-of-factly and without emotion. She knelt so they were on a level and spoke softly. "Mildred's cousin was killed this morning, Forbes, and she loved him very much. She is going to be sad when she comes home in a few days. We'll all have to be sweet and kind to her. Okay?"

"Okay. Did Mr. Rip love him, too? He's sad."

Following his pointing finger, Sheila saw that Rip's eyes were, indeed, sad, and he trembled with weariness. Rip caught their eyes and managed a small smile. "Evenin', son, Sheila."

Lamar reached down and patted Forbes's head, sending the child backing into a wall. "I'm on my way to speak to a VFW chapter," he explained to Sheila, "and thought I'd run in and see how Honey's doing."

"So did I," said Winona, her chin quivering with indignation, "and I don't know what's going on! I've tried to find Philip, but he's not around."

She shifted, and Sheila saw for the first time a discreet

"No Visitors" sign on the door. "When was that posted?" she asked.

Winona's carefully painted mouth tightened. "This afternoon, apparently. I sat with Honey for a few minutes this morning, and I hate to think of her in there all by herself. Faith can't be here all the time."

Lamar looked up and down the hall. "She isn't here *now,* and nobody else seems to know their head from a hole in the ground. I guess we'll have to come back tomorrow. Until then, don't lose any sleep over that boy's death, Mary. You know they all drive hell for leather. The surprising thing is more of 'em don't get killed. Co'se so many get knifed or shot—"

"Don't start that," Aunt Mary warned.

Lamar subsided, with a muttered, "Well, they do. If Stack were here, he'd say the same. Blacks, queers—taking over the country."

Sheila had forgotten over the years what a hidebound old conservative he was—and how angry he could make her. But Walt touched her elbow in warning, and she knew he was right: It was fruitless to try to change Lamar Whitehead's opinions. They were not merely his own, they were those of people who paid him well to defend them in court, gave thousands to elect candidates he championed, and lionized him as Patriot par Excellence. For Lamar, flag-waving bigotry was bread, butter, and power.

Instead of replying directly to Lamar, therefore, she murmured, "I do wish we could have at least seen those papers."

"I declare, Sheila, you are downright boring on that subject," said the same tiny woman who had been talking about it a minute ago. "We all knew Peggy personally, and she would have hated all this. If she were alive, she'd probably have burned them herself."

"But she isn't, and they could have been valuable, Aunt Mary."

"Pshaw! Probably grocery lists! Now let's forget them. Have you finished with That Man? Are you ready for dinner?"

Before Sheila could reply, Rip restlessly wheeled his chair around a quarter turn.

"I'm ready for dinner, Mary. Take me home, and let Gertie find something for you and Forbes, too."

"You do look worn out," Aunt Mary informed him with the privilege of an old friend. "Walt, you feed Sheila and I'll drive your dad home."

Lamar's laugh was as silver as his crew cut. "*You* drive him home, Mary? That'll be the day! Did you ever get a license?"

"No," Mary said serenely, buttoning up her black coat. "I got Jason instead."

"Thank the Lord for small favors," Rip rumbled, taking the brakes off his chair.

"I hope you didn't have other plans for your evening," Sheila told Walt as they got into his Buick. "Aunt Mary has a dreadful habit of running everybody else's life."

"No problem. What else would I be doing? I've watched more movies in the past six months than in my entire previous life."

He was a good listener and an old friend. She found herself pouring out to him the story of meeting Junior the night before, her liking for the young man, and their unkept appointment. When she'd finished, she knew that she was not yet ready to dismiss Junior and the Mitchell manuscript from her life.

"Did you have any place special in mind for dinner?" She hoped she sounded casual, not as tight and urgent as she felt.

Walt shrugged. "Thought we might hit the Steak and Ale up near Jimmy Carter Boulevard, unless you have a better idea."

She watched I-85 slide past. "How about Sweet Auburn Bar-be-que down on—"

"—Auburn Avenue," he finished. "Are you crazy? That's way downtown, and it's already dark."

She had suspected he'd be reluctant. Even in the enlightened nineties, few whites stopped on Auburn Avenue after dusk.

"You'll be sounding like Lamar in a minute," she told him.

"No, I won't!" he said hotly, turning momentarily to glare at her. The effect, however, was ruined by passing overhead lights that flicked in his glasses at regular intervals. "But you've got to admit there's a high crime rate down there, and some of those people don't like whites coming onto their turf."

"They've got long memories," she replied soberly. "However, I would still like to go, Walt. Mildred's cousin owns it, and I want to ask him for Elouisa Whetlock's address. Please?"

He passed the Druid Hills exit without slowing down. "You said going to Honey's was a wild-goose chase, but this one is—"

"—a paper chase," she finished for him. "I want to talk to Elouisa about those envelopes. She may have read the papers, or Honey may have taken them after all. Junior had a funny look at one point last night, and he stopped Aunt Mary from sending me after them right away. What if he knew they weren't there?"

"Wouldn't he have said so, then? Why go through the rigmarole of making an appointment with you?"

"Maybe he wanted to talk to me. Or maybe he thought he could get them back from Honey early this morning. He didn't know she'd been hurt. By the way, has she regained consciousness? Did you find out that much?"

"We didn't find out anything. Nobody would answer a single question except to say she was not permitted visitors. And speaking of not finding anything, you and I didn't find the envelopes at her place, either, remember."

"Maybe that's because somebody else took them first."

"That's a lot of maybes, Sheila. Why are you so all-fired determined about this?"

"Because—" She couldn't tell him the truth: Because Aunt Mary was determined to steer her away. Put baldly, it sounded childish. But she was baffled. Why was Aunt Mary

—usually the first to look for foul play—so adamant that Junior's death and Honey's fall were both accidents?

"Because I think there's more to this than we know yet, Walt. Besides," she added staunchly, "I liked Junior."

"Okay," he said, heading for the Claremont exit ramp, "but I'll wager you the price of our meal it's a waste of time. And don't you ever say another word about people who run other people's lives."

They heard Sweet Auburn Bar-be-que before they saw it. It was jumping with music and teeming with people who milled in the entrance, hitched extra chairs around tables, or stood four deep at the polished take-out counter—beneath a garland-decked mural of a hog looking sadly at a hole where its ribs ought to be. The air was so full of hickory smoke and sauce that Sheila was sure she could bite off a chunk. Over the music, a rich symphony of bass rumbles, alto counterpoints, and tenor tremulos called to one another and to waitresses in red jumpers and crisp white shirts, who scurried around and over stray legs expertly balancing aluminum trays piled high with red-and-white-checked paper trays of food.

A few people gave Sheila and Walter covert curious and even suspicious looks, but nobody stopped eating when they entered.

"See?" Sheila said softly over her shoulder, "the roof is still intact."

They found a vacant table beside the far wall, and were scarcely seated when a waitress bounced up to slap down paper Christmas napkins and take their order. "Is Anthony here?" Sheila asked when she'd ordered a slab of ribs, slaw, and buttered corn on the cob.

The waitress shrugged. "Probably cookin' out back. You need him?"

"Just to say hello. He's the cousin of a friend of mine."

Moments later, a man loomed over their table. "You wanted me?" His eyes had the wary expression of a café owner who expects to be hit up for a free meal by a casual acquaintance.

Not that Anthony Anderson would be a pushover. The owner of Sweet Auburn Bar-be-que looked like he sampled everything he served. Well over six feet and weighing more than two hundred pounds, he increased his height with a tall white chef's cap and emphasized his girth with an enormous sauce-stained apron that covered him from shoulder to knee and wrapped around his waist to tie in front. At the moment, sweat streamed copiously from his massive ebony brow onto cheeks the size of salad plates.

Before Sheila could speak, his face lit into a smile. "Sheila Beaufort Travis! As I live and breathe! Merry Christmas!"

"Hello, Anthony. It's been a long time."

"Shore has! I don't think I've seen you in—"

She held up a hand. "Please don't count. You'll make us both feel old. This is Walter Delacourt, of the Winsome Company. Give him one of your catering menus to take back to his office. You can't do better than Anthony's box lunches for board meetings, Walt. The ribs are superb."

Anthony snagged a passing waitress and sent her to fetch the menu, then asked, "What brings you down this way?"

"I wondered if you had Elouisa Whetlock's address and phone number. Mildred's not at Aunt Mary's—"

Anthony nodded somberly. "I s'pose you heard 'bout Junior?"

Sheila nodded. "That's partly why I want the address—to send flowers. I was dreadfully sorry, Anthony. We just met last night, but Junior seemed like a special young man."

"He sure was that, Miss Sheila. You wouldn't meet a finer one." He shook his big head sadly. "Anybody tries to tell you he drove reckless is talking through their hat. Junior didn't have a reckless bone in his body. Must have been something the matter with that car. Good thing you decided to come by tonight. I'll be out the rest of the week, to show respect."

He borrowed a guest check from a passing waitress, wrote down Elouisa's address, then lumbered back to his cooking pit.

Their ribs arrived so quickly Sheila suspected Anthony had moved their order to the head of the line. She had just taken her first bite when another man slid up to their table. The newcomer was wiry and tense, and from the damp state of his apron, Sheila deduced he was a dishwasher. From the way his eyes darted left and right all the time he spoke, she also deduced he'd lived his life waiting for something to catch up with him.

"I heard you axt for Cuddin' Anthony awhile back. You the Sheila Mildred Anderson knows? The one she called t'other night 'bout some papers?"

Sheila nodded around a mouthful of ribs. Before she could swallow, he had hunkered down on the chipped beige linoleum beside her chair, shoulder level with their red Formica tabletop. "I'm Demolinius Anderson, Millie's brother."

Sheila gave him a speculative look over her napkin. "Mildred only has a sister."

He shrugged. "Tell my mama that. Course, I been gone forty years. Jest got back Sat-dy nite. Millie might've neglected to mention my existence." He spoke pleasantly enough, but his slack pink mouth and darting, wary eyes reminded her of a frog watching bugs—and gave her an inkling of how bugs must feel. "Was you axing Cuddin Anthony 'bout them papers?"

"She doesn't have to—" Walt began. Sheila kicked him under the table. She wanted to know what Demolinius wanted.

He wanted something badly. That was obvious in the offhand way he rocked on the balls of his feet as if about to depart—without departing. To prime his pump, she picked up a rib and gnawed it as she offered a scrap of information. "I was telling Anthony how sorry I was to hear about Junior. Of course, you didn't know him, if you've been gone so long—" She dangled the sentence like bait.

He rose to it like hungry catfish. "Course I knowed Junior! Met him Sat-dy night, at Weesa's. He had her extra bed, so I bunked here. Guess I'll go back to Weesa's later tonight, now he's gone."

Would Demolinius sabotage Junior's car to secure himself a bed? He looked mean enough, and made no pretense of grief. On the other hand, he'd only met the young man Saturday night.

She continued to gnaw her rib and shot Walt a look she hoped said "Don't speak until he does."

Whether it was her look, the delicious ribs, or simply that Walt couldn't think of a thing to say to a dark-skinned man in faded jeans with muscles like wisteria vines and his life's history written in knife scars across his face—for whatever reason, he bent his head to his plate and throughout the whole conversation gave a good imitation of a man eating utterly alone.

Long ago in embassy circles, Sheila had learned to wait. Sure enough, when she was on her second rib, Demolinius asked, "Why didn' you come by Weesa's for them envelopes? I seen 'em still there yestidy morning, an' Ahnty Weesa was still 'specting you."

She wiped greasy fingers on her napkin. "We had an accident on the way. Icy roads." She gingerly lifted her shoulder. "I bruised my collarbone—"

He wasn't interested in her ailments. "Anthony don't know nothin'. Doan' *need* to know. You want dem envelopes, Demolinius is your man."

This was unexpected! Had the envelopes not gone up in flames with Junior? Could he have been running another errand before bringing them to her? Or did this crafty man not know Junior was carrying them? "Do you have them?"

"Might be able to put my hands on 'em, if it's worth my while."

He didn't have them. Certain of it, she sampled Anthony's cole slaw, willing the man to go. Instead, he leaned back and looked up at her, his eyes half-lidded and speculative. "Must be important envelopes. Another woman come for 'em early yestiddy. Said she'd save you some trouble." When Sheila didn't respond to that, he laughed, softly and privately. "Left like a jackrabbit."

"Why?" she asked, wolfing down the excellent mayonnaise slaw. "Why should she run?"

" 'Cause I was chasing her." He lowered his lids. "Tole her to set down them envelopes and git. She run out on me."

Sheila nearly choked. "Taking the envelopes?"

He laughed softly. "Not likely. Dropped 'em all in the mud and hared toward that taxi like a bat outta hell." He laughed again. In a less public place, the sound could have made Sheila's back hair stand on end.

Now, she was too disappointed to notice. Junior must have had the papers after all. She slowly buttered a roll and bit off one side before she inquired, "Why should Mrs. Norton want Elouisa's envelopes?"

A casual observer would have seen no change, but Sheila was watching Demolinius closely. For an instant, it was as if someone had yelled "Freeze!"

Then he asked, as if from polite curiosity, "Mrs. Norton? How you know who she was?"

"I knew she was there."

"What's her husban' name?"

"Winston Norton, but—"

Surprise and chagrin were the first genuine emotions he had shown. "I didn't know she was Mr. Stack's wife!"

Now it was Sheila's turn to be surprised, but she knew how to conceal it. "Widow. He died nearly twenty years ago."

He ducked his head and muttered to himself, "No wonder he ain't in the phone book."

She reached for another rib. "How'd you know Stack?"

"Oh—" he grew evasive "—I usta know him a long time ago. Why'd Mrs. Norton want them envelopes?"

She shrugged. "I haven't seen them, so I don't know."

"Well," he stood in one fluid, practiced motion and prepared to melt away, "if you still want 'em, I'm actin' for Weesa from now on. You got that?"

She shrugged. "I'll have to talk to Mildred first."

An ugly expression crossed his uglier face. "Mildred's got nothin' to say about it! You understand me, lady? From now on, you deal with Demolinius." He jerked one thumb toward the register. "I got no wheels to get anywhere, so that phone'll reach me." He slithered through the crowd with scarcely a ripple.

"Disgusting!" Walter curled his lip and shook his head.

"It's hard to believe he's Mildred's brother," Sheila agreed. "She's so refined, so—"

"Not him, you! You were eating like you were raised in a barn! What will these people think? You've got butter on your chin, barbeque sauce all over your hands—"

"Daddy *was* an agriculture professor," she reminded him with dignity, "but I was trying what Junior would have called intercultural communication: When eating with Demolinius, eat as Demolinius probably eats. Make him comfortable." She considered her stained fingers dubiously. "Maybe I overdid it a little." She scrubbed her hands with paper napkins from a metal holder on the table, but the flimsy napkins tore and stuck to her fingers.

"Gross," Walt said unflatteringly. "Here. Do your face, too." He held out two wet wipes brought with their order and summoned their waitress. "We're going to need more of these."

Chastened, Sheila made what repairs she could, then stood. "Let's go. It's nearly eight. Elouisa may go to bed soon."

Walt held his glasses with one hand and regarded her incredulously. "You heard what that man said! If you think we are going out there after that—"

"I most certainly do. I at least want to talk to her. But first, pay the bill. You lost the wager. I got more than I came for."

She hoped he wouldn't ask what it was, though. She wasn't yet sure.

On the way, Walter exceeded his usual careful, self-imposed speed limits and cast anxious glances from side to side.

"Slow down," Sheila told him once, crossly. "I can't find the street on this map. Why didn't you get one with bigger streets?"

"Why don't you get your eyes examined? Everybody else is getting reading glasses. Why should you be exempt?"

"I don't need reading glasses, I need for you to stop and let me find my place." She rattled the map menacingly.

He pulled to the side of the street and locked the doors. "Okay, but if anybody comes, I'm off like a shot."

"You're more likely to *get* shot," she retorted.

Eventually, they found the house due to luck, not Sheila's map-reading skills. As they mounted the cement steps to the small front porch, Sheila noted that, unlike most of its neighbors, the house's bricks were freshly tuck-pointed and its front door had a recent coat of paint.

No one answered their initial knock. "They're probably all over at Junior's," Walt muttered, shivering in his navy jacket. A sharp wind had sprung up in the past hour. It whistled over the hill that was the cemetery and down the little streets nestled around it.

"Do you not wear a coat on principle, or are you too cheap to buy one?" Sheila demanded, pulling her own close.

"Neither. I just keep forgetting them. I left one at work today, as a matter of fact. The office was warm, so I didn't think about it." Walt peered behind them at the few lights still visible up and down the street. "This is a horrible time to call on anybody, Sheila, about something as unimportant as those stupid papers. She's probably over at Junior's family's house, anyway."

Sheila agreed it was not the best time to call, but she wasn't about to admit it. Walt was perfectly capable of dragging her back to the car. "From what Mildred says, I don't think Elouisa can travel. We won't stay long." She knocked again, loudly.

"Who's there?" The voice sounded young, female, and scared.

"Sheila Travis, a friend of Mildred's. Elouisa knows me."

The girl who opened the door was petite and lovely, with caramel skin and tiny braids gathered into a cascading pile on top of her head. Her enormous eyes were full of tears. Holding a sodden handkerchief to her nose, she stepped back to let them in. "I'm Venetta. Junior's sister."

"Hello, Miss Sheila," quavered the shrunken woman in the recliner across the room. "Come on in. Venetta's stopping with me 'til the funeral."

That should keep Demolinius away for two more nights, at least. Relieved, Sheila offered condolences to both women and introduced Walt, who sat on one end of the love seat like a mute crane during the rest of the visit.

Deprived of any central place in the grieving family circle, Elouisa was in the mood to talk. The old woman prattled of this person and that person Sheila might know, then—when Venetta left the room—said with startling abruptness, "I guess you fin'ly come for dem embelopes."

Sheila nodded somberly. "Too late." She had a dreadful thought. What if Junior hadn't told Elouisa he was taking them? "You knew Junior had them in his car, didn't you?"

Elouisa cackled. "I knew he had *some* embelopes, but he ain't had de ones what I took. I ain't so wooly-headed as all dat." She hitched herself to a more comfortable position and plucked at the afghan covering her knees. "Yestidy *afternoon,* Junior and me had a talk. He said if dey was worth sumpin, they didn't need to be passed around. So he took 'em over to his college and he made a copy. Dat Junior uz one smart boy." She paused to wipe her eyes and spit in a can tucked beside her. "He put de real papers in a safe place. Den he got some embelopes jest like 'em and tromped all over 'em in de mud. Couldn't hardly tell the difference. Whut he aimed to take you dis morning was de copies, den if you wanted the real things, you could come get 'em."

Sheila swallowed to steady her voice. "Where are the originals? Can I get them now?"

Elouisa shook her head. "Cain' get to dat safe place at night. Come back tomorrer. Mildred'll be here in de mornin' and I'll send her wit' you to get 'em. 'Cose, dey might be one missin'."

Sheila, thinking the interview was over, had stood. Now she sat back down. "Missing?"

Elouisa nodded. "Miz Norton come by yestidy mornin'. Tuck one, I think. 'Less Demolinius, my nevvy, missed it when he picked up t'others outen de mud." Briefly, she repeated the story Demolinius had already told about Honey's morning visit.

"And you're pretty sure she took one envelope?"

Elouisa nodded. "I had five, and Linus brung in four. I didn' say nuthin' to him, but it doan' seem likely he missed none. He's pretty careful, as a gen'ral rule."

Sheila would have bet money on that.

Elouisa yawned. "I'd better git on to bed now. You come back tomorrer, like I tole you. Mildred's comin' by in the mornin', and you and she kin go fetch 'em den. Dat way, I kin die in peace."

Sheila couldn't help thinking, sadly, that she looked far more likely to die than Junior—but he'd beat her to it.

As she bent to shake Elouisa's hand in parting, she discovered that the old woman's thoughts had been running along similar lines. "Kin you fin' out what happunt to Junior? Weren't nothin' de matter with dat boy, and ain't nobody gonna tell me he drove so wild he run hisself offen de road. Junior drove good. He doan' drive fast and he doan' drive reckless. I keep wonderin' if dat wreck had anythin' to do wit' whoever he uz talkin' wit' out dere dis mornin'." She jerked her head toward the window.

Startled, Sheila knelt swiftly by the recliner. "Talking with, Elouisa? Who? What did they say?"

Elouisa leaned over until her grizzled hair mingled with Sheila's black. "I doan' know," she moaned, her voice heavy with grief. "Dey was talkin' too low for me to hear many words, and I cain' hardly see tru' de plastic. White pusson, dat I do know, wit' a deep voice—but could uv been a man or a woman. Black coat, pretty silver Cadillac."

Sheila's stomach tightened. "Tall, or short?

Elouisa shook her head in sorrow. "Like I said, cain' see much'—and didn' hear much, neither. Dey wanted dem embelopes, I know dat much, 'cause Junior said 'No, I promised Sheila'—real loud. Den dey both drove off." Her head fell back against the chair and her filmy eyes closed. When she opened them, they were full of tears. "Sheila, I done many bad t'ings in my life. But God's trut', I loved dat boy. He was fine. Fine! You fin' out who made him have dat wreck, and I'll pray for you ebery day I live. I shore will. You fin' out."

Sheila covered the palsied hands with her own. "I'm going to try, Elouisa. I am surely going to try."

•   •   •

They finally got away, Elouisa calling "You come back tomorrer, now. Doan' forget!" until the door closed behind them. As they drove away, Walt sighed. "You have the most peculiar friends—"

Like Elouisa a little earlier, Sheila laid her head back and closed her eyes, feeling tears stinging her lids. "I know, Walter. You, for instance."

"And you're really going back for those blasted envelopes tomorrow, then you're going to poke your nose around this accident trying to make something of it, aren't you?"

"Don't sound so peevish! If I hadn't poked my nose around your problems last summer—"

"There's a big difference between that and this." He spoke stiffly.

She sighed. "There certainly is. In that case, I was firmly convinced you hadn't done anything wrong. This time— Walt, who do we know with a deep voice, a black coat, and a big silver Cadillac?"

He shrugged. "Lots, probably."

"Name some."

He considered. "Mmmm. Well, now that I think of it, I can't think of anybody *you* would know. Charles Davidson, Max, and Lamar all have gray or silver cars, and Dad's taupe Continental can look silver in some lights, but none of them have Cadillacs."

"What about a woman?"

It took him a minute to catch on. When he did, he was so shocked he swerved nearly off the road. "If you mean Miss Mary—"

Said aloud, it did sound ridiculous. "I hope not, but—"

He held up one hand to cut her short. "Not another word, Sheila! I've had all I can take for one evening!"

He didn't speak again on the way home, turned down her halfhearted invitation to come in, and drove off with a frozen look she had seen before. Walter Winwood Delacourt was determined not to let any of this penetrate his own comfortable shell.

Sheila's own shell, however, felt blasted to pieces by a host of unanswered questions: When did Aunt Mary stop wanting to see that manuscript? Why? Who *was* talking to

Junior that morning? Someone who would have known whom he meant by "Sheila"? Had that person caused his accident? How? What on earth could be in a fifty-year-old manuscript that was worth killing for?

Mind roiling, Sheila took Lady for what the sheltie considered an indecently hasty walk, looking warily at familiar bushes that now seemed menacing. Back in her well-lit apartment, she started wearily to bed. This day had been at least two weeks long.

Just before she turned out the light, she remembered her answering machine. She padded into the study to check it.

There were two messages, and the first paled her cheeks.

Owen Green sounded so disgruntled she could see his face clearly, lips working in and out. "I really hate to tell you this, Mrs. Travis, but if I don't and you read it in tomorrow's paper, you'd never forgive me. You were right about something: The young man did not merely lose control of his car. He was apparently the victim of a drive-by shooting. They found a bullet hole in his skull. But don't you be looking for a perp, now—we live in a day of senseless, random killings, and this looks like another one. Happens all too often." He paused, then—remarkably—added gruffly, "Hope I didn't spoil your evening. Good night."

The second voice spoke the concise, light Japanese of Mr. Hashimoto, Sheila's boss. "I need you in San Francisco for the rest of the week. Masako is making reservations for first thing tomorrow morning. I will see you here in the afternoon. In case you fail to listen to your messages, Masako will call at dawn to waken you."

Sheila headed back to bed, muttering, "It would serve you right if I'd moved in with Crispin and didn't come home for a week." Then, snuggling under her covers, she had a sudden suspicion.

She reached for her bedside phone, and dialed the number Crispin had given her to retrieve messages from his answering machine when he was out of town. To her dismay, Mr. Hashimoto repeated himself exactly.

*When Henry Grady proposed to fellow Piedmont
Driving Club members that the majority of their land
be thrown open to the public for a city park, some
grumbled, "The whole point of buying the land was
to get away from the riffraff."*[13]

Three days later, high above Kansas's snow-swept fields,
Sheila smoothed the skirt of her black wool suit, reclined in a
first-class seat, and willed Delta to make this San Francisco-
to-Atlanta run in record time. She was being met by Sean
Bagwell and what might be an unpublished Margaret Mitchell manuscript!

Sean had been Crispin's idea. Before the sun came up
Tuesday, she had stopped by the hospital on her way to the
airport and persuaded a nurse to let her tiptoe in for just a
minute.

Crispin had been asleep, lying on his back, pain

smoothed from his face and that one recalcitrant lock of hair over his eyes. When she gently brushed it away, his eyes flickered open, puzzled. Then he reached up and drew her into his arms. She went willingly.

Eventually, however, she had to sit up and tell him where she was going, and why. Then she described her visit to Elouisa and her dilemma: "I can't pick up the envelopes until Friday. I know Elouisa thinks they're in a safe place, but Mildred's brother looks like he'd make short work of anybody who stood in his way, even a ninety-year-old woman. I don't like to bother Aunt Mary"—the truth was, she didn't want to share her suspicions of Aunt Mary with Crispin—"and there's no way Walt would go back out there today. He's miffed at the moment."

Crispin considered his cast ruefully. "I can't be much help."

"Of course not," she agreed. "I'm just unloading, that's all."

"Come here." He reached for her again. "I have a great method for taking your mind off your troubles."

Now that he was fully awake, however, all her old confusion returned. She bent and gave him a swift kiss. "I have to go in a minute. Please help me think, Crispin."

He grunted. "What about Sean Bagwell? He's a lousy poker player, but a good man. Call and fill him in, and promise if he sits on it now, you'll give him an exclusive later."

"Ummm." Sheila, too, had been impressed with the homely reporter—impressed enough to spend some time Monday afternoon in Hosokawa's library going through back papers looking for Bagwell's by-line. From what she'd read, Sean was a reporter in the Henry Grady tradition of commitment to a better and more compassionate Atlanta. "How could I get him?" she wondered aloud, checking her watch. "He won't be at work yet, and I have to leave in fifteen minutes or Masako will be frantic. I guess I can call from the plane. . . ."

Crispin fumbled in his bedside table drawer and produced a badly crumpled business card. Bagwell's home phone number was scrawled in pencil across the top. "Voilà!"

Sean Bagwell, once he'd shifted from saucy to serious, listened eagerly. "Sure!" he agreed. "I'll get the envelopes, read the papers—"

"Don't open the envelopes!" She repeated Lamar's cautions.

"Okay, I'll get witnesses, make copies, and read the copies. Then I'll call you in San Francisco. Can't think of a reason to fly me out on somebody else's expense account, can you?" he added wistfully. "We could consult on Fisherman's Wharf."

Crispin, who'd been resting his head on Sheila's shoulder, grabbed the phone. "Bug off, buzzard! This is *business*."

Sheila could hear Sean's bray through the line. "While the cat's laid up, big man, the mice lay it on."

"You lay it on very far, mouse, and Sheila will give you a karate chop to the left earlobe. She's deadly."

"She's wounded," Sean reminded him fearlessly, "and I don't take threats from one-legged men. You rest up. I'm saving my dimes."

Afterward, Sheila called Elouisa. Venetta answered. The girl gave her a number for Mildred—who understood how suddenly business trips can come up and how difficult they can be to get out of. They chatted briefly about Junior's death (Mildred sounded old and very weary), and Sheila explained why she couldn't come for the papers. "I'm also sorry not to be there for Junior's funeral, Mildred," she added sincerely. "I'm ordering flowers for Elouisa, and would like to send some to his parents. What about big bronze mums?"

"They'd be lovely, honey, but the wreath you sent to the funeral parlor is enough."

"Wreath? What—what did it look like?"

She heard the hint of a chuckle in Mildred's voice. "White and yellow glads—just like Miss Mary's."

"Mildred, when you get home, you find out where she's got my duplicate credit card, and you cut it up—do you hear me? This is the second time she's used it to send flowers in my name!"

"She's just trying to help you out, Sheila."

"You cut up that card. And now, about the man who is coming—"

Mildred carefully took Sean's name and description. "I'll tell Ahnt Elouisa to be expecting him, and she can call me when he gets there, so we can go together to get the papers."

Before she hung up, Sheila said hesitantly, "Mildred, don't tell Aunt Mary that the papers weren't destroyed until after I get them. Please?"

"Child, I don't plan to go home until Friday, and once I hand those papers to your friend, I hope to never mention them again."

They had both reckoned without Walter, however. When Sheila called her aunt Tuesday night to check in, as she usually did when she was away, she had heard voices in the background. "Rip and Walt came over for dinner." Aunt Mary paused, and Sheila suspected what was coming next.

"Where's Forbes?" she asked hurriedly.

"Isaac's taken him to the movies." Isaac used to take Walt to the movies, too, Sheila remembered. "Now, Sheila . . ."

"And Gertie?"

"She's filling in for Mildred tonight."

Of course. What else? Please come to dinner and bring your cook.

Aunt Mary continued without pause. "Walter was telling us about your visit to Elouisa, Sheila. Don't you think that was a bit thoughtless, considering the circumstances?"

"Elouisa was grateful, Aunt Mary. She was still terribly worried about those envelopes."

Aunt Mary's genteel snort spanned the continent. "Well, since the good Lord saw fit to send you three thousand miles to keep you from picking them up, I hope you will put those wretched envelopes out of your mind! Elouisa should just burn them. Don't waste time going after them when you get back."

"I won't," Sheila assured her.

Unfortunately, Aunt Mary had known her long enough

to know what that kind of honesty might mean. "Whom have you sent instead?"

Sheila considered lying, but she'd never known a lie that didn't backfire. "Sean Bagwell, a friend of Crispin's," she confessed. "A reporter from the *Constitution*. He was supposed to pick them up today—taking all the precautions Lamar suggested, so don't worry that we'll get sued."

"That," Aunt Mary informed her, "is the least of my worries. Why you let yourself get bullied into a silly errand like that—"

"You did the original bullying, Aunt Mary," Sheila reminded her. "And I didn't even mind. I'd love to see a manuscript that Margaret Mitchell may have written."

"Humph," said Aunt Mary, and hung up.

Now, winging over Missouri, Sheila felt excitement rising in her like foam in a freshly opened Coca-Cola. Very shortly she could be holding envelopes Margaret Mitchell once held! Common sense told her they could well contain nothing of importance, but right now she enjoyed imagining "What if it's real!"

She was lost in a pleasant daydream of hoopskirts and tall white columns when the child in the next seat crowed, "Oh, great! A logic puzzle!" She smiled at the delicate charcoal profile and silky black hair beside her. He did not notice. He was too engrossed in his puzzles.

When she had discovered that her seatmate was eleven, thin, and very intense, she had called down curses on whoever assigned the only child in a full first-class cabin to sit beside the only woman. Since takeoff, however, she had revoked her curses. Jubin Jacobs didn't complain about business or try to impress her with his importance. The boy asked intelligent questions and listened intently to her answers. Over lunch, which he'd unabashedly enjoyed while the overfed executives around him carped about airline food, Jubin explained that his parents were back in India for a year's sabbatical from Berkeley, so he was spending Christmas with his grandmother, an Atlanta psychiatrist. He then submerged himself without apology in the puzzle book he'd brought aboard. Sheila had been impressed as he whizzed through word search puzzles, crossword puzzles, and Mensa math puzzles. Now he held out the book in what was obviously a generous offer. "Do you want to do this one?"

She scanned it. From several pieces of apparently unrelated data she was being asked to determine which baseball position each of nine men played. "I never could do those," she told him regretfully. "I can't hold the facts in my head long enough to decide whether the man in the blue house owns a pony or a dog."

He laughed. "That's not how you do it! First, you make a grid, like this—" Chewing on his lower lip, he drew crossed lines in his margin. "Then you fill in the names down one side and the positions across the top." He struggled to write small enough to fit words on the tiny lines.

She opened her briefcase and handed him her legal pad. "Would this help?"

"Oh, yes! Thanks!" With a brilliant smile, he started a new, larger grid. "There!" he announced when it was complete. "Now we can solve this in no time."

"We can?" She still had no idea what he was doing.

"Sure. See the first clues? Bert is best friends with the catcher, so Bert can't be the catcher." He put an X in one box. "Tom is engaged to the second baseman's sister, so Tom can't be the second baseman." He put in another X. "Now you try it."

Sheila craned to read the story line. "Tom can't be married, either, if he's engaged. That matters later." She laid one finger on a pertinent sentence farther down.

"I told you you could do it!" His large black eyes shone.

She shook her head. "That was a lucky guess. I'll do some work, and you let me know when you get it solved."

She took out some reports and tried to concentrate, but her mind hopped like a flea from one thought to another. Would Sean run her by the hospital? Crispin had been feeling much better Wednesday night, and thought he could go home Saturday. After Sean left, would she fetch Lady from her neighbor's before she started the—

"Oho!" Jubin suddenly chortled. "Bob's the left fielder!

See? That's the first one I've gotten!" He bent again to his work, his thin fingers gripping his pencil so hard she marveled he didn't break it.

His enthusiasm reminded Sheila of Sean's.

The reporter had faxed a message to her hotel Tuesday. "Got papers, will read tonight. The safe place? A university safe!"

Yesterday noon he'd left a phone message, asking her to call him. When she finally reached him late last night, just after she'd spoken with Crispin, Sean was so bubbly she expected him to float out of the receiver in rainbow-hued spheres.

He spoke not in sentences, but in phrases run together with delight. "It's fantastic, although I'm no literary critic, and I'm only taking your word for it that the old woman took this from Margaret Mitchell herself, but it sounds just like her—it's only a fragment, of course, but the characters and story line are pretty clear, and a scriptwriter could make a *great* movie—murder, adultery, homosexuality, an old-fashioned love story—could have been written yesterday! But the flavor of Atlanta during the war is the best part—"

"The war?" she'd interrupted, surprised. "You mean it's not a sequel to *Gone With the Wind,* picking up where that left off?"

"Oh, no! It's entirely different. You'll see."

Sheila's enthusiasm waned. Having looked forward to finding out what finally happened to Scarlett and Rhett, she was utterly uninterested in a new cast of characters. "Scarlett's not in it at all?"

"No, but you're going to love it. It takes place—what?" He spoke to someone behind him, then returned to the line. "Look, Sheila, I've got to go. But take my word for it, this thing is fantastic! I can't wait for you to read it!"

"Don't you lose it," she warned. Sean's enthusiasm fired her own, and she was suddenly terrified something else would happen before she could see those pages for herself.

He gave his own peculiar bray. "Oh, I've made very sure of that. When do you get in? I'll meet your plane, carry your bags, and buy you dinner while old Crispin eats his heart out."

She doubted the last part, but gratefully accepted. She didn't have a car at the airport, and hated taking a shuttle bus. Besides, her shoulder was still a bit stiff and sore. She would appreciate a willing bearer!

Sean wasn't there.

Not at the gate, not on the concourse, not waiting for the shuttle train from her concourse to the terminal, not at baggage claim.

Jubin's grandmother was at the gate, a slender black-haired beauty in an exquisite peach silk sari. Sheila chatted with them briefly at baggage claim, but the boy's enormous bag came almost immediately, so she watched the two of them chatter off home while she stood, uncertain and annoyed, wondering why Sean and her own bag were so late.

While she waited, she idly watched the crowd. She was surprised to recognize a dapper figure with silver hair and beard at the next baggage carousel. "Hello, Philip!" she called. He turned, startled. Her first impression was that he looked furtive, but she revised it immediately. He looked worn-out. He managed a small smile, but his eyes sagged with weariness and something she could not define. If he'd been a dog, she'd have thought his master had just died. Often Philip Maxwell was the handsomest man in a room. Tonight he looked like a wreck. "Coming in, too?" she asked.

He nodded, then lifted a finger. "And there's my bag. Good to see you, Sheila." He hoisted a small bag and made a quick farewell. She watched him go, puzzled. Normally he would have checked to be sure she had a way home.

The idea of hauling her own suitcase off the carousel was so painful that she paid a porter to do it—then had no idea where to tell him to put it. Finally she chose a seat near baggage claim with a television overhead. At least she could catch the tail of the evening news while she waited.

She was half watching and half searching for Sean when an unexpected movement on the screen caught her eye, and she heard the usually blasé reporter say in a shaking voice,

"We interrupt this broadcast with a special report. A bullet has ended the life of Sean Bagwell, popular *Constitution* reporter. Bagwell's body was found within the hour near a housing project playground in central Atlanta, where he was completing a series about drug dealing in housing projects. Authorities speculate he got too close to the truth. Children found his body when—"

Sheila started to stand, but found she could not.

She jumped when someone laid a gentle hand on her shoulder.

"Sheila, honey? It's Lamar Whitehead. What are you doing sitting here? Are you unwell? You look a little pale."

Lamar beamed down at her like a kindly Father Christmas in a crew cut and red bow tie. Even his glasses, reflecting the overhead lights, sent out cheery shafts of greeting. He gestured toward a wire cart containing one garment bag. "I'm just getting in from Washington. Is someone meeting you?"

Sheila tried her voice, cleared her throat, and tried again. "No. I . . . I had a friend picking me up, but he, he's not able—I was just about to take the Gwinne H shuttle."

"Nonsense! Let me give you a ride to Mary's, and Jason can take you from there. Is that your only bag?" She nodded, and Lamar hoisted it awkwardly onto the baggage cart with his own. She felt too drained to help, but Lamar belonged to a generation that didn't expect her to try. He set off happily, cart wheels screeching badly enough to draw curious stares from everyone they passed.

Sheila was glad for the noise. It eliminated all possibility of conversation, and she still could not trust her voice. Sean dead? That ugly man with his impish humor, mop of dark red hair, teeth too big for his mouth, and clear-eyed vision of how Atlanta needed to improve herself?

When they stepped outside, she buttoned her coat and wrapped her scarf tightly around her throat. But it was not just the airport wind that chilled her. Like a robot she followed Lamar to his gray Thunderbird, got in when he held the door open for her, and heard him stowing their luggage in the trunk. He spoke briefly to someone, his voice light and indistinct except for the words, "I'll call you back later."

He bent in to set a cellular phone between them, then turned his back to the car and more dropped into than sat on the driver's seat, drawing in his legs slowly afterwards. "Touch of rheumatism," he confided.

Sheila gave him a small smile, shivered, and scrunched into her coat. She felt as cold at her center as at the edges.

"I'll have you warm in just a minute," he promised, starting the engine. "You must be bushed. Mary said you've been on the West Coast, and changing time zones can really take it out of you."

His kindness made tears sting her eyes. She felt as if all the stress of the past week—Aunt Mary's anger at Crispin, the strain of taking him to Rip's party, the accident, finding Honey, confiding in Crispin, Junior's death, the week's long and intense business meetings, and now Sean's murder— were compressing her into a small ball of ache. She gave Lamar a heartfelt, if tremulous, smile. "It's been a rough week."

He patted her arm gently. "How about if you join me for supper on the way to Mary's? She'll be done by now, and I'm famished." When she nodded, he asked, "What are you in the mood for—seafood? steak? Or how about Italian?"

"Whatever suits you."

"Italian, then." He slid a CD into the dashboard player. "I need to make a few calls on the way uptown, so you just close your eyes and listen to the music." Heavy music she didn't recognize filled the car. "Don't you just love Wagner?" he asked happily.

She didn't, actually. However, like the squeaky baggage cart, the ponderous music kept her from having to talk. She felt like echoing Rip's "Thank God for small favors."

Gratefully she closed her eyes while Lamar started home at what seemed a snail's pace. Peering from lowered lids, she saw that he had crept into the left lane of I-85 and was proceeding at a sedate five miles below the speed limit, chatting on the phone, while other drivers glared as they whizzed by on the right at ten and even twenty miles above it. She closed her eyes again.

She couldn't stop thinking about Sean's death, though. Would Crispin have been watching that same news report?

Crispin! Her eyes jerked open. Two deaths and Honey's accident in one week might be pure coincidence, but what if they were not? What if they were all connected, somehow, to the Mitchell papers? What if the killer had not *found* the envelopes? Would he or she assume Sean had taken them to Crispin—who lay helpless in a hospital bed? Picturing someone approaching with a hypodermic of air, or pouring poison into his IV, Sheila gave a quick, involuntary gasp.

Lamar shot her a curious look. "Are you all right?"

She nodded, brushed her aching forehead with her hand, and tried to sound casual. "I just remembered I promised to see Crispin on my way home. I'll have Jason run me by—"

"We can go now. I'd like to see how Honey's doing."

"That would be great. Thanks." Sheila closed her eyes again.

Who knew that Junior was bringing you the manuscript Monday and that Sean got it Tuesday? Someone who bears Crispin a great big grudge!

Sheila's mind recoiled from the thought. Aunt Mary might be thorny sometimes, but she could always be counted on to do the right, honest thing.

Good people may do dreadful things if they think they have sufficient reason, whispered the persistent voice.

But there IS no reason! Aunt Mary doesn't need money from the sale of the manuscript. What other motive could there be?

There's something she's not telling you.

Sheila turned her head on the headrest to stop the silent argument. She could not bear to think that Aunt Mary—the wonderful aunt who sent pink ruffled dresses to a skinny little girl with a firmly practical mother, who had introduced Sheila to theater, ballet, and glorious stores, who opened her home to a teenager—could shoot two people for any reason whatsoever.

Long ago, soon after she went to live at Aunt Mary's,

Sheila had started into the kitchen for a glass of milk and overheard Mildred telling a friend about Sheila's arrival. Curious, she had listened through a crack in the door. Tonight, she remembered what Mildred said:

"Last winter, when the child was in eighth grade, Mr. Tom wrote he was going to send her to a church boarding school up north to learn about American life. Miss Mary got a lemon look about the lips. 'That child won't learn a thing she really needs to know in that Yankee school!' she said. Next thing I knew, Sheila was coming to us—us! Two unmarried women going through change of life and crabby as all get-out—to attend the best private high school here in Atlanta. I could tell you who pulled the strings to get her in that school. Who's paying for it, too. Can't no missionary afford that tuition. The clothes they've bought since she got here, neither. Miss Mary's plumb worn them both out with shopping, plays, and concerts. I finally put my foot down. Told her, 'Give that child some space to breathe!' So she's trying, she really is, even though it goes against her grain. You might not know it to hear her talk, but Miss Mary fair *dotes* on that girl."

Sheila could stand her suspicions no longer. She reached for Lamar's phone. "May I call and tell Aunt Mary I'm coming?" Surely she could hear, in Aunt Mary's tone or inflection, whether she knew anything about Sean and his murder.

"Sure, honey. Let me show you how it works." Lamar reached for it, nearly sending them careening into a passing Ford.

"I can do it, thanks," she told him hastily. But her effort was wasted. No one answered Aunt Mary's phone.

At the hospital, the journey to Crispin's room seemed to last longer than her transcontinental flight. First Lamar had to find a double parking space, into which he carefully maneuvered the Thunderbird, straddling the line. After arthritically slow progress inside, they had to wait while new grandparents held the elevator door for a teenage aunt coming from the gift shop with a blue stuffed elephant. The elevator moved at a crawl and stopped three times to let off others (including Lamar) before Sheila reached Crispin's floor— wondering if hospital mortality statistics include people who die in their elevators.

She hurried out the door and strode to his room, whispering to herself, "He is fine. He is perfectly fine!" Nevertheless, her heart was racing by the time she pushed open the door.

A large woman in a hospital gown and hair net sat in Crispin's bed, placidly eating ice cream.

Sheila had endured greater shocks, but following the news of Sean's death, this was too much. Gasping, she backed out of the room and almost ran to the nurses' station. "Where is Crispin Montgomery?"

Her voice came out high-pitched and hysterical. A bored ward clerk looked up from her record-keeping and arched thin black brows in surprise. "Who?"

"Crispin Montgomery." Sheila took a deep breath and lowered her pitch. "He's supposed to be in room thirty-two!"

"Sorry, ma'am. Thirty-two is Mrs. Baines."

"Then where is Mr. Montgomery?"

The clerk shrugged. "Went home before three, I guess."

Sheila felt hysteria rising. "But I talked with him last night! He wasn't going home until Saturday. Besides, he can't walk or drive, and he lives upstairs, and—" She saw in the woman's eyes that continuing was futile. "May I use your phone?"

"Pay phone's down the hall on the left."

Sheila braced herself against the wall and punched the buttons with trembling fingers. "Be there, Crispin!" she whispered. On the fourth ring, his answering machine picked up. *"Sorry, folks, I'm out partying in Buckhead. Call me back Sunday."*

She hung up. "Be calm, Sheila! Nothing has happened to him," she muttered through clenched teeth.

But where could he be?

Looking for a familiar face, she spied the nurse who had taken Crispin his medication Sunday night. As casually as she was able, Sheila asked, "Do you know if Mr. Montgomery was discharged—and if so, where he went?"

Apparently she wasn't casual enough. The nurse appraised her shrewdly and sent a clear silent message: *If the man doesn't want you knowing his business, honey, it's not up to me to tell you.*

Sheila took a deep breath and aimed for the executive voice. "I spoke with him last night from California. He said he'd be released Saturday, and asked me to come by on my way home from the airport tonight. He's not in his room, and I've tried his home. Do you know whether he was discharged, or transferred to another room?"

"Discharged. Left about two. I helped him pack."

I'll bet you did, Sheila thought sourly. "Do you know who came for him?"

"Sorry."

Did she mean "Sorry, I don't know," "Sorry, I'm not permitted to say," or even, "Sorry, sister, you've lost this one"?

By now, Sheila was tired and drained enough to almost believe the last. Maybe Crispin had finally reached clarity on his own confusion. Maybe he had decided the two of them had no future together. Had he felt that leaving Atlanta while she was away would be easier for them both?

Don't be ridiculous, her commonsense asserted. *Crispin wouldn't go without Forbes. And if he'd tried to take Forbes, Aunt Mary would have called you.* Self-confidence partially restored, she turned again to question the nurse—but that wily woman was now behind a glass partition, out of conversation range.

Feeling like a battered volleyball, Sheila walked down the flight to Honey's floor wondering how to trace Crispin. *He'll call you,* her commonsense told her. *But what if someone took him?* Her fears replied. *The same someone who killed Sean and Junior?*

She reached the next floor and a conclusion at the same time: She had no idea where to look for him. In all their months of sharing so much, she had never thought to ask whom to contact in case of emergency. And she knew nothing about his family except that he was an orphan and had a legendary, surnameless Aunt Martha.

Lamar was waiting outside Honey's door. "The nurse says there's no change, and still no visitors permitted except immediate family. How's your young man?"

"He's been discharged." She didn't trust herself to explain further.

"Are we still on for dinner?" He looked anxious. "I was looking forward to it, but if you need to go somewhere else—"

She shook her head. Too much had happened in the past hour for her to think coherently. Numb, sore and bewildered, she would as soon eat dinner with Lamar as face her empty apartment and unanswered questions.

They returned to the Thunderbird and Lamar carefully maneuvered it from its double-wide space. As they left the garage, he leaned over and patted her arm. "You're looking worried, honey. Is something bothering you?"

His kindness got beyond her defenses. "Crispin was discharged, and the hospital wouldn't tell me where he's gone." She fumbled for a tissue, exercising considerable restraint to keep from pouring out all her worries and fears in a river of tears.

"Probably home," he suggested.

She swallowed and shook her head. "He can't climb stairs, and there's no elevator."

"Perhaps he left a message for you. Call your place and see." He handed her the cellular phone.

She dialed her own number gratefully. Why hadn't she thought of that?

Crispin's voice sounded indecently cheerful. "Sheila? It's Thursday noon, and a day for jubilation! I'm being discharged early!" She trembled with relief—and an unexpected spurt of anger. How dare he worry her so? *One more reason not to get married,* she thought resentfully. *Who needs that much worry about somebody else?*

Communing with herself, she missed an important part of his message, but she could get it later at home. For now, all she needed to hear was the next bit: ". . . place to stay.

I've got a college buddy who owns a peach orchard in Fort Valley. . . ."

She hung up and heaved a sigh of relief. "He's at a friend's," she told Lamar. "Let's go eat!"

He took her to a small Italian restaurant where he was obviously well known. Although several people were waiting, they were immediately shown to a corner table large enough for four, where Lamar, in Al Capone fashion, took a seat with his back to the corner. When he'd settled in, he exchanged a friendly wave with a man at the next table. "Ev'nin', Joe Frank. Sheila, do you know our former governor?" He added in a lower tone, "You don't get riffraff here like you do some places."

While they waited to order, other guests saluted Lamar or wandered over to greet him, giving Sheila a nod or ignoring her completely. It was so like a public meal with Tyler used to be that she felt right at home—and glad she'd decided to wear her black suit, paisley blouse, and heels on the plane. In this company, she would have been harder to disregard in jeans and an oversized sweater.

When he'd ordered veal scallopini for them both and approved a bottle of Frascati he'd selected to go with it, Lamar sighed. "Sure is good to get home from Washington." As he continued, Sheila translated: "Had to go up there to try to iron out a highway problem. Bunch of damned hippies" (YUPPY members of respected urban neighborhood organizations) "want to screw up" (politically defeat for the third or fourth time) "a crosstown expressway vitally needed in this city" (by suburbanites who want fast access to downtown jobs without paying city taxes). "I was in D.C. trying to talk some sense—" He paused midsentence to greet a dark-haired man. "Evenin', Mr. Sleet. I was just tellin' my friend here, we're gonna get that road through one day."

"Over my dead body," the man told him with a curt laugh.

"Another lawyer. Wrong side of the issue, but a fine

man," Lamar explained as the other left. "I defended against him just last week. As I told the judge, though—"

At that point Sheila realized she'd had enough wine to energize her, and she decided to steer the conversation. Lamar was no more bigoted than many politicians she'd met, and much less obstreperous to steer. He might give her information she wanted.

When he paused for breath, therefore, she asked quickly, "Are you a native Atlantan, Lamar? Have you known Rip, Charles, and Max all your life?"

"Most of my life. We all went to Boys' High together. And I was born and bred in Atlanta. My father's grandfather came to Atlanta in 1867, to start a sawmill."

She smiled. "Like Frank, in *Gone With the Wind*?"

Lamar chuckled. "Like half the population. Everything was burnt to the ground, you recall. People needed lumber."

The waiter slid salads before them. Sheila picked up her fork and asked, "When did you all meet Aunt Mary?"

His thoughts moved so slowly and deliberately she could almost see them. "Charles met her first, back when they were just little shavers. Families had summer places next door to each other down at Pawley's Island."

"Oh!" No wonder Aunt Mary knew Charles so well! The South Carolina beach house had been sold after her grandfather's death when Sheila was ten, but she still vividly remembered the children she'd played with during just one summer of blazing heat, tall dunes spiked with yucca, roaring surf, and seafood every meal. Even breakfast was whatever Gabe, the cook's husband, caught early. She was so lost in delectations of deviled crab and fried flounder that she had to tug herself back to what Lamar was saying.

". . . Mary over in Germany, back in '37. Stack Norton recognized her. He'd gone down to the beach with Charles one summer, so he knew her."

Sheila repeated a word she didn't understand. "Germany?"

"Sure, honey! Hasn't Mary ever told you about her carefree days as a graduate student? We all did two years of study in Berlin—got the last train out together, as a matter of fact, in '39! Close call." He drummed a lively tattoo on the tablecloth with liver-spotted hands. "Didn't Mary ever tell you?" he repeated.

She shook her head. It was impossible for her to picture a younger Lamar and Aunt Mary in that hectic time and place.

"Stack and I traveled over together. We'd been pals since first grade, you see, and when he heard I was goin' over for a couple of years, he up and wangled a fellowship in literature. Spent most of his time studyin' beer and frauleins, however."

Sheila shook her head in disbelief. "I didn't even know Aunt Mary spoke German."

"Oh, she kept her southern drawl, but she could make herself understood."

"And was she taking private lessons from the Führer in running the world?"

Lamar laughed so heartily Sheila could see his back fillings. "Mary could probably have *taught* Adolf a thing or two! But no, she was studyin' chemistry."

She paused with a cherry tomato halfway to her mouth. "Chemistry?"

Lamar was equally surprised at her ignorance. "Why, bless my soul, Sheila, Mary was quite good in chemistry! First place in a national competition. Never used it much, of course, except to help set up a blood bank lab during the war. Atlanta had one of the biggest banks in the nation, you know. Used to give a good steak dinner to members of their Gallon Club. That was incentive enough for—"

"But Aunt Mary," Sheila interrupted. "She actually became a chemist?"

Lamar shook his head and shoveled in salad. "No. While we were in Germany, her aunt died and left her a bit of money." Translated from southern understatement, that meant the modest fortune Aunt Mary had quickly parlayed into a large one. "Since she didn't have to work—"

"—and has a natural aversion to it," Sheila added with a twinkle, "she didn't."

Lamar chuckled. "She and Stack were alike in that. Both smart as whips, but both would take the long way 'round the Cape if it looked like less work."

"Did Aunt Mary come to Atlanta with the two of you?"

"No, but I was responsible for her comin', in a way. On the boat home, I told Mary she'd have a better time here than in South Carolina. She showed up a couple of months after we got home, and took to Atlanta like a duck to water. By now we think of her as one of us."

The waiter replaced their salads with veal. "What were *you* studying?" Sheila asked, mostly to keep him talking while she considered what else she really wanted to know.

Lamar cut a piece of veal and savored it before he replied. "German law." He leaned toward her confidingly. "You may not know this, Sheila, but my mother's father was German. Adolphus Bluher—owned a big printin' business. He came to this country when he was sixteen, leavin' his family in Berlin. Awkward for me later, of course, although Grandpa Bluher was carried away in '37. Same pneumonia that took my only sister." He chewed thoughtfully for a moment, leaving Sheila to imagine an enormous germ roving the streets like an overgrown rat, snatching unfortunates between its teeth.

"He left me his money," Lamar continued, "but asked me to spend two years in Berlin with his brother's family. It's a good thing that was before the war. I wouldn't have gone if I'd *imagined* what they were up to." He touched the small American flag on his lapel.

She started her own excellent meal, and took the conversation down another avenue. "Tell me more about Winston Norton. Was he always so—well, dishonest?"

Lamar was completely taken aback. "Why, I wouldn't call Stack dishonest, Sheila! A risk taker, certainly. But—oh. You mean that unfortunate episode after he died?"

That was carrying southern euphemism a bit far. Her face must have shown what she was thinking, for he hurried on. "Stack was a gambler, honey. He would never have figured on dyin' before he replaced that money." He leaned forward on his elbows, earnestly defending his friend. "Stack would have figured, 'If the symphony needs money and I have access to some, they ought to have it.' Then he'd make more to replace it. He made quite a lot in those days."

He fumbled at his waist, pulled out a pocket watch,

extended it to its full length, and peered at it. "Speaking of the symphony, I guess Clara and Walt are there about now. I got 'em some tickets. She wanted to go, and thought it might do him good to get out." He tucked the watch back in its pocket and returned to his meat and pasta.

Suddenly he stopped and smacked the table lightly in glee. "Did anybody ever tell you how *Stack* went to the symphony?" He scarcely waited for her to shake her head. "Never bought a ticket in his life—yet he went all the time. All the time!" He smacked the table again, to emphasize his point.

"They gave him tickets because he was such a good patron?" Sheila hazarded.

Lamar chortled. "Not at all. He just walked in! He'd show up in black tie durin' intermission, stroll over and have a drink at the bar with his friends—Stack knew everybody—then he'd follow the crowd back in. They seldom look at tickets after the interval, you see. So old Stack would hesitate at the back, as if looking for somebody, then take any vacant seat he saw." He chewed vigorously and punctuated his next sentences with jabs of his fork. "Not that he couldn't pay, mind you. And like you said, he gave so much to that bloomin' symphony he'd practically bought it over the years. But it was the risk he enjoyed. That's the kind of man Stack was."

A fond, faraway look came into his eyes. Then he came back to earth and gave his companion a rueful smile. "Took a few risks too many, of course. Got arrested a time or two for some of his pranks and brawls, and lost his driver's license for a year during the war—drivin' too fast too often. He was an excellent driver, but the police didn't see it his way."

Sheila, who had had similar discussions with officers in her own time, had her only glimmer of fellow feeling for the long-dead Stack.

Lamar, however, didn't give her a chance to say so. "Funny. People think of bankers as conservative, but the top notch ones are gamblers like Stack. Comin' up, his family never had much to speak of, but I never knew him to be without money to go on. Durin' the war? Why, he kept a runnin' poker game goin' down at Fort Mac—he was in the quartermaster's office, you know—and won enough to keep him in tailored suits, handmade shoes, beer, even gasoline while the rest of us drove on fumes! He and Honey lived like royalty after they were married."

Sheila was suddenly tired of this paean to a man who had cruelly betrayed his friends and left his wife destitute. "She's certainly not living like royalty now."

Lamar ducked his head and conceded, "Well, no, she's not."

Obviously relieved to have a distraction, he beamed up at two elderly women who'd stopped to greet him.

Sheila let them finish and depart, then mused, "Looks like Stack's family would have helped Honey."

"Well, that just goes to show you didn't know the Norton boys. Winston was the straightest of the four. Two are now guests of the government for income tax evasion, and the last I heard of Binky, he was living in Rio. No, if anybody should have taken care of Honey, it was her own family—or Stack's friends. But Maud got her back up about somethin', and the rest of us—well, we let it slide. We're going to have to do somethin' when she gets better."

He refilled their glasses and held his aloft. "Shall we say, to a better future for Honey Norton?"

Sheila could certainly drink to that. But thinking of Honey drew her almost inexorably back to Elouisa's theft—and Sean.

Lamar's thoughts traveled partway down the same path. "Speaking of Honey, did you ever get those envelopes everybody was so diddled about last week? The ones Mildred's aunt claimed she stole from Peggy Marsh?"

Sheila shook her head.

He didn't wait for a longer reply. Shoving his chair back and stretching his legs to one side, he considered the ceiling and ruminated in what he probably considered a fatherly tone, "Just as well. You can't trust anything somebody that old remembers—she could have gotten them anywhere. Besides, I knew the Marshes pretty well—far better than Charles or Philip did, for instance. I was in and out of Peggy's apartment all the time. Even helped her with a list she was compilin' of commie sympathizers in the South.

Peggy hated communists worse than anybody you ever saw. I was always sorry she didn't live to see the McCarthy years. For a while I even wondered if she'd been pushed under that taxi, but apparently not . . ."

He trailed off, visibly struggling to remember where he had been heading when he'd gone off on this tangent. Sheila prompted him gently. "You knew the Marshes—"

He brightened. "Oh, yes! So I am in a position to tell you that Peggy would *not* be pleased if any papers of hers came to light after all these years. She was a most private person, and ordered most of her papers burned at her death." He reached for his wine and sipped it, musing, "Fame proved a greater headache and heartache for Peggy and John than it was worth, in my opinion. They were a devoted couple, you know. Quite devoted. I've always envied them that." He sighed wistfully.

Sheila had had more wine than she should have, or she would never have made her next suggestion. "Why don't you marry Honey, Lamar? You're both alone, and you've known each other forever. You could look after each other in—" At last she stopped, horrified to be skating so near the edge of tactlessness.

Lamar, however, didn't act offended. Straightening his tie, he leaned confidingly over the table. "I've been getting a better idea this evenin', Sheila. I don't know if you and your young man have any firm plans, but if not—well, I could use a wife who knows her way around political circles and is charmin' company. You are both, and you've certainly kept this old warhorse in line tonight!"

She opened her mouth, but nothing came out.

He reached across the table and his mottled hand patted her own. "I won't say more now—I know you're tired. But I want you to know I've admired the way you are making the best of a bad situation, and I don't want you workin' for foreigners any longer than you absolutely must."

Sheila was still too astonished to reply.

•   •   •

When they finished dinner, Lamar stood, but motioned for her to stay seated. "I need to make a quick call," he told her.

By the time he returned, she'd realized that if Aunt Mary was out, Jason and the Cadillac probably were, too. She'd better call again. When she explained, Lamar beamed. "That's what had occurred to me, honey. There's no answer at Mary's, so I'll just run you home."

She dreaded—what? Amorous advances? A repeat proposal?

Instead, he played *Lohengrin* all the way to her apartment. The bridal march was the only remotely romantic part of the trip.

When they arrived he held out his hand for her key. "Just let me go in first, Sheila. I'll put your case in and check to be sure there are no unwelcome guests, then give you the high-sign. You women livin' alone can't be too careful, you know."

She was amused, but touched. The men of her own generation were many good things, but seldom gallant.

She wondered briefly if he planned to entrench himself at her place, but he was soon back, courteously holding the door. With an "Everythin' looks fine," he accepted her thanks and took himself off. Gratefully she watched him drive away—already chatting on his cellular phone.

Her apartment was chilly. She fetched Lady from her neighbor's and reported briefly that she'd had a good week but was tired.

Even a happy small dog, however, couldn't keep her apartment from feeling large and empty. The thought of Sean's death—mostly suspended while she was with Lamar —now pressed her down like a stone. Needing cheering, she went to her study to listen to the parts of Crispin's message she had missed.

". . . day for jubilation! I'm being discharged early. I tried to reach you in California, but you'd already left your hotel. I have a great offer of a place to stay. A college buddy who owns a peach orchard in Fort Valley had called last

night asking me to come evaluate some of his trees. I got the
message this morning, and when I called back to explain why
I can't oblige any time soon, he and his wife invited me down
to recuperate for a few days. They've got a big house and a
great cook, and their son broke a leg playing football last fall,
so he can help me get used to these blasted crutches. I've
accepted until Sunday. That ought to be long enough to get
me up and about. Give me a call when you get home, and if
you feel up to it, plan to come get me Sunday afternoon." He
left a number. She felt a surge of happiness that, for a moment, overrode her sorrow over Sean. Crispin wouldn't want
three hours in the car together unless he'd already done some
processing, would he?

It was too late to call now, and she hoped Crispin would
not get Atlanta news—including reports of Sean's death—
before morning.

She turned up the thermostat and made coffee, ignoring
a voice in her head that said, sounding remarkably like Aunt
Mary, "You drink too much coffee, dear."

Unpacking took no time. Then, restless and not the least
bit sleepy, she flipped on the television to catch what Aunt
Mary called "The Eleven O'Clock Crime Report." She
wished she hadn't. Sean's face filled the screen.

". . . found on the edge of a playground in late afternoon by children on their way home."

A film clip showed a woman reporter with tear-reddened
nose and eyes. "He said he'd gotten a tip about a drug bust,
and was going to cover it."

The television news anchor returned, glamorous and
suave, "Police department sources, however, say that no
drug raid was planned in that area for this afternoon. On the
international front, Bosnian leaders will meet tomorrow . . ."

Sheila clicked off the television and sat heavily on her
couch. Who had called Sean to lure him to that playground
this afternoon? Was it a genuine, if misinformed, tipster—or
someone else?

And, finally, *what had happened to those envelopes*?

She closed her eyes, leaned back against the couch,
sipped steaming coffee, and tried to remember their last con-

versation. What had Sean said when she'd told him not to lose them? *"I've made very sure of that."* What had he meant? Would one of his coworkers know?

Too anxious to wait for morning, she looked up the newspaper's phone number. Hopefully someone worked in the newsroom all night.

Someone did. He even knew Sean.

"I loaned him a stack of five manila envelopes," she explained, scarcely able to breathe, "while I was out of town. Would you mind checking to see if they are on his desk?"

"Sure. Hold on."

He was back in less than a minute. "What did you say your name was?" She repeated it. "Well, I don't see any envelopes, but I do see a Federal Express receipt with your name on it. Sean mailed something to you Tuesday at—" He read out her office address.

"Thank you very much!" Sheila hung up and poured herself a second, celebratory cup of coffee, then had to hold it with two hands to keep it from sloshing all over her.

For the next thirty minutes she paced her living room and debated. After the past strenuous days she could easily take tomorrow off, pick up the package, and take it to Aunt Mary's. Together, they could go to Lamar's office and open it in his presence. It made excellent sense.

The trouble was, she didn't want to wait that long to make certain the envelopes were there. What if someone else got to her desk first? What if they already had?

Don't be silly! Think how dark and empty that building is at this hour! cautioned commonsense.

"It could burn to the ground by dawn," she muttered aloud, heading for the jeans and sweater she had spurned that morning on the West Coast, "and Sumio Kubo will be at the security desk."

You haven't driven since the accident.

"At this time of night there won't be much traffic. I can drive slow. It'll be a good test for my shoulder. And I'm still on California time. I won't get sleepy for hours yet."

Driving was easier than she had feared. In record time she pulled close to the front door of the Hosokawa office building, parked under a halogen light, hurried up the shallow front step, and rang the bell.

Sumio, nearly a head shorter than she, peered anxiously up through the plate glass door. Then his small square face broke into delight. "Mrs. Tlavis!" he cried in English. "Come in, come in!" Bowing eagerly, he waved her inside.

By decree, Sumio could not leave the lobby except to make his rounds. Sheila, who was cursed with an irrational fear of the dark, found the familiar building dead, the air heavy and full of shadows that flitted just beyond reach of the few lights left on for security. When the elevator door closed behind her, she was very alone. The building brooded, still and wary, all around.

Nervously she hummed "Jingle Bells" as she rode upward, hoping Sumio's elevator monitor was a silent one! When the door slid open on the top floor to reveal a long dim hall edged with closed doors, she nearly turned back.

"I'm just going to my office," she said loudly, giving fair warning to any ghoulies, ghaisties, and things that might go bump in the night. "As soon as I get inside Masako's, I can turn on more lights," she added softly for her own benefit. Jingling her keys, she strode toward her office near the far end. Her feet seemed to move faster and faster on their own accord, until she arrived at Masako's door at a near run.

As light flooded the room, she felt joy akin to what God might have felt when "Let there be light" was followed by the actual thing.

In her own doorway she stopped and feasted her eyes. Sitting in the inconspicuous glory of a Federal Express box was what she had hoped to find: a possible Margaret Mitchell manuscript!

Reaching for her scissors, she ripped open the box and found—

"Glory, hallelujah, and thank you, Sean!" Not only the precious envelopes, but a second photocopy. She could build a fire and read the chapters this very night!

Meanwhile, Hosokawa International still felt vast and spooky. She hurried back to the elevator.

Her relief at reaching the ground floor and Sumio's smiling face was so great, she could have hugged the security guard if she hadn't been hugging the box. "Got what I came for," she said gaily, hefting it to show him. She rested it on his desk just long enough to sign out, then loped toward her car.

Juggling box and purse, she was trying to get her key in the door lock when she felt a sharp prick at her neck and heard a gruff voice. "I b'lieve you got somethin' of mine."

She froze, then thawed a trifle. She knew that voice.

"Demolinius? Where did you come from?"

His menacing chuckle was even less pleasant in a deserted parking lot than it had been in a crowded restaurant. "I was watchin' your place. Saw you leave, followed you over, and parked down by the next building, then I been waitin' behind your car. Doan' have to wait too long."

A thousand questions bounced around in her head. How did he know where she lived? Why would he have been watching her building? Why hadn't she asked Sumio to watch her from the door? And what the dickens was she going to do now?

Demolinius had a suggestion about the latter. "Give me that box, and I'll be travelin'. Doan' want to hurt you—Millie sets a store by you. But them're *my* papers now."

His calm assumption sent anger pumping through her veins. "They weren't even Elouisa's! She stole them, and now she's asked me to return them to the people they belong to."

"They belong to *me*. Weesa's too old to matter. You want 'em, you gonna have to bid like anybody else. Now hand 'em over!" The knife bit harder into her neck.

She jerked her head away, surprising them both. "Move that thing! I can't talk with it there!"

He jabbed her gently. "Lady—" his voice grew hard, with no attempt to sound pleasant, "—you got bigger things to worry about than that." What followed was blunt and obscene.

In one day Sheila had sat through a tense morning meeting and crossed a continent. She had endured the shock of Sean's death, the worry of Crispin's disappearance, and the tedium of Lamar's conversation. She had braved the darkened halls of Hosokawa, and now, with what might be a genuine Margaret Mitchell manuscript in her arms— The slime of Demolinius's profanity was suddenly too much!

"Put that knife away at least long enough for me to turn around," she ordered.

He backed up a couple of steps.

She dropped her purse and the box onto the top of her car, turned, and with one smooth kick disarmed him. In another second he sprawled on the parking lot, amazement written all over his face.

"Now get out of here, and don't bother me again," she told him.

Demolinius scrambled to his feet and scuttled across the parking lot, hate written in every line of his body.

Victory was not sweet. Hot pain shot across her back as she retrieved the precious box and her purse, opened her car, and dropped into the seat. She'd wrenched the same shoulder almost beyond bearing.

As she started the engine, however, she had no regrets. "Enough is enough," she muttered as she drove away.

*"Between 1943 and 1945, Mitchell wrote [her old
friend Cary Wilmer] long, typically rich Mitchellian
letters. She kept him posted on every turn of Georgia
social life, and these letters form a remarkable survey
of domestic history during the war years."*[14]

Sheila's fury and elation lasted about five minutes, then gave
way to shock—and terror. What was to prevent Demolinius
from following her? Teeth chattering, shaking all over, she
kept one eye cocked on her rearview mirror as she drove
painfully home. There, she hurried up the flight of stairs,
tottered inside, and double-bolted her door.

Her mantelpiece clock chimed a melodious twelve.

She fell to her knees beside the fireplace, threw logs on
the andirons, shoved some kindling and wadded paper underneath, and lit it. Then, clasping her arms across her chest,
she rocked back and forth on the rug trying to calm herself
until the fire caught. Lady, unused to a mistress cowering on

the hearth, pranced around her uttering sharp, piercing yips until Sheila clasped her tight—as much for her own sake as to quiet the sheltie.

In the process of giving comfort, Lady licked the spot on her throat where Demolinius's knife had rested. It stung. A trip to the bathroom mirror revealed he had drawn blood. "Oh, great," Sheila muttered, reaching for a washcloth and antiseptic. "I'll die from dog spit and Demolinius will gloat over killing me."

Grumbling made her feel better, but washing only her neck made her feel dirty all over. She peeled off her jeans and sweater and took a long, hot shower, then painfully drew on a gown and a soft wine wool robe and poured herself another cup of coffee—adding two heaping spoonfuls of sugar for shock. Lady accepted a couple of dog treats and trotted to her basket, content that her ministrations were no longer needed.

Making a wry face at the unfamiliar sweetness of the coffee, Sheila was finally ready to lie down on her living room sofa with Sean's photocopy. She fetched a light afghan and settled deep in the cushions. A yellow note stuck to the first page brought a lump to her throat. "Enjoy!" was scrawled in a spiky hand very like Sean himself.

Before she started reading the text, she scanned the first page and the lightly traced penciled corrections on it with a forefinger. Had Margaret Mitchell written them? It was still astonishing to realize there were people alive who would know. Imagine having actually *known* the famous author, and taking it for granted!

Sheila would gladly have traded the three presidents, one emperor, and numerous elected officials she'd ever met for an afternoon with the woman who had given her so much pleasure through *Gone With the Wind*.

Eagerly she started to read. She saw at once what Sean was trying to say before he was called away from the phone. This story was not about the Civil War at all, but about World War II. It told not about a spoiled young belle, but about four young lieutenants from wealthy white Atlanta families who, facing an uncertain future, were determined to snatch all they could from life before going overseas to fight.

Aunt Mary and her friends would surely recognize that hectic, frenetic Atlanta full of soldiers and swindlers, remember standing on freezing street corners selling bonds to build the new aircraft carrier *Atlanta* and partying all night because their partners were leaving at dawn and might never come back. They would resonate more than Sheila did to the characters' hatred of Nazis, communists, and fellow travelers.

Unfortunately, however, since Elouisa had stolen chapters at random, Sheila got very little of the complete story line. In one chapter, set at a June party in Buckhead, Cary anguished over whether to remain faithful to his wife, Pansy, a social butterfly, or leave her for Belle, a gentle, serious newcomer. "Ashley meets Melanie after marrying Scarlett." Sheila smiled.

She was disgruntled to find that her second chapter, however, not only occurred later in the story, but abandoned Cary for Ben, a young intelligence officer struggling with his feelings after being seduced by his superior. Sergeant Drake Cadwell—whom Ben described to his friend Nathan as "slithering white trash with commie leanings"—suggested that Ben give him copies of certain delicate documents to preserve his secret. "Ahead of her time," Sheila murmured, wondering how the author would resolve the struggles of the young man with both his homosexual superior and their blackmailer.

She would never know, for Elouisa's third purloined chapter moved to the Fort MacPherson quartermaster's office where Tim—assigned to keep records and order supplies, including enormous quantities of liquor designated for officers—was plotting a bootlegging business for dry north Georgia counties. Since he'd lost his driving license—

"Shades of Stack Norton!" Sheila exclaimed aloud, provoking a reproving "Woof!" from Lady.

—he had just persuaded a friend to come into the risky, lucrative business when Drake Cadwell appeared again. The sergeant threatened to turn them in unless Tim provided data on troop supplies and positions. Terrified, Tim complied—but did Cadwell keep his bargain? The chapter ended in a high-speed chase through the Georgia mountains with Federal agents closing in.

The fourth chapter was another party scene—or was it the same party? Both were in June, but was it the same June? Sheila wished the author had thought to number these chapters. She had no idea how to put them in order. At this party Drake Cadwell—inexplicably invited—got drunk and insulted Nathan's sister. Nathan whipped him soundly and then, enraged, clutched him by the shoulders and beat his head methodically against the hood of a parked car.

"Cadwell lay white and still," ended the chapter.

Sheila's final chapter.

She felt like a balloon that has been blown up and let go to whirl shrieking around the room. Except she didn't dare shriek. She'd have Lady hysterical and three anxious neighbors at her door.

Instead, frustrated and disappointed, she slammed the manuscript pages onto the couch, then groaned in pain and disgust. An imaginative Hollywood writer might put the meat of an entire plot on this meagre skeleton, but no one would ever know where the creator had intended to take her own story. Did Cary opt for adultery or fidelity? Did Tim and his partner get caught? Did Ben and his superior officer yield to the blackmailer? Did Cadwell die? Was Nathan tried for his murder?

Sheila would never know. And it made her mad enough to chew nails.

Once in Japan she had taken a late-night train home alone. Toward the end of the journey she had been the sole occupant of her end of the car except for a family who apparently assumed the tall white-skinned foreigner spoke no Japanese, for they were engaged in a whispered, highly rare public argument. The teenage son was furious, his parents tight-lipped and adamant.

"If you don't give your permission," the teenager hissed just as the train pulled in for Sheila's stop, "I shall kill myself!"

Sheila had wondered for days what permission the boy was demanding, whether his parents gave it, and if not, whether the boy carried out his threat.

Tonight she had the same feeling of coming alongside strangers for one brief, tantalizing glimpse into their private lives, only to be ejected like a child sent up to bed.

Meanwhile, it was three in the morning, she'd had a dreadful day—no, make that a dreadful week—and photocopies of penciled corrections Margaret Mitchell *might* have made had lost their charm. She yawned, tidied the papers into a stack on her coffee table, gave the manila envelopes beside them a pat, and went wearily to bed.

As she drifted off to sleep, her last thought was, "Those chapters certainly aren't valuable enough to kill for."

The phone woke her.

She opened one eye to peer at the clock. She had slept past nine? She must still be on California time.

When she reached to answer, pain made her flop back onto her pillow with an involuntary moan. Her entire shoulder was in spasm. The phone trilled on.

Summoning every ounce of willpower she possessed, she reached across herself with her left arm and picked up the receiver.

Lieutenant Owen Green, Homicide Division, was furious. She could tell, because his voice was deep, rich, and full of sorrow, and he wasted no time on greetings.

"Mrs. Travis, you know Sean Bagwell?"

"Why?" she asked, desperately massaging what shoulder muscles she could reach. Through a crack in her blind she saw that the day was gloomy and gray. She felt gloomy and gray, too.

"Got shot yesterday down at one of the projects. I've been turning over rocks to find out what happened, and your name turned up under one of those rocks. He wasn't supposed to meet you there yesterday, was he?"

"Of course not!" Disoriented and in pain, she was belligerent. "I was in California—neither in a housing project nor under a rock. And before you ask, I met Sean once, through a friend."

"Lordy, woman! Now it's people you meet once. You are a walking disaster!"

"Wait a darned minute!" She sat up, swung her legs over the side of the bed, and fumbled for her slippers. She wouldn't take this attack lying down. "Sean ran an errand for me Tuesday, I'll admit that. And he was planning to pick me up at the airport last night. But—"

He grunted. "Figures. People who plan to pick you up might as well go to confession and ask for last rites."

"Lieutenant Green, I'm appalled by Sean's death, but I resent your implication that I caused it. From the little I saw on television last night, he was gunned down while investigating drug deals. Isn't it likely that—"

His answer chilled her soul. "What is likely, Mrs. Travis, is that he was shot with the same gun that killed James Turner—also known as Junior. We retrieved a bullet from the ashes of Turner's car that matches one we've taken from Bagwell. Looks like I've been handed a case of double murder, and the only thing connecting those two murders is one Sheila Travis!"

"It's not me," she told him soberly. "It's a manuscript."

When she had explained, Green said nothing for a full half minute. She could hear the scratch of his pen. Then the lieutenant grunted. "Sounds like a rabbit trail to me. From what you say, it's only a piece of a book. Hardly worth having. Besides, even if the killer got Sean's photocopy, he didn't get the original."

"I know, but he—or she," Sheila added, to be fair, "wouldn't have known that at the time. And I can certainly picture somebody trying to take it away at gunpoint. I had something similar happen to me just last night."

"What?"

She had never seen that mournful basset face look amazed, so she couldn't imagine it. His surprise, however, sounded less like the "How dreadful for you" kind and more like the "Why the hell didn't you mention this before?" variety.

"Sorry I didn't mention it before," she retorted sourly, "but you were accusing me of murder."

"Not of murder, Mrs. Travis. Of being the catalyst for murder. It does seem to follow you around."

She winced, remembering something her father used to say about his elder sister: *Trouble follows that woman like fleas a dog.*

Green was still talking, ". . . about this purported attack on your life."

"It wasn't purported and it wasn't an attack on my life. Just an attempt to hold me up for the manuscript."

As she described what had occurred, again his pen scratched across Atlanta, compliments of Southern Bell. "Well, we'll pick up Demolinius Anderson for questioning. Maybe he knows something about these two homicides. Any idea where he stays?"

"You might find him at Sweet Auburn Bar-be-que. It's run by his cousin."

"Uh-oh," Green muttered unhappily. "Anthony's a Lodge brother of mine. Won't take too kindly to my bringing in his relative."

"He may pay you to take this one away," Sheila assured him.

"That manuscript is probably absolutely worthless," Green concluded sourly, "but I'm going to need to see it. I'll drop by a little later in the day." Without waiting for her permission, he hung up.

With awkward, agonizing maneuverings, Sheila pulled on slacks and a warm green sweater. Then she drew the vertical blinds leading onto her deck. Since the apartment was on a hillside, the deck was high above the ground and private. It was also, on this December morning, too cold and bleak to be inviting. Above a distant pond the sky was heavy with dark clouds, and a strong wind whipped the water into shallow waves.

She turned and confronted the ashes of last night's fire. Strange how the notion of building a cozy fire never included a reminder that you'd have to clean it out the next day. She found a newspaper, raked the ashes onto it, and stuffed the bundle into the garbage with a twinge of guilt. She probably ought to be sifting them onto a garden somewhere to replenish the earth. Instead they would lie forever on top of a layer of plastic in some unsightly landfill, contributing to the earth's desecration—

"You're not focusing on the problem at hand," she scolded herself sternly, dumping last night's stale coffee and starting fresh. "You need to be thinking about—" a ring "—answering the telephone!"

Aunt Mary was all in a pucker. "Sheila, are you ill? Your assistant said you aren't going in today."

"Good morning, Aunt Mary. No, I'm taking a day of compensatory time. I've been trying to get that concept across at Hosokawa, and thought I'd set a good example."

"I hope you always set a good example, dear, but don't shirk your responsibilities. Hard work never hurt anybody."

This from a woman who never appeared to do a lick of it! How she accomplished the reading and correspondence involved in running her modest empire, her family never knew. They never caught her reading anything more strenuous than a murder mystery. Speaking of murder . . .

"Aunt Mary, did you hear? Sean Bagwell, the man who picked up Elouisa's envelopes—"

"Sheila, would you please stop harping on those envelopes? If I'd known you were going overboard about them, I'd never have suggested you run out for them last weekend."

"Suggested? You *ordered* me to drive through a blizzard after them, and to come right back! I don't know when you changed your mind, or why—"

"I realized what a fool's errand it was. I hope you will never mention those silly things to me again. What I called to say is, Forbes and I are leaving Sunday for Florida, right after church, and you still haven't come by to pick up your parents' gifts."

For a fleeting instant Sheila wondered if Aunt Mary had gotten Crispin's permission to take Forbes with her, but Christmas plans were close to the bottom of her agenda right now. "Aunt Mary, listen! Sean Bagwell was murdered yesterday, shot with the same gun that killed Mildred's cousin."

"Whatever on earth do you mean, *gun*? Mildred's cousin ran his car off the road." She sounded so absolutely certain, and the pause of dismay before her first sentence had been so infinitesimal, that Sheila almost believed her. As it was, she struggled to interpret that pause. Was Aunt Mary dismayed to learn that Junior had been murdered, or dismayed that the police had discovered (and Sheila now knew) how he'd died?

"Owen Green says Junior was shot in the head, Aunt Mary, then lost control of his car. They're treating it as a drive-by shooting."

"Then that's probably what it was. I am sorry for his family, but why must *you* go poking and prying into all this?"

"For the same reason you usually push me to poke and pry! Two men have been killed, and I want to know why. Especially since I may have been somewhat responsible for their deaths." Her words slowed as she spoke that dreadful truth aloud.

But Aunt Mary's reply was immediate and blunt. "Horsefeathers! You had nothing to do with any of this. You are just imagining things, because you are run-down and peaky and worried about That Man. You have far too much on your mind. Leave this to the police."

"For once, Aunt Mary, the police have asked for my help. Lieutenant Green is coming over this morning. Once I have satisfied him that I didn't actually commit the murders—"

"Nonsense!"

"Of course. But once he knows that, he's going to want to know who else knew Sean was picking up those envelopes. Who did you tell?"

"Whom, Sheila. Whom did I tell."

Sheila sighed. "Whom did you tell, Aunt Mary?"

"Why, no one, dear. Oh, I may have mentioned it in passing to the folks who were here—"

"Rip and Walt?"

"Well, ye-es . . ."

"Who else, Aunt Mary?"

"Oh, the usual. Dorothy and Charles dropped by and brought Philip and Winona. Lamar stopped to say Crispin's car was almost ready, and he stayed a while, too—oh, and his granddaughter was with him. Practically threw herself at Walter. And while she's a charming young woman, I am not certain that Walter needs—"

"Aunt Mary, we are not discussing what Walter needs. What you are saying is that your whole gang knew. Did you tell anyone else? Because if you did not, then I am very much afraid—"

The voice that interrupted was as cold and unstoppable as a glacier. "A drive-by shooting and a drug-related death, Sheila, have nothing to do with my dearest friends, and I do not ever want to hear you refer to them as a 'gang' again. The very idea! If it will make you feel better, however, I shall ask Charlie to do a bit of discreet checking into the two deaths. Meanwhile," her voice thawed slightly, "you may as well come to dinner. Mildred will be back, and we're having a roast. But wrap up. Forbes likes to call the weather service, and the latest forecast is rain and gusts up to twenty-five miles an hour, with a windchill factor near zero."

Aunt Mary sounded as if their previous conversation was over. But she had made a mistake. She knew that Sean's death had been attributed to a drug deal. Did she also know —or suspect—who had really killed him?

Sheila would have loved to accept the dinner invitation and pretend, as Aunt Mary was pretending, that none of this really mattered. But Sean mattered. Junior mattered. And most of all, Aunt Mary mattered. Taking a deep breath, Sheila forced herself to speak lightly as she threw down a gauntlet. "I'll see about dinner, depending on what Lieutenant Green has to say after he sees Margaret Mitchell's Papers."

There was silence on the other end for three seconds by Sheila's watch. Then Aunt Mary asked, her voice elaborately casual, "Sees them, dear? I thought—"

"—that they'd been destroyed, along with Sean? No, he mailed me the original and a copy before he died. Get your friends together, and we'll all read them together this evening."

"No!" Aunt Mary was done with pretense now. Anger rippled through the line. "Build a fire and burn them right now, Sheila! Do you hear me? Burn them! If you don't, you could—ruin our whole Christmas!"

Sheila sighed. She could ruin a whole lot more than that. "I can't burn the papers, Aunt Mary. But I will take them to the Mitchell family lawyers this afternoon. I'm sorry." She meant it. Whatever was going on, she was deeply sorry it had begun.

Aunt Mary said nothing. Sheila pleaded, "Before we hang up, tell me why these papers have upset you so."

"The papers haven't upset me, Sheila. What upsets me is having you turn against my express wishes that we drop the subject. I have never known you to be so pigheaded."

"Well, since I'm already being pigheaded, let me ask you about one thing more. You don't have to answer if you don't want to, but I wish you'd tell me about Dorothy and Charles's engagement party."

It was an impulsive guess, based on her remembrance of the strange reactions of Aunt Mary's friends to Lamar's mention of the party last Saturday night. As she had hoped, the unexpectedness of the subject caught Aunt Mary off guard. "Heavens, Sheila, that party was a long time ago. Parties tend to run together." She sounded dubious, not very interested.

"Try to remember, please? What did you wear?"

"Black piqué," promptly—then, uncertainly, "or was it organdy?"

Piqué. Sheila was sure of it. Sure Aunt Mary remembered the party, too, and had begun to make connections. "What happened?"

"Happened?" Aunt Mary's laugh was offhand, almost frivolous. "Why, dancing, eating, toasts to the couple. Just your ordinary engagement party."

"What month was it?"

"June, I believe. Yes, I'm sure of that, because I left the next day for home to celebrate your father's sixteenth birthday."

Sheila took a deep breath and plunged into deeper waters. "Was there a fight or anything—out where cars were parked?"

"What on earth would make you think that?" Aunt Mary's voice was as light as a June breeze. "Why, hardly anybody *had* a car. Gasoline was rationed, you know. Most of us took streetcars, or went in groups. I had to save gas coupons for weeks for my trip to Kennedy's Landing."

Sheila was unwillingly diverted. "Who drove you?"

"I drove myself."

"But you can't drive."

"Of course I can! Just because I don't doesn't mean I can't."

It didn't, of course, but— "You told Lamar Monday you never got a license."

"Oh, a license." That Aunt Mary dismissed as a whim of some negligible bureaucracy. "I didn't have a car back then, but Stack Norton's brother Binky lent me his. Now, Sheila—"

"Was there a fight at the party, Aunt Mary?"

"Not that I saw."

Sheila had heard that tone before. "Was there one you *didn't* see?"

"I cannot speak about what I did not see." Sheila had also heard that tone before. The subject was closed.

She veered and tried again. "Who else was at the party besides you, Dorothy, and Charles. Rip and Georgia, I suppose?"

"Of course. Her parents gave the party. Fancy was very fond of Dorothy—and of parties. Max was there, too, I suppose."

"Winona?"

"Oh, no, they got married out in the Pacific during the war, and only came back here to live after it was over, in Philip's mother's house, over on Habersham. Mrs. Maxwell had died in '43, you see, freeing him to serve. He was her only child, and they didn't take the only sons of widowed mothers. But—"

Sheila, knowing why Aunt Mary was babbling on like a brook, stepped in midstream. "We were listing who was at the party. Lamar must have been there. What about Honey and Winston?"

". . . I don't remember. There were over a hundred

people. You can't possibly expect me to remember them all! But Stack and Honey wouldn't have been together. She wasn't out yet, and he was grown. They didn't get together until two years later, after her debut."

Aunt Mary sighed at the memory. "La, Sheila, the poor girls of that generation scarcely knew what it was to come out. Instead of luncheons, teas, and dances, they went to classes on rolling bandages and driving ambulances. I've always felt sorry for Honey and her classmates—and grateful that at least the Japanese waited to bomb Pearl Harbor until after the '41 Junior League Follies. It was a magnificent show —the last real fun anybody had for years."

Southerners might well presume that Japan had scheduled Pearl Harbor for the convenience of the formidable Atlanta Junior League, but could Sheila work that into a seminar as an example of Japanese courtesy?

It was time to slip in her big question. "Was Margaret Mitchell at that engagement party?"

"Sheila—" When Aunt Mary used that tone, it was easy to visualize her drawing herself to her full five feet and lifting her chin like a duchess, "—I've already told you I don't care to discuss Peggy Mitchell Marsh any further!"

"But you did know her? She knew all of you? Came to your parties?"

"Of course we knew her! *Everybody* in Atlanta knew her! Peggy was a tireless volunteer, especially during the war, and she and John lived right across the street from the the Driving Club, so we'd run into them at lunch sometimes. They both had such bad health by then, though, that they seldom came to parties. She may have come to that one because of Fancy, but the Marshes were private people. We who knew them owe it to them to preserve that privacy. Burn those papers, Sheila, whether they are hers or not! It could," Aunt Mary added, reluctantly and ominously, "save your life."

Sheila hung up, poured herself a cup of coffee, and found she was ravenous. "Used all my little gray cells," she told

Lady. She fried two eggs, made toast with butter and jelly, and even cooked four slices of bacon. If Aunt Mary's fears were correct, she wouldn't live long enough to have to worry about cholesterol.

She built another fire, hoping to cheer her spirits. Maybe the leaden sky at her back wouldn't look so bad with orange and red flames near her toes. Halfway through the eggs, however, she set down her fork with a mild oath. She hadn't felt so alone since the day of Tyler's death. *Forlorn,* that was the word. She and Aunt Mary had always discussed mysteries together. They might not agree, but at least they had a common purpose. This time—

She went to her study phone. No matter how he felt about Aunt Mary, there was one person she wanted to talk to.

He was, his hostess cheerfully informed her, still asleep. "Said the hospital left him a week short on sleep. Shall I wake him?"

"No, just tell him Sheila called. I'm home, and should be here most of the day."

She hung up feeling worse than before.

She was on her second mug of coffee when Owen Green arrived, wearing a dripping raincoat and a shapeless brown hat, and rubbing his bare hands to warm them. The lieutenant watched mournfully as she poured him a mug.

"Do you ever look happy?" she asked impulsively, offering sugar and cream. He took them as if they were the last condiments of a dying man. When he stirred in three sugars and a generous dollop of milk, she added, "It's a wonder all that sugar doesn't sweeten your disposition."

"I'll be sweeter when I get this case behind me," he informed her glumly. "Happier, too." He sat heavily in a chair and said, with an air of melancholy, "Let's have a look at those papers."

He reached out to set his mug on the coffee table—on top of the precious original envelopes!

"Wait!" Sheila snatched them up, then winced with pain.

He gave her a level look. "You get hurt last night?"

"Pulled a shoulder I'd bruised earlier in an accident," she admitted.

"Other fellow get hurt?" No smile, but was that look in his eye the trace of a twinkle?

Sheila laughed. "His pride, at least." She handed him the photocopied chapters. "These are what you can read. These," she patted the envelopes, "are the real thing, sealed and initialed. I've been advised by a lawyer not to break the seals."

"Humph." Green settled himself deeply, balanced one ankle on his other knee, and scanned the pages with amazing speed. Then, sipping the coffee, he grimaced in distaste.

"Cool," he grieved. "Reheat it, please, and then explain why you have let your imagination run away with you once again. Almost anyone can kill for almost any reason, but to think anybody would shoot two men in cold blood to get their hands on these pages—" He shook his head and handed her the mug. His dewlaps quivered and the bags under his eyes sagged. She expected any moment to see tears in his big brown eyes.

She topped off his coffee and handed it back. "I agree."

"You do?" Apparently, even being agreed with disagreed with him. He rubbed one hand across his grizzled kinky fringe and worked his lips sorrowfully in and out. "I cannot tell you how disturbed I am to have been assigned to this case. Drive-by shootings are not my thing. Drug killings in deserted playgrounds are not my thing. Neither of them gives me a snowball's chance in hell of finding the perpetrator. However, my superiors say try, so try I will. But—" He leaned forward and jabbed the air with one skinny brown forefinger. "I will not spend time following rabbit trails. Do you understand? And this so-called manuscript—" he slapped the papers beside him "—is a rabbit!"

"It could be part of an unpublished Margaret Mitchell novel," she pointed out stubbornly. "As such, it could be extremely valuable."

"Only to her heirs. Who else could hope to sell it?"

She nodded and started to shrug, but considered the consequences and settled for a second nod. "You're right again, of course. It was taken from the Marsh home, so it obviously is theirs—*whoever* wrote it. Any court in the country would agree. Even Elouisa agrees. I'll take it to their lawyers this afternoon—if you don't need it."

He held up both hands in protest. "*I* certainly don't need it, and you don't need it around if it's as dangerous as you think it is. Take it to their lawyers, by all means. But one more question. Does the family of the woman who stole it want anything for it? Not that they deserve it, but—"

Sheila smiled wryly. "Only Demolinius."

"Oh, my God." The groan was a prayer. "Was this thing originally stolen by another relative of Anthony's?" When Sheila nodded, he groaned. "Mrs. Travis, what have you gotten me into?"

"*I* haven't gotten you into anything, Lieutenant Green. Your superiors assigned you, remember? But to continue what I was going to say, Anthony's cousin Mildred, my friend, wants her aunt's part in it hushed up entirely. She's terrified the Mitchells will be furious with the old woman for taking the papers."

"She'll be lucky if furious is all they are." His fingers drummed the papers beside him and he worked his lips in and out again. Finally, lugubriously, he spoke. "Nothing in here worth trying to hide fifty years later."

"Murder?"

He shook his head. "Looked like manslaughter to me, and if it happened—*if* it happened, I say—it could as easily have been a fair fight that the author escalated for his or her own purposes. Besides, can you imagine the time and manpower it would take to trace the dateless murder of a nameless sergeant in an unspecified year? That's *before* we start looking for the killer. Do you have any idea how many troops passed through this city during that war?" He didn't wait for her to nod. "And there were ninety-seven murders in '46 alone. Did you know that?"

The barrage of questions was wearing her out. She shook her head quickly. "No, but I agree. Tracing a murder, if there was a murder, would be almost impossible at this date unless it's already on the books, and nothing else in there would matter fifty years later. How about another cup of coffee?" She hoped he'd decline. She might get him out the door without having to mention Aunt Mary at all.

He shook his head. "Don't need more coffee. I need to get out of here." He stood, but remained where he was, slapping his hat against one thigh. "Looks like our best bet is still Demolinius. He's the only person hoping to benefit from those papers. I ran a check on him before I came over. Had a bad record back in the forties and early fifties. Knifings, robberies—left town because he was wanted for questioning in an arson case. I checked by Anthony's after I talked with you, but they haven't seen hide nor hair of him since Wednesday. Said he got him a job and moved out, leaving no forwarding address."

She rose to see him to the door. "I'd bet you that's how he's lived his life. He must have gotten a good job, though. Monday he said he had no wheels, but he had a car last night. He said he followed me to my office from here."

He looked at the glass doors onto the second-story deck. "Man climbed over that once, I seem to remember. Isn't as safe as it looks, if somebody's determined. Maybe you ought to go stay with that meddlesome aunt of yours until this is over. If," he added morosely, "it ever is over."

"I'll be fine." She spoke with more conviction than she felt.

He sighed and carried his mug to the sink. Carefully rinsing it, he muttered over his shoulder, "I can't offer you protection, you know, but we'll look for Demolinius. He's the only person likely to have killed to get the manuscript back. Otherwise, like I said, Mrs. Travis," he dried his hands and shrugged on the still-damp trench coat she handed him, "it's a rabbit. Take my word for it. But you make good coffee. Thanks." He jammed his hat over his bare scalp.

Gathering his coat around him like modern-day armor, he trudged to the door—then turned and growled in barely suppressed rage, *"This manuscript business is a rabbit!* I know it, and you know it! But because it's the only thing that might connect two probably unconnected murders and," he added grudgingly in a lower tone, "because you've had a few mighty lucky guesses—down on Peachtree, out in Snellville, and up in Dunwoody—I'll follow it up." He dragged out his notebook and uncapped a gold Cross pen. "Who knew James Turner was bringing you the manuscript?"

It had come. Sheila caught her lower lip between her teeth, trying to think of any way to make this sound better. She couldn't think of one. "His cousin Mildred, my aunt Mary, and a few friends she told."

"What friends?"

When she named them, Green's lips rounded in an indrawn whistle. "You *do* want to get me in trouble, don't you? Do you know what my job'd be worth if I falsely accused any of those folks of murder?"

She nodded soberly. "Not to mention my own hide."

He shook his head, then poised his pen once more. "And who knew Bagwell would be picking up the manuscript?"

She gave him a wry smile. "Same folks. They were all at Aunt Mary's when I called to tell her. Oh, and Crispin Montgomery, a friend of mine—but don't get excited. He was in the hospital when Junior was killed and on his way to Fort Valley when Sean was shot."

"He can prove that? Got witnesses?"

She nodded.

His lips worked in and out while he turned it all over in his large domed forehead, then curved in a smile so quick that she almost missed it. "Well, it looks like Mildred, your aunt Mary, and her friends had better have good alibis. I hope to God I won't need to ask for them. I'd counted on working another five years before retiring. Good day, Mrs. Travis."

After he left, Sheila roamed the apartment, her mind playing with various scenarios. Had one of Aunt Mary's friends lost his money and imagined he could sell the manuscript for enough to recoup it? Not likely. These few chapters would represent only a drop in any of their deep financial buckets. Besides, as businessmen, Rip and Charles would know almost as well as Lamar the legal problems involved with trying to sell this particular manuscript on the black market, and a doctor couldn't practice these days without a working knowledge of the law. Not to mention that all four men were highly respected for integrity. Why would any of them risk that for this?

They wouldn't. So it was not the *value* of the manuscript, but the *content* that had spooked somebody. Why?

On the theory that doing two things is better than doing one, Sheila prepared a moist heating pad and flopped onto her bed to think while she tried to relax the knotted muscles in her back.

Now. What about this new manuscript could be important? As in any good literature, the book's main themes were simple and universal: thwarted love, illicit sex, murder, and danger. That plot could have been written by Margaret Mitchell, or by a writer friend who had left chapters for the famous author to read. The characters could have been any four soldiers. Or they could have been lightly based on true stories and situations. Sheila had read somewhere that *Gone With the Wind* was based on Mitchell's ancestors and family stories. These soldiers certainly could have been taken directly from real life. Wasn't it Mark Twain who joked that he wrote true stories, then changed the names? But if the book *was* true stories about real people, the soldiers needn't have been Aunt Mary's friends.

But they were the only ones who knew about the manuscript, her inner voice reminded her. *The only ones who knew Junior and Sean had it.*

It all came back to that. Either the two deaths and Honey's assault were unrelated, or they had to do with the manuscript. If she decided they were connected with the manuscript, she needed to look among Aunt Mary's friends for a murderer—with Aunt Mary fiercely dogging her every step and conversation.

"If only Stack Norton were alive—" she muttered, massaging her shoulder. "He's very like Tim in the book. . . ."

Her mind explored that possibility like a tongue probing a tender tooth. Maybe the chapter Honey took had convinced her that the book was telling Stack Norton's story.

Would any of Stack's friends kill now to protect his reputation?

"What reputation?" Sheila demanded aloud. "He was a rat! Besides, why would one of Stack's friends attack Honey?"

Lady took the words as invitation. First she stuck her nose onto the bed. Meeting no reprimand, she wriggled her soft body up to lie beside her mistress. Sheila was too busy thinking to notice.

Five men, counting Stack, and five risky situations if you counted the bootlegger's accomplice. Why did that sound familiar?

"A logic puzzle!" she exclaimed aloud, scrambling off the bed and sending poor Lady tumbling to the floor.

Taking a pad, ruler, and pencil to her dining table, Sheila carefully made a grid:

	Charles	Max	Rip	Lamar	Stack
MUR-DERER					
ADUL-TERER					
HOMO-SEXUAL					
BOOT-LEGGER					
ASSIS-TANT					

After a moment's hesitation she added three more names: Dorothy, Mary, Honey. She also added one more category: Single Woman. This meant she had two more people than categories. She knew one person she hoped to eliminate.

For half an hour she sat, remembering snips of conversations she'd had in the past week and jotting them down, putting *x*'s on her grid. (Reader, can you work the puzzle yet?)

At the end, she *could* make the puzzle come out without using Aunt Mary. But who else (1) thrived on excitement, (2) was richer after the war than before it, (3) was a newcomer to Atlanta during the war, (4) never married or showed serious interest in the opposite sex, (5) used to have a dreadful temper, and (6) was a crack shot—in other words, who might fit *any* position on the chart?

Sheila was aghast at that conclusion—disturbed by the entire process. How could she assign *any* of her honorary aunts and uncles, people she'd known for years, to the categories she'd *x*'ed under their names? And even if they had fit one of the categories fifty years ago, which of their "crimes" was so dreadful that any one of them would kill today to prevent exposure?

"The accidental murder of a blackmailing sergeant?" Sheila was unconvinced. She was looking for a heinous, despicable crime.

Perhaps there had been a second murder, one that appeared in Honey's chapter or that someone feared *might* appear in a chapter Sheila had—the murder of someone so important that revelation would rock Atlanta even today. Had one of Aunt Mary's friends committed such a murder, or helped to conceal it?

She wrinkled her forehead, trying to remember what she had heard recently, just this week, about unsolved murders. Oh! The notebook she and Walter had made in high school, describing four of Atlanta's unsolved crimes in the forties. It was still there, on Rip's overflowing bookshelves.

Having no better idea, to Rip's she would go. With any luck, she'd get there and back before Aunt Mary started looking for her niece among her friends.

• • •

She had painfully changed into a navy-and-green plaid wool skirt and low navy heels and was trying to coax her unruly curls into order when the telephone rang. It took her half a minute to recognize the hysterical voice as Mildred's.

"Tell me again, Mildred. Slowly."

"The po-lice are here, questioning Miss Mary! Say a kid saw her car down at some housing project yesterday, with two people sitting in it having a fight, then right afterwards a man turned up there dead! They haven't said so yet, Sheila, but I can tell—they think Miss Mary or Jason may have killed him!"

Sheila shivered, in spite of her sweater. "Why do they think it was Aunt Mary's car?"

"Kid who saw it said it reminded her of a fairy queen or somethin'. Been reading Shakespeare in school, policeman said."

Sheila instantly made the connection: MAB. A vanity plate in more ways than one.

"I'll come right over," she said, reaching for her purse.

"Can't, Sheila. The detective told me not to call you, that he wanted to handle this without your . . . uh . . . help. But I knew you'd want to know. I've also called Mr. Whitehead. Didn't like to call her regular lawyer, but seeing Mr. Lamar's a friend. . . . He said he'll get here as fast as he can."

Thwarted, Sheila decided to carry out her original intention. "Call me as soon as you know anything else, Mildred. I'm going up to Rip's. You can reach me there."

When her black Maxima rolled down the I-85 exit toward Peachtree, however, it seemed to turn of its own volition left toward Aunt Mary's instead of right toward Rip's. Sheila pulled into the apartment parking garage and sat for a moment considering the culprit Cadillac. She wondered what Owen Green would say if he saw her in the apartment. She even, hating herself for what she was doing, went over and peered through the windows of the car.

"Looking for what—powder burns?" she asked herself in reproof. She was relieved, however, that the Cadillac looked as pristine as ever.

To avoid meeting Green, she rode the elevator to the next-to-top floor. Then she took the fire escape to the penthouse's kitchen entrance. She found Mildred baking, her usual remedy for low spirits. This noon her shoulders drooped over the mixing bowl, and she looked thinner than when Sheila saw her last.

Sheila gave her a quick hug. "You doing all right?"

Mildred shook her head mournfully. "I don't know, Sheila. It's almost more than a body can stand. First Junior—" She broke off and pressed her lips together tightly, breathed deeply. "That was one precious boy. I don't think I'll ever get over his being gone."

"How's Elouisa?"

"She's making it. 'Bout all any of us can do. But it's hard on her. Junior's sister's moved in with her for the time being."

"I met her Monday night. Met your brother Demolinius, too."

"*That*'ll never make you rich and famous. What was he doing?"

"Washing dishes at Anthony's restaurant." She didn't bother to tell Mildred about the rest. Mildred didn't need another stone on her worry pile.

Mildred made a sound somewhere between derision and admiration. "He's not washing dishes now. *Says* he's working for somebody he used to know. I don't know what he's doing, though—and my good sense tells me I don't *want* to know." She kneaded her bread fiercely. "Seems like all our troubles are piling up, doesn't it? The Bible says we aren't tried beyond our ability to endure, but this week somebody's got me overestimated."

With a big sigh, she rolled out her dough. "You know, Sheila, the Bible also says the sins of the fathers are visited on children to the third generation. It's the literal truth. Ahnty

Weesa stole the envelopes, but Junior died for them. And now Miss Mary—" She swiped away a tear and burst out fiercely, "Why'd she have to put his old *A* on her license tag, anyway? Don't anybody but me know what it stands for, and I wouldn't know if I hadn't seen his dumb old card!"

"What card?" Sheila asked, curious even now.

"An old birthday card, signed 'To my darling little Mary Albertine from your Grandfather Albert.' Oh!" Mildred gasped, suddenly realizing the treachery she'd committed. "If Miss Mary ever finds out I told you—"

"She won't, Mildred. But no wonder she keeps it a secret."

Mildred managed a small chuckle. "I only use it when she steps a bit out of line. All I have to say in company is 'Miss Mary Ah—' and she comes right 'round!"

"I don't blame her." Sheila tucked the information into a recess of her mind as she tiptoed to the swinging door leading from the kitchen into the front of the penthouse. Pressing almost imperceptibly, she made a tiny crack through which she could see Owen Green's tan trench coat sleeve resting on the fat arm of her own favorite chair. Across from him, Aunt Mary sat on the couch, small feet planted firmly on the floor. No one was speaking.

Sheila let the door swing back into place and whispered to Mildred, "Where's Forbes?"

"Spending the day with a friend."

"And Jason?"

Mildred nodded toward the back. "Waiting in his room."

As Sheila started toward the door leading to the staff rooms, Mildred caught her sleeve. Her look was long and stern. "You're not thinkin' of bustin' Jason out of here, are you?"

"Heavens, no! I just want to talk with him a minute."

"Okay. But if Miss Mary or that detective find you in there—"

"One minute," Sheila promised, hurrying down the back hall.

She rapped lightly on the last door. "Jason? It's Sheila. May I come in?" She took a grunt for assent.

Jason didn't sleep in this room. He just used it to pass the hours between working on the car and Aunt Mary's infrequent trips and errands. Painted beige, it contained a day bed covered in brown corduroy, a caramel carpet, a desk and a straight chair, a bookshelf filled with books, tapes, and CD's, a high-quality CD player, a Nordic track, a weight set, and a television. The only window had a chocolate brown Levolor blind, no drape. Sheila knew without asking that Aunt Mary had given him free rein in decoration and furnishings. Aunt Mary had no patience with what other people called earth tones. "Dirt colors," she called them. "Lower my spirit and make me want to go wash."

Jason's spirits looked about as low as they could get. He lay sullenly on his bed watching CNN, looked up only briefly as Sheila entered, then dropped his eyes back toward the screen. "They ready for me again?"

"No, they seem to have reached an impasse. Nobody's saying a word, and Aunt Mary has her chin in the air."

He gave a short, soundless laugh, but also said nothing.

Sheila sat on the edge of his desk chair. "Jason, I don't have much time. Why *was* Aunt Mary's car down at the housing project yesterday afternoon?"

He shook his head but didn't look at her. "Wasn't."

"Someone saw the tag. Could someone have borrowed the car—or the tag?" Now that was an idea! Borrow a license plate, commit the murder, and presto—a suspect!

Jason, however, did not encourage that solution. Without moving a muscle, he managed to convey that a wall had risen between them. And he said nothing.

"Jason! Where were you all yesterday afternoon?"

He shook his head. "Don't have to answer to you, Sheila, just Miss Mary. She knows where I went. She sent me."

"She sent you to shoot a man?" Sheila demanded.

He kept his eyes glued to CNN as if the day's news was of far more importance than his own whereabouts during a murder he might have committed. She longed to shake him.

"Did anybody else use the car, Jason? Just tell me that."

He swung his legs over the side of the bed and glared at her. "I ain't tellin' you one blessed thing! You got us into this mess, and God only knows how Miss Mary is gonna get us out!" He stalked to the window and turned his back. The interview was over.

Indignant and troubled, Sheila returned to the kitchen. "Struck out on that one," she reported gloomily to Mildred. "Jason won't say *where* he was yesterday."

"Gettin' the oil changed," Mildred said matter-of-factly, setting her bread dough out to rise. "I heard him tellin' the detective."

"At the Cadillac dealer's? Why didn't he just say so?"

Mildred shook her head. "Miss Mary don't use the dealer any more. She's bought stock in one of those jiffy places, and you know Miss Mary. She shops places she owns a piece of."

Sheila was puzzled. "Then an oil change wouldn't have taken more than half an hour."

"He was gone all afternoon," Mildred volunteered. "I know, because I kept trying to call here, and got no answer."

"Then Aunt Mary must have been with him." Sheila was enjoying the picture of her dignified aunt waiting in a mechanic's office while her oil was changed, but Mildred canceled it out.

"No, she'd gone to the dentist. Gettin' her teeth cleaned."

Sheila felt a chilly ripple down her back. "I thought she did that Monday morning."

Mildred shook her head and started washing up. "No, she went out someplace else, early for her, then met me at the play."

"Do you know what time she got her teeth cleaned yesterday?"

"Her calendar says two o'clock."

Plenty of time Monday to kill Junior, plenty of time yesterday to shoot Sean.

Sheila sighed. To herself as much as to the housekeeper,

she said, "Let's don't worry until we have to. I don't really think Jason killed anybody. And we both know Aunt Mary didn't."

"Not unless they riled her considerably," Mildred agreed.

"Though war might rage about him, [Berlin Coca-Cola bottler] Herr Keith was as single-minded as any loyal Coca-Cola man in America. . . . 'We had a good business volume in spite of factories being blown up.'"

The moment the Allied victory was announced from Berlin, he sent this cable to Atlanta headquarters: "Coca-Cola GMBH survives. Please send the auditors."[15]

A steady drizzle was falling by the time Sheila reached Buckhead. Steering, even with her good arm, was agony. Only determination to find a few answers kept her driving. It was past noon, and she considered stopping somewhere for lunch, but decided Rip would be delighted to have company. Gertie always fixed more than enough.

Only when she pulled up to Rip's front door—six granite steps and an uncovered terrace away—did she remember she had no umbrella. Holding her purse over her head, she dashed to the door and jabbed the bell.

Gertie answered, flour on one cheek and an unusual pucker of worry creasing her forehead. With something less than her usual delight she gestured the uninvited guest into the foyer. "Mr. Rip 'n' Isaac are out, Sheila. . . ." She backed toward the Christmas tree. Looming tall and unlit, it made the foyer look forsaken and desolate.

As Sheila brushed rain from her hair and assessed how much it was frizzing, her hopes for lunch took a plunge. Years ago Gertie would have taken her into the kitchen and waved her to a counter stool for a bowl of hot soup, a slab of cheddar, and a slice of Pepperidge Farm bread with butter. But Gertie had her pride. She would not feed an embassy widow a pickup meal in her kitchen. Not even a very hungry embassy widow. Unless Gertie had something in the fridge she considered appropriate for a guest, Sheila would have to eat on her way home. "I just wanted to look at a book in Rip's library for a few minutes. May I?"

"Sure." Gertie stepped back with obvious reluctance. A shade of her usual courtesy returned as she offered, "Want a Co'-Cola?"

"Sure. Rip still on a weekly delivery route?"

"Sure is, honey. We cain' do without our Co'-Colas around here."

Sheila went on back to the library. Real Thing lifted his head curiously from the rug, then went back to his snooze. Real Thing had never been known to show the slightest interest in anyone or anything except dinner and Rip.

As Sheila had known he would, Rip had left a CD in the player. She turned it on. The encompassing sound of E. Power Biggs playing Bach filled the room. With the rain, the heavy organ chords were the perfect background for reading about old unsolved mysteries.

"That's his shut-out-the-world music." Gertie handed her a well-iced drink in an official glass, brought with the half-full bottle on a Coca-Cola tray. Sheila wondered if Rip had willed all his memorabilia to the new Coca-Cola museum downtown. If so, they'd have to expand considerably.

"I think I drank my first Coke at Rip's," she remembered, drinking thirstily, "in a mug with a teddy bear on it."

Maybe it was the teddy bear that softened Gertie slightly. She reverted to her old self long enough to order, "See can you find something a bit more cheerful. That music with this rain gives me the willies."

"I like it." Sheila refilled her glass before suggesting, "Close the door, and I'll turn the volume down."

"You want a fire? Isaac laid one this morning." Gertie pointed to the logs waiting on the andirons and hovered, delaying her exit.

"If I do, I'll light it. Don't let me bother you." *And please go away so I can do what I came for,* Sheila added silently. But then she recalled something she wanted to know first. "Gertie? Do you remember if Rip was home all day Monday?"

Gertie twisted a corner of her apron, trying to remember, then shook her head. Worry, which had subsided while she was fetching the Coke, returned doubly to furrow her forehead and slump her stout shoulders. "Sure wasn't. Had Walt drive him downtown to see Dr. Max, and didn't call Isaac to pick him up all day. Miss Mary finally brought him home at dinnertime. Isaac was real put out." She hesitated, then said in a rush, "Sheila, I know strokes affect the mind, like—Mr. Rip's been gloomy and moody a lot. But these days, seems like somethin's eatin' him for lunch and dinner! Somethin' more than his being sick. And this latest notion of his . . ." She broke off abruptly. "I'll be in the kitchen if you need me."

Deep, determined strains of "What a Friend We Have in Jesus" triumphed temporarily over Bach and the dull thud of rain on the boxwoods, then subsided as the kitchen door swung shut.

Sheila moved to the window, greatly disturbed. Could Rip have hired a car Monday, driven to the housing project, met with Junior, and killed him? "Of course not!" She spoke aloud and firmly—to convince herself. Real Thing opened his eyes halfway to give her a noncurious stare. "Elouisa would have noticed his wheelchair," Sheila told him. "Besides, Rip can't walk, much less drive."

Are you absolutely certain of that? It was her own inner voice, not Real Thing, that asked, but she replied to the dog anyway.

"Certainly! Aunt Mary would have mentioned anything as exciting as Rip's beginning to walk again. I'm worse than she is," she muttered, turning her back on the bored animal. "I see murderers not merely behind every bush, but in every wheelchair."

She forced herself to look, really look, at the view outside the streaming panes. The rain was pounding the dry brown grass and ruffling the aplomb of a fat old magnolia, but enormous rosy camellias glowed like jewels in the gray. Sheila had never seen that window when something was not blooming beyond it. Rip loved flowers almost as much as he loved music, pranks, and Real Thing. What a waste, for such a talented, life-loving man to spend his days cooped up in this one room! And what treachery for her to even suspect him of killing Junior.

Better him than Aunt Mary, warned her silent voice.

Resolutely Sheila sought out the old green notebook and dragged a wing chair nearer the window to avoid turning on a lamp. Bathed in cold gray light, with Bach resounding off the bookshelves, she settled down to the business of resurrecting old crimes.

Even after all these years, she thumbed through the notebook with pride. She and Walt had been meticulous in gathering data. They had read old newspapers and interviewed people who had been around during the forties. They had, however, concentrated on people over sixty. World War II had seemed such ancient history! With a rueful smile, she now realized that Walt's parents and Aunt Mary would have done better. They'd been, then, about the same age as Sheila and Walt were today. Those war years were closer to them in time and memory than the well-remembered sixties were to her now.

She quickly scanned the first case they had researched. Surely none of this week's events had anything to do with ten dead elephants and one dead clown at Ringling Brothers' Circus in Atlanta in '41.

Their second case was really two: the Winecoff Hotel's

mysterious fires of 1942, in which nobody died, and 1946, which destroyed the building and killed over a hundred people. She found it equally hard to connect them with Elouisa's stolen envelopes.

The third case was possible, she supposed. One of Aunt Mary's friends might have shot banker Henry C. Heinz, son-in-law of Coca-Cola's Asa Candler, in 1943. A man had confessed and served time for the crime, but had he been framed, or paid to confess?

Most promising was the highly publicized 1947 murder of Margaret (another Peggy!) Refoule. She had been discovered bound and strangled in the shallow waters of Peachtree Creek behind her home not far from this very house. Sheila looked at the water currently streaming past the window and shuddered. Peggy Refoule's husband Paul—Frenchman, artist, and war hero—was suspected, but college art students insisted Refoule was teaching a class at the time his wife was killed. Was Honey Norton one of those students? Or had there been a war-related connection between Rip or Charles and Paul Refoule in France?

"That murder happened after the war," she reminded herself.

Immediately her inner voice replied: Gone With the Wind *continues past the war. Maybe this book does, too.*

She was still considering the possibilities of that when Real Thing gave a low "Whoof" and Rip wheeled himself through the doorway.

"Heard you were here! Raining frogs and chickens outside." His tongue was thick and unruly, and his heartiness seemed forced.

Nevertheless, she expected the next sentence to be "Stay for lunch?", to which she would reply, "I'd love to." Over lunch she would tell him Aunt Mary was being questioned by Owen Green and why. She'd ask about the Refoules and the Heinz murder, and maybe she'd get some answers.

In anticipation, she teased, "Thought I'd catch you in your slippers and your red-checkered shirt on a day like this!"

Rip shook his head. He reached down slowly to scratch

Real Thing beneath his long silky ears before replying. "Had an errand. Find what you wanted?"

"Sure did." She held up the green notebook. "It's a report Walt and I wrote in high school."

He grunted. "Can't imagine you two writing anything of lasting value." He stopped. Could he be waiting for her to leave?

She had never before felt unwelcome at the Delacourts'. Piqued and curious, she drew the conversation out. "We didn't, but our research was impressive. Unsolved Atlanta mysteries from the forties. Do you remember the Refoule case?"

He nodded shortly. "Wondered if her husband did it."

"So did half of Atlanta, apparently. Did you know them well?"

"Georgia knew Peggy Refoule." Again, he stopped abruptly.

She stood and went to the bookshelves, biting her lip as she pondered various reasons why Rip, normally garrulous even after his stroke, was so eager for her to go.

She turned and made a frontal attack. "What's going on? Is my being here causing you a problem?"

He hedged, ducked his head, mumbled, "Got folks for lunch."

"Why didn't you just say so? A simple 'Hello, Sheila, sorry I can't offer you any chow, but I've got guests' would have done. You know that."

Head still bent over his lap, he absently fondled Real Thing's uplifted chin. The silence grew long.

She ought to have picked up her purse and said a quick farewell, but something kept her standing by the shelves. Perhaps it was the dejected slant of his shoulders. Or maybe it was the way his head was half-cocked toward voices, sounding vaguely familiar, that grew steadily louder in a distant room.

She had heard them without hearing until one said, shrill and clear, ". . . go home!"

". . . come to me, then!" That was Faith Andrews. It had to be. So was the other—?

"Honey Norton?" Sheila hazarded, surprised.

Rip nodded and shot her what looked like a guilty look from under his bushy brows. "Brought her to stay a few days, but—" he shook his head in hurt bewilderment, "—she doesn't want to."

Apparently not. Few words were clear, but the tone was furious. She caught "no business" and "run my life" before Rip said, urgently, "Help Faith, Sheila. Honey—end of her rope."

She might well be. Getting that hysterical was dangerous for someone recovering from a concussion. Sheila rested one hand on Rip's shoulder in quick reassurance and hurried toward the living room.

It was not a cozy space at the best of times—too vast, with a huge fireplace surmounted by a pink marble mantelpiece carved in odd, exotic flowers with spiky petals. The same flowers, in plaster, surrounded a ceiling almost as high as the heavens. As a girl, Sheila had been terrified the plaster blossoms would crash down and pin her to the cold dark floor whenever she and Walt had pretended the clusters of sofas, chairs, and coffee tables on blue-and-green Persian rugs were desert islands separated by wide muddy seas. Opulence, not cozy comfort, had been the vogue when Walt's great-grandfather built this house. The living room was seldom used except for large parties, so nobody had bothered to alter it.

Today, the heavy gold draperies increased rather than cheered the gloom. Enormous landscapes, somber in thick brown and gray oil, looked heavy enough to fall at any moment, dragging chunks of plaster with them. There was sufficient empty space, however, to provide proper scope for an angry woman.

Sheila paused in the entrance, unnoticed. Honey Norton, wearing a camel dress and a white turban bandage, strode between the chairs, flailing her arms in agitation. "I don't want his charity!" she cried to her sister Faith, standing uncertainly nearby. Faith, Sheila noted automatically, wore a tailored pantsuit in russet tweed with a creamy silk blouse. Honey's dress was a fine and expensive wool, with a flared skirt that swirled gracefully about her legs as she raged.

"It's not charity, Honey." Faith spoke in a let's-be-reasonable tone she probably used with students questioning a performance grade when they hadn't practiced. "He's got Gertie and Isaac here, and loads of space. And he says he'll enjoy your company."

The tone might work on students, but it carried no weight with her older sister. "I don't *want* his company. I don't want *any* company! Don't you understand?" Honey was pale to the point of exhaustion. Surely only fury kept her from toppling to the floor.

Faith, too, seemed strained almost to the breaking point, and was so pale her freckles stood out like measles. "I understand one thing well enough: You are too weak to go home alone." She sighed and said in the tone of one repeating something she's said several times before to no avail, "So come to me. You don't even have to talk to me if you don't want to. I'm gone most of the day. But I'll ask Dorothy to let me have Bertha, or even get Hattie to come back—"

"I . . . will . . . not . . . go into . . . that *house!*" Honey's words came in queer little gasps, and then she caught sight of Sheila. Her eyes widened. Then she sank abruptly into the nearest chair, head on her knees.

Sheila reached her as soon as Faith did. As they bent over the pale, still form, Faith uttered a series of garbled explanations. "Rip's just trying to be kind. Don't know why she's so set against it. Don't understand—"

Honey spoke dully, without raising her head. "You don't understand a blessed thing."

The back of her neck, shorn of its tawny glory, was very white, crisscrossed with tiny wrinkles like a mud flat at low tide. Bent low and cruelly exposed, it looked like that of a queen waiting on the block for her executioner.

Sheila pulled a pillow from a nearby couch and shoved it gently under Honey's forehead. "Lie still for a minute until things stop whirling. You're still weak."

Honey obeyed. As the minutes passed, however, and she still did not lift up her head, Faith looked from that pale vulnerable neck to Sheila. Worry filled her dark eyes. Sheila wondered if suspicion filled her own.

"Why don't you go ask Gertie for a hot cup of very

sweet tea?" she suggested. If Faith thought Sheila should go herself and leave the sisters alone again, she gave no sign.

As soon as the kitchen's swinging door swished behind Faith, Sheila bent and touched Honey lightly. "You can come up now. She's gone."

Honey raised her head. Relief made her gray eyes even larger. "Thank you. I couldn't take much more, and didn't know what else to do."

Sheila sat on a nearby chair and spoke casually. "I hadn't heard you were well enough to come home. Does Aunt Mary know?"

Honey shook her head. "Max said this morning I could be discharged. Rip and Faith were there, and Rip said he'd bring me here. I tried to call Mary, but Mildred said she couldn't be disturbed, and they kept insisting I should come with Rip. . . ." She broke off and rubbed blue-veined hands across her cheeks. When her fingers touched the swathing bandages, a spasm of pain crossed her face. "I must look dreadful."

"No, just pale. Your hair will grow back."

Honey gave her a quick, uncertain look, then shrugged. "I don't suppose it really matters to anybody but me."

"Matters to me."

Rip had wheeled himself silently into the foyer behind them, Real Thing padding along. Now Rip rolled across the floor and came to a stop beside Honey's chair. Real Thing lifted his muzzle and sniffed her knees, then rested his chin on them. Honey stroked his head, her marvelous eyes fixed on her host. Sheila could have been in Japan, for all the attention any of them paid her. "Beautiful as you used to be," Rip told the bandaged woman gruffly.

Honey looked down into Real Thing's eyes, in her lap. Her mouth twisted in a smile that looked more like she wanted to cry. "That's been a long time, Rip," she said haltingly.

He reached out to tilt her chin gently until her eyes met his. "Too long, Honey. I'm a crock now, but I want to help."

She pressed three fingers to her lips but could not stop fat tears from spilling onto her cheeks. She gave him a long, searching, puzzled look. Then she finally asked, so softly

Sheila scarcely heard, "Why didn't you help me before? When I really needed it?"

"I didn't know." He leaned forward in his earnestness, nearly tipping out of his chair. He didn't seem to notice.

"Didn't know?" The words were wrung from her in a sharp cry. Real Thing gave a puzzled, worried "Woof?"

Rip shook his head. "I just heard Monday night about Maud's will. If you'd only said . . ."

"Oh, the *will*!" She flapped one hand to show how unimportant that was. "By then, what did it matter?"

"You matter," he said, almost repeating his entrance line. In the silence that followed, Real Thing lay down on Honey's feet. Sheila decided it was time for her own exit. She rose and started toward the foyer on tiptoe, but it is hard to melt away when you are five foot nine and walking on bare wood.

Their eyes rose with her. Honey reached out and caught her hand. "Don't go, *please*? I've forgotten your name, but I know you are Mary's niece. Don't leave me."

Sheila hesitated. "You two have something to discuss—"

Honey tugged her hand. "No. Sit here beside me, please. I've known Rip since I was a little girl. What could we have to say to one another after all these years?" Her laugh was high, brittle, and mirthless. It ended in a crooked, unhappy smile. "I used to think he hung the moon, but he never even answered my letters."

He reached out to grip her shoulder so hard that Honey winced and drew away. "What letters? You never—"

"Here's the tea." Faith strode into the room bearing a tray. Her square strong hands poured out a cup, stirred in two lumps of sugar, and held the cup out to Honey.

Honey ignored it. She and Rip were staring at one another in bewilderment.

Sheila stood and motioned the other woman to follow her. "Faith and I need to help Gertie with lunch," she said firmly.

Neither said a word. Had they not heard her, or did they not know Gertie would rather die than accept help in her kitchen?

• • •

The cook was stirring corn chowder at the stove when the two women came in. "Is there enough for me, too?" Sheila asked, bending to give the creamy mixture an appreciative sniff.

Gertie raised her head and shot Sheila an appraising look. "I got plenty, but who all's staying?"

"I think everybody, but you might delay things a few minutes."

Gertie snorted. "From the soun' of things awhile back, I was 'fraid I'd have to delay 'em longer 'n that—or throw all this out. Mr. Rip doan' eat much when he eats alone." She jerked her head toward the back of the house. "You all go wait in the liberry. I'll keep my ear cocked, and when they sound ready, I'll have Isaac call you. Want another Coke?"

Faith looked chilled to the bone. "How about coffee?" Sheila suggested. Faith managed a small nod.

On a familiar top shelf, Sheila found two blue-and-white mugs shaped like corsets and held them up with a smile. When Faith saw what they were, she smiled, too. "Walt nearly died of embarrassment when Rip ordered these," Sheila told her. "What was that, Gertie—Winsome's thirtieth anniversary?"

"Sumpin' like that. Miss Georgia wasn't too fond of them, neither. Only let him keep the two here."

Sheila poured the tiny corsets full of coffee and handed one to Faith. "Go on back to the library and light the fire. I'll be there as soon as I make a quick phone call."

"Did Green leave?" Sheila demanded moments later, before Mildred had completed her last syllable of greeting.

Mildred wasted no time, either. "I was just about to call you up there. Miss Mary says for you to go home right this minute and wait for her call. You lock the door and don't let nobody—"

Mildred broke off with what sounded like an "oof!"—or was it merely a cough?

"Let me speak to Aunt Mary for a minute, Mildred."

"She isn't here. I got to go—" Mildred must be worried if she was slipping into casual grammar.

Sheila's stomach clenched. "Where *is* Aunt Mary, Mildred?" Could Owen Green have possibly thrown her dainty aunt into the Fulton County Jail?

"She and Mr. Whitehead went down to Mr. Charles's office for a little while. Miss Mary said not to expect her back until later, and she said to call you at Mr. Rip's and tell you to go home and wait. Don't do *anything* until you hear from her."

Sheila was bewildered. "And Detective Green just left? Without taking her or Jason with him?"

"Yes, ma'am."

Now Sheila *knew* something was the matter. Mildred had never called her ma'am in all the years they had been friends. "I got to go," Mildred repeated. "You do like Miss Mary said. Go home right now, and lock—" Again she broke off with a cough.

Sheila didn't try to hide her annoyance. "I've been asked to lunch here. I'll go home when we're through."

"She *said* to tell you to go home *now,*" Mildred insisted firmly. "You know how she gets if—"

"You've told me," Sheila said lightly. "You're off the hook." She hung up before Mildred could say another word.

In the library, Faith sat on the sofa, one leg tucked beneath her, sipping coffee before a crackling new fire. Sheila inhaled deeply of fresh coffee and burning logs and went to the hearth, nursing her mug and enjoyed the gently throbbing heat on her calves.

Faith looked up questioningly, and Sheila gave her a rueful smile. "My aunt's as much trouble as your sister! Earlier today, the police were asking Aunt Mary if she'd shot a man yesterday afternoon. Now, Mildred says she's out gallivanting with Lamar and Charles. If she isn't worried, I don't suppose—"

"Yesterday afternoon?" Faith's mahogany eyes widened. "She was with Honey all afternoon. Came right after lunch, and I took her home just before six."

Sheila hadn't known how worried she was until her knees buckled with relief. She sank to the other end of the couch and demanded, "You're sure? You were there?"

"Not all the time, but the nurses were in and out. I'm pretty sure they said she'd been there all the time."

Why didn't she just tell them, then? Sheila wondered silently. *Why pretend, even to Mildred, that she was going to the dentist?* But whatever game Aunt Mary was playing, she was so far concealing it successfully. The best thing Sheila could do was continue to seek answers here.

"That's a relief," she told Faith with another smile that made a joke of it all. "It's great to see Honey doing so well. Did she ever say what happened last Sunday?"

"No, not a word. Whenever I tried to ask, she'd change the subject."

"Why did you all insist on no visitors? Because they'd cut off her hair?" Faith and Honey both looked like they had more sense than to let vanity keep out their friends.

Faith's reply surprised her. "We didn't. Dr. Maxwell said he wanted Honey to rest, so to let absolutely nobody in. At first, in fact, he was even going to exclude me, but I put my foot down. Nobody's been in all week except Miss Mary. And Rip, this morning. Dr. Maxwell called him, I think, although I'm not sure why. As you can see, Honey doesn't want Rip's help—or mine," she added somewhat wistfully.

"How did Aunt Mary get past the sign?"

Faith chuckled. "She just came. She's spent every afternoon with Honey, and Dr. Maxwell knew, so I guess it was all right. It certainly helped me out—I could teach most of my classes. Yesterday Miss Mary brought some of Honey's clothes over, too."

That costly camel dress had not been hanging in Honey's impoverished closet Sunday afternoon, but if Faith didn't know that, Sheila wasn't about to tell her.

To give herself time to think, she sipped Gertie's strong, wonderful brew—trying to figure out why someone as naturally indolent as Aunt Mary would devote a week's afternoons to the tedium of sitting with an unconscious woman.

Unless— "When did Honey come out of the coma?"

Faith looked across the rim of her own mug. "Monday night. Early evening, actually."

"And she's been conscious ever since?"

Faith nodded.

"I hadn't heard that." In fact, hadn't the nurses told Lamar Thursday evening there was no change?

Another puzzle: Why would a medical system that sends octogenarians home the day of a hernia operation permit a mildly concussed woman to loll around in a private room for nearly a week?

"Philip never suggested that Honey go home?"

Faith shook her head. "Not until today. I offered to take her to my house, but as you may have heard," her wide mouth curved in a wry smile, "Honey's not fond of the family manor."

Sheila gave her a sympathetic grin. "I noticed. Has she always been that way, or just since your mother died?"

Faith sighed. "As long as I can remember. She seldom came home when I was growing up, not even after Stack and Daddy died. I used to think she was just busy with grown-up things, but after I grew up, I realized it was more than that."

Sheila agreed. Visiting one's mother *is* a grown-up thing. And hadn't Rip said, "Maud doted on Honey"? "Did your mother disapprove of her marriage?"

"Heavens no! Mother adored Stack. She was shocked after he died, of course, by what he'd done, but he used to come by our house more often than Honey." Faith stopped, struck by a memory. "He even bought her Mother's Day presents. His own mother was dead, you see."

"Did you stay with them when your parents were out of town?"

"No, the few times Mother left me at all, she left me with Aunt Carrie, her best friend. Rip's aunt, actually. She had this big old house full of china thimbles and hand-crocheted doilies."

Sheila chuckled. "Can you picture Rip growing up with china thimbles and lacy doilies? She raised him, didn't she?"

"Did she? I didn't know that. She almost never mentioned him. We'd have tea parties with cookies cut out with a thimble and pink lemonade, or we'd dress up her four Bye-Lo Babies. Remember them? Soft cotton bodies, but real bisque heads, hands, and legs?" She considered her big hands ruefully. "Can you picture me cuddling a Bye-Lo

Baby? I wasn't much for dolls, but I'd pretend for Aunt Carrie. She adored playing with them."

Sheila laughed. "Did you teach them to play the piano?"

Faith shook her head. "No, but I first started playing at Aunt Carrie's. That's one of the few things she told me about Rip—he learned to play on her old piano. She'd let me bang away long before Mother would. She had one of those round stools you turn around to raise, and I remember dragging myself up by the stomach onto that stool when it was nearly as tall as I was."

This was getting them far from the topic of the day.

"Did Honey ever tell you whether she went for those envelopes last Sunday?"

"Oh, yes! Tuesday morning she was sneezing, and said she'd gotten soaked Sunday going over to Elouisa's. And I'm sorry." Faith pressed one hand to her cheek in dismay. "She told me to call and tell you the papers weren't worth going after. 'Tell Sheila not to bother,' she told me. But I forgot until this minute. Sorry!"

"That's okay."

Was Honey lying because she knew (or suspected) what had happened to her stolen envelope? Because of what it contained? Or because the concussion had caused her to genuinely forget?

Faith wouldn't know. Better to move the conversation along. "Did she talk about Stack at all?"

Faith finished her coffee and set the mug on the coffee table with a thoughtful frown. "Not that I remember. Why?"

Sheila wished she could blurt, "She didn't happen to say he killed a man in Buckhead during World War Two?" Instead, she said carefully, "I wondered if after the party she'd gotten to thinking more about the war—what Stack did during it, how they met, things like that."

Faith grinned. "They probably met in diapers—or when Honey was in diapers, anyway. She was seven years younger than Stack, you know. How does anybody meet?"

Instantly Sheila was whisked through time and space to June, a Dunwoody cul-de-sac, where—in a crowd waiting for news about a murdered woman—she'd first met a tall man in mirror sunglasses with a lock of hair falling across his forehead. Resolutely she pulled her thoughts back to this dreary December day.

Isaac spoke formally at the door. "Luncheon is served."

For family meals and small parties, the Delacourts used the solarium at the back of the house. Its soft brick floor, two walls of glass, yellow swags patterned with pastel birds, and a cart of Gertie's vivid African violets were cheerful no matter what the season or weather.

Today, however, Isaac had put a round table beside the huge dining room's long front windows. He'd had to turn on the three-tiered crystal chandeliers because the rain and tall boxwoods eliminated most of the light, and even a screen around the table couldn't quite cut off the enormous emptiness beyond.

Sheila didn't know whose idea it was to eat so formally, but appreciated the someone who'd gone out in the icy rain to cut three blood-red Professor Sargent camellias to float in a crystal bowl on the creamy damask cloth.

When Honey pushed Rip's wheelchair into the room, Sheila's secret hopes for some restoration of their childhood friendship were dashed. He looked baffled, and she looked totally drained. Real Thing, padding at Honey's heels, looked sadder than usual. No one spoke as Honey wheeled him to the space reserved, chose the seat across the table, spread her napkin across her lap, and sank into a private reverie. Real Thing again flopped at her feet.

Rip gave Faith a quick look, both appraising and somehow shy, then ducked his head and began the tedious task of spreading his own napkin over his useless legs. Sheila guessed he was embarrassed at the rows he had inadvertently brought about. Faith fidgeted with her silver.

"Looks good, Gertie," Sheila told the cook, who ladled chowder into Royal Doulton gold-and-white bowls and set the tureen near Faith's plate. The words were almost lost in the big empty room. Gertie gave her a glum smile as Isaac brought in hot homemade biscuits and a salad, then they returned silently to the kitchen.

Looking at the small servings being offered and remembering the high-piled plates at Anthony's Sweet Auburn Barbe-que, Sheila wondered—not for the first time—why wealthy people serve such small portions. This morning, even after her huge breakfast, she could finish off almost everything on the table. Worry always made her hungry, and even if Aunt Mary hadn't killed anybody yesterday, what had she done back in the forties?

Her concern must have communicated itself to Faith, for after five minutes broken only by the musical clink of silver on china, she looked at Sheila and asked softly, "Shouldn't you tell them about Miss Mary? If she's in trouble—"

Sheila shook her head in warning. Then she gave Rip what she hoped was a reassuring smile. "She's not in trouble. She's probably in her element. Tell me," she addressed her host with more enthusiasm than she felt for the task, "how long have you known Aunt Mary?"

Rip seemed glad to turn away from his invited guests to the uninvited one. With something like his old zest he replied, "Long enough. —met just before the war. Something wrong?"

She ignored the question. "You met when she first came to Atlanta?" He nodded. She took a ragged breath and asked, "Was she dating anyone back then?"

Either she had alleviated his worry or he had already forgotten it, for he looked concerned only with buttering his biscuit without dropping it. Meanwhile Honey was breaking her own biscuit into tiny pieces and making little doughballs on her bread plate. "Engaged. —Frenchman she'd met in Berlin."

"Engaged?" Sheila nearly dropped her spoon in surprise.

Rip's eyes were on Honey's busy fingers. "Marc Dumier," he said absently. "Mary was crazy about him, until—" he raised his hand and let it flop, "—Dunkirk." He stopped, staring through the camellias to a past only he could see. At last he heaved a heavy sigh and his stroke-tied tongue tried valiantly to tell a complete story. "Sent Charles and me to . . . family before we shipped home. Hard—but . . . insisted. Kept in touch . . . years and years. Sent food parcels . . . visited couple of times." He shook his head and returned to his chowder. "Never cared a flip for anybody else."

"Why didn't I know all that?" Sheila asked the table at large.

He grunted disparagingly. "Prob'ly never asked. Kids! Think we're born same day you were." He gave Faith, who had not said a word, a mute nod of apology and bent his head over his bowl. Honey looked from one of them to the other, but said nothing.

Sheila, meanwhile, was mulling over what Rip had said. It was true. Except for a short time in Charleston,* she'd never given much thought to Aunt Mary's youth, or her parents' either. She was vowing to ask questions during the holidays with her parents when Faith asked, "Would you like more chowder, Rip?"

With shaking hands he gestured to his bowl. She lifted and filled it, set it painstakingly back in place. "Sheila and I were talking about your Aunt Carrie earlier. Did you know you and I learned to play on the same piano?"

Rip eyed her uneasily. His gaze slid to Honey. "That right?"

Faith bent her head to her own chowder as she replied, "Well, sort of. At least I played as a child on the piano you learned on."

He stopped eating and sat back in his chair. "So you like music. That's fine!" Sheila wondered if he had forgotten who Faith was, or that she had provided the music for his party last weekend.

Honey, meanwhile, had lifted her eyes and was watching him anxiously. "Rip—?"

She spoke just the one word, but it seemed to convey a whole message. He leaned forward and rested his weight on one forearm. "Okay, Honey. You eat, now—build up your strength." So far she had not taken a single bite.

Honey said with forced gaiety, "I'll eat if we don't have to talk about the past. Think of something else, somebody. Something up-to-date!" She fluttered the fingers of one hand

---

* *Murder in the Charleston Manner.*

through the air, and a few crumbs drifted onto Real Thing's wavy red-and-white back.

Sheila had opened her mouth to say "We could talk about last weekend, and those stolen envelopes" when the doorbell rang.

"It don't do no good to trifle with the Lord, 'cause if akse him for somethin' He likely to sen' mo' than you can handle."

Margaret Mitchell letter, July 21, 1945[16]

Isaac hurried from the kitchen to answer the door, greeting the guests in his usual soft rumble. At the sound of people in the foyer, Faith looked up curiously. Rip swore mildly. But Honey's white face turned a shade paler and her already enormous eyes widened in terror.

"I must go!" she cried, trying to rise. Her foot caught in the carpet under her chair, and she fell awkwardly back into her seat. "I have to go!" she insisted. "They mustn't see me!"

"Why, Honey!" The voice at the door was clear as a bell. "It's so good to see you up and about!"

Sheila saw first a shaft of light reflecting from the silver head of an ebony cane. Then Dorothy Davidson came into the room with her gentle shuffle-hop, graceful in a deep rose knitted ensemble with a striking pattern of gray leaves down the sweater front. She must have left her coat with Isaac.

Behind her, Winona, bundled to the nose in a bright green raincoat, sailed through the doorway.

"Come on in!" Rip waved his good arm and bellowed, "Isaac, bring chairs for Dotty and Winona! Want a Coke? Or coffee?" he asked his new guests. "Put a dent in the food, but—" he gestured at the almost empty table, "—welcome to what's left."

"We've eaten." Winona tramped toward the table and took up a position behind Honey's chair. Honey bent her head and began to eat her chowder, which was surely cold.

Isaac brought two more chairs from the long table at the far end of the room. "Would you ladies like some lunch?"

Dorothy took the chair he held behind her. "No, but coffee would be lovely."

"Nothing for me." Winona sank into the chair Isaac slid beneath her ample derriere and breathed as deeply as if she'd run a marathon. Her surprisingly little feet were encased to-day in rain-spattered violet suede. Where her coat gapped open, a violet suede skirt was stretched tight across her lap. It would have better suited young Clara than Winona's heavy thighs.

Winona took Honey's hand as if taking her pulse. "How are you, dear? Feeling better?"

Honey drew back slightly. "I'm a trifle woozy, still, and my memory's not completely back, but I'm much stronger."

"Want her to stay here," Rip growled. "Can't go home alone."

"Of course not," Dorothy agreed.

"You'd have to ask Philip," was Winona's opinion.

By then Isaac had brought Dorothy's coffee. He bent over Rip's chair. "How about if I serve everybody coffee in the library, sir? Fire's more cheerful than—" He gestured at the streaming windows on one side and the immense dining room on the other.

"Good idea." Rip rolled his chair back from the table. "Coffee for everybody?" As he started out of the room, Real

Thing rose and padded beside him. The others followed. Proceeding down the hall, Rip looked up at Dorothy. "What brought you here . . . day like this? I'd have thought . . . curled up with a dirty book."

"I don't read dirty books!" She gave him a teasing swat but did not, Sheila noticed, answer the question.

They took their places—Rip near the fire in the wheelchair, Honey and Winona on each end of the couch, Faith in the big wing chair Sheila had left near the window but which was now drawn nearer the fireside, Dorothy in the other wing chair across the hearth. When Sheila started to take the seat between Winona and Honey, Winona slid over to the center. "Here, I know you like to curl up in corners, and I want to sit next to Honey."

Honey gave her a weak smile.

Sheila had the oddest notion that Dorothy and Winona had come, like guardian angels, to stand between herself and Honey Norton. But which of them were they protecting? And why?

She got a partial answer almost immediately. "Fiddlesticks," said a familiar husky voice in the hall. "You don't need to announce us, Isaac. We'll just go on back."

"Oh, good," murmured Dorothy. Her relief was obvious.

Sheila grimaced. Now she knew who had sent Dorothy and Winona—just not why.

Aunt Mary entered followed by Charles, Philip and Lamar, her three aged musketeers. As Sheila looked around the room, a jump rope chant started in her head: *Murderer, bootlegger, partner, gay. Adulterer, mistress, who do you say?* She knew, or thought she did, who to say for each—if only she could be sure of Aunt Mary!

At the moment, her aunt was crossing the library carpet to say reproachfully to Honey. "We met Philip on the doorstep, and he said you were here. You promised to call me before you left the hospital!"

Honey raised one hand in wan salute. "I tried. You had guests, and they—" she lowered her arm and gracefully gestured toward Faith and Rip, "—said I should come here."

Aunt Mary swept the two with a considered look, then her eyes saw Sheila and became like black fire. "What on earth are *you* doing here? I told Mildred to tell you to go home. You have no business here. Go—!" She swept one arm toward the door like a diminutive Fury.

Sheila shook her head and said to the others, levelly, "We'll have to excuse Aunt Mary this afternoon. The police think she killed a man yesterday. Perhaps she did."

Silence.

Then babble. Dorothy's "Nonsense!" was drowned by a simultaneous "No!" from Winona and a roar from Rip: "What?" Charles patted air like an impotent teacher with an unruly kindergarten—"Now, now"—while Lamar cleared his throat above the din. Faith and Honey stared about them in bewilderment. Philip tugged at his tie as if it had suddenly slid up of its own volition to choke him.

Aunt Mary walked with the rigid dignity of royalty to a chair Isaac had brought from a corner and set beside Dorothy. She seated herself thoroughly on its firm cushion before saying coldly, "Sheila is exaggerating, as usual." Her chin was high in the air.

Sheila raised her own. "Was Lieutenant Owen Green in your apartment this morning?" Aunt Mary did not reply. "Did he tell you that your car was identified down at a housing project yesterday just before Sean Bagwell, a *Constitution* reporter, was shot there?" Still no answer. She chanced a direct hit. "Did he ask whether you committed a murder during World War Two?"

"No, she didn't!" Charles Davidson stepped fully into the room, smoothing the wisps of hair crossing his pink scalp. He dropped his hand to touch his mustache reassuringly. "I did."

Sheila nodded. Sunday night Dorothy had said that Charles's sister and her husband had come to lunch that day. He was the only one of the friends to have a sister during the war. And while she was surprised that he had summoned the passion to commit murder, she was not surprised that he had had the chivalry to defend his sister's honor when necessary.

Charles wasn't looking at Sheila. Instead, he had crossed the hearth to address his shocked wife. "I've been with Lamar this past hour setting down a confession, dear. I don't know what it will mean for me, but you will be amply provided for." He shook his head. "You cannot know what a relief it is to have it in the open." He peered about him for a chair.

Isaac, stunned as the others, recovered enough to shove the desk chair in next to Faith. Charles folded his long legs and perched stiffly on the very edge of it, contemplating liver spots on the backs of his folded hands. Isaac hurried from the room. He returned with straight chairs for Philip and Lamar. These he set at each end of the couch, making a rough semicircle around the hearth. Then he shuffled out, a shaken man.

"Was it a sergeant?" Sheila asked, calm amid the agitated silence of the others. "Someone who insulted your sister Meredith?"

Charles peered at her through bushy brows, without lifting his head. "I've always suspected you were half witch, Sheila. He was a private, but otherwise you've got it right."

"Did it happen here, during your engagement party?"

"No!" Dorothy gasped, but Charles nodded.

"I'm sorry, my dear," he said heavily.

Dorothy stood. "Change seats with me, Faith. I want to sit next to my husband!" She moved to the other wing chair and took his hands in both of hers. "Imagine!" she said, "You, Charles!"

He bit his lips and gave her a look of mute shame, but she returned a smile of frank admiration. "I never would have thought—for Meredith? Imagine—Charles!" She beamed at each of the room's occupants in turn.

Baffled, but flushing with pleasure at the unexpected, implied praise, he finally lifted his head and looked Sheila fully in the eye. "How did you know?"

It was time to tell them. "I've read what Walter calls 'the purported Margaret Mitchell manuscript.' "Whoever wrote it, it's about World War Two, not the Civil War, and the author had a similar murder in one chapter Elouisa stole."

She was not surprised when they all glanced quickly at one another, as if assessing possible future revelations. She was surprised, however, that at least one of them—an innocent one—did not ask the obvious question: What else was in it?

Rip broke the silence. "Got it here?"

"No."

His eyes were shrewd, reminding her of days when he had built and run a corporation. "Any way . . . convince you to burn it?"

"Sheila—" Aunt Mary began, but Rip waved her to silence.

"Shush, Mary. Let her answer. Burn it, Sheila? Bury old sins?"

Lamar shifted in his seat, as if about to speak, but said nothing. Sheila sighed. "It's not old sins that bother me, Rip, but recent ones. Two men tried to bring me that manuscript this week. Both were shot and killed."

Again a hubbub of dismay and disbelief filled the room. Above it, Philip asked, "You're sure their deaths were connected with the manuscript?" The doctor's voice was a little hoarse, his cheeks pale above his silver beard.

"Come over here, Philip." Winona moved closer to Honey, leaving a space between her and Sheila barely large enough for her slight husband. He shook his head, and remained where he was.

Meanwhile, Aunt Mary seared Sheila with a look of pure indignation. "Of course she isn't! Sheila, I beg you, forget this nonsense and go on home. Surely you have laundry to do after three days out of town."

Sheila sighed. "Do you want to tell us why your car was at that housing project yesterday?"

Aunt Mary's lips settled into a thin line.

Charles leaned forward and gave Sheila a weary look. "Maybe you'd better tell us what else was in the manuscript."

•   •   •

When she'd finished, Faith drew her brows together. "That doesn't sound like enough to construct a whole book from. Why should it threaten anybody?"

"That's what I wondered, too," Sheila agreed.

Nobody else spoke until Honey, bending to contemplate jewel-like flowers in a milk glass bowl on the coffee table, murmured softly, "The mills of God."

Sheila leaned across Winona, uncertain she'd heard correctly. "I beg your pardon?"

Philip nodded and said gruffly, "All coming round at one time. I've felt it for several days—haven't you?" He looked around the room. Rip gave a small nod. Charles did likewise. Honey gnawed her lip. Dorothy looked at the floor. Winona was busy scratching a small scab on the back of one plump hand. When no one else spoke, Philip continued, almost as if talking to himself. "Too much happening for coincidence. Not just the manuscript, either."

Charles gave a curt bark of laughter. "A general coincidental stirring of conscience."

Faith spoke thoughtfully. "One archbishop said, 'When I pray, coincidences happen.' "

Rip grunted. "Nobody prayed for this." He wheeled his chair around to face the window. "Looking for confessions, Sheila? Why you're here?" he asked without turning around.

"No, Rip. I don't know why I'm here. The soldiers in the story aren't necessarily any of you, but nobody except the people here knew about the manuscript, so who else could have killed—"

"My friends aren't killers!" His roar was so like the old Rip that she instinctively recoiled as she had years ago whenever he'd lost that famous temper. "Let 'er rip!" had real meaning for Rippen Delacourt's friends.

Then, unexpectedly, he continued mildly, "Got one more story right, though. Stack bootlegged in north Georgia durin' the war." At a sound halfway between a gasp and a gurgle, he turned. "Now, Honey, don't look like that. Shockin', but before your time."

But she was laughing, eyes twinkling. "Oh, Rip, I'm not shocked, just surprised. Fort Mac should never've put Stack in charge of liquor if they didn't want some of it siphoned off!"

Lamar's light chuckle rippled. "Damned right." He turned to Sheila. "Stack just stole a little, used profits to set up the business. Bought at army rates, sold high. Made a tidy little pile. Went on until a scandal broke. They caught a spy on the base, and Stack shut down. Didn't want 'em thinkin' *that* was what he was doing." He stopped, then recalled there was something he'd forgotten. "Put back what he took, though—first thing. Stack wasn't a thief, just a—"

"Wheeler-dealer?" Sheila suggested wryly. "You said much the same thing last night."

" 'S true." Rip scratched his nose. "Give Stack a half-open door, always pushed through."

"Who knew he was doing it?"

"Hell, Sheila." Rip again. "Everybody knew. All of us, anyway."

"Who drove for him after he lost his license?"

When she'd asked, she realized she didn't want to know. She was afraid she knew the answer.

Instead, Dorothy leaned forward. Fluffing her already perfect hair, she gave Sheila a smile both dazzling and intimate. "I did. Did you know that, Charles?" Obviously astonished, he shook his head. She twinkled at him, "I quit after we got engaged—got scared you'd find out, and I knew what a stickler you are for propriety. I didn't want to lose you! But I made one last run, to pay for our wedding. Going down the aisle I looked at you up front, so proper and solemn, and wondered what you'd do if you knew the whole shebang had been paid for by bootlegging. Instead, all the time, you—"

He lifted her hands, which still clasped his, to his lips in a kiss both gallant and sorrowful. "Solemn, Dorothy, but not very proper. Not proper at all."

Her voice was soft. "A hothead and a bootlegger, that's what we are. What's going to happen to you?"

"Nothin'." Lamar spoke with confidence. "We'll get Meredith to testify, show clear provocation. That manuscript might even help, Sheila. I'll want a look at it."

Dorothy and Charles were still speaking softly. ". . . only another fifty years," she said, then became aware everyone was listening. For the first time since Sheila had known her, the poised Dorothy Davidson blushed. Then she stood, leaning slightly on her silver cane. "My car's here, Charles." She turned to the others, her eyes sparkling like a girl's. "I think, if you all don't mind, we'll be goin'. We have some talkin' to do." She left, Charles at her elbow.

Lamar also stood. "I think I ought to be goin', too. Got some work to do on Charles's case before it's ready to present." He waved to the room at large and took himself off.

When they'd gone, Rip turned back to the room. "Didn't know Stack roped Dotty in, but should have guessed. Always liked fast cars—like her daddy." He chuckled.

In the silence that followed, Philip stood. "I want to tell you all something, too. Something that may become public soon." He spread his hands, then rubbed them rapidly together as if generating energy for what lay ahead.

"Peggy—or whoever wrote that book—got something else right. The young intelligence officer seduced by his superior."

Winona uttered a short cry and half rose. He waved at her as if to push her back, and continued. "Except it wasn't an intelligence officer, it was a young doctor, and he wasn't seduced, he was, well, willing. Mama had just died, and—" He turned his back to them and spoke to a small china shepherdess on the mantelpiece. "It all came back to haunt me last Saturday, when I read that my old friend is dying of AIDS in D.C. I went up Wednesday night. Ran into Sheila at the airport coming back Thursday, as a matter of fact. I was up arranging for him to be transferred here, under my care." Someone gasped, but he didn't turn to see who it was. He was addressing the shepherdess again, his voice low, as if only he and the delicate, china girl were present. "It was long ago, but I owe him that much. He meant everything to me for a while." He turned back to the others. "When it ended, I . . . I wound up in the psychiatric ward of a naval hospital. Winona nursed me—" He broke off, bewildered. "What on earth is the matter with you?"

The others followed his gaze, and saw that Winona had turned a deep puce. Her green eyes bulged with fury. "How

—dare—you?" she raged, her voice harsh and ragged. Tears ran down her cheeks, making mascara trails through the rouge. "How *dare* you? Pouring out your confession like some schoolboy caught peeking in the girls' dormitory window, while I . . . I've spent my *life*—Have you no pride? Have you no shame?" Her thick body crumpled, racked with ugly, rasping sobs.

Sheila had guessed about Philip. Charles had killed the soldier, Stack had sold liquor, and Lamar and Rip—she'd eliminated them, too. But it had never occurred to her that Winona knew. That massive gossip who never kept anybody's secrets? How had she managed to live for years with such momentous ones and never give out a single clue?

"I'm grateful, Winona," Philip said gruffly, frowning at her unseemly display of emotion. "I was about to say I'm grateful."

"Grateful?" Her voice was full of venom. "Grateful is *nothing*!"

He reared back, offended. "I've given you my life, the boys, everything you've ever asked for. What more did you want?"

Aunt Mary coughed gently. "Winona is talking not about something she wanted, but something she's done lately, aren't you, dear?"

Sheila held her breath. So Aunt Mary had not been as impervious to what was going on as she had led Sheila to believe! The others gaped mutely at Winona. Even Philip had lost his voice.

Winona's sobs continued. Spasms gripped her stout shoulders. Finally she managed to nod and gasp, "For nothing! All for nothing." She stood and stumbled from the room, tears streaming down her fat, splotched face. In a moment they heard a car start and roar down the drive.

Philip watched her go like a man dazed. "She took my car!" he exclaimed, amazed. "What on earth has she done to make her act like that?"

Aunt Mary said softly, "Honey must have called her—"

"I called Philip." It was the first time Honey had spoken for quite a while, and her whole body was trembling. She put one hand to her bandaged forehead, as if struggling to remember. "I had gone to Elouisa's, and managed to get one chapter of the manuscript. The last chapter, I think. And it—it was about me!"

"You? Why should you think it was you?" Faith demanded.

"Never mind why. It was my story," Honey said stubbornly. "I didn't know what to do. I wanted to burn it—like you said, Rip. But if it was really a valuable manuscript, I didn't like to destroy it. So I thought you might know, Philip, if you can stipulate that something not be published until after your death."

"Why Philip?" Faith persisted. "Why not Lamar? He's a lawyer."

"Because Philip knew," Honey said simply. "He was the only one who did. But he'd gone to make rounds. I didn't like to tell Winona, so I just said I'd gotten the papers and they were about when Philip and I were young. Winona said she'd send Philip. But then she came herself, wanted to see the pages. I didn't want her to see them, but she tried to take them, and—I don't remember any more." She buried her face in her hands.

"Good God!" Philip's face was ashen. "She hit you? Left you unconscious? You could have died!"

"Think like a husband, not just a doctor, Max," Aunt Mary said sharply. "Winona was protecting *you*. She worships you, you know."

He bent his silver head. "And I've let her, to my eternal shame. Did you suspect, Mary? Could you possibly have suspected Winona of harming Honey?"

His old friend nodded, but it was to Sheila that she spoke. "I knew in the corridor Sunday that it wasn't any of us, and I'd been to Honey's to pick her up Saturday night and seen that her apartment has good security. It was very unlikely that she had let in an intruder. Eventually I realized that the most likely person it could have been was Winona."

Sheila nodded. She'd reached the same conclusion. Mary continued, "I felt sure she must have done what she did thinking to protect you, Philip and I was afraid she'd still try to silence Honey if she could."

Philip rubbed his eyes. "I hope I wake up in a minute and none of this ever happened."

The others silently agreed. Rip turned his chair once again toward the window, shutting them all out. Aunt Mary and Sheila both looked into the fire, while Honey sat like an alabaster statue. Tears streamed down her cheeks.

Faith rose and went to her. "You need to rest, Honey. Come home with me. I'll put you to bed, and—"

"No!" It was a scream from the pits of hell. "I will never go into that woman's house again! After she told Peggy—exposed me—"

"Exposed what?" Faith spoke soothingly, still trying to protect her big sister. "Nothing you did as a girl could possibly matter after all these years. Come home!"

Honey didn't move. Her large gray eyes were fixed on Faith with despair and horror.

Sheila caught Aunt Mary's gaze and understood, finally, why her aunt had desperately tried to prevent her from being here. As one by one her childhood giants toppled, she felt as if she were standing on a plain watching Mount Olympus crumble. She yearned to jump up and dash elsewhere—*anywhere*—before the final collapse, but she'd waited too long to leave.

Honey licked her lips and looked imploringly at Aunt Mary. "Do you know?" Then at Philip. "Does everybody know?"

Aunt Mary nodded, but "I don't know," Faith said flatly. "Maybe I don't *need* to know—whatever it is. What I *do* know is that you are letting an old quarrel with Mother deprive you of—"

"She wasn't your mother!" Honey blazed. "*I* am your mother! We went up to North Carolina for you to be born, and when we came back she told everybody she'd had a baby. But it was *my* baby," she clapped one fist to her breast, "my own little baby, and she never let me . . . never let me . . ." She stopped, her chest heaving.

Color flooded Faith's square cheeks. She shrank as if to contract herself away from the words and the pain. "That's monstrous—and not true!" Her eyes raked the room, came to rest on Philip.

He nodded his silver head and said gruffly, "I'm afraid it is, Faith. I confirmed the pregnancy myself."

"Then who—not Daddy!—?" She could not go on. She dropped to the couch and looked toward the window for escape. What she found instead was a square face suffused with guilt, and a pair of eyes very like her own. They regarded her with compassion. "You?" She leaned toward Rip and said it again, incredulous. *"You?"*

He nodded. "Came home for Thanksgiving, just before shipping out overseas." He lowered his eyes to his lap, where his good hand was playing with the useless fingers of his crippled one. "Georgia had the flu, and Honey was so sweet—"

All color drained from Faith's face, leaving only the freckles and her large dark eyes. "This is monstrous," she repeated in a whisper. "Mama, Daddy . . ."

"You haven't lost them, dear," Aunt Mary reminded her.

Faith shook her head and dropped her face into her hands. The room grew so silent it could have been empty. A log fell in the fireplace. Real Thing raised his mottled head and waited to see what would happen next in the unpredictable world of humans.

"I've seen my birth certificate," Faith protested, still not believing. "You can't fake something like that!"

Honey's laugh was brittle and without humor. "We didn't have to. I was named for Mama, and born on her birthday. When they came for the information, she took the form and filled it out, giving Daddy's name as the father. She wrote in her own birth year, and I signed it. Nobody asked if it was right. They were short-staffed, you see, with the war."

"But why did I never know?" Faith's voice was almost a whisper. "Why didn't you tell me?" She shoved back her thick red hair.

Honey's lips twisted into a parody of a smile. "I couldn't. I promised Mama and Daddy at the beginning, when I was scared and—" she looked quickly at Rip, then back to her hands "—alone. First they said I must give the baby away, but then they said they'd raise you, if I would never try to get you back. They made me promise—and I was so desperate not to lose you, I agreed. Later, after I got married, I *begged* Mama to let me have you. I wanted you so much! And you were tiny. You wouldn't have remembered those first two years. But Mama said Stack would divorce me for trash, and Daddy reminded me I'd promised." She took a deep, ragged breath and hurried on. "After Stack died, I begged her again. You'll never know how I begged." Her chest heaved, and she raised a sodden, flushed face. "But Mama said again I must keep my promise, for your sake. She said—she said it would ruin your life if you knew. *And now it has!*" She wept.

Faith touched her lightly, then drew her hand back as if from scorching heat. She turned to confront Rip. "But you— you—?" She stopped, not even knowing yet what she wanted to ask.

He jutted out his lower lip. "I didn't know until this afternoon. I swear it."

Honey's voice was barely audible. "I wrote—"

"Never got it. I told you!" He wheeled his chair toward her, then stopped. "Maybe—" he shook his head. "Maybe the letter got lost."

She shook her head and raised a tear-streaked face to his. "I wrote every week! They couldn't *all* get lost!"

"I wrote, too," Rip said in the tone of one who has said it before. "You didn't get my letters—"

Aunt Mary cocked her head to one side, as if in thought. "I wonder," she mused aloud, looking into the fire, "if Maud and Carrie may have intercepted the mail."

"Aunt Carrie?" The words burst simultaneously from Rip and Faith. Honey looked shocked.

Aunt Mary addressed Rip. "She was the one person Maud might have confided in, and I was just remembering how much attention she always paid Faith. They each thought the world of you, and of Honey, too. But they also loved Fancy, Delaney, and Georgia. If they intercepted your letters, they no doubt thought they were doing it for the best."

"But how could they?" Honey pleaded, compelling Aunt Mary to look at her by her very intensity. "Rip was in France."

Aunt Mary tilted her silver head to one side. "I suspect they must have taken Charles into their confidence, at least a bit. Told him you were corresponding and it wasn't wise, perhaps. Didn't you say last week, Rip, that Charles fetched your mail in France?"

Rip nodded soberly. "Offered right after we got there. Went every day. I never thought—" He wheeled abruptly back to the window, visibly shocked to the core by that betrayal.

Honey rose, went to stand behind him, and laid a gentle hand on his shoulder. "If he did it, Rip, he did it because he cared for you. Charles is an honorable man." Rip put up a hand and clasped hers, but did not reply.

"Maud and Carrie were honorable women, too," Aunt Mary said. "They both aged after the war. Several people mentioned that. We will never know what it cost them to keep you apart."

"Mama stopped loving me." Honey spoke wistfully, her thoughts far away.

Faith pressed two fingers to her lips, then took them down and shook her head. "She always cried on your birthday. She had your picture beside her bed when she died."

Silent tears streamed down Honey's elegant cheekbones.

Aunt Mary spoke briskly. "Maud's courage matched her convictions. It so seldom does."

"But when Rip came back, when Stack died, when Georgia died—why . . . ?" Faith stopped, as if unsure how to frame the question.

Honey looked at Rip, her face pensive, but she said nothing.

He turned his chair and faced his newfound daughter. "When I got back, Honey was married." His voice revealed the desolation he must have felt. "Hadn't heard from her, didn't know—thought . . . hadn't really cared."

"Not cared!" The cry was wrung from Honey, but Aunt Mary waved her to be quiet. Rip continued as if he had not heard.

"Saw her—parties, Driving Club—across a room. Never spoke, never acted like she knew I was alive."

"I knew," Honey said, her bandaged head bent toward

him. She timidly stroked his hair. "I thought you were sorry—"

He patted her arm to quiet her. "Never, Honey. Never." He sighed. "Georgia—muddled along, best we could. Then, several years later, had Walt. Had given up on kids. Later, Georgia got sick, died—" He sighed again and smiled sadly up at the woman beside him. "Thought about calling, many times. Kept your number in my wallet. Never got the nerve. Thought you didn't care." He shook his head and said one sentence distinctly. "Years have a way of passing, whatever you do."

His voice ground to a halt. Honey gave him one final pat and returned to her seat beside Faith. Faith moved a bit more toward the center, as if not yet able to sit so near. Philip, shifting in his chair, caught Rip's attention. "You knew? All these years?" Rip growled.

"Not who the father was. She never told."

"Never?" Rip asked Honey.

She shook her head. "Only Mama, and only then because she kept worrying that the man had—wasn't clean. She worried on and on about that the day I told her I was pregnant, until finally I got angry. . . ."

Her voice trailed off. There seemed to be nothing further to say. They all sat in silence, then, listening to the rain drumming on the boxwoods, the fire crackling on the hearth, and the thoughts of their own hearts. Honey and Faith both wept silently, unashamed. Sheila brushed a tear from her own cheek, and noticed Rip surreptitiously doing the same. Philip's head was clasped between his hands. And Aunt Mary? She was fumbling in her purse for something.

Sheila sneaked a look at her watch, and was about to stand and make her farewells when Real Thing raised his head for a gentle "Woof."

Walter walked in. He lifted his hand to hold the left side of his glasses and peered about the room. "A party! Why wasn't I invited?"

"It's a grown-up party," Aunt Mary informed him with dignity. Sheila knew she was trying to draw his attention away from the sodden duo on the sofa.

Grateful that she could both help and achieve her own

ends, she herself stood. "I'm a gate-crasher, too, Walt, and was just leaving. Walk me to my car?"

On the way down the hall, she asked (just for something to say), "Is it tonight you and Clara go see *A Christmas Carol*?"

He nodded gloomily. "You know, Sheila, that woman is going to kill me."

"Nonsense!" She reached into the closet by the door for her raincoat. "She's good for you."

He shook his head. "The only woman who was good for me was Yvonne. She was helpless—needed my protection. Clara wears me out."

Sheila laughed. "Good for her! And be honest, Walt. Yvonne could take care of herself. That shy helplessness was an act, and ought to have taught you something: Real people don't need protecting. Or—" thinking of Rip and Honey "—some do, but only because they've been terribly wounded. Be gentle with your dad tonight," she added.

He took her coat and held it for her, about a foot too high. "I know about wounded people," he said stiffly. "My poor mama—"

She sighed. "Lower, please. My shoulder's sore." As she buttoned the coat, she said bluntly, "Your mother is dead, Walt. So is Yvonne. Clara is alive, and if I'm not mistaken, she's misguided enough to be falling in love with you. Poor girl, I hope she gets over it."

She turned to go, but he grabbed her arm—her sore one. When she cried out in pain, Walt let go, but braced his hand against the door to block her exit.

"Why? Why do you hope she gets over it?"

"Because you'd probably spend your life trying to change her. Delaney Winwood, from what I've heard, devoted his marriage to toning down Fancy's liveliness. Your mother wore herself out trying to remake Rip in her father's image. They both married wonderful, vibrant people, then did their best to stamp out that vitality. Did your mother ever, just once, laugh at your father's jokes? No. She spent her life outraged by Rip, and finally died of outrage—just like her father."

"They had bad hearts," Walt replied hotly.

"*Hard* ones," Sheila replied with equal heat. "Unless you can learn to enjoy Clara, don't marry her. You'll die of outrage, too." She jerked open the door and headed into the welcome coolness of the rain.

Walt shrugged as he opened an umbrella and held it over her. "So see? We're back where we started. That girl is going to kill me."

But as he held her car door and slammed it behind her, Sheila noticed a certain lightness in his face she had never seen there before.

She, on the other hand, contemplating the gloomy, streaming drive back to her apartment, felt as though the clouds above would press her into the earth itself. The whole exhausting afternoon had not smoked out one motive worth killing for. Would she get a second chance?

"Even in her lifetime many Atlantans had not known what to do with Margaret Mitchell. The problem grew with time."[17]

Sheila drove around to Rip's kitchen entrance. Beyond the back door was a round pea-gravel courtyard surrounding a black fountain Fancy Winwood had ordered in Italy years ago. Today the half-clad nymph in the fountain's center, poised on one toe with slender arms outstretched, seemed ready to fly back to Calabria out of the freezing rain.

As Sheila had expected, Aunt Mary's silver Cadillac sat in the courtyard, Jason reading at the wheel. Gertie and Isaac would have invited him in, but Jason usually preferred his own company and a book. She climbed out of her car and dashed to the other, sliding into the front passenger seat before he knew she was there.

"Hello." She wiped rain from her face.

"Is Miss Mary coming?" He tucked the book down beside him and bent toward the ignition.

"Not yet, just me, and I'm only staying a minute—long enough for you to tell me exactly what happened yesterday afternoon. And," she added as he started to shake his head, "don't give me any more high-and-mighty business. I have to know."

His dark, handsome face grew sullen. "I told you. I went on an errand for Miss Mary."

"To get the oil changed." A muscle tightened by his mouth, the only indication she had surprised him. "Where did you go after that?"

He stared over the steering wheel without a word, his jaw rigid.

"You were free after the oil change," Sheila pressed him. "Did you stop somewhere for a Coke or a beer?"

He glared across the few feet separating them. "So what if I did? What difference does it make to you?"

"Not to me, Jason, to Aunt Mary. Somebody borrowed her car, didn't they?" Shifting to look out the side window at the water streaming down Fancy Winwood's freezing nymph, she asked casually, "What did they do, knock you out?" She turned quickly enough to see his nostrils flare and knew she had scored another hit.

"Not in a fair fight, surely," she persisted, deliberately massaging his ego. Jason worked out every day, was proud of his body. "Was it something in your drink?" His sullen silence was her answer.

She leaned toward him. "Have you told Aunt Mary, Jason? You may be shielding a murderer."

"He wasn't a murderer, he was a *thief*! If he'd wanted to murder me, he—" Jason pounded the steering wheel and bellowed, "Look, I don't know who it was! The bar was full of guys—drinking, talking, watching a game on television, passing the afternoon. Nobody special, nobody I knew, nobody who knew me. So I order a second beer, they pass it down the bar. Okay? I didn't see anybody put anything in it, but the next thing I know, I'm waking up in the back seat 'way down near Grant Park. That's all I know. Except it was nearly dark, my wallet and all my money were gone, and I felt like I'd been run over by a ten-ton truck. But look, Sheila, I've given this some thought." The old Jason again— quick, eager, and, she was relieved to note, friendly. He'd finally forgiven her for having to walk her dog.

"What did you think?" she asked, really wanting to know.

"Well, Grant Park's not too far from that project where the body was found. Maybe the fellow stopped there to roll me. Maybe we were the two guys the witness saw in the car. Maybe Miss Mary's car being near where that murder happened was sheer coincidence."

It made sense. She told him so. She even half believed it. Maybe, she thought wearily, gritting her teeth against the pain in her shoulder, it had been an entire blessed week of coincidence.

Sheila drove home slowly, fighting a depression that threatened to engulf her. Only part of her mood was weariness. Part was the crumbling of old idols. And part was a dread of what else might crumble if the murderer was ever unmasked.

As her black Maxima climbed the hill toward home, however, her heart lurched. Crispin's Jag sat in her visitor's space! Was he able to drive? Had he come home early?

A welcome-home light shone in her living room window. Smoke snaked from her chimney through the rain. Eagerly she turned off the engine and mentally surveyed her larder. Thank heavens Crispin was a man who wouldn't mind a grilled cheese sandwich and canned black bean soup laced with sherry and sour cream. Once inside, she need not go out again.

Ignoring the pain in her shoulder and postponing all thoughts of manuscript and murder, she dashed through the downpour and took the steps two at a time.

Below, another car pulled into a vacant space. She scarcely noticed.

So engrossed was she in getting inside that she didn't hear stealthy steps behind her. She had her key in the lock when the muzzle of a gun nudged her neck. "Okay, lady, where are them envelopes?"

Demolinius.

Numb with shock, Sheila could scarcely speak—much less think how, with one weak, sore shoulder, she could possibly disarm him. But what about Crispin, scarcely able to walk, waiting inside?

"They're . . . they're at a lawyer's." Knowing what a poor liar she was, she willed him to believe her. She also spoke a trifle louder than necessary, hoping Crispin would forego heroics and call the police. "I took them by this afternoon."

"Hunh-uh, lady. I was at your aunt's place when you called Mildred. I heard you say you were staying for lunch at Mr. Delacourt's. Lordy! I remember that house from 'way back!" Demolinius crowed in self-congratulation. "So I went straight up to Buckhead to wait and follow you. You ain't been to no lawyer's. Where're them envelopes?" The gun pressed closer for emphasis.

Inside the apartment, the sheltie began to whine at the door.

"Look, Demolinius," Sheila tried desperately, "those envelopes don't belong to me or to you. They belong—"

"They belong to whoever's got 'em," he said flatly, giving her another ungentle shove with the gun. "I mean to make sure that's me. Now come on, open that door." He shoved her again.

What could she do but turn the key?

Inside, Lady danced around her feet, yipping nervously with a trace of embarrassment. The smell of wood smoke and coffee filled the hall. So did another, less pleasant odor. No wonder the sheltie was embarrassed. Seeing the intruder, she backed up and growled.

"It's okay, Lady," Sheila said hastily. She certainly didn't want a dead dog. Lady, living up to her name, immediately stopped growling. She wagged her tail at the unexpected guest.

"Move!" Demolinius ordered. Together they went down the short hall beside the galley kitchen toward the living room at the back. Then Sheila stopped, as speechless with surprise as she had been earlier with shock. Lamar Whitehead sat on one of her dining room chairs before a merry fire. In one hand he held a sheaf of paper from the Mitchell manuscript.

Instinctively, Sheila glanced to the coffee table and gasped in dismay. She felt sick in the pit of her stomach. Of the two stacks—original and copies—she had left there, only one original envelope remained. As Sheila and Demolinius entered, Lamar fed another precious page to the greedy blaze.

With an oath, Demolinius shoved Sheila aside and leapt toward Lamar. He landed instead on the dog's pile on the carpet, skidded, slipped crazily, and fell. The gun skittered from his hand and slid across the carpet toward Lamar. Lady went into a frenzy of barking.

Lamar bent with difficulty to retrieve the weapon. Puffing with exertion, he stood and said querulously, "Sheila, pen up that yapping animal and clean up her mess!"

Pain clawed her injured shoulder as Sheila shoved the wiggling, protesting sheltie through the study door. She considered following and shutting the door behind them both, but only for an instant. The door was hollow and had no lock. Besides, Demolinius no longer had the gun.

But what she heard behind her was not reassuring. "What you doing here?" Lamar demanded softly. "I told you to meet me downtown at six."

"I'll be there by six," Demolinius said sullenly. "This lady's got sumpin' I want, first. Sumpin' belongs to me."

"What's that?" Lamar's tone was mild and curious.

Sheila turned back in time to see Demolinius pull himself to his knees and reach for the dirty envelope that still lay on the coffee table. "Them papers. They's mine."

"Don't be ridiculous." Lamar waved him back with the gun. "Those papers have nothing to do with you. Now get up, boy, and take off that shirt. You stink of dog doo."

Gingerly, Demolinius pulled the stained shirt over his head. His bare chest and shoulders, like his face, were a map of past fights. He wadded the shirt and flung it toward the kitchen, sent an equally offensive shoe after it, then crouched on the carpet, eying Lamar warily. His fingers convulsed and opened against his chest.

Lamar still held the gun.

He had not bothered to pull the blinds. On the far wall, two large windows showed a late afternoon as charcoal as dusk. Rain slanted onto a small lake down the hill. Rain also pelted the sliding doors leading to the deck, its *scritchy-scratch* the only sound in a room that was too bright, too hot, too charged—in spite of Lamar's apparent mildness—with dangerous emotion. From outside, Sheila thought flippantly, this room would be lit up like the set of a badly produced play—except they were two stories above the audience. Nobody could see the actors.

Nobody had given her a script, either. She would have to improvise.

She could not keep her hands or knees from trembling, but years of embassy parties had given her good control of her voice. It was perfectly level and merely curious as she said, "I didn't realize you knew Mildred's brother, Lamar." She leaned against the closed study door as if chatting with two about-to-leave visitors. As if all her visitors held guns while saying farewell.

Lamar's glasses twinkled in the firelight. Above a blue bow tie his face was cherub pink. "Oh, yes, Demolinius and I go way back, and he's done a bit of work for me these past few days."

Work like killing Sean Bagwell? Work like accosting her in the parking lot last night? But why should Lamar Whitehead try to prevent her from getting the manuscript?

And why should Lamar destroy it now?

Even as her common sense was urging her to simply ease these unwelcome guests out the door, she wanted answers. To get answers, she would have to keep Lamar talking—which shouldn't be difficult. Always garrulous, he had gotten around to ". . . used to work for Stack, too. Did some driving for him, didn't you, Linus?"

Demolinius still crouched on the floor, seething with silent fury. He nodded abruptly; his eyes were locked on the papers in Lamar's hand.

The other two played out the act as if he were not there.

Sheila forced her legs to carry her casually from the study door to the wall between the kitchen and the living room, a trifle nearer the coffee table. "How did you get in, Lamar?" she asked pleasantly.

He beamed a five-hundred-watt smile and nodded toward a key on the coffee table, sitting beside a half-full mug of coffee. "I played a little trick on you, honey. Made an impression when I let you in last evenin' and had a copy made this mornin'." His look was almost boyishly sheepish. "I'd hoped I could run by while you were at work today and take a quick peek at Peggy's papers." He paused, waiting for —what? Approval? Praise? When she said nothing, he confided, "I was a bit taken aback to find you at Rip's, but then right after I got back to my office, the mechanic called to say your friend's car was ready. I decided to bring it over to surprise you—and snatch a look at the papers while I was here. But I didn't expect you so soon. I thought you were going to Mary's for dinner."

"Did you pay for Crispin's car?" *Keep him talking!*

"Oh, yes, but don't worry about that, honey. He can make that right whenever he wants to." He nodded past her toward the kitchen and added apologetically, "I made myself at home. Saw you had a pot of coffee, so I heated it up and had a cup. Hope you didn't mind."

"No, that's fine." Drinking somebody's coffee was nothing when you'd already let yourself into their house. He hadn't apologized for that, she noticed.

"Good. You make great coffee, Sheila." He set down the papers, picked up the mug, and took an appreciative sip.

She yearned for a cup so badly she could almost taste it, but to get coffee, she'd have to turn her back on the remaining Mitchell pages. Was that what Lamar hoped? He seemed to be waiting for something. Or was he, like she, improvising —wondering what to do with the rattlesnake at the other end of his gun?

Impulsively, she decided to test that theory. "Shall I call

the police to pick up Demolinius?" She half turned toward the kitchen phone.

"You don't need to do that, honey." Lamar gestured idly toward Demolinius with the weapon. "Just wait outside, Linus. I'll be ready as soon as I finish my little job in here." He picked up the sheaf of pages remaining in the next-to-last chapter. "There's nothing in this manuscript worth bothering the Mitchell lawyers about, Sheila. I doubt if Peggy Mitchell even wrote it. We might as well burn the silly thing and save everybody a heap of trouble." He turned deliberately toward the licking flames.

Before Sheila could protest, Demolinius scuttled across the rug. "You cain' burn them papers, Mr. Lamar! You cain'!"

Lamar got to his feet. "Co'se I can. Just watch." And with that, he flung the remaining pages he held onto the burning logs. Flames spurted up to embrace them.

"No!" Demolinius launched himself toward the pyre.

Lamar fired.

Demolinius's back arched. He twitched, and was still.

Lamar stood like a man of ice, only his eyes moving waiting for—what? An outcry? A horde of curious neighbors at the door? Sheila wished with all her heart that they would come, boiling with curiosity and outrage. But she knew the shot had gone unheard. In midafternoon, all her neighbors would be at work.

Lamar must have reached the same conclusion. "My, my!" He wiped the barrel of the gun on his trousers, "Did you see that? The booger was coming for me! Made me shoot him in self-defense."

"I—we'd better call the police and tell them so." Would she reach the phone before she started to throw up? Could she even walk? Her knees were rubber.

"In just a minute, Sheila." Lamar bent toward the one remaining chapter.

"No!" Without thinking, Sheila lunged and kicked the envelope to the far end of the room, beyond his reach. Then she froze. For Lamar had raised Demolinius's gun to point it straight at her. He held the gun with both hands because he, too, was shaking.

They confronted one another for a very long minute. Then he lowered the gun and ducked his gray crew cut apologetically. "Sorry, honey," he said softly. "I don't know what came over me."

"I think you'd better go," she said as evenly as she could. "I'll call the police about Demolinius when you are gone."

He held up the gun—not to aim it, but as if to remind them both that he had it. "I want you to burn that envelope first, Sheila. Please."

She would always wonder where she got the courage—or folly—to shake her head. "It isn't mine to burn, Lamar." Without taking her eyes off him she edged toward the sofa, lowered herself on the far cushion, retrieved the battered envelope, and shoved it beneath her.

He lowered the gun and raised his other hand as if he were arguing a case before some imagined bench. "I knew Peggy Marsh, Sheila. Personally! She was a *private* person, would have wanted—"

Sheila was suddenly extremely tired of this charade. "Peggy, schmeggy, Lamar! Who can say what Margaret Mitchell or any other writer would want fifty years after their death? And why should you care? You aren't even in the book!"

As soon as she'd said it, she knew he was. Snatches of conversation and history abruptly fell into place. Sheila knew what he had done: Committed the only crime his friends and supporters would find totally abhorrent.

Before she could avert her eyes, he read her gaze and understood that she knew. A dull red flooded his face. Pulling a handkerchief from his hip pocket, he dabbed his forehead, which had broken out in a sheen of sweat. Behind his glasses his eyes blinked rapidly. As a little girl, Sheila used to blink like that when she got to corners, willing traffic lights to change. What did Lamar hope to change?

He wadded the handkerchief back into his pocket. He tried to smile, but achieved only tautly stretched lips across his capped white teeth. "This makes things quite a bit more difficult, Sheila. I hope you appreciate that."

"They're difficult enough already," she said, trying not

to look at Demolinius sprawled motionless on her Persian rug.

Lamar sat gingerly on the other end of the sofa, near the fire, his eyes on the gun resting casually on one thigh. He said nothing for what seemed an eternity, then leaned toward her confidingly. "Last night, honey, when I suggested we get married—did you give that any more thought? I was perfectly serious, you know."

She shook her head. "It's not a solution, Lamar."

He sighed. "I just thought it might be."

"No." No matter where Sheila sent her gaze, it invariably crept back to the crumpled heap that used to be a man.

Lamar sighed a second time, then raised the gun. "I am so sorry, my dear." Sheila braced herself to die.

Then he spoke again—a politician unable to resist the opportunity to make one more speech. "I surely do hate to shoot you, Sheila. I've been fond of you for a long time. But" —his voice pled with her for understanding—"there are some things more important."

"Like what?" she demanded. How long could she draw him out? How long did she have to live?

"Patriotism. Honor. A lifetime devoted to this great country of ours. I am needed here. There are those who count on me to lift their voices in the halls of government."

She licked her lips and prayed her own voice would still work. "Then how did it happen, Uncle Lamar?" The child's title slipped out unbidden. "You—the quintessential American, southern statesman! At least tell me *why*."

Lamar wavered, considering. With her whole being she willed him to lower that gun.

At last he did, and nodded. "I'd like to tell you. I've never even dared write it down, lest I have an accident and someone find it among my papers." The implication—that she could be told because she would not be around to tell— was impossible to miss.

"You remember I told you . . . It's a long story. Would you like some coffee, my dear? I'll fetch you a cup."

She accepted. Not because she thought she could swallow, but because it might delay death long enough for her to think of some way to prevent it. Lamar carefully filled a mug for her, refilled his own, and carried them one at a time (with the gun in his other hand) to the coffee table. He even went back for two paper napkins. Perhaps Miss Manners would let him write a chapter on Courtesy to Those One is About to Shoot.

As he was resuming his seat, Sheila felt emboldened to reach behind her for the afghan she'd left over the couch the evening before. Was it less than twenty-four hours ago? It seemed like several years. "Would you please cover, ah, him, too?" she asked.

It was an awkward task while holding a gun on her, but Lamar made certain that poor Demolinius was fully concealed before lowering himself arthritically to the other end of the couch and starting his story.

"As I told you last night, when Granddaddy died, he left me everything he had—on the condition that I spend two years in Germany with his brother's family." Lamar's voice deepened and took on a thick German accent. " 'I do not intend dat he should luff his own country less, but only dat he should respect odder nations as vell.' So I went, as I told you, in the fall of '37. You cannot imagine what Germany was like back then. There was an energy—a conviction that der Führer would restore Germany to the power she had once known . . ." His face brightened at the memory.

Was he so lost in reminiscence that she could get the gun?

No. His fingers gripped it tighter as he continued. "I lived in Berlin with Mama's first cousin Dietrich and his son Diet, who was sixteen. Young Diet was very involved with Hitler Youth. He urged me to go with him to hear der Führer *sprechen*." Unconsciously Lamar shifted languages.

"When der Führer spoke, everything he said you believed. A magnificent man, with the oratorical gift. My heart within me quickened! I for Franklin Roosevelt no respect had. He and his busybody wife our nation to—"

She missed a word. Probably the German equivalent of riffraff.

"—would give! Hitler of a pure race spoke, a nation of God–created superior people." Lamar's voice fell reverently, then he sighed. "Impulsively, I a Nazi student group joined. Our group leader Karl Schwartz was."

He stopped and flushed. "Forgive me, my dear. I believe I must have abandoned English for some time now. Did you understand any of that?"

"Most of it." She sipped her coffee. It could have been melted mud for all she knew, but it provided a brief distraction from the gun gently tapping his knee. "What happened next?"

Beneath her, the envelope corners grew sharp. Even though these could well be the last ten minutes of her life, her hips clamored for relief. When she shifted slightly, however, the papers crackled. Afraid the sound would recall them to Lamar's attention and shorten his story, she coughed.

"Smoke bothering you?" He glanced toward the fire.

She tensed to jump for the gun, but he turned back too soon.

"I came home," he continued, "as I told you, in '39, and finished law school. Like everyone else, I followed the European war avidly. Unlike many, though, I secretly believed in Hitler's dream for Europe. I even speculated on how it could be superimposed onto the democratic process." He stopped, sank into a too-brief reverie, then shook his head sadly. "An idle little exercise, and not one I've ever spoken aloud." He leaned a little nearer, his eyes hopeful behind the polished lenses. "You are easy to talk to, honey. Are you certain you won't reconsider my offer?"

She was tempted. Marriage, even this marriage, might be preferable to death. But before she could speak, he shook his head. "No, I could never be certain of your loyalty."

"You're a fine one to talk!" she blazed, stung into indiscretion. "You—a spy!"

He recoiled as if she had struck him. "Never a spy, Sheila! Merely an informer. Stack and I were both assigned to the quartermaster's office, and Atlanta was a major army depot, you know. Bedding, food, clothing, transport—we supplied them all."

She smiled—desperately hoping to distract him from her

flare of temper. "The old army way. Take a lawyer, and set him to counting sheets."

It worked. He chuckled. "You've got that straight, honey. Well, to make this long story short—"

"Take all the time you need." She meant it!

However, he glanced at his watch and shook his head. "No, I have a dinner engagement. Just a bit more, now."

She scarcely heard the next part. ". . . letter from Diet . . . if I was still playing for my old ball team . . . give him Diet's regards . . . Sheila? Are you listening?"

"Oh, yes. You were to give him Diet's regards." She had no idea who was to get the regards—but then, she was unlikely to take a final exam.

Nevertheless, she dragged her numb, wandering attention back to Lamar, who had hit the easy stride of an old man telling a good story. "I didn't give the letter much thought until a few weeks later. Then, at a downtown bar, Karl Schwartz slid onto the next stool. He ordered beer in perfect English and ignored me, while I squirmed and wondered what to do." Again Lamar pulled out his handkerchief and mopped his brow. "Finally he addressed me, introduced himself as Carl Black from Chicago, and started to chat. We went to dinner and—" he shrugged, "—in the end I did what he wanted. Not spying!" he insisted. "Just providing information about what supplies were being sent where, and when."

Where supplies went, troops were sure to follow.

He must have read that in her expression, for he pled, "I love this country, Sheila! But I vastly preferred Hitler to Roosevelt. Still would, for that matter. Any right-thinking American would!"

"The concentration camps?" she protested in spite of the risk. "The gas ovens?"

He wiped his forehead again. "I didn't know about those then. I've never been convinced der Führer knew about them, either."

At that moment she knew how perilous her situation truly was. Any man who believed *that* could give himself all sorts of excellent reasons to shoot even an honorary niece.

"But how did you keep from getting caught?" She willed her voice not to tremble.

His mouth set in a bitter line. "Nobody ever noticed me back then. In law school, on base, even in Buckhead where I was born, I could stand in a circle of people and nobody would remember I'd been there."

As Aunt Mary couldn't remember if he'd been at Charles and Dorothy's party, Sheila recalled.

For an instant the look in his weak eyes wrung her heart. Then they blazed behind his lenses. "Folks thought I was a fool. Well, young lady, I fooled *them*—and knowin' that gave me the confidence to become what I am today." He raised the gun's muzzle again. It was no longer Uncle Lamar, but Lamar Whitehead, Political Power Broker, who confronted her on the other side of the ugly little gun. "Now, Sheila, please burn that last chapter."

Jump! screamed every fiber of her being. That was impossible. But out of desperation was birthed one frail hope.

"Very well." She pushed the coffee table further away from them and rose slowly, fumbling for the envelope beneath her. Holding it in her left hand, she opened it, pulled out a page, and glanced at it wistfully. "I just wish I could know if Margaret Mitchell penciled in these corrections in her own hand." She slanted the page slightly toward him.

As she had hoped, Lamar tilted his head up to look through the bifocal bottoms of his lenses. "Let me see. I knew her writing well."

And as he reached for the pages, Sheila chopped his right wrist with her right hand and smacked him across the face with the envelope in her left.

The gun exploded. The sliding door shattered. In the next room, Lady began to howl. Fear lent strength to Sheila's injured shoulder as she clasped Lamar's wrist and wrestled desperately for the weapon.

Just as she gave his hand one last vicious shake and the gun fell to the carpet, a voice spoke from the hallway: "Don't reach for it, Lamar! I've got you covered!"

•　　•　　•

Aunt Mary stepped into the room. Firelight gave her silver curls the same sheen as the tiny silver pistol in her hand.

Lamar sank back on the sofa. With a whimper, he buried his face in his hands.

Sheila staggered to the far wall, gasping for breath and clutching her agonized shoulder.

"Sorry I'm a bit late, dear. Traffic was heavy." Aunt Mary's deep voice was infinitesimally shaky. "I hope you've got a good explanation for this, Lamar."

Slightly reassured, he looked up at his old friend. "Put down that gun before you shoot somebody, Mary, and let me explain." He started to rise, but she raised her pistol a fraction higher.

"Don't get up."

Behind her in the narrow hallway, Jason and a young man Sheila didn't recognize lent reassuring bulk, but the young man kept an anxious distance behind the tiny elderly woman with the pistol. "It's okay, man, she's a crack shot," Jason murmured, moving closer.

Aunt Mary spoke to them over her shoulder. "Has Lieutenant Green arrived yet, Crispin? Mildred was supposed to have him to meet us here."

Sheila heard only one word. "Crispin?"

Jason and the young man fell back and Crispin limped in —pale, casted, and on crutches. Like a schoolboy, he raised one hand. "Present. Green's just arriving, Miss Mary." Grinning, he shoved a lock of dark hair off his forehead. "Good to see you alive and kicking, love."

The smile Sheila gave him was wan. "I had my doubts for a few minutes there," she said softly.

"I wouldn't have hurt her for the world!" Lamar protested. "If she had just been reasonable. . . . Mary! Stop wavin' that gun and let me explain before you go callin' in the police!"

Aunt Mary's brown eyes flashed. "Don't be tedious, Lamar." Her gun quite steady, she added, "Jason, you and Buddy go send in Lieutenant Green, then wait in my car."

As they left, she gently nudged the afghan hump with one gray leather toe. "What on earth is this?"

Hot bile rose in Sheila's throat. "Not what, Aunt Mary. Who. It's Mildred's brother, Demolinius."

"Oh, my! Did you shoot him, dear?"

"Of course not! Lamar did."

He lifted a defiant face to his old friend. "In self-defense."

Aunt Mary raised one silver brow in response. Sheila turned away.

Crispin limped over to her. "Here, lean on me," he told her. When she complied, she found she was trembling so badly they both shook. "You okay?" he asked.

She nodded, not trusting herself to speak. Crispin wrapped his arms around her, crutches and all. He was nuzzling her hair when Green entered, accompanied by two uniformed policemen.

Aunt Mary quickly slipped her gun into her purse. She took the wing chair across from Lamar, giving the scene the appearance of four friends having a quiet chat—except for the shattered glass door and Lady, still howling piteously, in the study.

"Somebody hush that dog," Green ordered.

One of the officers opened the door and Lady bolted toward Lamar, barking and growling deep in her throat.

"Lady!" Sheila had to shout three times before the dog heard her. Only then did she trot over and cower against her mistress, uttering exhausted little whines.

"So. What's going on here?" demanded Green.

"Theft," Aunt Mary said crisply. "This man was trying to steal something that belongs to my niece."

"It wasn't theft, Aunt Mary."

"But if he followed you here to take that silly manuscript—"

"He was here when I got here."

Sheila began to explain, starting with her arrival at the apartment. It took a while, for Lamar persisted in interrupting until Aunt Mary quelled him with a look. Sheila was grateful for Crispin's arms around her. If he removed them, she might melt boneless to the rug beside the corpse.

When she got to the part about Demolinius's death,

Green lifted one corner of the afghan, then scowled and let it drop. "Anthony's cousin, I presume?" he asked glumly.

Sheila nodded. "Mildred's brother."

"Oh!" Aunt Mary's little hands fluttered in distress. "I forgot to call and tell Mildred we're all right!" She rose and trotted to the bedroom phone.

She returned just in time to hear her niece explaining why Lamar so feared the manuscript. Aunt Mary's lips pursed in disbelief. "Lamar a Nazi informer? Under our very noses? Pshaw!" Her tone implied she would have been as easy to convince that he'd swum the Atlantic.

Crispin chuckled and started to murmur something into Sheila's ear, but she pressed a finger to his lips. In spite of all she had been through, she was touched by the two old friends facing one another across the coffee table. They could have been alone in the room.

Mary's eyes raked Lamar from head to toe, then she shook her silver curls. "I still can't believe it, Lamar."

But she did. Her next sentence betrayed her. "How on earth could you *do* such a thing?"

Lamar squared his shoulders. His face was pink and earnest, and wet with tears. With vast dignity he replied, "I believed in him, Mary. God help me, I believed in Adolf Hitler."

"God had better forgive you," she replied bruskly, "for I cannot." She tottered to the shattered glass doors and turned her back on them all, looking suddenly old and frail.

Lieutenant Green touched Sheila's shoulder. Gruffly, he asked, "This Demolinius—you saw him shot?"

She nodded. "Like I said, Lamar was going to burn the manuscript—"

She realized, to her surprise, that she still clutched the remaining envelope to her chest like threatened treasure. "Here." She held it out to the lieutenant and shuddered. "I never want to see that thing again."

Green gave her a sour smile. "We'll probably all see more of it than we want to in court."

He reached for it, but Lamar lunged forward, wrenched it from Sheila's grasp, and flung it onto the fire.

Green rushed to retrieve it just as Lady, misunderstanding, dashed between him and the blaze with a menacing growl.

The envelope and its precious contents, brittle with age, burst into flame.

Tears stung Sheila's cheeks. "How could you?" she cried. "You weren't even in it! The spy in the story was a sergeant!"

Lamar's face mottled with rage. "Peggy shouldn't have done that to me. I can stand almost anything except being *ignored*!"

The pages turned to ashes in seconds.

With a sigh, Owen Green waved to his subordinates. "Get him out of here."

Lamar, satisfied, held out his wrists. "I'm ready, Lieutenant." He darted one quick look at Mary Beaufort. But she was staring rigidly outside.

Green considered Lamar gloomily, then turned to Sheila. "You know, of course, that with a self-defense plea, he'll be on the streets by tomorrow. Especially if that's Demolinius's gun. I've heard Mr. Whitehead in court, Mrs. Travis. By the time he tells his story, the judge's gonna consider him a public benefactor and your hero."

Sheila shook her head. "He's no hero. And while he couldn't have killed Sean—he was in Washington all day yesterday—I think he did kill Junior. There's even a witness."

Lamar swiveled. "Witness? Nonsense!"

But he was uneasy. Everyone in the room could testify to that. Sheila hoped they couldn't also testify to the fact that she was bluffing. Would Elouisa really be able to identify Lamar as the man who talked with Junior, or his car as the one that followed Junior toward the cemetery?

Aunt Mary spoke without looking away from the window. "Trace the registration on that gun, Lieutenant. It may be Lamar's." Her voice became an angry rasp. "And charge him with intent to murder my niece."

"—*and* breaking and entering," Sheila added. "I never gave him a key to this apartment. And theft."

Green nodded. "And destroying vital evidence. That might hold him a while." But he didn't sound too sanguine.

"Just until we can investigate—the other." Aunt Mary whispered the last two words, as if she could not bear to say what she was thinking. She could not yet face Lamar himself.

"Mary!" he cried once, imploringly. Then, led by the two officers, he turned toward the front door.

At last, his old friend relented. "Wait. I'll walk you out," Mary said gruffly.

When Sheila and Crispin were finally alone, she couldn't speak. Her throat was clogged with a lump of something. Crispin steered her to the couch and limped to bring her a glass of water. She gulped it gratefully, but it did not wash down the lump.

"While you recover, shall I tell you how the cavalry arrived?" He sat awkwardly across from her, his casted knee thrust before him. She managed a nod. "Well, you'd called and said you'd be here all day, but when I tried to call back, you weren't. Then on the noon news I heard about Sean, and that police thought he'd been killed with the same gun that killed Mildred's nephew. Knowing how apt you are to get involved in things like this, I got antsy. I decided I'd rather recuperate up here than down there. Buddy—my friend's son—agreed to drive me up, and when we got here, you still weren't home, so I had Buddy take me over to Miss Mary's—"

"You *were* worried!" She managed a tiny smile. "Risking instant annihilation—"

He chuckled. "Right. But the ogress was out to lunch. Mildred said you were probably still up at Rip's, and called to check. Then she told me to wait a while until Miss Mary called back, so Buddy and I settled down to a bowl of soup. Next thing I knew, Mildred was whisking away the soup and ordering us to meet Miss Mary here at once. Apparently she'd called Lamar's office, thinking you might have gone there, and they said he'd gone for the day to pick up my car. Miss Mary got it in her head that he'd decided to come here and steal the manuscript to sell. Buddy and I made good time coming over, but Jason must have burned up the free-way. Your aunt was already out of the car before I arrived."

"But how did you all get in? I never gave you a key—"

"Miss Mary let us in with hers."

"Hers?" Sheila asked, bewildered. "Where did *she* get a key?"

Aunt Mary entered just in time to hear. "I keep it on my ring, dear. For emergencies." Serenely, she perched beside Sheila on the couch.

After every crisis there is one small, often unrelated thing, which is the proverbial straw on an overburdened back. For Sheila, this final invasion of privacy was it. A torrent of anger slammed over her. She opened her mouth—then saw Aunt Mary's face. It was pale, and much older than it had been at the beginning of the week.

"Are—are you really all right, dear?" the husky voice trembled.

The illicit key was instantly forgiven. Sheila crumpled like a child. Burying her face in her hands, she wept with abandon.

"Lamar . . . Uncle Lamar—"

Aunt Mary's hand stroked her hair. "I know, dear." Her own voice was rough with tears. "Sin, repentance—most of us have learned a lot about that this past week." She sighed. "Lamar's still got a lot to learn." Sheila felt the small fingers in her black curls, twisting them and tugging gently. Then Aunt Mary cleared her throat. With some of her accustomed briskness, she said, "We arrived in time to hear you at the end, Sheila—using his own vanity to bring him down. A wise idea. Very few people would have thought of that."

Sheila sniffed, then chuckled. "Just you, huh?" She sniffed again. "Aunt Mary?" she said hesitantly. "I think you need to check your shoe. I think you've stepped—"

"Oh, fiddlesticks!" Aunt Mary exclaimed in real distress, lifting her size fours. *"That dog!"*

That evening Sheila sprawled in her favorite chair in Aunt Mary's rose-and-ivory living room, feet on the ottoman. "I may never move again," she announced, holding up a glass of sherry and watching the light shimmer through the liquid gold.

Aunt Mary, in a forest green velvet hostess gown, was curled into her favorite corner of the couch, feet tucked beneath her. She sipped her own sherry and regarded her niece thoughtfully. "I really think you should, dear. The suburbs are so dangerous these days. There's a lovely apartment downstairs here—"

Sheila shook her head. "Not downstairs, Aunt Mary. I may think about moving closer in—" She shuddered. "I don't relish my present apartment just now. But," she stretched and slid lower in the chair, "like Scarlett, I'll think about that tomorrow. Today I have a few questions for *you*. First, are Rip and Honey going to live happily ever after?"

Aunt Mary shook her head. "Nobody knows. Faith is very hurt and bewildered, and Honey is dithering."

"Perhaps, in time—"

"There isn't time!" Aunt Mary flared with unusual fierceness. "Rip is old, and sick. Honey must see that and leave Faith to work out her own problems!"

Sheila nodded. "So tell me how Charles knew Honey's apartment had stairs. Remember, at the hospital—?"

Aunt Mary arched her brows. "So you noticed that? I asked him about it. For some time now, he's been buying Honey's pictures. Told her he had a buyer, and probably gave her twice what some of them were worth. Charlie's one of the few truly good men I've ever known."

Sheila gave her a level look. "He's also got a queasy stomach, and a rigid propriety. I wonder who convinced him to conceal that dead soldier's body, and helped him do it? The same person he called when he'd decided to confess?"

Aunt Mary considered a more important issue, the state of her shell-pink nails. "I really must get a manicure before we leave town."

Sheila flexed her shoulder, winced, and tried another tack. "Was it you who ordered no visitors for Honey?"

"Yes, because of something Rip told me. He spent Monday beside Honey's bed, and Winona tiptoed in midmorning to sit for nearly an hour. Rip got worried she'd be there all the time and drive Honey mad. I had other reasons, of course, but I agreed with him that Honey would be better off without visitors. Now," she reached for her phone. "If you are quite finished, dear, I have to make a call."

Sheila leaned back and closed her eyes. Someday she would ask about Marc Dumier, but not today. She was too tired. She heard Aunt Mary say, "Jane? I have four buyers interested in your mobiles. My financial advisor suggests—"

Sheila didn't hear any more. She was fast asleep.

She woke an hour later to find Crispin and Forbes in the doorway, very alike with their dark curls, long lean bodies, and smug expressions. When Forbes saw that she was awake, the boy sidled over and looked at her sideways. "Crispin bought a present for you. I saw it! It's little, an' sparkly, an' the most specialest thing you ever saw! He's gonna give it to you in a minute—" He pranced in his excitement.

Sheila's startled eyes flew to Crispin's. He smirked. She frowned, but her limbs were too heavy to move.

Across the room, Aunt Mary was giving Crispin a regal glare. He lounged against the fireplace, turning from the niece to the aunt. "First, Miss Mary, Forbes and I have a couple of proposals for you. We think you ought to take him to Florida with you for Christmas—"

"She was going to anyway," Sheila informed him drowsily from across the room.

He waved her to silence. "Don't interrupt, Sheila, I'm negotiating. You take Forbes to Florida for a few weeks while I recuperate, Miss Mary, then in the spring, we want you, and Sheila too, if she will, to come to South America with us."

Forbes jumped up and down. "We'll tramp through jungles, and sleep in hammocks, and feed crocodiles—"

"Feed them your hands and feet," Sheila warned him.

To her amazement, however, Aunt Mary said in a considering tone, "I haven't slept in a hammock for years. Perhaps I will. But now, Forbes," she put out one hand, emeralds twinkling in the lamplight, "it's time for your bath and a talk about manners. You should never tell someone what they are getting for Christmas."

Forbes shook his dark head, obstinate. "It's not for Christmas, Aunt Mary, it's for tonight. And I don't want to go until she opens it. It's the *specialest* present. I wish I had one!" He turned to Crispin. "Can I—" he stopped, gave Aunt Mary an angelic smile, and amended it, "may *I* give it to her?"

Crispin hesitated, then reached into his pocket and brought out a small blue jeweler's box. "Sure. She may take it better from you than from me."

Sheila watched the child approach, dark eyes shining and one lock of hair dangling in his face. She could feel herself flushing all over, overwhelmed by a myriad of emotions. Confusion: *We haven't discussed what I told him Sunday night. He knows I'm not ready for this.* Anger: *How dare he do this so publicly?* But also anticipation, excitement, and a deep winging joy.

She took the small blue box with trembling hands. "Thank you, Forbes."

She smiled. Then—as she opened the box—her smile turned into a peal of delight.

Nestled on white velvet was a brooch of red and white glass stones: "Life is Uncertain. Eat Dessert First."

1. William R. Mitchell, Jr., and Van Jones Martin, *Classic Atlanta: Landmarks of the Atlanta Spirit* (Savannah: Martin-St. Martin Press, 1991), p. 58.

2. "Scarlett Started It," in *Atlanta Journal Magazine* 1/5/41, p. 4.

3. Wylly Folk St. John, "The War-Time Scene," in *Atlanta Journal Magazine* 1/30/44, p. 9.

4. Darden Asbury Pyron, *Southern Daughter: The Life of Margaret Mitchell* (New York: Harper, 1992), pp. 586–587.

5. James Dickey, "Looking for the Buckhead Boys," in *The Whole Motion: Collected Poems 1945–1992* (Hanover, N.H.: Wesleyan University Press, 1992), p. 310. Used by permission of The University Press of New England.

6. Ronald P. Hopan, quoted by Maria Saporta, "City, business finally teaming up on housing," in *Atlanta Constitution* 2/9/91 p. C-1.

7. Yolande Gwin, *Yolande's Atlanta: From the Historical to the Hysterical* (Atlanta: Peachtree Publishers, 1983), p. 15.

8. Elizabeth Lockhart Davis and Ethel Warren Spruill, *The Story of Dunwoody: Its Heritage and Horizons 1821–1975* (Self-published, 1975), p. 185.

9. Doris Locherman, "Sonnet Bonnets," in *Atlanta Journal Magazine* 3/25/45, p. 16.

10. Estelle Clemmons, quoted by Clifford M. Kuhn, Harlon E. Joye, and E. Bernard West, in *Living Atlanta: An Oral History of the City 1914–1948* (Atlanta: Atlanta Historical Society and University of Georgia Press, 1990), p. 337.

11. Elizabeth Candler Graham, *The Real Ones: Four Generations of the First Family of Coca-Cola* (Fort Lee, N.J.: Barricade Books, 1992), p. 337.

12. Kuhn, Joye, and West, op. cit. p. 314.

13. Davis and Spruill, op. cit. p. 184.

14. Pyron, op. cit. p. 518.

15. Pat Watters, *Coca-Cola: An Illustrated History* (New York: Doubleday, 1978), pp. 170 and 176.

16. Richard Harwell, ed., *Margaret Mitchell's Gone With the Wind Letters* (New York: Macmillan, 1976), p. 390.

17. Pyron, op. cit. p. 594.

ABOUT THE AUTHOR

PATRICIA SPRINKLE lives in Miami, Florida, with her husband and two sons. She is the author of *Murder at Markham, Murder in the Charleston Manner, Murder on Peachtree Street, Somebody's Dead in Snellville,* and *Death of a Dunwoody Matron. A Mystery Bred in Buckhead* is her sixth Sheila Travis mystery, and she is currently at work on her seventh, *Dubious Death in Duval.*